CONTEMPORARY AMERICAN FICTION

SALARYMAN

Meg Pei graduated from the State University of
New York at Binghamton, and has won writing
awards from *Newsweek*, *Scholastic*, and the Illinois Arts Council. This, her first novel, was the
recipient of the Friends of American Writers
Award.

MEG PEI

SALARYMAN

PENGUIN BOOKS

PENGUIN BOOKS
Published by the Penguin Group
Penguin Books USA Inc., 375 Hudson Street, New York, New York 10014, U.S.A.
Penguin Books Ltd, 27 Wrights Lane, London W8 5TZ, England
Penguin Books Australia Ltd, Ringwood, Victoria, Australia
Penguin Books Canada Ltd, 10 Alcorn Avenue, Toronto, Ontario, Canada M4V 3B2
Penguin Books (N.Z.) Ltd, 182–190 Wairau Road, Auckland 10, New Zealand

Penguin Books Ltd, Registered Offices: Harmondsworth, Middlesex, England

First published in the United States of America by Viking Penguin, a division of
Penguin Books USA Inc., 1992
Published in Penguin Books 1993

10 9 8 7 6 5 4 3 2 1

THE LIBRARY OF CONGRESS HAS CATALOGUED THE HARDCOVER AS FOLLOWS:
Pei, Meg.
Salaryman/Meg Pei.
p.   cm.
ISBN 0-670-83979-5 (hc.)
ISBN 0 14 01.7826 0 (pbk.)
I. Title.
PS3566.E333S25   1992
813'.54—dc20   91–30433

Printed in the United States of America
Set in Bodoni Book
Designed by Francesca Belanger

To Judith and Salvatore;
and to Fletcher

Acknowledgments

The writing of this book was supported partially by a grant from the Illinois Arts Council.

Thanks also to S. L. Heidenreich, for all those clippings.

Prologue

I come from Tokyo, I do. You know me, you've seen me and my colleagues running about your city, touring your national parks and landmarks, investigating, investing, spending and flexing our yen. Japanese. Salarymen. Who are we? Do you care?

You may resent us, you may make fun of us; you may like our food and quaint customs, think of Mount Fuji and geisha girls, Toyotas, transistors, temples, or perhaps World War II and Pearl Harbor. Your nerves may prickle as our corporations spread across your land, gobble up real estate, the entertainment industry; our odd names on billboards everywhere, our cars on freeways, our technology in every home. . . . When will it end? Or will it? I don't know, I can only speak for myself. Will you listen? For I do have something to say, a dimension to add beyond that caricature stereotype of a Nip in a business suit, or a bucktoothed four-eyed Nip with a camera around his neck, or the Nips you saw screaming

"Banzai!" in your John Wayne movies. The faceless crowds of Tokyo; the factory Nips soldering engines in documentaries about us, the economic animal. Karate Nips, tourist Nips in packs. Those, you see, are Nips. I am flesh and blood—five feet six inches, 145 pounds, type O, to be specific. We are all flesh and blood, not Nips.

So listen up closely, as I reveal my first guarded clue to myself, the salaryman, in a haiku:

> *Even the small fish*
> *swim without ceasing toward the*
> *far and distant shore.*

That is my motto.
Do I have your attention? Fine; thank you.
I will now begin.

PART ONE

There has always been a strangeness to me, no matter how I try to pace myself to move with the everyday crowd. The strangeness comes from within—you cannot tell by my appearance, the way I talk or what I say, but rather it is phosphorescent, like a fungus, only to be seen by those with keen eyes in the dark.

They say that my father, when stuck for inspiration, would listen to Brahms's Third Symphony, the Poco Allegretto movement. My father, though he wrote in kimono with antiquated ink sticks, was always spouting the glory of Western influences: Brahms, Satie, Chekhov, Balzac. Yet he never in his life left Japan.

I remember the day he killed himself, a very bright, oddly warm day in December, and how my mother ran out to the small bomb shelter behind our house and remained there until dusk, whining and whimpering like an old dog. When she emerged, her clothes were damp and streaked with soil; she immediately began preparing miso soup for my supper, dipping her head slightly forward into the steam from the kettle so as to loosen her swollen face. My father had left her long before and taken up with a series of other women, but that did not seem to matter. His suicide had been a double one; he'd taken along his fifteen-year-old mistress, who he'd insisted had great depth. Fifteen-year-olds, as we all know, are very deep, or should I say narrow (and tight), particularly between the legs. Still, my mother maintained her strange, saintlike vigil. She had been the first, her child had been a boy, and even though she had had to learn of her husband's death through the newspaper as she sat on the floor of our tiny, train-banked house, she seemed to find solace enough.

To this day schoolgirls decorate his grave. A certain literary society holds a ceremony each December 10, at Kinosaki, where he died.

I have not been able to eat miso soup again without a slight thickening of the throat. Warm days in December put me on edge, as though I'm about to be struck by lightning; the Brahms symphony I can never hear all the way through, unless I am drunk. When I was sixteen, about to go to college, I went to a bookstore to find one of my father's works. My hands were stiff as I opened the flyleaf and stared dully at what could have been a picture of myself, at what I would look like in twenty years. Disheveled hair (thinning hair!), haggard eyes and solemn, downturned mouth. The weak words inside embarrassed me and filled me with disgust:

> Sickness is our only escape, the body's vacation forced upon itself. . . .

> Suicide is for the very weak or very strong. It is obvious which side I fall on. . . .

> Certain mornings I yawn and smell the decay of my own flesh.

A man was peering over my shoulder, curiously, almost as if he knew. I closed the book and returned it to its shelf, then went home and smoked five cigarettes in the bomb shelter, with its tiny stores of rice and water. I was new to smoking and became a little dizzy. Outside, the Amerasian girl next door did cartwheels on the grass and listened to the Beatles on her radio. "Love Me Do." The Amerasian girl was a curiosity in our neighborhood, both admired and chastised because of her mixed race. Normally I would go and spy on her, but that day I was not feeling right. My lungs ached. There was a petrified mouse in the corner of the room, by the tarp, so well preserved it was like a museum specimen. Its paw was raised, waving. I wondered how it had managed to die like that.

Back in the house, I sat skimming through my chemistry text, pretending to be engrossed. I refused dinner, refused to talk, and that evening found it easy to be cruel to my mother, for the first time in my life.

My mother. She was a good woman, very simple, like the food she served in her Tokyo Line snack shop—just noodles, omelets, sandwiches; nothing special. I helped in the shop as well, I had no alternative, and when I expressed an interest, she taught me how to cook. She lost her beauty early and went to fat, but then food was a constant for her, both a reliable pleasure and a source of steady income. She was small, round, really barrel-shaped, her features and skin thickening into coarseness as she got older and more mechanical, as she lost interest in how she looked. She had crooked teeth. When she was a girl, however, she had been very appealing, from what I understood, healthy and strong, with all the force of her youth behind her like a mountain well. My father picked her up when he was in his rustic phase, bored with Tokyo; she was a maid at an inn he visited, aged sixteen. It went on for a little while—from mid-spring to late autumn—long enough for her to get pregnant. Then he went back to the city, bored with country life.

He set her up in the snack shop and sent her money every month, but he refused to acknowledge her anymore, except for whenever he wanted to see me, once or twice a year. She would spend hours getting ready for these visits, powdering, doing her hair, soaking her hands in ice water to reduce the puffiness, but it never worked. He had become bored with her too. I only know all this through the novel he wrote about the episode, *Among the Birches*, and not through her. She talked about him as if he were a little god—all his great works, none of which she had the capacity to understand. I know and anybody else who cares to read the book can know, in depth, how badly my mother was treated. This is a nasty thing about being related to a writer—anyone can know you, about your secrets and most intimate details. Sometimes they don't even have to pay the price of the book; you might be public domain at a library. It is a little chilly, and miserable. It is a little like walking around forever, naked and locked out of your own house: everyone sees your crevices and your beauty spots—you have no place to hide.

In school, every literature or composition teacher I had singled me out. "How well you write, Shimada," they would say, yet always with this postscript: "But then again you had a head start." I began to hate these classes. Still, I worked very hard, because I also hated our house and helping my mother in the shop, always sweating into steam pots, always hurrying; the pauses, the rhythm of your heart run by trains gliding in and out, depositing hungry commuters at your door, which was open from five in the morning till midnight. Our house stank of food, of onions and yesterday's broth, fish guts in the garbage, oil, coffee. It was in the woodwork, the bedding—you couldn't get away. Even outside, the odor hovered around a landscape of crisscrossing tracks and telephone wires, clotheslines connecting one shabby little station house to another. Ratty gardens, mulch heaps. Not poverty, which might have been an excuse to do nothing, but tireless struggling working class.

My mother, tiny steamroller that she was, slept three or four hours a night, always doing something, humming, clattering in the kitchen, ironing my school uniform, her little otter eyes cheerful and bright. Her life revolved around me and the commuters. As I got older and began to look more like my father, she treated me with a strange reverence. A frightening tenderness. "You're his," she would say, clucking to herself, as if now all the world could see whose son she'd had. She would comb my hair to the left, the way he did, a shock of it falling forward, poet style. "Huh," she would say, admiringly, then as soon as she'd gone I would part it in the other direction, neatly toward the right, so that I could be myself.

My mother died the year after my daughter was born; she had a heart attack out in her garden, picking turnips. Early in the morning, before rush hour, no trains—I like to think that there was silence for a moment as she lay there, facedown in the dirt. I also like to think that she was happier than she had been over the course of her life: she had her savings and her snack bar (in which, sadly, she had just installed a new counter she'd never wipe), her home, a son who seemed successful and wore business suits, a friendly daughter-in-law and a grandchild. I drank a lot for a month or so to blur the sight of her shiny face, a planet I had lived with for so long, and also to quash the sense of relief I felt inside. There was sadness too, keen and sharp, and I imagined it on my heart all brown and soft, like a bruise on a nectarine—but the relief was sharper. I had never wanted to fail my mother, and I hadn't, for to fail her would only have deepened the sense of failure she had herself. Because of her and simultaneously to get away from her, I had studied furiously in school, at university; I took a job with a large corporation, with its myriad benefits and its familial structure; I married young, I set myself up—I didn't want her to worry about me anymore; I wanted her to relax. And then she died, keeled over without warning, almost as if her function had ceased. Again for a little while, after the cremation, I felt hollow, everything I'd achieved now somewhat vaporous and unimportant, without her there to perceive it. But I continued.

We kept her photo in an alcove in the apartment, and at first I made a point of nodding to it each morning as I left for work. So solemn, uncharacteristically so—like most unsophisticated people, my mother tended to look strained before the camera. Captured like that, she seemed sadder than she had been in life, almost pathetic. Eventually I avoided the photo altogether. I preferred to remember her bustling around, having her evening beer, hoisting pots of noodles and sacks of buckwheat flour, laughing at her customers' jokes. She was not a gloomy person. Japan was rebuilt by such people, eternal scavengers, salvaging and piecing together ruins. Tough people. I was glad to have half of that in me. The coroner said she had gone instantaneously, she had not lingered. Ah, yes, the ultimate thing I loved about my mother.

She died an honest death.

My father, Kazuo Shimada, was born on the first of September, 1923, the day of the great Tokyo earthquake. His family's house was leveled, everyone in it killed—his father, his grandfather, the maid—and the ruins of the home looted. My father's family had dealt in Western antiques. Very little remained of the clocks and curios, china and crystal they had collected over the years. My father, however, still inside the womb, had gone on a spur-of-the-moment trip—his mother had gone on the trip, that is, accompanied by her mother. Originally the grandfather was supposed to go, but when the mother-to-be complained of shortness of breath, everyone decided that the mountains would do her good. They were in the Hakone range, south of Yokohama, visiting a great-aunt, taking in the air, my father's mother in the last month of her pregnancy. She said she felt tremors and then went into labor. No one else felt them, but she insisted that she did. They chose not to tell her what had happened till afterward, after she had delivered a healthy boy. The trip was an unsettling coincidence, a sudden switch of pawns on the chessboard. Had the women stayed at the Tokyo house, they and the unborn baby would have died too. It was a tremendous stroke of luck, but rather than view it like this, my father chose to take it as a sign that he was not meant to be born. The feeling troubled him all his life: fatalistic, undeserving, he dragged it around with him like forcep marks. He also used it as an excuse to treat people badly. This was how he was.

Up until age seven, I visited him every year, though I don't recall much of what we did. He had a mistress at that time, Reiko, whom I liked better than I did him. Reiko was just about to be dumped for Seiko, his last and youngest mistress. Reiko was on the tall side, willowy, with a long, oval face. My father had bronchial problems and was always coughing. His studio had a sweetish odor I never could quite pinpoint, and then later I learned that the smell was from herbs he put into his Chinese vaporizer. Scrolls and scrolls of paper, all over. As I said, I don't recall much, aside from sitting on Reiko's lap in the subway car, visiting museums and amusement districts, falling asleep at café tables while my father drank late into the night.

"When you're older and you want to learn things, you'll come live with me," he always promised. I would smile and hide my face when he said this—I didn't feel at ease with him, but I liked how solemnly he spoke, as if I were the most important thing in the world. I was his Son. That was my mother's trump card. She used it craftily and got nothing for herself, but she did get an inheritance for me, money for college. My father died and left me that money and some royalty rights. He wanted me to become a scholar, I supposed, but my mother and I both knew that college money had to have a direct payoff. I studied English, business, international marketing relations, while my father howled from beyond. I had got into a good university, and I worked hard. Keiji, my best friend, whom I met shortly after enrollment, remembers me then as "endearingly serious."

When I was just at college, the first month or so, I heard from my father's old mistress, now a Mrs. Ogawa running a kimono shop on the Ginza, Tokyo's exclusive shopping district. Reiko had married but was already a widow—her husband had been much older than she, in his late sixties, and hadn't lasted long. Her family had run the kimono shop for over a hundred years, and being widowed and childless, Reiko took over. She had, more or less, approached me about losing my virginity. Discreetly, of course. She was older now, close to thirty-five, almost of my mother's generation but better preserved. Much better preserved: she had kept her figure, stayed slim. Perhaps because of her old-fashioned husband, she still perfumed her sleeves, used almond oil on her hair, powdered the nape of her neck. For some reason she gave me a feeling of importance, being so classic, a murmur from a time when men and women were very separate, when women more or less lived for men. Delicately, as an art—flowers turning toward the sun and all that. I am not saying I approve of that era—I prefer the broken barriers, the ambiguity of now—but when one is eighteen, things are very urgent and undone, and to shy boys the simplicity of the past holds a certain appeal. I think she may have been planning our encounter for a long time, watching, unfolding expectations along with obi sashes and bolts of cloth, waiting for me to grow up.

She had me come for a visit during my first semester—her shop was nearby, her apartment closer—under the pretense of giving me some of her late husband's books. I wore a suit that afternoon, the first really adult clothing I ever owned, and as I walked there I noted how a lot of women glanced at me. This I liked, the attention, although I still had difficulty glancing back and found it ironic and depressing that someone who was looked at so often had never touched a woman significantly. I was so self-conscious it was as if I were balancing an egg on top of my head. I had picked up a new mannerism to cover my awkwardness: the mask face. Seem preoccupied, seem indifferent. They only looked harder. That was my out-on-the-street face for many years, before actual preoccupation took its place. I recognize the look on many younger people today and cannot help but wince.

It was a slow afternoon, pleasurably so. Mrs. Ogawa had a certain body type—girlish, very small breasts, long waist, flat hips—which because of its spareness had resisted age. Over that winter I visited her often. She merely let me practice, asking nothing for herself, provided me with a set of training wheels of sorts: it had no future, this thing, yet it had a colossal sense of the past. For her it was a step backward, a reactivation of her youth. Her house was very traditional as well, with few modern touches, so unusual for a person in appliance-happy Tokyo.

Here she also taught me certain graces that she felt might come in handy later in my career, certain subtleties you would not learn in a classroom, like the conversational importance of listening and questioning, as well as the significance of silence; how to hold a Western knife and fork, use a soup spoon, spread a napkin across your lap; not to talk with your mouth full and to rise when greeting ladies. That blue and gold were my best colors; how to identify the styles of the various classical composers; the importance of washing one's hair and not overdoing it on fried foods, how a vegetable soap might be good for my complexion. We spent many hours together during that brief period. Each time I left her and emerged back into reality, I was almost disgusted to see all the modern fashions, the things like pay phones and vending machines, which cheapened my own existence. Although I sometimes felt him watching us, hovering, for once in my life the fact that I was following in my father's footsteps did not bother me. I was grateful for the opportunity, saw it as sort of swimming in the same lake he had. I stopped the visits just after I met Taeko, my wife, but there was no hysteria or animosity; I even referred Taeko to the Ogawa shop for her wedding kimono, where she received a family/ friend discount. My training wheels were off, I could ride free, assert myself with women to a normal extent. Reiko understood. I remember the whole period in a sepia tone, segmented, as if I had acted for a season in a play set in the Meiji era: I had played a student in a cap and a uniform; Mrs. Ogawa had played herself.

I send her something every New Year's, something delicate and frivolous—a basket of candy and fruit, a crystal ornament, perfumed soaps. I have also referred many business associates to her, but I have not spoken to her on the phone or face-to-face since shortly after then. I have a great deal of gratitude for her beyond

the sexual sense—surely that would have evaporated soon enough.
It regards the matter of self-importance: how one can never truly
acknowledge others until he has a feeling of confidence in himself,
a frame in which to center things, to hang from in shaky situations.
Mrs. Ogawa provided this for me, enabled me to lift my thoughts
out of the murky pool of my skull, shake them dry and turn them
outward. Of course she had the motive of her own vanity, as well
as her continued association with a legend, even after his death,
but I accepted that just as I accepted her husband's books. An
unexpected part of my father's legacy, I took it for what it was and
enjoyed it. There are so few people who are kind without motive
—you will drive yourself crazy trying to find them or trying to be
that way yourself.

◆

My name is Jun Shimada, and for eight and three quarters years
I was an employee of the Yamamoto Corporation, the number-five
electronics firm in the world. After I left, it became number four,
but I do not take that personally. I was a Salaryman. The French
have a better term for it—*un homme d'affaires*—but the French
have a better word for everything and tend to be individualistic.
A Salaryman (*sararīman*) is a midlevel executive who does not so
much follow the nine-to-five punch-punch of the time clock but
rather draws a set sum of money, working long hours to advance
the corporation he is part of and thereby eventually advance himself. Just as many cogs move the machine, many bees fill the hive,
many cells fill the body with their tiny labors—such is how it
works.

 I joined Yamamoto right after I graduated university, at the
Tokyo office. The year following, I married; the year following that,
our first child was born. At Yamamoto, I, like all new recruits,
plunged right in. I began doing surveys galore, marketing and
demographics, spent a short time in Legal Affairs to learn the ins
and outs, was sent to the big home plant in Kobe, where each
evening they sing the corporate hymn, then went back to geographic

strategy and analysis of American markets. I was promoted on a regular basis; my status increased, and so did my hours at the office. It was inescapable. Salarymen put in fifteen-hour days oftentimes, yes, but don't feel sorry for us. Not every minute is spent at a desk. Socializing is inherent in the job: e.g., a meeting with O. from Asahi Real Estate may run into dinner and drinks, pushing things toward eleven P.M. (we eat rapidly, but we do not rush mealtime); or a conference with K. and A. and H. from the Osaka office may be conducted on the golf course, on a Saturday morning, or perhaps at a tearoom, in the midst of several young women. I could never quite understand all the hoopla over us industrious Japanese: any German or English or American businessman worth his salt puts in similar hours, only he is working for himself, following a lonely ego course—whereas we charge in a pack, yipping and urging each other on.

For many years, nothing pleased me more than a good day's work. Having had such a cloudy background, I felt driven to prove myself as levelheaded, a *doer*, not a quivering intellectual like my father. I loved the beginning of the day, small pots of tea and newspapers being distributed to everyone; the noisy activity, the clutter, three of us sharing a phone. I enjoyed the sense of accomplishment at the end of the day—pages that were blank now filled with numbers, a mass of data compressed into concise reports, items on a list ticked off, trash cans filled with financial sheets, doughnut wrappers, empty coffee cups and cigarette stubs. To have my pencils sharpened, my desk heaped with papers, typewriters clacking around me, phones ringing, all used to give me a jolt akin to vigorous exercise. I quote my Yamamoto office manual, page one.

Every day must have a plan, a track upon which to guide the restless colt of one's ambition. He who does not plan fails and flounders. Life, within the office and beyond, should be organized, structured: our times are too chaotic to allow one single day to pass in a casual, haphazard fashion. Plan for now, and thus plan for the future. Wild ambition is useless in itself.

Money went into the bank; my wife and I accumulated kitchen gadgets, TVs, radios, clocks (all Yamamoto products); I began to buy better suits. My fifth-year anniversary passed, and I was given an Omega watch and treated, along with the various other members of my starting group, to lunch in the boardroom. I remember the meal well: first, because it was foreign—prime ribs, asparagus, pâté, chocolate truffles that nearly gave us all a rush (we are not used to sweets), and a *vin rouge* bottled the year of our hire. The second reason I remember the lunch is because what happened following it changed my life.

Things became a little boisterous toward the end, as they always do, a general high-spirited drunken flush, and we began singing the corporate anthem, with old Yamamoto, our president, leading from the head table. I myself was somewhat subdued, trying to drink a cup of black coffee and pull myself out of the sugar coma I had dropped into, just sort of bobbing along with the waves, smiling. I admired the fine linen cloth beneath my elbows, the china and the silverware monogrammed with a golden *Y*, the lead crystal, the embroidered napkins—this was the Western service, used for special occasions. I puffed on a cigarette, suddenly feeling quite relaxed and at ease with myself, proud to be part of such an organization. The new watch on my wrist ticked smoothly, self-winding. My stomach was full; I was young, healthy, intelligent; I had a wife and a baby daughter, a clean home, acquaintances. All was right with the world. I turned to my neighbor, warmly, then in shock realized it was old Yamamoto himself, his black eyes glittering. My face stiffened. I had never been so physically close to him before; our knees were touching. I transferred my cigarette from one hand to the other, then, before I could think, dropped it into my china coffee cup, where it made an ugly sputtering noise.

"S-sorry," I mumbled. I fished the butt out and dropped it into an ashtray, wiping my fingers on my pants. "Excuse me, sir— wine's gone to my head."

"That's quite all right." Yamamoto was staring at me in the usual piercing manner, surveying the remains of dessert on my plate, the pink truffle wrappers. I had had four. "Everyone deserves a celebration."

I had no idea why he had sat down next to me, and curiosity was making me fidget. I thanked him for the watch. He smiled. I thanked him for the meal, and he nodded with a quick, pecking motion.

Yamamoto has always reminded me of a hawk: an older one, of course—he is nearly seventy—but one still quick and shrewd in assessing his prey. All my life I have been afraid of birds; when I was a baby, supposedly one tried to peck my eyes out. I don't remember this to be truthful, but perhaps it explains my nervousness toward them. Yamamoto, with his snowy tufts of hair and sharp bright face, was forever putting me on edge.

I waited.

"Shimada, your English is impeccable, is it not."

Another habit of Yamamoto's—turning a question into a statement. Though he may have phrased his words as a question, the intonation never followed suit. I think this came from his years of giving orders in the army; he was quite the decorated officer. I had seen his official war portrait at his penthouse home in Tokyo: Yamamoto young and imperious, the narrow but erect shoulders of his uniform covered with stars.

He repeated himself. I stammered something about how one never really knows another language, that it's a career in itself, but he cut me short.

"You speak better than anyone in the corporation. I've seen your translation work. And I myself put you into Executive Training."

This was true. Just the last year I had been assigned to several hours a week of coaching those executives going to America, helping them with idioms and smoothing out the awkwardness of their accents, although ironically enough I had never left home. I had had a tutor early on, however, a Mr. Solomon Levy from Long Island, who had come to Japan on a Fulbright to study tea whisks and never left. For an American he was relentless, worked me like a mule. Even his name—*Solomon Levy*—as well as *Long* and *Island*, was difficult to pronounce, like having a rubber band on the tip of your tongue.

"It has occurred to me that someone like you is not reaching full potential at the home office," Yamamoto said, while around him several members of the catering staff began clearing away the remains of lunch. I noticed the looks of my co-workers as they filed out of the room to go back to their desks—some worried, some envious, but all staring doglike nonetheless at the sight of me and Yamamoto. They probably thought I was becoming a president's man. He continued.

"I think you might do better with your language skills where you can use them best. Now, you know we've just opened a New York office, and I'm planning to venture there for a while and establish things. You were aware of that." I nodded. "Well, within a year or so I want to open another branch in Chicago, and then Los Angeles. I'd like you to accompany me on the project. I need someone who can communicate, who can help me build an American staff. Tell me, are you interested?"

An actual question from him. I felt a strange paralyzed tingling through my fingers; my arm, propped in its awkward position, had fallen asleep. The United States: I tried to visualize the map we had studied at school—yellow for the east coast, blue for the middle, green for the west coast, and small black *v*'s for the mountainous regions. To live in the United States, drive its highways, watch its television shows. I stared at Yamamoto blankly.

"I don't expect an answer from you now, but I do ask you to consider it. You understand. And keep it in confidence—I'm only choosing nine or ten. I want a young group with me, open-minded."

There was a screech of wheels from a cart heaped with dishes. The floral centerpieces were being taken away. I paused for a moment, now knowing what to say, then reached for my cigarettes, but the pack was empty. Besides, it was poor form to smoke in front of a superior unless he initiated the action. I pushed my hand through my hair instead and forced myself to look the hawk in the eye.

He leaned closer. "I realize this is an unusual place to raise the issue, but I figured you were in the proper spirit. I wanted to catch you at that moment. Forward-moving, looking toward the future."

"I am," I said.

"Of course you are. You're an adventurous type, Shimada, I can see that. A pioneer spirit. This is a new frontier for us, you know."

He pushed himself away from the table and stood, one hand resting lightly on my shoulder. The room was now deserted. A warm breeze smelling of coffee came from the hallway and ruffled the boardroom drapes.

"Stop by my office later, and I'll give you more information. Exact locations, times, what you would be doing. Initially I'd like you in New York—we'll provide you with temporary housing—and then after a year or so, on to Chicago." He smiled broadly. I was surprised to see he still had most of his own teeth. "I'm sure your wife will find it very exciting."

Taeko. I had not even thought of her. A small red flag fluttered inside my head. Taeko was no pioneer.

Yamamoto put his hand on my shoulder again, this time with more force.

"Think about it. It's a wonderful opportunity. I'll speak to you again tomorrow, after you've given it more consideration."

I stood also and bowed as he walked away, limping slightly but with ramrod posture, his head back. He paused to hold the door open for one of the catering girls. I allowed myself a small grin, finally: The room had been filled with men, my co-workers, many more dynamic, more aggressive than myself, but Yamamoto had sat down at my side. I swayed, still a little dazed. I saw a bunch of rose petals from the flower arrangements, fallen on the carpet, and impulsively I scooped them up and folded them inside my handkerchief. They were tender, a soft pink, like the lobes of a baby's ear. They seemed a good enough omen to me: birth, beginnings, a new start. To go to the United States . . . I would talk to Taeko about it that night, as persuasively as I could. I stuffed the handkerchief into my pocket and with difficulty tried to keep from smiling further.

Yes, I will admit that much. I was indeed smiling when I took the bait.

They say a tree or shrub cannot be transplanted without damage to its system. Of course many things are transplanted and survive, but there is always that initial period of shock and readjustment, roots paralyzed, groping for their old soil. My wife, Taeko, was that way. When I broke the news to her, firmly yet cheerily, as if announcing a wild vacation, she stared at me in disbelief but kept silent. I took the silence gratefully and rushed around getting ready to go out (I was treating her to dinner and dancing, a sort of softening of the blow), only when I came out of the shower and set myself up to shave, she was still on the striped armchair I had left her in. I had on my robe, my hair was wet, a nice September breeze was puffing about. I felt very clean and happy. It was growing dark. Taeko had her eyes closed, and her face was stony and hard to read. I chucked her under the chin.

"Come on," I said. "The reservation's for eight. Don't you want a bath before you get dressed?"

No response. Her legs hung off the chair, boneless, as though she'd lost the use of them.

"Taeko?"

The weight of her surprised me, falling forward, clutching me around the waist. I nearly lost my balance. She held me so tight I could just breathe—I had not known she was that strong. Her head bashed into my thighs, and her fingers clawed my buttocks.

"Don't make me go!" she screamed, so loud that the blare of the television next door stopped, the radio from above was lowered.

Our neighbors were listening. I cringed. "Don't! I can't live there—I don't want to go!"

"Taeko, shh . . . shut up." I tried to slip my hand over her mouth, but she twisted free, the mass of her hair whipping around like the tail of a wild horse.

"No!"

"Quiet, before somebody calls the police," I whispered, holding her head at such a painful angle that if she did move again she would snap her neck. I didn't mean to be brutal, but it was the only way to subdue her. The skin around her face was so taut her features seemed to be ripping forward, like an infant being born. She was stamping on my feet—I had never seen her like this. I guided her, still in the headlock, back to the armchair, scraping my knees on an end table. Our apartment was so ridiculously small, everything was piled on top of everything else.

"Now calm down. Do you want me to go without you?"

She was trembling, the area between her narrow shoulder blades damp with sweat. I touched the gauzy fabric of her blouse, mystified. I had never known Taeko to perspire so before.

She wriggled. "Let me *go*."

"How can I?" I said. Her muscles were still rigid. Having just come from the shower, I had no underwear on. I eased up, drawing my robe closed. Taeko sat forward, rubbing her face, and as the blood returned to her cheeks, she began to cry. I sighed and leaned back. We were obviously going nowhere that night.

"Why do we have to move there? I don't understand," she sobbed. "Why can't we stay here, where we belong. We don't belong there, we'll be foreigners, stupid foreigners who can't speak English. And the crime is terrible in New York. Something will happen . . . I know it!"

Her nose was running. I wiped it with the sleeve of my robe. She flailed away and turned on me again.

"New York! Out of the blue. You must have asked for a transfer," she hissed. "You want to get promoted."

"Well, yes, but I was offered the transfer," I said. Was that such a terrible thing, I thought, to want to get promoted? Why else was I there? Her bitterness puzzled me. "And yes, I accepted. You want me to do otherwise? You don't want me to get promoted? Do you want me to tell Yamamoto himself, oh, no, my wife's afraid to do anything exciting. She only wants to read about foreign places and go see foreign movies—she doesn't want to visit them. Taeko . . ."

I cradled her head, whispering, trying to impart my own excitement. "Think of what we can see there. The Empire State Building. The Rocky Mountains. We can take Etsuko to the Grand Canyon and Mount Rushmore. All the museums you can visit, and the space we'll have in our new house. A house! This time next year, we can be living in a house. How long would it take us here? Huh? Don't be frightened. You'll experience so much."

"No!" she sobbed. "I don't want to!"

"Taeko," I said again, softly, and with my finger brushed the curve of her left ear. "Is that really true? That you'd rather stay here than be with me?"

She stood up with some stiffness, adjusting her blouse and bra straps and putting herself to rights, while I waited for an answer. I simply could not understand. To me it all seemed a tremendous and incredible opportunity, to be able to live and work in another place, to have so many things to do and see, to bypass tiers and tiers of established hierarchy at Yamamoto and report directly to the man himself. This would be the greatest accelerated step of my life—to go beyond the subway commute and no parking spaces of Tokyo, to get out of this tiny hotbox we lived in, to have a house. To go where not everybody was the same, with the same, repetitive culture; where very few people would know about my father. Ever since Yamamoto had raised the subject, I had felt increasingly claustrophobic, to the point where had I been able to get on a plane that night, I would have done so without a second thought. I waited for Taeko to answer, my nerves bristling. I simply could not comprehend why anyone would not jump at the chance. I was wild on the subject; I had lost perspective. Although I tried as I looked around at the low-ceilinged square we lived in, with its flimsy walls, I simply could not comprehend. It wasn't that I didn't want her to be happy; I merely thought she was too afraid to try. She had always been indecisive—she came from a sheltered background—and she had transferred her dependence on her father to dependence on me. Taeko was the only person I ever habitually told what to do, and I thought that now once again it was my job to push her forward.

"Well," I insisted. "What do you say?"

But she gave me no answer. Instead she went and got herself a glass of wine, which she drank straight off, offering none to me and staring with such dead blankness I felt I had disappeared. Dusk was turning to night, and the pallor of her face was frightening. I reached for the lamp.

"Don't," she said. "Please."

"All right."

She sat on the floor, still staring through me. I moved my hands around, restless. I didn't even have Etsuko as a buffer—thinking we were going out, we had asked Taeko's mother to take her for the evening.

"Do you want to go to dinner?" I asked, hoping again that perhaps an elegant meal would cheer her up. "Maybe that's an easier question for you to handle."

"No, I don't think so," she said. "I won't be very good company."

"Well, I'm stuck with you either way." I laughed, to silence. I groped around, desperately wanting to make her stop all this, to shake it out of her.

"Taeko . . ."

"Mmm, how unusual for you even to be home this early," she mused. "And to want to eat at a restaurant. I should have known it was bad news."

She poured another glass of wine, her eyes glazed, and sighed between sips, each sigh longer than the next.

"Has someone died?" I exploded. "Am I leaving you for someone else? No, it's just the opposite. I could go without you—how would you like that? It's not a permanent transfer, maybe five years at the most. Would you like to be apart that long? It's an option. We'll have half a marriage. I'll see you for two weeks out of fifty-two, during home leave. How would you like that?"

"I don't know."

"You'd consider it?" I was jolted. To me, after my upbringing, the most important thing was family: that I should have a base to revolve around; that my daughter should feel very sure of my presence. My hours at the office were lengthy, yes, but still I was there. She would know I was there, daily, as her father and not some strange figure dashing in and out yearly for a fortnight.

I finished what wine was left in Taeko's glass. "You'd want a marriage like that?" I asked.

"I don't know," she said again, without emotion, and laid her head in my lap.

More breezes came through the sliding glass windows, exciting the wind chimes into music. Cheap, made of hollow bamboo and invisible nylon thread, the chimes were nonetheless very evocative. We had had them forever, it seemed. When we moved, Taeko did not bring them with the other things, and when I asked her about them she looked at me in the new, dead way and said that she had forgotten them on purpose, that she didn't want to be reminded of home.

Taeko, you see, was not a typical salaryman's wife. She was not a wild free spirit, no, but there was a certain deep and stubborn streak that asserted itself in quiet ways. An art student at university, she had been passionate about her studies yet at the same time unfocused and unsure about her own talent, which was in painting and drawing. She had, I was later to learn, got into the school through what we refer to as the "little door," really a sizable contribution from her father, who owned a chain of furniture stores. Not that Taeko was stupid, but as I said, she was unfocused and her grades not spectacular; she dropped out shortly after our marriage, tired of the incestuous circle of the art department and claiming that she could learn more on her own.

Why she had sought me out was a mystery to me at first; I worked at a student job in the slide library, was fairly conservative and was irritable in the presence of art majors, who tended to hold business students like myself in contempt, calling us "cogs." And I sneered right back at them, at their sophistry, saying to myself that art is a machine too, with even smaller and cheaper cogs. These were the sort of people my father loved, I assumed. Bohemians.

Taeko, being winsome and decorative, was the darling of the leaders of this crowd—their little doll, whom they dressed up in odd fashionable costumes and hats. She didn't seem to speak much, but she was always there with them, smiling or staring calmly into space. She was slim and soft-skinned, with a heart-shaped face and a small, serious mouth. I noticed her right off but never indicated any interest—she seemed a specific appendage of their ringleader, an exotic, almost Burmese-looking guy named Sakamoto, who was said to have great talent. But one day, when she had come into the library alone and was returning a set of Cézanne slides, she handed me a sketch she had done of me at my desk. It was not bad; perhaps my eyes were spaced too far apart, but nonetheless I was enchanted. Flustered as well, that this type of girl would pay attention to me. Normally I attracted the straightest of the straight. I held back a little, thinking it was a joke on Sakamoto's part, a setup, but then hope got the better of caution, and I asked her to a coffeehouse. She accepted. She had a slow and lovely way of talking, and we did talk, then and on subsequent meetings. We began to date. She wore her hair then in a braid over one shoulder, smelled like ginger grass. When she spoke, the lower half of her face—the solemn mouth—barely moved, yet the eyes were excitable. I remember snatches of things that she said:

"Oh, yes, your father's photo is in the literature library. He's in a suit, holding a lily. Now that I know who you are, I see the resemblance. I always did like that picture."

"Sakamoto? Mmm, yes, he's very talented. He's fearless, that's why his painting is so good. Everything I do is self-conscious. He has a lot of girlfriends, not only me. He's very charismatic, I suppose, though we're pretty much through. He's used me up, done as many portraits and studies as he could, and now he's focusing on a girl who studied in Paris. She's much more talented than I could ever be. And I knew Sakamoto was never serious about me. I simply went along for what he could teach me. You're so much kinder and more attentive. And so serious. I like that."

I puffed with pride. It amazed me, hearing about Sakamoto, to see how far these types could get—these cultural gurus—and I was thinking of not only Sakamoto but my father. They aged, yet their mistresses or disciples or whatever did not. They were replaced; there was always a fresh supply—girls willing to be used up like tubes of paint, sheets of paper, even to die with their master, like my father's last involvement. Was it that only the very young and naive were capable of putting up with the pretensions of these types; or was it only the very young and naive who could understand the purity of their emotions? I couldn't figure it out; I saw developing in myself certain monogamous tendencies. I liked the thought of focusing in on one target for a number of years, and I was already focusing in on Taeko. I had no family; I was eager to get married. Taeko, while obviously not the best choice for a businessman's wife, still had a steadying effect on me, on my coursework. She made me feel I was not working out of a vacuum, talking to myself. My mother was still alive, of course, but I wanted to break free of her: her love was desperate.

I continued to pursue the relationship.

"It must be difficult," Taeko once said, "studying business. Stuff you hate. I don't envy you."

"Hate?" I objected. "But you're wrong—I don't hate my studies. Some of the subjects are dull, yes, dry, but I can handle them. They put things into perspective. Maybe you might hate the idea of accounting or economics, but I don't."

"Mmm, of course," she replied. "And you're going to work for a corporation?"

"Yes, I am." I had a tone of defensiveness to my voice. "I want to be secure."

She nodded, but her words were unenthusiastic. "I might be a hindrance to you, with a job like that. I don't think I'd have the right attitude."

"Oh, don't be such a pessimist," I insisted, squeezing her hand and toying with the soft fingers. "Keiji's going to work for a corporation too," I said, referring to my best friend. "You like Keiji. He's not a monster. You'll do fine. Really. You don't give yourself enough credit."

"No." She nodded again, thoughtfully. "I suppose I don't."

Her family absorbed me in slow stages, the process quickening somewhat after our engagement. I liked being there, seeing her father and mother, her three sisters, their old-style Japanese home with modern Western bathtubs. Her father, although somewhat abrupt and formal at first, warmed to me after he had thoroughly investigated my background. Despite the circumstances surrounding my birth, my father had given me his name. Taeko's father approved of my aspirations and the fact that his daughter had got away from her artist friends. Though I'm sure he would have preferred to pick Taeko's husband for her, he seemed pleased enough with our "love" match. I liked to visit them, flip through the photo albums of Taeko and her sisters at various ages, hear all their childhood stories and see old home movies of their vacations.

"Oh, come on!" Taeko once protested, laughing, as I asked to look through the teenage album again. "You've seen it ten times —you're worse than a little kid with bedtime stories!"

I also liked to watch Taeko's mother and father bickering agreeably, feed the fish out in the pebble pond, help Taeko's younger sister with her English grammar. They were so established, so clean—so distant from the railroad tracks; there was a friendly sense of leisure about them I longed to enjoy myself.

"You have such a pleasant family, Taeko," I often remarked. Generally she would agree or just nod, but one reply I remember in particular.

"Mmm, yes, but Father's too strict."

"Oh, he's just protective of his daughters." I smiled.

"Maybe." Taeko stroked her eyebrow, again and again, as if trying to erase it. "But I am dying to get out of the house," she added. "Become an adult."

Shortly after my graduation we were married, a traditional affair: Taeko wore a kimono, I wore a suit. Taeko had already dropped out of university and taken a job at the Western Art Museum, counting pictures or something. She quit after the wedding and threw her creative efforts into decorating our apartment. She seemed very happy, playing house; her dress was more conservative now, her hair no longer in a braid but in a bun, her art supplies in a case in our one closet. My co-workers leered at her whenever she came to meet me at work, taking her at face value, which to them was about all she offered; and my mother worshiped her. We spent more time together then, Taeko and I. My hours were not so long—I was generally home by seven; I had more energy, particularly after my evening bath. I remember how I jumped up and down in nervous happiness and broke a vase when she told me she was pregnant. Etsuko was born, and a bit of stress invaded our lives—the apartment seemed smaller, Taeko began to have back pain—but it was nothing tragic. Time worked it out. And then, well. I could still see her expression when I had told her we were moving to the States, how her features stiffened and that tiny spark of resentment came into her voice. She was not the same after: it was as if I had slapped her. No more excited, happy stories about her day when I walked in the door; no more nibbling on my fingers to wake me up on weekends. Poor Taeko, she cried every night for a month. And when I left for New York, initially on my own, six months after the talk with Yamamoto, Taeko and I faced each other stonily, half exhausted, as if we hoped never to see each other again.

But of course we did.

◆

The flight from Tokyo to New York seemed akin to a journey to another planet, thirteen hours nonstop, sealed in the hermetic tube of an airplane. They drew shades over the windows to simulate nighttime and played soothing koto music, served sashimi, rolled a full bar up and down the aisles. I always find it amusing to think of people eating and drinking thirty thousand feet in the air.

I was very wired; I could not sleep. Next to me, Keiji dozed on and off, did a strange yoga exercise, pressing the heel of his hand against each of his ears from time to time, and listened to English conversation tapes on the earphones of his Yamamoto tape player. We were venturing off on our own at first—actually, *I* was venturing off on my own: Keiji had no family to speak of. Keiji Narata, whom I had known since college, had had radicals for parents and spent most of his early years at concerts and protests, until his father and mother were killed in a motorcycle accident, leaving him to be raised by grandparents. I considered Keiji another person touched by strangeness, but unlike me, he did not hide it very well. My first encounter with him—the memory could still make me chuckle ten years after—had been in a first-year economics class, the first test of the semester, in fact, which everyone was in great dread of. I knew Keiji by sight, but I had not spoken to him yet. He broke the ice when another of our classmates, a pale, lanky guy who took scrupulous notes, swayed forward and threw up as the exam was being passed out. Anxiety, I supposed, although the instructor was nonplussed and made him take the test anyway. While we were waiting for a janitor to come and clean up, Keiji pointed to the mess and whispered to me in English: "Din-ah is suh-erved. . . ." He drawled this in a British butler's accent. The remark shot my remaining tension all to hell.

He was an odd fellow, Keiji, extremely tall for a Japanese— nearly six feet—thin yet powerfully built, with proud, angular features. Unmarried and bitingly sarcastic, he did not fit the mold at Yamamoto but was kept on because of his incredible marketing savvy, particularly toward Western markets. He had taken the job for the money, he insisted, wanting to be financially independent, though it was soon obvious after we both started that Keiji was not just another suit on the rack. While he truly loved his work, he despised the salaryman code—the conformity of dress, behavior, life-style—and he fought it desperately. After hours, he dressed in a kamikaze fighter jacket and rode a motorcycle, frequented some of the roughest bars in the city, was a member of an avant-garde cinema club and strange troupe of sensory-release adventurists who covered in head-to-toe body stockings, hung suspended upside down for hours from ceilings on cords. He was a thrill seeker. And it had also occurred to me, only because I knew him so well and because he hinted at such from time to time, that Keiji was bisexual. We did not discuss it openly—there was a certain line of confidence neither of us crossed—yet I had a feeling. Of something. Perhaps for someone as highly tuned as Keiji, one sex was not enough. He was attractive to women, though he rarely went out with them. My own wife even confessed that she found Keiji's aloof attitude "intriguing," a casual comment she made only once yet with such a low thrill to her voice I actually was jealous for a minute.

Still brash and resistant, Keiji was being sent overseas for different reasons than myself, more or less in the way family black sheep used to be shipped off to Australia. And besides, Yamamoto needed him in the States. Keiji had uncanny insight into "things American," or rather what aspects about our culture Americans would gobble up. Keiji called me by my family name, and I called him by his first. There was a certain enduring irritability to our friendship, like that of an old married couple. And now we were off to the U.S. Taeko and our daughter, Etsuko, and Cho, the dog, would come later, after I had got settled, and most reluctantly, I might add.

There was nothing to be done about that.

So I did not sleep. I merely drifted in and out of a series of hallucinations—that there were schools of fish outside the window, that the clouds were frozen waves. A woman across the aisle spilled tomato juice all over her silk dress; I felt sorry for her and thought of offering her my handkerchief, then remembered it was the one with the rose petals wrapped inside, now dried to dull brown husks, so I gave her my cocktail napkin instead. I had brought the withered rose petals with me deliberately. It did not seem wise to start my adventure without them.

By the time we landed, I was ready to spring out of my seat. My legs had become wood limbs from nearly a whole day of sitting, and I dragged them stiffly down the aisle. The stewardesses were like bobbing flowers on a receding shore.

"Sayonara . . . ," they called.

Keiji and I entered the blast of Kennedy Airport, rush hour, hugging the sidelines and trying to determine where to go next. I had never seen such a mixed crowd in my life, heard so many different languages and raucous voices. A sea of dead-faced limo drivers beyond the arrival area held signs with the names of the people they were supposed to pick up; we were not being met. We headed straight for the customs line. A black man in a flannel shirt and heavy boots, from a construction crew working nearby, approached Keiji with money in his hand and said, "Say, man, can you bust up this five?" Keiji blinked, uncomprehending. It took me a moment to figure out what he meant, and I translated for Keiji, who hopped up and down, delighted, then dumped several small one-yen pieces into the man's outstretched palm. I laughed too; the man walked off, his face hard, glaring at us as if we were crazy.

"What else did he expect?" Keiji said. "We're right off the boat."

I nodded. My own money was inside my sock in a leather pouch, a departing gift from my co-workers, who all seemed convinced we would be killed within minutes of landing in New York.

Keiji was about to pass through customs. He turned toward me briefly before stepping up to the counter and, eyes crossed, saluted the American flag. There was an odd, tight look to his face, and I knew that he was even more excited to be here than I was.

I thought of Yamamoto's speech suddenly: "You're an adventurous type, Shimada, I can see that. A pioneer spirit. This is a whole new frontier for us, you know."

The sound of his voice came to me amid the chaos. No doubt Keiji had received the same sales pitch, I thought, perhaps even word for word.

A christening party. We were being given our American names. Seated around the marble boardroom table of the Manhattan office, we laughed uproariously as each of us was assigned his alter ego. Yamamoto, having a grand old time, was handing out smiley-face buttons with the names inscribed so they would be easier to remember and so we could practice on each other. We were to use these American names exclusively with American associates, who tended to have trouble pronouncing our real names and distinguishing first name from family name, or even male from female.

I was John. Keiji was Ken. Michio was Mike, Tomohiro Tom, Atsu Ed, etc., etc., and Yamamoto himself had accepted our collective suggestion of James.

"I like that," he pronounced, smiling. "James Stewart, right?"

"Or maybe James Dean," Keiji countered. Yamamoto glowered for a moment, then let go of a laugh. We then again all laughed. He continued on and reached the end of the list with Ichiro, our intern.

"You are Henry," Yamamoto said. His eyes twinkled. He handed Ichiro's button to Keiji to pass down, only Keiji slid it like a hockey puck across the table. Yamamoto frowned. Ichiro was frowning also.

"Oh, I don't like that," he said, so softly we could barely hear him. We were all surprised to hear him speak up; Ichi was so young and quiet, maybe twenty-two years old, with a long, boyish face.

"What's that?" Yamamoto asked.

Ichi nodded, stammering. "Excuse me, sir, I don't like that name—do you suppose I could have another one?"

We were all still shocked into silence. Keiji, however, was regarding Ichiro with a bit more interest. We assumed a talking-to would commence. But for some reason Yamamoto did not seem upset.

"You don't like Henry?"

"No, sir."

"Doesn't like Henry. Huh. You have another choice?"

"No, sir."

"Well . . ." Yamamoto paused, finger to his temple. "Where do you sit, young man?"

"On the west wing." Ichiro was practically whispering now, head bent. I could see he was sorry he'd spoken up.

"Ah, sure, by the copy machine?" There was a squeak of a response. "West wing by the Xerox." He coughed. "Well, then, we'll call you Xerox. Is that better, you think?"

We were all laughing again, relieved; even Ichiro giggled as we patted him on the back and greeted him jovially as Xerox.

"You like Xerox?" Yamamoto said.

"No, sir."

"You want Henry back, then?"

"Yes, sir."

Yamamoto clapped his hands like a magician and imitated a cloud of smoke. He was laughing also.

"Henry it is, if you insist," he said, then put on his own button and said, "Let's practice," and we all nodded at each other across the table and began, seriously, with a round of introductions.

◆

Things changed, in an uncomfortable downward spiral. The bright hopes I had for working in the States never quite materialized, though I waited patiently for things to improve and take shape, to emerge from the period of adjustment, which was like a vast wind-storm that kept changing direction. For some reason, perhaps because of my looks or my manners—the flat, handsome exterior I projected—Yamamoto had picked me out as his pet. Not protégé—which implies forward movement, learning, an eventual assumption of power or talent—but pet, to be treated lightly and assigned all sorts of frivolous duties. Although at home I had truly enjoyed detailed work, anonymous work, compilation of statistics, review of surveys, marketing plans—how I loved marketing work, the thought of all those little black-haired consumers from Hokkaido to Kyushu gobbling up the latest fads; and how I looked forward to studying American markets, so regional and diverse— suddenly I was taken out of marketing and given the rarely used title of Special Projects Assistant: i.e., Pet.

In the Manhattan office, my desk was not in the maze, with the others, but rather within the corporate suite, right next to Yamamoto's New York assistant, Miss Ozaki. ("Secretaries" are generally men in Japanese businesses, men like me.) Right out there in the open, most decorative. You could not smoke or put your feet up or take off your jacket—no privacy, but you were allowed to help yourself to the executive stock of Perrier, croissants in the morning, tea and cakes in the afternoon. This was little consolation, as I had been excluded, distanced from the others. I would rather have been out there with them, eating bagels and doughnuts, and I found myself forced to act humble to them all the time, just to keep their friendship. My responsibilities seemed to be as follows: to dress as tastefully as possible and to be impeccably groomed (something like a hotel concierge); to act as intermediary and occasional spy between Yamamoto and the American and Japanese workers (but never to become too involved with real matters, lest I give something away); to handle Yamamoto's phone calls to any English-speaking persons, as he was not comfortable with the language yet didn't want a mere assistant involved; and lastly and most distastefully, to handle the "special projects." This could be anything from the translation of a report to going and picking out shirts and socks for him, as he didn't like to deal with rude American clerks and had a theory that even in the best stores Japanese were always overcharged. The lists I compiled these days were names of U.S. golf courses and airports, top hotels, boutiques, Japanese dentists.

I found myself hiring the Yamamoto chauffeur (fortunately they spared me that job) and attending many cultural events with either Yamamoto or his wife, or with both. Here charm and witty conversation became prerequisites, as did the ability to divorce myself from a performance or a meal and write down whatever memo or order Yamamoto was dictating.

People outside the company mistook me for an idiot son or son-in-law, too foolish to have a real job but ornamental enough to serve some purpose. I resented this, deeply, but then I would see how a little smirk of what almost looked like pride would stretch across Yamamoto's face when such a mistake was made, how his voice was more relaxed with me than with other employees, how he took an interest in my family life to the point of intrusion. He had no children—presumably this was his fault; he had had two wives. I had no father, and I was so ingratiating. Chromosome X combined with Y to form Z in vitro: I was his son. He had adopted me, my wife, my daughter, singled us out. While he tended to call many of his younger employees just that—"son"—with me it was pronounced with a particular richness, a dynastic sound.

Other men, more cunning and ambitious than myself, men with a full set, would have milked the situation dry, coasted along till the right moment, then taken over. Not I. I didn't want power; power made me nervous. I couldn't handle it, like strong drink— I couldn't even handle my wife. Instead I fidgeted and balked, I refused privilege; I kept looking longingly at the bullpen I had come from and walked around as if my tie was too tight. The unhappy prince. All I really wanted was to be busy and anonymous, functional, just another employee—Yamamoto might know my last name but not my first. Exposed so long by the bright light of my father, like a mole I kept searching for shade.

I had my little rebellions, like using the common washroom instead of the executive one, thrilled to be back with the others as they crapped while reading the *Wall Street Journal*. I never missed a chance at lunch or after-hours drinking with the others, for fear they might label me standoffish, and I paid for a lot of these drinks (my salary was slightly higher than theirs, though they didn't know it). I also took a sullen pleasure in the way I dressed, figuring that if I was going to be decorative I might as well do it up, and I stepped into the heretofore unknown regions of patterned ties, black rather than blue suits, cufflinks. This pleased the others, as once I presented myself in a clownlike role they relaxed around me, called me *GQ* man and admired my argyle socks, the dab of Hayashi pomade I smoothed onto the sides of my hair, my two-tone umbrella. Yamamoto never said anything. Sometimes he gave me the Look, sternly, but in general he was indulgent toward his stylish son, who cut such a memorable figure, like a hood ornament.

He loved to have me around. My desk was within yelling distance of his suite (he disliked the intercom—for an electronics mogul, he was very old-fashioned), and if I was not at my desk—perhaps bitterly smoking a quick cigarette in the employee lounge—my name would be announced over the paging system, echoing over four floors: *Jun Shimada, report to the executive area. Jun Shimada, report to your office* . . . , and I would scramble back, to everyone's further amusement.

Just once I made noises of unhappiness to Yamamoto, after a particularly trying day wherein my duties had ranged from the drafting of a tentative budget for the executive area to having *Y.Y.*—Yoshi Yamamoto—embroidered on the cuffs of all his dress shirts. The Yamamotos' maid couldn't do this: she didn't speak English well enough; and besides, Yamamoto wanted it done by a specific Italian tailor, who apparently refused to talk to women. Mrs. Yamamoto was planning a dinner party that week and needed someone to talk to the caterers. Give it to Shimada; he knows what a finger bowl is. Miss Ozaki seemed able only to type and take messages, make tea, and page me on the PA system. She was useless. I glared at her, sitting there with her little gray upsweep, as I spent an hour taking notes on caviar. Yamamoto strolled in from making his rounds—he liked to swoop around and be "public" at some point during the day—and paused before me, concerned.

He had just caught me slamming down the receiver in a most unprofessional manner.

"Is there a problem, Shimada?" he asked. "You look a bit piqued. Come inside. We'll talk."

In his office I blurted out something about whether perhaps I could go back to doing the more mundane tasks I was better suited for, back to research or translation, how I truly wasn't worthy of performing such glamorous duties. I sat there, going on and on, and Yamamoto nodded, seeming to listen while leafing through his mail. But already he was sorting certain letters into the red file folder I received each day: the Shimada file, worn and tattered, often stuffed to bursting. Just the sight of it there made me lose all hope.

He pushed the folder toward me, and I accepted it, placing it stiffly on my lap. It was a test, which I failed. A truly earnest man would have left the folder there and continued pleading his case. But I took it; I didn't have the nerve not to. To Yamamoto this confirmed that these were my true duties—these silly things—that I was perfect for the job, intelligent, discreet, but thoroughly unambitious. No killer instinct. I nearly apologized for wasting his time.

He regarded me warmly. He was in a rare jovial mood, all smiles and contentment: he must have just made a killing someplace.

"I rely on you a great deal, Shimada," he said, hands up, fingertips touching in contemplative prayer fashion. "You are indispensable to me. If I felt you were unworthy of your duties, I would have reassigned you long ago. You're doing a fine job; no need to worry. And there aren't many men in this corporation I would allow such a vantage point."

"Yes, sir."

"Your duties will become more sophisticated very shortly, when we open the Chicago office. Lots of traveling back and forth. You've never been to Chicago, have you."

"No, sir."

"A good city in its own right. Not so abrasive as New York."

"Yes, sir."

We went off on a tangent about my daughter and what musical instrument she might start on, seeing as she was nearing the age to begin all that, almost four. I got up and held the red folder to my heart.

"Tell Miss Ozaki teatime," Yamamoto called, yanking on his blinds to let in the afternoon sun. There was a note of further enthusiasm to his voice. Yamamoto loved his cup of tea.

I relayed the message and watched her jump at it. The red folder bulged before me, waiting, but I pushed it aside, as I hadn't yet finished all the items on the day's list.

The executive office was so formidable no one dared to come in and chat. The waiting-area sofas were uncomfortable and rarely used, the room so quiet you could hear the central air going on and off. I looked around, all alone, and opened up my wine list again, then with effort turned back toward my enemy, the phone, to make my next call.

◆

Sweep it under the rug. A Western saying, perhaps, yet so Japanese. Don't confront, question, or attempt to expose—simply continue as always, maintain face, and hope the storm clouds will pass. You might think it odd, but we are a cautious group, not fond of rocking the boat. Causing a scene, a stampede—maybe that is the key to it all, our being so perpetually packed, so crowded, into trains, stadiums, housing space: no one wants to step out of line. Certain levels of polite miscommunication can continue for years, because it seems so much easier to suffer in silence.

Such is how my wife and I went on, speaking yet not talking to each other. Nowadays I recall certain incidents with a cringe of my shoulders, incidents I was fully aware of at the time yet unable to deal with, happy that the press of daily activity was swallowing them up, cushioning them, carrying them away . . . or so I hoped. Perhaps it was my guilt—I had brought her here, I was responsible for her unhappiness—and perhaps it was my growing frustration with my job that kept me from acknowledging the guilt, made me flip it inside out, into resentment. It was her fault. I was dubious about my work because I was always worrying about her problems. I can see possibilities, but I'm no psychiatrist. I only know that the problems intensified; for both of us it seemed easier just to sweep them under our new beige rug and gradually avoid all levels of contact: first conversational, then physical; even the meeting of eyes became awkward. Slowly but steadily the plaster stiffened—suffocating, uncomfortable—yet I reiterate how much easier it was to sit still and let it harden than to try and break out.

Through the company, we had found a house—a small, blue-gray Cape Cod in a North Shore Long Island neighborhood that was becoming increasingly Japanese. Though I say "small," the home to me seemed Texas size after so many years spent in my mother's little hut, my various dormitory rooms, and the box of an efficiency Taeko and Etsuko and I had shared. It had a yard, a garage, a laundry chute (Etsuko's favorite place during games of hide-and-seek), a cellar, a den for me and an area in which I encouraged Taeko to take up her old hobbies of sewing and painting, to no avail. I even bought her a new easel, a box of Sakura watercolors and brushes, but she seemed more interested in painting her fingernails and toenails, slowly, repeatedly, lost in moody absorption; sometimes she changed the color every day. By the end of year one in the States, her shelf in the medicine chest was crammed with thirty shades of nail polish. Once I found a mosaic she had done, strange and abstract, a shattered geometrical face on a piece of Etsuko's posterboard, and as I examined the colors closely, I could tell by their lacquer and sheen that she had used nail polish as her medium. The following day the mosaic was in the garbage, under a blob of coffee grounds. I did not bring it up, I did not ask why or how or what, because she had not shown me the piece outright.

She was defensive about her work, insecure; the more I asked about it, the less communicative she became. "It's not a *hobby*," she had flared once. I bit my tongue, nearly answering, No, it's nonexistent, that's what it is. I had hoped the new surroundings would provide inspiration—not, to be truthful, because I thought she had great talent, but because painting and drawing seemed to soothe her, give her a sense of purpose. Give her something to do besides complain about New York. It did not. The easel and the watercolors went untouched, the brushes never came out of their plastic wraps. Our house was sparsely decorated: just the bare essentials, no special touches; Taeko was not sewing, sightseeing, or doing much of anything. Not learning English (she watched the Japanese TV station), not making new friends. Although the other relocated wives at Yamamoto had formed a small support group, Taeko refused to join them. Only once did she participate in an outing—to go shopping at the all-Japanese Yaohan Plaza in New Jersey. That was about as far as she was willing to venture.

Other scattered bits: Etsuko, aged five, at dinner, calmly observing to me over her spinach, "Mommy's dumb. She won't talk English like you and me"—while Taeko, thank heaven, was in the other room. A phone call I received early one Friday evening at work, from Keiji, who was in the building lobby. "You'd better get down here right away," he advised. Apparently Taeko, who was coming into the city on the train to meet Keiji and myself for dinner and the new Itami movie, had had an upsetting incident with an impatient female conductor. Keiji said Taeko had arrived sobbing. I was in a meeting, and by the time I reached the lobby, he was with her over by the corporate sculpture garden, leading her around and talking a mile a minute. He had calmed her with one of those rare, keen flashes of sensitivity he could show in times of crisis, their little fingers linked in what seemed almost like a secret handshake.

"Poor kid," he later remarked. "She's too isolated out in the suburbs—she'll never pick up. You should move to Manhattan. Force her out, give her something to do. Throw her to the sharks —she'll survive." Taeko rejected the suggestion. She was afraid of New York and its crime stories; on the streets she flinched and shuddered as if she were in a horror house.

"Don't be ridiculous. There are a million people walking around, surviving—just try," I urged. "Be on your guard, but see all there is, give it a chance. Bring Etsuko in to the museums, to the stores. You'll both have fun. You had fun in Tokyo."

"No. It's not the same," she countered. "I don't speak English; I can't learn it in a week. People make fun of me. I hate it. These women are so abrupt here, they think I'm an idiot. Etsuko's teacher said I should learn English with little children's books!" Taeko's eyes became red and teary at the recollection. "She says I should try to set a better example. It's so humiliating!"

I had so much to do in those days—I was forever ferrying visiting executives to and from the airport, escorting them to limousines and preparing itineraries for them; going to mixers and productivity seminars; running errands for Yamamoto. I went home to change clothes, it seemed; cooked my own dinner and ate it on a TV table while the dog and I watched the eleven o'clock news. I then went upstairs to lie in bed next to an already sleeping wife, then got up at six A.M. to start the whole cycle again. Taeko, who had previously had the distractions of her sisters and her girlfriends in Tokyo— shopping, movies, little pseudo-European pastry shops—now focused on my absence. I became the full target of her misery.

"Bye. See you Saturday," she would say to me, dully, on Monday morning. Or once, when I told her how much I liked living near the ocean, she replied, "Oh? When did you notice? Driving back and forth from the train?" She hated participating in corporate affairs, complained that the other wives were stupid and that nobody cared who she was or what she thought, so I stopped including her. And the chasm between us deepened.

"I thought you were different," she observed one weekend morning as I was stepping out for a Yamamoto outing with my golf clubs.

"Oh, yes? How so?" I asked, pausing.

Her face, desperate and dejected, floated before my own. "I thought you cared about other things in life—I thought you had perspective. You're such a company man. A cog, like Sakamoto said you would be."

It was an attempt to make me angry; I recognized it as that—she was frustrated, lashing out. I rubbed the last bit of sleep from my eyes impatiently and slapped my hand against my chest. "Look, it's my job, and I try to do it well. You don't understand the pressures of a real job—you do nothing all day but resent me. Make me out to be the villain, the idiot, the hypocrite. How do you think I feel? You don't care. I spend my whole life being *friendly* for this corporation to support you and Etsuko, to keep us going."

She seized my arm, her white tabi socks scuffing along the floor in great haste to keep up with my exit. "I'm sorry I mentioned Sakamoto—I'm sorry! But we don't have to live so well, really; I'd rather we had less money, less things, and more time together."

"You spend the money fast enough, though," I teased.

"Oh, but it's my *hobby*," she said back derisively, and then let me go. "What else is there to do?"

I hesitated for a moment, almost tempted to chuck the whole outing and my clubs, spend a Sunday with her in utter laziness, watching TV on the couch or simply lying on the grass out in the yard. But I couldn't, I simply could not manage something like that—I would have been guilt-ridden throughout, preoccupied with how to make up for my absence in the coming week. And I was still annoyed with her calling me a company man. She didn't understand the constant scrambling I went through all day long, the commute, one project after another—she, artist fashion, assumed I was doing it for my own ego. Did she ever care, give a damn, say, Oh, aren't you tired? and What happened today, what kind of nonsense did you have to put up with? No, it was more in the vein of: Home before midnight? Is it a holiday?

So I went to my golf game, stewing. I did not like golf, and it was obvious that I did not like my job either. I had blamed it at first on the trauma of adjustment to the new office, yet I leapt forward willingly into the newer trauma of helping to set up the

Chicago branch. Frequent commuting ensued—I was home for perhaps two weeks a month—yet I pumped up great enthusiasm for the project, telling myself it was another adventure, another foreign place. And to be truthful, I almost enjoyed the travel, which gave me an excuse to escape from home. Taeko began to experience more back problems and visited one Akira Saito, an orthopedist recommended by the Japan Bureau. Saito was handsome, extravagantly virile, and unmarried. He put her on a slew of painkillers, and she became very fond of them very quickly, their numbing effect. It seemed to me that she was visiting him more than was necessary, but I paid the bills and said nothing. Likewise when she told me she was pregnant again.

When I called from the office during the day, when Etsuko was in school, I rarely got an answer. The phone rang and rang. "What is it that you do all day long?" I asked once, lightly, while she was changing Omi, our new baby, with great effort. Taeko squared her shoulders and dumped the dirty diaper into the garbage pail. "Oh, sleep," she said equally lightly, and did not elaborate.

More swept under the rug. We were soon to be tripping under the bulges beneath our feet.

◆

Chicago, "Queen and guttersnipe of cities . . ." Where I first stepped off the beaten path, a path I knew so well I could have been a guide. Clearly I remember the nondescript December rain, the sound of a harp I followed up the stairs, summoned, although I knew it was hell and not heaven I was ascending to. The pain —a sharp, acidy feeling in the hollow of my chest—intensified as I saw old Yamamoto and his wife already seated, looking more than a bit uncomfortable in oversize chairs that tipped them slightly toward the delicate tea things on the table before them. A wedding party passed in a brightly colored stream, on its way to a reception; a small crew-cut boy in a miniature tuxedo looked at me and whispered, "I hate my shoes, I hate my shoes, I hate them both. . . ."

There were no other Japanese in sight.

Yamamoto waved, rose on stiff crane legs and motioned me over. The room was full of Water Tower shoppers, stopping off for tea at the Drake, with its fountain and its crystal chandelier: the after-museum crowd, the pre-theater crowd; the leisure class, all sitting very primly, munching sandwiches with the edges of their front teeth. The smell of wet fur intermingled with the other odors I always associate with expensive hotels: perfume, leather luggage, flowers, a bit of car exhaust from the cabs idling outside the entrance.

I made my way to the table, still in my trench coat. I had hoped to sneak a few minutes in the bathroom to collect myself—my bladder felt like a bruise, it was so full, and I had just got a haircut and was afraid there might be short black snips all over my face. There were mirrors all around, but they were distant, clouded by gray glass. Besides, it was too late to do anything now: Yamamoto had fixed me with his bird-of-prey stare and would keep staring at me until the meeting was over. Since arriving in the States and having him so relentlessly on my back, I had come up with a new analogy, beyond the hawk: to be with him was like having a needle in your arm—you could do nothing but wait, tensed, watching with patience as the blood left your vein slowly, until the needle was withdrawn and you could sit back, weaker, a bit sore, but glad to have it over with, have your arm back, even with its swollen pinprick.

"*Konban wa,*" I said. I bowed, greeting Yamamoto and his smiling wife, who had been a movie actress for several years and prior to that a famous Kyoto beauty. Still beautiful in an overdel-icate way, she was thin, with translucent skin powdered white, small bow-shaped mouth and a heavy twist of hair I estimated must reach to her hips when undone. She wore a black dress with a ruffly lace collar. You could barely hear the words she spoke, everything as frail as the teacup she held, perched just above its saucer. A large diamond on her finger blanched the flesh around it, made it look dead. The diamond caught the light from the chandelier and sparkled repeatedly, reflecting odd jags of color here and there. It was a little showy, but I was glad to see she had it, to sustain and anchor her small hand. She deserved something, I felt. After all, this woman lived with the needle in her arm every day.

As I removed my coat and gloves, I saw a flicker of disapproval cross Yamamoto's face at the sight of my new Italian suit and multicolored tie. The Look. The tie was not outlandish; its colors were muted, dull dark purple, green, blue—the colors of an oil slick, but still colors, not the usual salaryman uniform Yamamoto preferred, sober and monochromatic. Which is silly, because Asians can wear colors like nobody else. Mrs. Yamamoto seemed to like the outfit, though. Her eyes rested on me fondly, and her smile deepened.

"I'm so glad you could join us—"

"Did you get the Mont Blanc fixed yet?"

Both of them were speaking to me at once, though Mrs. Yamamoto deferred to her husband and went about pouring me tea, reaching across my lap. She placed a gold strainer on top of my cup and lifted the pot gently, tilting it forward. I caught a vague odor of perfume in her movements—stark, floral, like refrigerated orchids. Yamamoto sat upright and inclined his smooth white head in my direction, then repeated what he had said.

"Did you get the Mont Blanc fixed yet?"

I nodded. "He'll have it done by Monday." (The nib of Yamamoto's favorite pen had chipped.)

"What about the tour of the Field Museum?"

"Set up for next Thursday. It's a luncheon—your calendar was clear."

"The translation of the article in *Newsweek?*"

"All ready. Everything's finished, everything. Finished, done, all done." I paused, swallowed a mouthful of saliva. Although I had been working with Yamamoto closely for three years now, I was still flustered by him, even to the point of stammering. "I requested vegetarian for you at the Field Museum lunch, and mineral water. Otherwise it was quiche."

"Good. I want to close in on that netsuke hall endowment before Toshiba does." He turned impatiently to his wife, who was making small plucking gestures at his sleeve. "What? What *is* it?"

"You'll have to call the waitress. We need more hot water and pastry for Shimada-san."

Yamamoto, calling for service, stopped himself in midclap, gestured with a sharp snap of the wrist instead. His wife craned her neck anxiously, lips in a half-pout, overcome with worry at the sight of my empty plate.

"Did she see you?" she asked. "I don't think she noticed."

Yamamoto frowned. "Quiet. They saw me. Here comes somebody now."

It was the steward. Yamamoto ordered another round of tea and finger sandwiches and asked that the dessert cart be wheeled over so that we could choose sweets. The words drifted cautiously from his throat, like smoke rings, carefully formed, as opposed to his Japanese, which shot straight from the stomach, every word a small shout. Mrs. Yamamoto spoke very little English and, when she did, spoke like a child, head bent. My own English was correct but had a vague New York accent from Solomon Levy, and since I had lived on the Island it had only got worse. I thought that funny: I was in New York, Solomon Levy was in Tokyo. We had switched birthplaces, more or less. I would have to send him a postcard someday soon.

"Is your wife coming to Chicago to visit?" Mrs. Yamamoto asked, setting down her teacup in anticipation of having it refilled. There was a dull smear of red on the rim. "Or is her back still troubling her?"

Yamamoto broke in. "She may be moving here permanently— have you mentioned that? Or maybe you should wait till it's definite, seeing as she's so high-strung."

"Yoshi . . ."

Yamamoto narrowed his eyes at his wife. "It's true. You've met her yourself. She's very nervous."

"He's right." I smiled, picking a piece of lint off my trousers with elaborate nonchalance. Taeko was becoming all nerves and moods, a network of wires that didn't connect. There was nothing seriously wrong with her back or her neck or any of the places she complained of having pain in: it was psychosomatic, an excuse to take Darvon or Valium and make visits to the doctor. Of course old Yamamoto, with his general intolerance to any form of sickness, saw right through it. Half the times he had seen Taeko recently she was drugged, and he had expressed his disapproval outright, just as today he might comment on my choice of tie.

"She's homesick for Tokyo," I added, hoping that might soften them up. "I think she's still going through a period of adjustment."

"Nonsense!" Yamamoto said. "It's been three years; surely she should have adjusted by now. She can have things here that she could never have dreamed of in Tokyo—a large house, clothes, all kinds of foreign movies and theater and art museums. She was an art student once, am I right? Living so close to New York City, you'd think she'd find enough to keep her happy."

"But surely she misses her family," Mrs. Yamamoto said. "It's not easy to be uprooted."

"She has her family with her—two children and a husband. This is a whole new frontier, this country—we've never had opportunities before like we have here."

For a moment I was afraid we might have to endure what I had dubbed the Banzai #1 speech, which Yamamoto had expanded on greatly since he had given it to me following my fifth-year anniversary lunch. America, the New Frontier, the Second Empire . . . Fortunately he trailed off as a plate of scones and sandwiches was set down before us. Our waitress, whom I had not seen in the room previously, moved about the table with a swift grace, emptying what cold liquid remained in our cups into a china water jar and pouring fresh hot tea through the gold strainer, just as Mrs. Yamamoto had done.

The waitress's hands were slim, almost mannish, nails trimmed short and fingers callused at the tips, as if she played some sort of instrument. At first glance she startled me, in the muted light of the chandelier: broad face, broad mouth, eyes that tilted slightly at the corner. She looked almost Japanese, like a Japanese school-girl, particularly in the waitress uniform. Her hair was cut on an angle, in a bob, straight, smooth, dark enough to be black. She reminded me of the Amerasian girl I had gone to school with, who had lived next door to us, whom I had been obsessed with for years to the point of heartbreak but to whom I had never spoken.

I watched her closely, how she smiled and nodded through the ordeal of Mrs. Yamamoto's deciding between an éclair and a na-poleon; how she retrieved Yamamoto's plaid muffler from where it had fallen, then draped it over the back of his chair, without a word and all in one smooth motion, as though doing a plié. As she filled my cup, her forearm lightly brushed the skin of my knuckles, and I felt my hand tighten in involuntary reflex. Once distanced, she looked what she was—white, Western; I saw how the eyes were heavy-lidded and wide, yellow-brown, almost hazel in color. Still there was that strangeness, pale eyes looking through an Asian mask. I realized I was staring. Mrs. Yamamoto seemed to have noticed, too, and glanced at me sharply. I swallowed, brought a dry biscuit to my mouth, then put it back on the plate. The girl had left; she was wheeling the tea cart to the table opposite: two young men, obviously lovers, and an ancient regal woman in a fur hat.

"I saw one of your films the last time I was home," I said to Mrs. Yamamoto, hoping to deflect her attention. "The one about the Yoshiwara."

She smiled, delighted. *"Sin Street?"*

"That's it." Actually I had not seen the whole thing through; I had fallen asleep with a cigarette in my hand and almost burned the house down. Mrs. Yamamoto had played one of the geisha, a small part. Still, she was so hungry for attention it was worth a shot. "And on the public television station, not just the Japanese channel." I took a quick sip of my tea, which was scalding, and managed with great effort to keep from coughing it up all over myself. The girl was actually looking at me now; her eyes met mine leisurely from time to time, in the way one might observe a drifting cloud. It was torture not to look back; I felt as if I were being forced to hold my breath. I sighed. "When was that film made, twenty years ago?"

"Try thirty!" Yamamoto laughed.

"You haven't changed a bit," I said. Mrs. Yamamoto flushed and pressed her hand against mine in protest. The diamond flickered.

"Don't lie to me; I can't bear it. Thirty years on a woman is a century's time. How old are you, Jun?" she asked.

"Thirty."

"Oh!" Mrs. Yamamoto pretended to shudder and leaned back wearily in her chair. "Only a baby then, probably not even walking . . ." She drifted off, eyes shut.

"You should flatter me, not her," Yamamoto said. He reached for his wallet and counted out several bills onto the silver tray where the waitress had placed the check. "By the way, make sure I call Tanaka tomorrow. Is he in town yet?"

"Till Tuesday."

"What about Kurahashi?" The girl appeared and discreetly removed the tray. She looked at me again and smiled. Her lips were very full. I had a vision of them pressed against my eyelid.

"Well?"

I turned back to Yamamoto. My heart was slamming into my chest, and I was perspiring. "I don't know," I said.

"Then find out."

I nodded and took a small notebook I carried around to remind myself of things, then paused for a moment, pen in hand. This was a new notebook, all its pages blank. Instead of writing the names Tanaka and Kurahashi, I wrote my own, with my business address and phone number. I returned the pen to my pocket, then smiled and pointed to the harpist, who was covering her instrument with a canvas sack and lifting it onto a small platform to wheel it away.

"My, she must be strong," I remarked. The Yamamotos both turned to watch, while I slipped the notebook to the floor. Its cover was a maroon leather that blended in well with the carpet. Surely nobody would see it lying there until later, after we had left.

I finished my tea quickly, as Yamamoto seemed eager to go. We were all continuing on to the theater together, *Kabuki Othello*, sponsored by the Yamamoto Corporation. Yamamoto purchased a cigar, then went out to see if the limo driver was there; Mrs. Yamamoto disappeared into the powder room, and I excused myself as well—by now I had to go so badly the pain was spreading into my flanks. The girl was nowhere. I had hoped to say something to her, a simple goodbye or good night, just to reestablish my presence—the Japanese man at that table, the Japanese man who had forgotten his notebook.

In the bathroom I ran cold water over my wrists and stared at my reflection in the mirror. Sure enough there were small black clippings from my haircut, like tiny insect legs, scattered here and there over my face. I wiped them off irritably and shook my head. "Tanaka, Kurahashi, Tanaka, Kurahashi . . ." My face had a wild look to it, tribal. For a moment I almost did not recognize myself.

Things had become very bad, you see. I was starved for attention, eyeing tea waitresses. I was disgusted with myself, yet I could not shake her image from my thoughts.

"*Tanaka, Kurahashi, Tanaka, Kurahashi.*" I was never going to remember. I bolted back into the stall and tore off several sheets of toilet paper, wrote the names and wadded the tissue into my coat pocket. Five more hours of the needle in the arm. I inhaled and exhaled several times, to revive myself, then left the bathroom—careening into Mrs. Yamamoto, freshly lipsticked and powdered. I escorted her through the lobby, past the girl and the main entrance. Mrs. Yamamoto clung to my arm with a frail insistence. I did not look back.

The sleep I was in was like warm water—it filled my lungs and my throat. I pulled myself out of it and looked up at a white plaster ceiling, divided with cracks and rust spots. There was a heat between my legs; my hand groped uselessly at my thigh. For a split second I thought it was Taeko lying beside me, my wife, but then I remembered. The spine was clearly defined on this back, a small vaccination mark on the shoulder, the hair not quite black against blue-flowered sheets. It was the girl, the tea waitress, Gina—that was her name. A siren wailed outside and faded into the distance. I was not even sure what part of the city this was, it had all happened so fast.

Up until the evening it had gone like clockwork, perfectly orchestrated. Although she had not called me—the concierge had —she was nonetheless leaving the Drake the next day just as I was arriving to pick my notebook up. I waved before I could stop myself. A small smile of recognition pulled at her mouth, and she nodded.

"Here for tea again?"

"Tea? Oh, no." I launched into the story of the notebook while clutching at my gloves, all the time realizing I was stammering slightly, as I did when I talked to Yamamoto.

"Of course—you're Mr. Shimada. They should have your notebook at the desk, over there." She pointed. "Here, follow me."

I followed. She was wearing jeans, straight-legged, with socks folded over what looked like army boots, large hoops in her ears, a man's leather jacket. Quite a departure from the prim waitress uniform, I thought, although the outfit did not displease me. She walked with confidence, stalking across the tapestry-like carpet, banging on the bell of the desk until a clerk appeared. She and the clerk laughed and bantered back and forth; to me it seemed that she and this clerk—tall, sharp-faced, his sleeves too short to cover his wrists—knew each other quite well. I waited. He produced the book, and she smiled broadly as if she had figured out my motives, then together we made our way back to the revolving door. No harp was playing; this time it was a piano, an elaborate rendition of "Laura."

There was snow in the air. "Oh, it's freezing!" She began hopping up and down on the sidewalk and zipped the leather coat shut. "It wasn't this cold when I came in this morning—the temperature must have dropped thirty degrees." A vague puff of frost drifted from her red lips, then evaporated. "That's Chicago for you," she said.

I knew I had to do something, immediately—within minutes she would be walking off to the elevated, the bus, maybe an evening out. I had to at least get her name; I could not keep coming back with a mouthful of excuses like a schoolboy. I didn't have a school-boy's free time. I cleared my throat.

"I—"

"Is it this cold in Tokyo?"

I paused, flustered. "What?"

"I said is it this cold in Tokyo?"

"No, not really. Tokyo weather is more like New York. Milder, not so much wind. I believe they're in the same climate zone." *Why* was I saying that? Climate zones, for God's sake. I took a cigarette out of the case Taeko had given me the previous Christmas—silver, with the character of my name engraved in front. The sight of it disturbed me, and I shoved it back into my pocket, then thought perhaps I should have offered the girl a cigarette. "How did you know I was from Tokyo?" I asked.

"A guess. I probably only know of ten other cities in Japan, as stupid as that may sound."

"That's about nine more than the average American," I said. "Although that's changing lately." I placed the cigarette, unlit, in my mouth. The girl actually seemed to be stalling, waiting for me to do something, although she was not looking at me directly any-more and instead stared ahead at the passerby across the street. The Amerasian girl from my schooldays had had a habit like that too—of course I never talked to her myself, but I had always noticed that when she did speak, her eyes looked beyond the other person, easily distracted, gaze always shifting, clear and full of light.

"Name them," I said. I hunched against the wind and brought a match up to my cigarette, and as I took the first puff, I felt whatever membrane of shyness in my throat burn away so I could speak. "Name only five of your ten cities and I'll buy you a cup of coffee."

She laughed, pretending to give the matter great thought. "Five for a cup of coffee; all right. Tokyo—"

I laughed too, foolishly. "Tokyo doesn't count."

"Fine. Osaka, Kyoto, Yokohama, Hiroshima, Nagasaki . . ." She trailed off at these last two, embarrassed. "Honshu—"

"Honshu's an island, but still you named five. Not bad."

"You think I'm an idiot," she said. "I do know about Japan, really."

"Is that right?" I stopped smiling and took a step toward her; we had been standing fairly far apart, like people on stage. Her hair blew around her face.

"Five cities!" I yelled, clapping my hands. She was scowling at me now, and I wondered if she was offended. I didn't care. I had come this far, I had to continue, shove it over the edge. I went further. "Name the emperor and I'll take you to dinner."

There was a piercing blast of a cab whistle from the doorman at our side. I waited, tensely, feeling a trickle of sweat run from my abdomen down my leg. I had offended her, I could see that. She was probably afraid I thought she was a prostitute, asking her to dinner before I even knew her name. Pushy Japanese, trying to pick up women like soldiers in a foreign country. I began composing an apology, head bent, but, before I could say anything, heard her speak first.

"Hirohito," she said. She looked at me directly now, and then I caught her glancing at my hands in search of a wedding ring. The left one was mercifully still inside its glove, hidden and warm. It was fairly obvious, my ring, a wide gold band. Surely she had noticed it before.

Halfway through dinner, I began to feel sick. The restaurant was overheated, and the Greek food, alien to my stomach, would not digest. I was terrified that somebody I knew might see me: a group from Yamamoto, one of the secretaries, mail clerks, or, worst of all, Yamamoto himself. Although I flew to Chicago only once or twice a month on business, I was still disturbed by the high rate of coincidence: I always seemed to be bumping into a fellow executive on the street or in department store lobbies, stepping out of a cab just as one of them stepped in. That very morning, while I was buying stamps, I had seen the Filipino maid from the Hotel Nippon, where the company put me up—the very woman who took care of my room—on line in front of me, mailing a package to Manila. Spies. It was as if I were in a small, protective ring of people, like the circle games we used to play at school, a group of only twenty or so, but still I could not manage to break free.

I drank a lot of wine to loosen myself up and to encourage Gina to drink more. She was very calm, expertly pulling apart her shish kebab, asking polite questions about my work and my country and telling humorous anecdotes about pouring tea for the wealthy day after day. Her voice was low and murmuring—half the time I could not hear what she was saying, but the sound of it soothed me, like ambient music. Beneath her soft sweater the outline of her breasts was just visible—they seemed round, firm; a gold pendant settled in the narrow valley between them. I had no idea what I was doing. I had never involved myself in anything like this before, except with one girl, Miho, a receptionist at the office in New York, but she had been highly sensitive and discreet—she had later married a co-worker of mine and moved back to Japan and, as I had read in last month's corporation newsletter, just had a baby boy. The affair had happened after the birth of my son, Omi, when Taeko and I were beginning to fall apart. The affair had had such a practicality to it, almost like physical therapy, that I had never really considered it wrong.

This was wrong. If this Gina was stupid, neurotic, obsessive, she could ruin my whole life. Surely she seemed reasonable enough, sitting there nodding; she looked healthy, laughed a lot, but you could not trust that. Plenty of women *seemed* reasonable enough until you undressed them and went inside their bodies, and then it was as if you triggered some sort of neurochemical response, a manic-depression, just by scraping the vaginal walls. If something like this got out—an affair with a Westerner, so young, *a tea waitress* at a hotel—I could lose my job at Yamamoto, Taeko could divorce me and never let me see my children again: I would be ruined. Even though my job was aggravating at times in its personal-secretary aspects, it was still employment, and it paid very well. And Yamamoto liked me so much. . . . No, I would not do it. I sat up in my chair and pushed the plate of food away abruptly, as if to finalize my decision.

"Is something wrong?" She was staring at me with concern, eyes lazy. The glass of rhoditis wine before her was drained empty, a half lip print on the edge where it had touched her mouth. Like Mrs. Yamamoto's teacup, blotted with red. She smiled.

"I've been rambling on for fifteen minutes, only because I know you're not listening."

The thudding in my ears subsided. I suddenly heard, as if sound had been turned on, the din of other voices and silverware against dishes, waiters yelling *O-pah!* as they theatrically set fire to pan after pan of saganaki.

"I'm sorry; I forgot to make a phone call at the office." I glanced over at the jungle of potted trees that led to the rest rooms. "There's a pay phone over there," I said, pointing. "I think I'll go take care of it now. Excuse me?"

She nodded, toying with her pendant, a watch. As I got up, I caught sight of a group of dark, sleek heads, men in suits, cigarette smoke. I swayed forward a little, panicked, but they were not Japanese; they were probably Greeks, regulars of the restaurant. A rush filled my mouth. I made my way past the phone booths and into the men's room, then stood hunched over the pink shell sink and splashed water onto my face. I was so hot! Fever flesh, like sunburn, spread all the way down into my throat.

"You're *sick*," I said, taking out a roll of antacids and chewing several of them at once. I was by myself, the row of stalls behind me vacant. "Go on, leave. Get out of here and go home."

The churning in my stomach ceased. I took a breath, smoothed my hair back in place with my palm, then paused. My hair was nearly one quarter gray, and lately—when I took time to notice—I saw gray stubble in my morning beard. Last year there had been only a few shoots, the year before that nothing. My face still looked young, still a young, good-looking face: taut, handsome, only a few wrinkles at the corners of my eyes from smoking and a tendency I had to squint from time to time. My mother had always said I would get handsomer as I got older. I wondered how old the girl thought I was.

Back at the table, I moved quickly, paying the bill and thanking her for joining me, trying to inject a note of finality into the endless evening. Snow had been falling outside for some time, and it covered everything with a glittering persistence. I hailed a cab. Gina stood by my side, unwrapping one of the candies that had come with the check, scarf draped over her head loosely, like a hood. In five minutes she would be gone: a clean escape. I would never see her again. The throb of relief, however, became a blank feeling as I thought of my empty bed in the hotel room, so impersonal, its only female touch being the hands of the Filipino woman who put on fresh sheets.

The cab came, and I stepped forward to open the door, my intention being to send the girl off in one cab, with fare, then call another for myself. But I lost my balance—the sole of my shoe hit a patch of ice—and I slipped. The girl caught me, just a light touch at the elbow, fingers momentarily around my wrist. Her laughter smelled of peppermint and condensed in the air before us, her white teeth sharp, with little pointed cat's incisors. I got in the cab with her. It would only be a ride, I told myself, nothing more, to make sure she arrived home safely, then I would tell the driver to take me back to the Nippon. I had not seen much of Chicago's neighborhoods and was curious to see where she lived. Besides, I was not feeling well, and the cold air, blowing through a crack in the rear windshield, would do me good. I nodded to the driver and settled back in my seat. Gina settled back also, her leg against mine, smiling lazily and looking me straight in the eye as she announced how very happy she was that she lived alone.

I followed her upstairs like a dog in heat. It had been so long. Sexual pleasure—wild, uncontrollable—was something I remembered vaguely, in the way one might remember a vacation.

She walked in and locked the door but did not turn on any lights. I heard her slip off the leather jacket and the boots, then jumped as she touched her fingers lightly to the sides of my face.

"So nervous," she whispered. "Do you need to get drunk?"

I was holding her back, without much force, using the palm of my hand. Before I could think, the hand had moved and covered her breast, while almost simultaneously her tongue slipped into the hollow of my ear. I moaned, then collided with the wall behind me. She was saying something, her voice like a violent western wind.

"I'm drunk," she said. "Let me show you. Really." She felt for me between the legs, and again I jumped. "You don't want to go home alone, I can tell. You're stiff."

"No—"

"You want me to love you, don't you." She glanced down at my face—she was a few inches taller, if that, but that did not discourage me. I had, however, forgotten what she looked like. I could not see. The dark pressed us together, heightening only smells and body parts.

"I'll do it, right down to the last whisker on your face. You just say the word Go."

A solid core of warmth replaced the panicky feeling in my stomach. Smooth hair and flesh, small muscles, swellings, curves, indentations. I groped for them all. I was choking slightly, trying to take in too much at once. I paused and allowed her to peel off my sweaty clothes.

"Go," I said.

"I don't have any diseases. You should ask, you know." She draped my tie over the doorknob, which pleased me greatly. The tie was one of my favorites, black with a red stripe. A shower of small change fell from my pockets. "Hmm. Laundry money," she said.

We had gone to a bed, a futon. I remember I thought it interesting that she had one. Moonlight outlined this room, sparsely furnished: the futon, a bureau, a wastebasket. I sank back against rough-textured sheets. The girl sat on top of me, a warm anchor.

"You undress now," I urged. It made me nervous to be the naked one.

"Not so fast." She began to kiss me, strategically, then to stroke and rub various sections of my body until I was near frenzy. Each time I tried to break free, she held me down. She seemed quite strong.

"You said you were going to let me do it!" She sat back on her haunches, almost petulant. I could see her now, the bobbed hair, the strange half-breed face. "I'm not finished."

"But you're teasing," I gasped.

She bounced, nearly snapping my kneecaps. "I am *not*."

I managed to roll her over and take off most of her clothing. "You don't understand," I was mumbling, climbing on top. "I don't need that now; I can't stand it. Later you can do whatever you want, I promise."

I had worked my way in. The loose sensation of gliding on ice overcame me; my body was liquid; I was about to lose balance again.

"Wait!" Her voice seemed several feet away. I forced myself to listen. "Talk to me in Japanese."

"What?"

"You heard me. Talk to me in Japanese!"

Japanese. I searched my mind for something to say, then logically came up with numbers. "*Ichi, ni, san, shi* . . ." I continued to ten, watching her struggle. She wriggled around on the flat mattress, delighted. "*Juichi, juni, jusan, jushi* . . ." By thirty, she was moaning and arching underneath me, hips like a machine; by forty, I was afraid she had passed out. I did not care—I could not think anymore. Every nerve had become an arrow, all pointed in the same direction. A yellow haze drifted before me and broke into a bath of sweat, sweat so rank I could smell it, feel it like an adhesive between us. I fell. I dozed lightly against her, then allowed her legs to wring the last impulses free. Winded, I rolled over, eyes shut. Talk to me in Japanese, I thought, and smiled to myself briefly, feeling as though my mouth was stretched out of shape.

I woke to the eyes of a cat, small delicate paws perched on my hip. It seemed to be after midnight, quiet, radiators breathing heat in small gasps and the queer violet light of a snowy sky glowing in the room. A clock was ticking someplace. I sighed, stretched my legs beneath the blanket and swallowed several times to clear the sour taste from my mouth. I felt very good now, purged, as if I had been taken apart and reassembled, with all the bad cogs thrown away. The cat was still staring at me, having retreated a slight distance, its tail curled nearly around its front paws; its fur was a thick smoke-gray color. The sight of it standing there made me crave a cigarette, only I would have to find my coat to get the pack, and none of my clothes seemed to be within reach. I sat up. Jun Shimada in a strange woman's apartment, a young woman at that, American. There was something so climactic to it, as if all the hundreds of movies seen and novels read against my will in college had pooled into this one night: I was no longer viewing, I was acting, having an adventure—the film had jumped its sprockets, the page between my fingers buckled of its own accord and torn itself in half.

I began to explore, walking on the balls of my feet so as not to wake her, closing the bedroom door with its porcelain knob and wandering into the living room. Turning on the light, I almost gasped; an origami mobile hit me in the head. The walls of the room were covered with a bizarre collection of posters, huge, like billboards, all of them Japan-related. There was a tattoo artist, hairless and painted to the anus with dragons and intricate swirls; two Tokyo hoods; a geisha of the Meiji era, with blacked-out teeth; a tourist map (no wonder she had known her cities!); and a poster of the actor Eiji Okada in *Woman in the Dunes,* looking helplessly up out of his sandpit. At this point I froze, feeling as though I, too, had stepped into some sort of trap. Taeko had several times remarked how I reminded her of Eiji Okada, whom she did not particularly like; then a woman at work, one of the office ladies, or clerks, as you call them, had said the same thing. I squinted at the poster, trying to see the resemblance. Maybe around the mouth but nothing more: Okada had always seemed so haggard, and there was a flatness to his face. It made no sense, but the girl had obviously picked me out—that was why she had been looking at me at the hotel. She was crazy. Books from and about my country filled the built-in shelves; I examined them closely but did not find what I wanted. Nothing by my father. Only modern authors, modern, racy covers—names I did not recognize. I moved on.

She had very little furniture, and because the apartment was so spare, the floors were cleanly swept, gleaming, even the leaves on the plants shiny and free from dust. A bicycle was parked in the foyer; in the kitchen I caught sight of a percolator pot and a set of butcher knives, a wok, a calendar from Dai-Ichi Kangyo Bank and a sink that dripped. It was not until I saw the lower half of myself reflected in the toaster that I realized I was still naked. My body had such a good feel—charged, tingling—as if I had taken a sea swim and then a long shower. Even in my thirtieth year it had not ceased to amaze me how the release of certain fluids could produce such contentment. I laughed, quietly, to myself. A Japan freak; the Eiji Okada Fan Club: how ridiculous, but still so lucky for me to have stumbled upon something like this.

I followed the cat back into the bedroom. The girl jumped as I walked in, pulled out of warm unconsciousness, her skin moist, her eyes—at the corners—oozing small tears. She sat up as I sat down, took a sharp breath and looked at me blankly until she remembered.

"I set the alarm for seven," she said, suddenly quite calm. "Is that early enough?"

"Yes, thank you." I was embarrassed that she should go to such trouble. "I may have to leave earlier, though, to change and get my briefcase. Shave, too. You understand."

"Whatever . . ." She was drifting off again, facing the wall. She didn't seem to care when I left, six or seven; I could probably have left now and she wouldn't have noticed. But she did want me out, that was clear enough—she had set the alarm clock, put a jarring exclamation point at the end of the sentence to eject me from her bed. I wondered if I should leave now. She stretched at my side and moved farther away, one leg off the mattress. Miles away. I frowned. I felt restless, unanchored—I might as well be by myself at the Nippon, staring out the window at the view of the river and the iron drawbridge that opened and closed all night. Better that than this cold white back with its vaccination pock, curled up indifferently away from me as if I were not even there and this was just any other night.

"Gina." I said her name, with caution, for the first time. There was no response.

"Gina?"

The back remained smooth, forbidding, the two sharp shoulder blades prominent beneath the drum of skin. I prodded my forefinger between them.

"Come here."

She allowed herself to be dragged over, her head to be placed against my chest. I felt a momentary comfort from the weight of it but still could not sleep. Alone, hollow. There was a body next to me, but what did that mean? I imagined myself standing on a white surface, elongated, stiff, casting no shadow. Giacometti-like. My wife had had a book on Giacometti in college. It had always depressed me.

I pinched the girl roughly on the thigh.

"Ow!" She was quite awake, looking at me in either anger or confusion, I could not tell which. Perhaps disappointment. Had I been her first Japanese? The shock of waking and finding a haggard real Japanese in your bed, not Eiji Okada, small hands pinching, slanted eyes blinking in the dark—what was that like? I glanced down at the suddenly strange proportions of my body—scrawny torso, short muscular legs—and covered myself with the sheet. I smiled morosely. American men had bigger sexual organs, I was sure of that.

"What do you want?" she said. She had her hand on me, on the only part of my body I felt self-conscious about, a small swelling at the base of my stomach, a paunch. All in all, I was fairly thin and elastic, but the paunch had developed over the years from so much deskwork, so much drinking after desking and not any real exercise beyond golf—a corporation activity. I tensed my abdominal muscles, hoping she would move her hand away, but she did not; she seemed to be nestling the paunch protectively, like the soft spot on a baby's head. What was it about her? What did *she* want? Her build was not unlike that of my wife or of the few other women I had slept with; her voice was gentle, her skin soft and pliant, but all this crazy Japan paraphernalia—and she had been almost uncontrollable underneath me, all muscle and bone, driving me on. She had not received, she had taken, and now she was fondling the soft spot on my body in the way I might fondle her breasts.

"Stop!"

I grabbed her with a violence I was immediately ashamed of.

"I—" I broke off. I could feel her breathing now, warm stirrings against my neck. She moved her head back with effort.

"What?"

"I don't know."

"You're not sick again, are you?"

"No."

"Then what?"

Her eyes seemed larger in the moonlight, very much like the moon itself—pale, with a ring of frost. I jerked her hands up and forced them through my hair.

"Go on," I snapped. "Just pretend you like me. Hold me. I think I made a mistake. Hold me down so I forget about it till morning."

I pulled the hands around my waist and encircled myself with them, hooked my legs around the longer legs, suppressed an urge to bite the round shoulder.

"I'm not a prostitute," she said, although there was no trace of nastiness to her voice. She giggled. "A geisha."

"No."

"You've been to geishas?" I did not answer. Her fingers rubbed at my scalp in a rough massage that made my spine tingle with excitement. Familiar odors crept up between us, warm body smells. I sighed.

"That's not so bad, is it?" I asked. "Listen to me: I sound so shaky. I sound like an old man." I continued. "Please, put your lips against my eyes. Kiss them, kiss them shut."

"All right."

She was murmuring. I lay back against the pillows, eyes closed.

"I *do* like you," she said. "I'm not pretending."

I smiled. "Uh-huh. Hold me." I waited, allowing her to slip her arms underneath me. "Tighter. Break my back."

The knot inside my chest loosened, melted into a sweet viscous liquid that soothed my ragged stomach. A wave of fatigue followed. I was suddenly quite tired.

"Thank you," I said. "I think I'm okay now."

She let go but remained with me. I sensed her staring at me curiously but was too tired to care.

"I do like you, Mr. Shimada."

"Mr. Shimada!" I laughed. I stroked her hip gently several times, then rolled over and fell into deep sleep.

I was fine at the office after I had had a second cup of coffee, washed my fingers to eradicate the disturbing sex scent, and sat before a pile of spreadsheets, allowing the ticker tape of work to refeed itself through my head. I was in my cubicle—I had a cubicle in Chicago; I was not exiled to the executive area—working on a special project for Yamamoto: a breakdown of the corporation's ethnic makeup: 20 percent Black American; 15 percent Hispanic;

55 percent White / White Ethnic; 10 percent Other (including Japanese). Numbers: so exact—I took great pleasure in the control I had over them, like trained fleas. Still, within an hour I found myself thinking of Gina again, the bright color of her sweater and the curves underneath it. A vein in my throat pulsed uncontrollably. I made small talk with Hiroshi, the finance whiz, about the inefficiency of the Chicago subway, then accepted an envelope from Yamamoto's Chicago secretary, which I opened with a sick start. Inside was an airline ticket for my next flight to New York. I had forgotten completely that I was going home the next day. Tomorrow evening I would be having dinner with Taeko, walking around my house with all its pleasant elements, playing with my children and the dog. Tomorrow. The coffee became an acid drip. It was too soon. Blows were falling, one right after the other.

Hiroshi asked me if I wanted anything from the newsstand in the building lobby, and I glanced up at him blankly.

"They sell Mild Seven down there now, isn't that great?" he said. "I can't get used to American cigarettes. The closest things, I guess, are Camels."

"No."

Hiroshi blinked. His hair, parted in the center, was pure black, not one thread of gray. "No, what?" he said.

"Luckies. Try Lucky Strikes."

"L. S. M. F. T." He laughed.

"What's that?"

" 'Lucky Strike Means Fine Tobacco.' Or maybe it's 'Makes Fine Tobacco'—I don't know exactly. But it's on every package, don't you look?" I shook my head. "You're not very observant," he said.

He left. I stared at the page of tiny figures before me, then began to re-input them into the computer. I typed several exclamation points and the letters S-H-I: *shi*—death. At the sound of Yamamoto's voice barking through the corridor, I backspaced, erased the letters and sat waiting, shoulders tensed, for the blast to reach my cubicle, full force, like a hurricane, relentless and scattering debris.

But he had stopped en route. I heard him out in the hall, asking one of the cleaning women what she had got "her babies this year for Christmas," and then I saw him listening keenly to her embarrassed replies, still in his coat and hat.

◆

Taeko met me at the airport, with Omi and Etsuko. She was leafing through a magazine in the waiting area, wrapped in a bright-red coat I had never seen before, hair pulled into a knot at the top of her head. I noticed her before she saw me; my first welcome was from Etsuko, who ran toward me laughing, her arms outstretched like a jet.

"Daddy! *Okaeri-nasai!*"

I swept her up and hugged her, careful not to blow smoke into her small triangular face. There was no smoking on short flights these days, and I had been dying throughout the trip, cigarette held between two fingers as soon as they'd made the landing announcement, as soon as I'd seen the lighted span of the George Washington Bridge.

Etsuko attempted to straighten my tie and rubbed her nose against me. "Mmm, Daddy smells nice. Daddy smells like Chi-cah-go!"

I held her back awkwardly for a moment, caught off guard. What did she smell? Etsuko, though only seven, was highly sensitive, *my* child: I recognized in her many mirrors of myself. Her frail weight was now against my hip, and her eyes, blinking happily along with my own, made me feel transparent. I tickled her behind the knees as a distraction, and she howled.

"Make the fox face, Daddy. I want to see it."

I smiled, voice very low and conspiratorial. "Not now," I said. "Wait until we're in the woods, later; then we'll become foxes."

"Okay!" She giggled. "Here comes Omi!"

Taeko was bringing the baby over, although Omi was not really a baby anymore and could walk well enough on his own—a chubby boy, dark, wearing a Mets hat sideways on his little coconut head. I hid behind Etsuko for a moment and took a quick breath.

"Right on time," Taeko said. She did not kiss me but instead stood jostling Omi, tapping the toe of her shoe repeatedly against the red carpet. "How was your flight?"

"Fine."

"Any luggage to pick up?"

I let Etsuko down and patted the garment bag slung over my shoulder. "No, this is it."

"Good."

Her mouth stretched itself into a small half-smile, then straightened again. We began to walk toward the parking area, Etsuko first, running in and out of the crowd, then Taeko and Omi, then me. Omi rested his head on his mother's shoulder and watched me like a little monkey on a caravan. Omi with his soft face, its features so unlike my own.

"I got a letter from Megumi yesterday," Taeko was saying, still turned away from me as we stood on the escalator. "She's moving into her own apartment next week."

Megumi was Taeko's sister, a merry career girl back in Tokyo, with a job at NHK.

"Well. Where's the apartment?" I asked.

"Roppongi."

"Not bad," I remarked. "She must be doing quite all right."

"She *is* doing quite all right."

"That's what I said."

"You sounded sarcastic."

I focused ahead on Etsuko, standing, shyly fascinated, next to a group of nuns in old-fashioned habits.

"I always sound sarcastic; you know that." I sighed and placed a hand on her shoulder. She stiffened. "It's the frustrated cynic in me coming out."

"Maybe."

"How's your back?"

She shifted Omi, as if he had suddenly become quite heavy.

"Not so good," she said. "The cold makes it worse, I think. I have more trouble in winter."

"Sure." The wide planes of her face, so beautifully symmetrical, turned away from me once more. Her mouth was sullen and shut.

"Been to see Saito?" I asked.

"Mmm; last week." I could barely hear her. She was mumbling in that half-exhausted way of hers. Her fingers toyed with her knot of hair.

"What?"

"I said last week."

I smiled. "That's nice," I said. I stopped short, still smiling. We had reached the car.

Although it was late, I prepared dinner, mainly because I wanted something to do, to have the familiarity of the kitchen around me, things simmering, oil smoking in a pan. It was only spaghetti, but it made me happy. Taeko was an adequate cook, but unadventurous and timid with her spices. Half the gourmet gadgets in our home had been bought by me, presumably for Taeko, but both she and I knew that in reality they were presents to myself.

The precious distractions of our children kept us from further conversation. Omi had been picking up more words every day, none of them English. Etsuko had made me an ashtray in art class—small seashells glued to what looked like an old tuna-fish can. We all watched the *Japan Variety Hour* on channel 31, then Omi had his bath; Etsuko pretended to fall asleep and thereby avoided her bath, and I roamed around the downstairs rooms by myself, feeling out of place.

I had been away only two weeks—the same month was showing on the scroll calendar in the hall, the same arrangement of chrysanthemums was in the vase beneath it—but I was far removed. I prowled about, leafing through the mail, then I grew tired and went into the kitchen to heat myself some sake, which I poured into an old cedar cup that had belonged to my father. The wood was rough against my lips, and I was comforted by the thought that my father's lips had touched the same spot. Perversely comforted; no doubt he had been at his worst whenever he sipped from this cup. I had always kept it as a sort of negative homage. I toasted him at that moment, *"Kampai,"* quite coldly.

Taeko was not coming downstairs, I guessed—I no longer heard the sound of footsteps up above; I no longer heard any sound, except for the dog whining softly in its sleep. I continued to drink. The sake was cold now, but once inside my mouth it burned a pleasant familiar trail down to my stomach, loosening my thoughts. I began to feel more at ease—after all, this was my family, my house; I had lived there for three years, been married for eight. Gina, the girl, was twenty-five. I had thought she was younger, but then remembered something she had said at dinner about being born on the day John F. Kennedy was shot, and I had mentally calculated her age. Beyond that and her physical appearance and the fact that she was a tea waitress at the Drake, I knew nothing about her, and it disturbed me to realize how much importance I placed on a stranger, actually wishing I was with her now instead of in my own home. I was an idiot, I thought. I resolved never to see her again: I was not going to fix up my problems like that; yet still I knew with the certainty of a cold coming on that I would break the resolve as soon as I could.

I set the sake cup on the coffee table and went upstairs. Etsuko had flung off all the covers and lay in a diagonal across the bed; as I straightened things and pulled her back onto the mattress, she sat up, butting her head into my chest.

"Are we in the woods yet?" she asked.

"Uh-huh." I assumed she was dreaming.

"You said you'd make the fox face when we were in the woods."

"Oh, sure." I tightened my mouth, raised one eyebrow, and pretended to sniff the air around us. We had been playing this game for several years, after she had decided I looked like a fox in one of her storybooks. "The fox smells . . ."

"Mice!" Etsuko finished. "But he can't have them!" She made little squealing noises into her pillow and kicked her legs back and forth.

"Suki, shh," I said. "You have to be quiet in the woods. The fox will get in trouble. Now go to sleep."

Her small body was straight and tense as a little soldier's, eyes squeezed shut. I cupped her cheeks, smoothed the black bangs across her forehead.

"Daddy?" she said, just as I rose to leave.

"What?"

"I'll make breakfast tomorrow, okay? It's my job now. Don't you do it—wait for me. I'll make egg pancakes."

I nodded. "Egg pancake" was Etsuko's name for omelet. "All right. We'll make them together," I said, and closed the door.

What a beautiful child. It was not that her features were so beautiful, they were average, small except for the mouth—she had inherited my mouth, wide and downturned, instead of Taeko's pouty flower bud, which would have suited a girl much better. Still, there was something about Etsuko, a serenity, that livened her thin face and made you want to watch her. As a baby she had cried so little we had thought she might be deaf, and even now she rarely showed any normal childish signs of impatience or jealousy or a need to talk back—she was just placid; it was apparently inherent, like blood type or the sheen to her hair.

I continued down the hall. I had no urge to look in on Omi. In my own bedroom, Taeko seemed to be asleep, hair fanned out around the pillow and a dull almondy odor of cold cream surrounding her. Exhausted, I sank down upon the bed, dragging my clothes off and letting each item drop onto the rug. Taeko did not move. Her face, in the moonlight, was visible to me, and I could tell by its absolute immobility that she was only pretending to be asleep. I leaned on one elbow and very lightly ran my finger from her shoulder to her hip. Nothing. The green film of her nightgown remained slack—she did not even seem to be breathing anymore.

Taeko. Since the birth of Omi she had put on weight, mostly around the hips, but still I found her desirable in a way no other woman could match, not even the girl Gina. The quintessential Japanese beauty: taut jellyfish breasts, thin limbs, skin the color of oyster shells, nearly hairless. The full swelling down below made it even worse—before, she had been flimsy underneath me, ready to break, but now she would be an anchor, capable and firmly planted. But it was not worth it. I leaned back against the headboard, arms crossed. After the violence of two nights before, I was in no mood for necrophilia.

I do like you, Mr. Shimada. . . .

I made my breathing heavy, as if I, too, had fallen asleep, yet still I watched. A few minutes later Taeko opened one eye, then, upon seeing me seated there like a judge, quickly shut it, murmuring and rolling over.

"Don't worry, I won't bother you," I said. I laughed, disgusted. Her body, foreign hills and valleys beneath the sheet, was motionless. A bottle of Darvon stood on the nightstand, next to a glass of water. Maybe she really was asleep, I thought, a restless drug stupor, but as I turned and settled into my side of the bed, I was sure I heard Taeko sigh, slowly, in what was undeniably relief.

As I lay there, I recalled the birth of Omi. Our second child had been a trial, labor dragging on for twenty hours, and rather than sleep at the hospital, on the cot provided for expectant fathers, I had gone home, made hamburgers with Etsuko and helped her with her English alphabet. Then I went to work on my income tax return, grateful for the distraction. Etsuko, who did not seem particularly upset over the absence of her mother, interrupted me once to bring in a glass of lemonade, which she set down very carefully on the desk, littered with receipts and federal forms. I nodded and took a quick sip. "Very good," I said, smiling. "And I was just thinking of how thirsty I was."

Etsuko nodded back, watching solemnly and waiting for me to finish. She was serious even then, at age five; I remember thinking how it was too bad she resembled me, had the same drawn expression. For a man it was all right; a man would be labeled "thoughtful"; but for a girl—it was almost as if she were being sentenced to a life of shyness and introspection. She continued to stare while I drained the glass, and I stared back. I crossed and uncrossed my eyes, puffed out my cheeks like balloons, then pretended to pop them with my fingers. Etsuko giggled softly, showing her small front teeth.

"You're silly," she said. "What are you doing?"

"Drinking lemonade."

"No, you're not. You're done." She sidled over to me and looked dubiously at my calculator and page of figures. "You're doing math?"

"Taxes."

"What are they?"

I sat up with mock authority and cleared my throat. "Taxes are what everyone must pay to the government in a country. You help the country that way, to build bridges and parks, roads and other things."

Etsuko touched one of my pencils, then leaned on my shoulder. "We pay taxes to Japan?" she asked.

"No; now we pay them to the United States. We don't live in Japan. You have to pay taxes to the government of where you live."

"Government?"

"Yes, government. That's a group of people who make laws. You know what a law is, right? You saw that on TV."

"Yes." She took a deep breath, remembering. "Something you can't do. But Mommy says we're moving back to Japan."

My mouth tightened. I wondered exactly what Taeko did say to Etsuko all day long; unfortunately she was with her most. I kept my voice calm.

"Oh, I don't know about that. Maybe we'll stay here awhile." I smiled and smoothed Etsuko's hair, cut short like a helmet. "We'll be pioneers."

"Pioneers?"

"People who go to new places and settle there. Strong people. Like something else on TV you've seen, that show you watch, *Little House on the Prairie*."

She giggled again, leaning her full weight on my arm in protest. "We're not like that!"

I nodded, and with my hand made her nod back. "Yes, we are, sort of. Now go get ready for bed. I have too much work to do to talk to pretty girls."

Her pale face darkened, and she ran out of the room, embarrassed. Several minutes later I heard the roar of the vacuum cleaner in the hall, and I glanced at my watch. Ten-thirty. I got up and went to investigate.

"Suki!"

Etsuko was attempting to push the vacuum cleaner around, struggling as if with an oversized dancing partner. Filling her mother's shoes, no doubt. I unplugged the cord.

"I thought I told you to go to bed, bumblebee. Come on, we can do this tomorrow. It's late."

"But—"

Her mouth became a round red O.

"Bed!"

Halfway up the stairs, she stopped and wound herself around the banister. "What kind of baby do you want, Daddy, boy or girl?"

"Oh, I don't care." I pretended to check and see if the front door was locked, so as not to look her in the eye. "Either kind will do."

"I don't want a sister," Etsuko said, confidingly.

"Well, you might have one, so don't say that. Now go to bed."

I sounded much harsher than I'd intended, but it had been a long day. Etsuko wilted away from the banister like a dying vine and continued, hangdog, to her room.

Not right to take it out on her, I thought. On my way back to the taxes, I glanced through the curtains of the bay window, at a fat orange moon bright as daylight. I should be at the hospital now, not home, or should I? I sat at my desk, reshuffling credit card receipts and noting how all of them dated nine months earlier were from Chicago—I had been there throughout July, helping to set up the new branch office. Taeko had been menstruating when I left. Her periods were regular, almost to the minute, but very painful, often leaving her bedridden. I always knew when she was that way; I could tell by the tone of her voice. She had not menstruated when I came back. Several weeks later she told me she was pregnant, and now she was in labor under a bloated orange moon. Protracted labor: she was suffering. That morning the obstetrician, Dr. Sugarman, had beamed. "Boy, she's right on schedule, John—April fourteenth. Babies and taxes, they won't wait."

I had smiled back obligingly, then after a decent interval left the beige-and-blue waiting room. So it was, I thought. So it was.

Dr. Saito was in that waiting room when I arrived next morning. He was smoking a long, thin cigarette wrapped in brown paper. His square face looked a little puffy from lack of sleep, his body diminished by the plain white physician's coat. Saito was a powerful guy. I had seen him undressed once or twice in the steam room at the club, where he played racquetball and I played golf, and I couldn't help but admire his barrel chest and muscled arms, skin nearly two shades darker than my own, even in the dead of winter. This was Taeko's orthopedist. As he explained it, the cushions between her vertebrae were shrinking, so that the disks pressed together, causing excruciating pain. The problem had started when Etsuko was born and had intensified with this second pregnancy. That would explain his presence here in the waiting area this morning. Of course it would.

Upon seeing me, Saito's heavy-lidded eyes squinted through a cloud of smoke. He extended his hand.

"Congratulations, Shimada," he said. "I assume they told you over the phone."

"Yes."

"Your first son. You must be pleased." He stabbed his cigarette out in an ashtray filled with sand and ruffled his hair through his fingertips. His hair was thick and abundant, shooting up in stiff black tufts; it covered his arms and his legs and, if I recalled correctly, even his chest in a dark thatch, unusual for a Japanese. But Saito was like that, abundant; he could probably impregnate a woman just by looking at her. Or was that wishful thinking on my part? The very odor of him was hormonal, dense and spermy, heightened by heavy cologne. I felt boyish and unsettled, standing at his side. I straightened myself to my full height.

"Where were you?" he asked.

"I had to drop my daughter off at school."

"Oh. No bus?"

I bristled; what the hell was it with this man, the bachelor doctor, questioning me like that? What did he know of parental responsibility—big, grinning bachelor doctor with a ridiculous number of female patients.

"I didn't want her to take the bus. She's upset with all that's going on, and I thought it important that I drive her."

My fist clenched in a tight knot; both Saito and I seemed to notice it simultaneously. I loosened it, one finger at a time, glancing at Saito's broad body and realizing the absurdity of such a gesture.

"Of course," he said. "I just happened to be on rounds and checked in. They said she was having a bit of trouble. You know she's very delicate, your wife."

"Yes." I took out my cigarettes and lit one, tossing the match into the ashtray where a number of Saito's brown stubs lay crushed. Seven or eight of them, at least. He had been here for some time, it seemed, waiting.

"Yes, we're both delicate," I continued. "A very frail pair of people, you might say."

"Huh. Well, come on. . . ." Saito thumped me on the back and steered me over to the nursery window, where we stood together, our collective breath slightly fogging the smooth glass. There were several newborns in a row, nearly all white, one black, two Asians. None of them appeared to be moving; they stared with bleary new eyes, up into the womby light. My eye rested on the smaller Asian baby, and I felt my throat swell up with affection. Tiny pointed face, buttery skin and red mouth—it looked just as Etsuko had when she was born. Although I am not a religious man, at that moment I prayed intensely that this was my baby—it would have to be mine if it looked like that. But Saito was looking farther down the row; the baby I was praying for was a Korean, its tag marked

Ho. The baby Saito pointed out, tagged *Shimada*, began to kick one froglike foot in the air. This child was very dark. Its head seemed larger and more developed than the others, hence all the trouble coming out. Round and very dark. It resembled a baby ape. I looked slowly at the child and then at Saito, whose brown wrists shot strong and covered with hair from the cuffs of his white jacket. Saito's mouth was pursed tightly, as if he wanted to smile.

"Big, isn't he?" he said.

I nodded, assessing my own pale reflection in the nursery window, then I turned and strolled out, with my cigarette dangling from my mouth, both hands again fists, shoved into my pockets like stones.

"Where're you going, Shimada?" Saito called. "To work?"

I ignored him and kept on walking. There was a heat like vomit rising slowly in my throat. I had to get out of there, into the cool air beyond. The smell of Saito was positively making me sick.

How does one live with such a fact? I don't know; in the same way one lives with a bad tooth, or piles, or maybe even an ulcer. I was afraid she would leave me if I raised the issue, leave me out of honor yet destroy me in the process. I didn't want to make a wave; I told myself she couldn't possibly love Saito, she had done it out of utter frustration. My only demand was that we name the child Omi, after a friend of my mother's older brother. I chose the name deliberately, because the man had been such a bad influence—postwar Tokyo hood, into gambling and petty thievery; there was even a rumor that for some time he had been a pimp. Always borrowing money, always trying to drag my uncle down. It seemed a fitting label for this child, for whom I felt nothing. Although I expected Taeko to put up resistance to the name, she kept quiet; in fact, she spoke very little these days and spent almost all her time in bed, pale and flaccid, breasts perpetually oozing small drops of milk like cloudy tears. I ignored the child's presence and let Taeko drag herself up whenever it cried, nor did I respond to any of Etsuko's nervous questions about this new intruder into her

life. For a while I even moved the extra tatami mattress into my
study and closed the door each night so as to muffle the baby's
cries; it was easier that way, I felt. This wasn't my son—why
should I lose any sleep over it? Although I still did.

◆

At work the Monday following my return to New York, I sat alone
in the boardroom with its view of lower Park Avenue and the Empire
State Building and stared at my hands. A seagull passed, tilting
in the wind, flying uncertainly at this height of forty-seven stories.
Within minutes I would be sitting in on a meeting with the bank
men about purchasing an office complex in Connecticut, Yamamoto's newest venture—he was extremely fond of Connecticut these
days, thought it was such a good, clean little state.

I yawned, feeling I had a mouthful of straw. My hands lay useless
on the table before me; soon they would have to assume their active
pose, either clasped together firmly or scribbling down notes. I
liked my hands, the simple sight of them. They were heavily veined
and spatulate, a small bump on the right index finger because of
the odd way I held a pen. No amount of curbing in elementary or
middle school could keep me from gripping my pen, Neanderthal
style, and over the years the bump had thickened and become
quite important to me: my scar of independence.

I had the boardroom doors closed, for privacy. Very swiftly, and
as if it were typed on an agenda, I called Chicago information and
got Gina's phone number and address. It took three attempts before
I got the spelling of her last name right—I had seen it only in
glimpses as I passed in and out of her lobby. I wrote the number
on the inner flap of a matchbook advertising a trucking school.
Just having it agitated me slightly. I wondered how long I could
keep from calling. I would be home now, lifeless, for a month.

There was an interruption, a buzz through the intercom from
Miss Ozaki to let me know the bankers had arrived. I hung up,
clasped the blemished hand over the other one and sat upright,

the young man of business, le petit homme d'affaires, ready to nod and curry favor, wondering only briefly if it was still so cold in Chicago and whether Gina was wearing the leather jacket, the lobes of her ears chapped pink.

A thought of Keiji dangled, spiderlike, in my mind as I caught a blast of atonal music from a passing car. Keiji music. The bank meeting had run into after hours at the Pelican, a salaryman bar on Thirty-fourth Street, and having packed Hirota and Shoichi laughingly into a cab, I was at loose ends. A rare happy feeling hummed through my veins: the bankers had liked me. Hirota, a heavyset man with bifocals, had a daughter about Etsuko's age; and Shoichi, the older one, white haired,—at first caustic, presumably another Yamamoto—had softened like wax upon hearing "Lili Marlene" on the jukebox, with which he sang along drunkenly, one finger raised.

"I haven't heard that in years," he gasped. "Why, last time, I was hooked up with a German girl during the war. What a mess . . ."

He laughed, and a tear ran slowly down his cheek. "*Robust*, she was. I never thought I'd get out of that one alive."

A final meeting with Yamamoto was arranged, to be held at the site of the proposed plant, now a boarded-up A & P.

"Connect-eee-coot!" we yelled to each other at parting. During our discussions we had all had trouble getting it out—even I had come up with some interesting variations. Shoichi leaned on Hirota fondly and waved through the cab window, nose pressed against the glass. It had been raining; the streets had a glazed look, smeared with red and green light.

I stood on the corner of Park and Thirty-third, contemplating my next step. The office towered behind me—black, irregularly lit—like a big domino, but I did not want to go back there just now. I had an urge to walk. It was still early, about seven o'clock, and to begin the drive back to Glen Cove now would only tangle me up in the end of rush hour. Besides, there was really nothing to go home for. The mere thought of it was unsettling, like a draft on the back of my neck.

I hesitated for a moment, then ducked into a doorway to avoid a group of Yamamoto men heading toward the Pelican. All were dressed like myself: tan trench coats, plaid mufflers, Totes rubbers pulled over their wing-tip shoes—custom-fit, small-size, extra-width, like their suits, tailored "especially for the Japanese man." I had had lunch with three of them earlier; did I have to see them again? I waited. Video monitors in the Pelican window flashed returns from the Tokyo Stock Exchange. It had been a good day; I had checked the screens myself. The group huddled and conferred, then moved with enthusiasm through the chrome-and-glass entrance, bathed in purple neon light. They let out small whoops. Drinking would run past midnight, no doubt.

I took off running as soon as they were inside, frantically, in a way I had not run since compulsory exercise in high school. Water from puddles sprayed up behind me and stained my pants. I stopped after a few blocks, hunched over momentarily to light a cigarette, then continued in the same direction, downtown, where Keiji now lived. I'd finally heard from him since he'd left Yamamoto. Been *fired*, to be specific. Of that incident I could remember the exact date, the hour, the minute, not only because Keiji had been my best friend but because I had known he was going to be terminated before he did. I suspected Yamamoto had let it slip out, as a test of my loyalty, one week in advance of the actual firing date. A "special" ethics project. So for one week I had had to walk around with that bottled up inside me, talk to Keiji, eat lunch with him, watch him working diligently on a project he would never see finished. But I couldn't tell him—Keiji was not the sort of person who would take the news quietly—he would barge in and cause a scene; Yamamoto would know right away that I had violated a confidence. That I was not to be trusted. He was aware that Keiji and I were friends, and he had never approved of the liaison. "A bad influence corrodes like nothing else," he once remarked. The only thing that propelled me forward this night was the memory of Keiji's face, deadpan, and the last words he had said: "Don't worry, sonny; actually the old shit's just done me the greatest favor of my life," after which he had gathered his things and walked out, humming.

Afterward, the sight of his empty cubicle had put knots in my stomach every time I passed it. I had tried to call him on several occasions, but he had disconnected his line and left only a post office box for his forwarding address. Sometimes for no reason I would break into a slow, cold sweat at the thought of him—there was so much trouble for him to get into in New York. What kind of person was I, what kind of friend? I imagined he must despise me. A summer had passed, and an autumn, and then finally, within the past week, I had received a plain white envelope at work with his new address and number—no name, just a thumbprint. It was from Keiji, there was no doubting that. I had never been so happy to receive a piece of mail.

He lived near Chinatown, on the top floor of what had once been a public school, its classrooms converted into studios and apartments—cold, dank, dim; the halls smelling, even now, of small children. I saw what looked like a rat skulking on one of the landings as I climbed the iron staircase, but it disappeared before I could be sure. Hearing a rustling overhead, I froze, looking up. In the gloom I could just make out the long figure of Keiji dangling over the railing, a slight reflection bouncing off the frames of his glasses, thick and oblique.

"*Gozen-sama!*" he yelled. The sound echoed and flew all around us. "You weren't kidding—you escaped! You should be in the pachinko parlor with the boys. What're you, drunk?"

I had stopped at a phone booth on my way to warn him I was coming. Although it had ruined the surprise, it was probably for the best; dropping in on Keiji unannounced was never wise—you never knew what he might be up to.

I paused to catch my breath.

"You climb these stairs every day?" I wheezed.

"Six, seven times a day." He pulled me by the hand up the last flight. "Soon I'll be ready for the Olympics."

"Or the Iron Man."

"Or an iron lung. Wanna cigarette?"

"Shh," I protested. "You'll kill me."

"No such luck," Keiji said, and we both laughed awkwardly as we bumped each other in the dark. Keiji kicked open the steel door to his apartment and waved an arm, smiling. "Well, this is it. My home."

I looked at him first, before the room. He had let his hair grow so that it reached his shoulders and had also grown a beard, really more of a tuft, underneath his lower lip. Pencil mustache. The hair gathered into a queue, Chinese style; the old tortoiseshell glasses gone and replaced by two circles of wire balanced on the end of his nose. He was still gaunt, still nervous; he still gave the appearance of being tightly strung. His face and voice carried the same tones of arrogant disbelief that had made him so unpopular at Yamamoto, but now, with the long hair and black turtleneck and glasses, the attitude was more fitting—imperial. It suited him well.

His apartment was a room and not much more: exposed wiring overhead, dusty floors, a refrigerator, a closet, windows grimed with street soot facing out to a network of fire escapes. He had furnished the room with a cot, a card table and two chairs, an aquarium, a Yamamoto TV set, black-and-white, from the days when Yamamoto produced nothing but televisions and transistors. No source of heat. The utility sink was heaped with dishes and cheap bamboo chopsticks; the air smelled sour, of garbage, spoiled milk, dirty clothes and a further deeper smell—a familiar one— the smell of determined solitary living. I swallowed, remembering when I had last been in a room like this. It was my father's studio in Tokyo, his filthy haven: soiled kimonos, teacups, sake casks, fish bones and cigarette ashes all over the place. A mess that did not want anybody to clean it up. I had never liked to go there and intrude. My father always seemed so much happier when we were leaving.

"You're repulsed, I can see that," Keiji said softly. "But to be honest, I really don't care."

I focused momentarily on the aquarium, its gurgling of water and goldfish, a few strands of algae floating eel-like along the surface.

"Do what you want; don't worry about me. Does it get cold?"

"Sometimes. I wear a lot of sweaters."

"Roaches?"

Keiji shrugged. "You get used to them. Everybody has roaches in New York. I'm so good at killing them you wouldn't believe it. I use my bare hand—splat! I don't even give them a chance to get away while I'm trying to find a magazine or a shoe."

I looked back at the pile of dishes in the sink, the smears of yellow-brown on the wall above it.

"Which hand?" I asked. Keiji raised the left one, long fingers spread wide. "Ah, southpaw." I laughed but made no move to take off my coat.

"I'm happy now," Keiji said.

"I don't doubt it. You look happy, or happier." Keiji would never look happy in his life, I thought. Another aspect of solitary living, much more pleasant, entered my mind: Gina's apartment, its hollow neatness, radiators hissing warmth. Such a lurid episode—only about twelve hours of time—yet I kept reviewing it over and over again like a film clip.

I swung around abruptly on the heel of my shoe and clapped both hands together.

"Have you eaten yet?" I asked. Keiji said no. "Let me take you to dinner. You pick the place."

"All right." Keiji found his coat and scarf and a pair of gloves, which I noticed were not wool or suede or leather but gardening gloves, made of white canvas, with square, puffy fingers.

"They were two dollars at Woolworth's, so I bought them," he explained, turning his hands back and forth. "They do the trick. Money's money. Gloves are gloves."

"But you're wearing gardening gloves!" For some reason, I found this hysterical. I stared at Keiji's big white hands and slumped against the door, laughing. "Hah! I can just picture you in Woolworth's, economizing. You're nuts!" I pulled on his arm as we were walking out, an arm so taut and sinewy it was like pulling on a rope. "You know, I miss you every day at the office. Nobody cracks me up the way you did. Really."

"Shit, you're easily amused," Keiji said, but he was smiling as he tramped down the stairs, heavy boots stamping sideways as if he were scaling a mountain, led me through the hallway darkness and out into the street. He walked with authority. The air was wet and heavy and began to thicken with odors of oil and meat and vegetables as we approached the heart of Chinatown. I followed, uncomplaining, through a maze of alleys and garbage, pleased to see that Keiji, for once, seemed to know where he was going.

I offered him a piece of gum as we walked—sugarless—but he rejected it because of its bright-green color. "No, thanks," he said. "I mean, really, I'm not sure if I'm supposed to chew this or put it on my clothing so I don't get hit by a car at night. And NutraSweet, that's Cancer City. I think the U.S. government is using it for mind control over its people. You know how it breaks enzymes into basic elements, wood alcohol and all that. By the way, did I tell you I applied for citizenship?"

The restaurant was one of hundreds in the neighborhood, hidden above a grocery store, about the size of a living room. "Only Chinese eat here," Keiji remarked with his usual arrogance upon entering the dingy place. "This isn't for the round-eyes or the tourists."

He appeared to be right. Several Chinese were seated here and there—two elders sipping soup, a couple, and a group of workmen at the table in the center. They all glanced up to stare coldly at Keiji and me, then went back to eating.

"I guess they still dislike us, even here," I said. Keiji nodded. "We're still the evil dwarfs."

"Evil dwarfs—where'd you hear that?" We were moving toward a table in the back. Keiji sat down first, folding his long legs underneath his chair. "I'm no dwarf," he said.

"True. But you're an aberration in all areas."

"Shut up. Besides, we brutalized half their country," he continued. "Can you blame them? Koreans hate us too. It wasn't so long ago, you know."

I leaned back in my chair and said nothing. I had learned some time ago not to discuss politics with Keiji, who was inflexibly liberal. I myself did not mess with politics, except when they affected business. I knew my history and my current events, but as far as real opinions were concerned, I did not have many. I went along with what promoted the corporation. I had found this chameleon attitude helpful in my years at Yamamoto; because I had had to be so conservative at first, swallowing down what few theories I had picked up at college, I eventually decided to abandon them all and become neutral, thereby saving myself both the displeasure of lying and the effort of political thought.

I closed my eyes and listened to the loud atonal waves of Chinese bouncing around me, like singsong violin music. It had been strange walking here, lost in a crowd of so many faces similar to my own—straight black hair, Asian features—the closest thing to Tokyo I had felt in years. But it was not the same, really—there was too much clutter and chaos. The Chinese were a very different people, rougher, louder, almost coarse. I had always been intimidated by them. On the way here, two young kids, maybe Vietnamese, stood hawking flesh magazines on a corner. "Oriental pussy, Oriental pussy," they called to us, in English. "Oh, none of that for me," Keiji replied, stone-faced. "We've seen that all our lives; why should we want any more?"

"What looks good?" he was asking. The hostess—the woman who owned the apartment whose living room this was—stood waiting for our order. She was short and stout, moon-faced and suspicious. She did, however, warm to Keiji, who spoke fluent Mandarin.

"Oh, I don't know. Duck. Duck and maybe some chicken livers. You decide. Something very good, to wash this bad taste out of my mouth. My stomach's backing up."

Keiji rattled off several phrases, and the woman nodded and left. There was a loud burst of laughter from the workmen as they passed around a roll of something in tinfoil, their table already heaped with plates and bones and empty beer cans.

"You know what that is?" Keiji asked.

I yawned. "Opium?"

"Don't be silly. It's raw pork. Ever had it?"

"No." I looked at them with sudden concern. "Aren't they afraid of trichinosis?"

"I'm sure it's fresh. They know what they're doing."

"I hope so."

"Sometimes you have to take risks."

"If they're worth taking," I said. I lit a cigarette with the citronella candle flickering between us, putting my face deliberately close to the flame to show Keiji I wasn't afraid to take risks. "It's like fugu, I guess. You know the saying, 'I want to eat fugu, but I also want to live.' "

"I haven't had fugu since your wedding," Keiji said. He blinked his eyes reflectively several times and took a long sip of the beer the woman had set down before him. "By the way, how is Taeko? You haven't mentioned her once tonight."

"That should tell you something." I swallowed half my own beer, right off. The earlier drunk from the Pelican had worn away, leaving me irritable and cold sober. I puffed on my cigarette slowly and watched the workmen attack a platter of fried chicken feet; I could hear the sound of their crunching, the snap of cartilage, all the way across the room.

"What are you doing now, to support yourself?" I asked Keiji, eager to change the subject. "You were out of touch for so long I was afraid something bad had happened."

"To me? Never. I'm tough. Once I was fired, I immediately

began to cheer up. It was liberation. Sometimes you have to be kicked in the ass to be liberated."

The woman returned with the appetizers. I noted how her hands and wrists were covered with small red welts, some pink, some brown—burns from oil splatters, no doubt, in various stages of healing. My mother had had hands like that. Just the sight of them made me melancholy.

Keiji bit into a cabbage roll so hot that steam accompanied his next words. He paused and took a sip of water.

"I have an easy job, almost no pay. I sit in a gallery that sells hideous prints and postcards, and I read. They let me park my Harley in there and listen to the radio. It—"

"Your Harley!" I interrupted. "What happened to the old Yamaha?"

Keiji made a face. "Oh, I sold that rice grinder. I wanted a real bike. Anyway, the job takes care of the rent and nothing more. Hardly anyone comes in. Also I work for a mover sometimes on the weekends. That keeps you in shape, dragging couches and pianos in and out of walk-ups." Proudly he flexed the long muscles of his arms beneath the black turtleneck. I slumped back, beginning to feel a little flabby—like a small, unexercised pet. "I'm all right," Keiji said. "You have to remember how much money I have in savings. A ridiculous amount—I can't believe they paid me that much."

"You deserved it. You were the best ad man we had," I said. Actually Keiji had been making an average salary, about five thousand dollars less than I made. But he had no wife and children, no house, no car, no two-hundred-dollar monthly phone bills riddled with calls to Tokyo. He was a loner. Everything he earned was his own.

The appetizer plate was swiftly replaced by the main-course dishes, and another round of beer was set down. I gathered a wad of meat between my chopsticks and chewed slowly, allowing each chicken liver to pop sweet and full of juices in my mouth. The food was reviving me; the place did not look so dismal anymore, the people didn't seem half as hostile. I sat with elbows propped on either side of my plate and began to eat ravenously.

"But what's happened to your life's focus, Keiji?" I asked. "Don't you have any goals left?"

Keiji glanced up sharply, glasses fogged.

"Hey, fuck you and your goals. I have no expectations of me, and that's the way I want it. I don't have to get married to some stupid little bitch just because everybody else is married to some stupid little bitch, I don't have to have children, I don't have to spend money or wear suits or pal around with a bunch of assholes from Japan all day long. I don't have to get my hair cut. I don't even have to wear a watch if I don't feel like it."

I glanced at my own watch, the present from Yamamoto for my fifth anniversary. It was nearly ten o'clock. "I get your point," I said. I did not mind the outburst or feel personally offended. Keiji had always been explosive, even in college, quick to lash out but even quicker to repent. I waited for the usual cavalcade of apologies. There were none, however; Keiji's mouth remained shut, opening only to eat. After several minutes of silence, during which he pretended to be engrossed in deboning his fish, he finally spoke. His voice was shaky.

"I remember that Yamamoto bastard, trying to force me to go to social club meetings or to hook me up with his niece. Once he said, 'You, what's wrong—how come you're thirty and still single? Is there something funny about you I should know about?' Pompous sonofabitch. As if he were something to look at, with all his excess—penthouses and limousines, that has-been movie star wife he parades around like a prize dog. Big deal. As if I'm supposed to be impressed by that. All that phony concern about his employees and their problems, when all he's really interested in is sniffing out trouble, finding the subversives."

"The needle in the arm," I said softly.

"I'm through with that. I hated that place from day one. I hated it in the Tokyo office, and I thought maybe if I came here it wouldn't be so bad—you know, a different environment—but it was worse. He's ten times more protective. He wants to bring Tokyo over here. Every *real* ad idea I had was shot down—was I supposed to be happy doing catalogue work? Forget it. You can keep your money."

"All right."

"And what are you now, anyway? You look worn out. You're on a treadmill. Yamamoto's bag carrier, that's what you are. Yamamoto's lackey."

"All right, Keiji, enough!" I swept my hand out as if to silence him and in doing so almost knocked over the citronella candle. I had spoken loudly, more so than I'd intended, and all the Chinese were staring. I pretended to ignore them. The food in front of me was suddenly tasteless and unappealing, and fatigue from the long day was setting in, making my eyes itch.

"I heard you the first time," I said. "Don't keep tearing me down to justify yourself."

"Sorry," Keiji mumbled, his mouth full of rice. "But—"

"I don't want to hear it," I snapped. I fumbled again in the pocket of my trench coat for my cigarettes and took one out secretively so as not to display the ostentatious silver case. My hands were trembling, and I could feel myself growing excited. "You're just as intolerant with your bohemian life-style as any salaryman," I said. "You can only live in abandoned buildings, only wear varying shades of black, only hang around with other blasé bohemian people, who all think the same way you do. The convention of always defying convention. How bourgeois. How boring. And what's wrong with wearing a watch, enjoying the division of time, seeing how much you can get done in fifteen minutes? To control the chaos of a day. What's wrong with wearing good clothing, expertly fitted; what's wrong with having a beautiful home, a VCR for films, a stereo for the purest-sounding music—what's wrong with that? I like control, I like the organization of things. But I'm not inhuman for it, am I?"

I broke off, exhausted, several strands of hair fallen out of place and hanging between my eyes. My damn hair. It was like a bunch of weeds sometimes.

Keiji sighed. "You're missing the point. You'll see it my way someday, I know it."

"Oh, no, not that someday business—tell me now. What is the point, then, besides the fact that I'm a money-grubbing jerk?" While I was speaking I made a circle with my thumb and index finger, to indicate money, and then I heard my own voice and was surprised by the ragged edge to it. It was almost as if I was begging him for an answer.

"The point is . . ." Keiji raised one chopstick ceremoniously, then lowered it back to his plate. "The point is there is no point. So there."

He used the stick to fling a black shiitake mushroom at me, and it landed with a plop on the immaculate silk of my new Brittany tie. "There, there's your debating medal. You win the argument, Shimada, what do you think about that?"

"Is there something funny about you I should know about?" I said, doing my best Yamamoto bark.

We smiled at each other half hostilely for a moment, frozen, then laughed and raised hands and yelled for two more bottles of beer.

At parting, I clamped Keiji's hand between my own. The rain had dissipated into a fog that huddled around us thickly.

"Just remember, if you ever need money," I said, making my eyes solemn and my voice very grave. "If you ever need money, you can go straight to hell!" I hugged myself, laughing.

"Thanks," Keiji said. "You're a prince."

"But if you ever cut that braid off, send it to Etsuko. She could use it for one of her dolls—she'd love you forever. That I'm no kidding about."

"All right." Keiji glanced around and shoved his hands into his pockets. The gardening gloves were gone. "How are you getting back?"

"Oh, I'll walk."

"But it's after midnight, isn't it? Don't be stupid, Shimada—this isn't Tokyo." A cab was cruising by in the distance. Keiji whistled shrilly several times through his fingers, and after the fifth or sixth attempt the cab turned, its high beams making us squint. I hurried over and opened the door.

"I'm always taking cabs," I complained. "I don't get enough exercise anymore."

"This isn't the hour for exercise," Keiji said. "Do sit-ups at home. You're a real target with all those nice clothes on."

He leaned through the cab window while the Arab driver, oblivious, waited and watched a Jerry Lewis movie on a small portable TV.

"It was good to see you," I said. "Call me, now—often. Don't let six more months go by."

Keiji's face was somewhat strained, two deep creases puckering the long seam of his mouth. "You don't feel awkward, after what I said?"

"About the money?"

"No, later."

I pretended to search for my wallet. "Awkward? About that? No, not at all. Why should that make a difference?"

He was staring at me directly, so it was difficult to lie. His face was taut and shiny, as though it were about to burst; it reminded me of the skin on a grape.

"I suppose I did. I was never sure about you. I couldn't tell if it was just a phase. You've always wanted to be different, you know."

Keiji nodded. "This isn't a phase."

"I believe you."

"Good." He stepped away and allowed the cab to make a U-turn and begin the drive back uptown. I watched as he cut through an alley to his apartment, walking on a diagonal with the same bullying swagger he had always had—the walk of a bully who had been bullied all his life, now out looking for confrontation, seeking it, even in densest fog.

Although it was nearly one A.M. by the time I reached the office, I was keyed up, still not quite ready to go home. I phoned building security and had them open up the executive lounge, took a shower, then sat in the steam room and dictated a summary of the bank meeting into my tape recorder. I dressed, combed my hair back, and left the tape to be transcribed on Miss Ozaki's desk. The office was deathly quiet, but I swore I heard the wheeze of the telex machine, repeatedly, though the door had been locked and required special clearance to get in.

I drove slowly and cautiously—even though there was little traffic, the Long Island Expressway was dangerous, with poor visibility, mist swallowing the lane markers and dripping from the border of trees. I thought of Keiji. Yes, I had suspected on and off over the years, but the solid truth itself was difficult to accept, like trying to swallow a hair. Keiji *was* gay; so that was that. It was not just tendencies, as I had imagined, not just for kicks. Bloodhound Yamamoto had sniffed it out and then persecuted him for it, trying to force him into something, match him up like an odd sock.

Keiji, so sinewy and alert. Keiji with his wild ideas, which had cut right into the American market. Gang of Four and rap music for the cassette commercials; kodo drummers and cartoons for the C6-30 compact stereo system. He had handled Young Consumers. Keiji hip-hopping around his cubicle with a pair of headphones which he wore as often as he possibly could, even to lunch. All that new-wave coloring and lettering. Keiji would explain for hours how music was color, every note a different shade.

I began to wonder stupidly—I could not stop myself—whether Keiji had ever been attracted to me. I had considered this before of course, at certain moments over the years, seeing certain expressions in his eyes. If anyone could get me to think in such terms, I supposed Keiji would be the one—it would be satisfying; he would make a great effort. But no, there would be something missing, a certain pliancy I had to have. Of course I would never, I couldn't—although I allowed myself to think of Gina in those terms, in a long, elaborate way. A moth flew into the windshield and became a brown smear; I shook my head, startled, and looked up. I had missed my exit. I would have to take the next one now, for Oyster Bay. Of all times to be lost; I was a creature of habit —even one missed exit made me nervous. I had no idea where I was going.

When I did arrive home, around four, I was surprised to see Taeko still up, lying prostrate on the couch in the lavender kimono I had given her the week before, for New Year's. The kimono was already soiled, its front damp with water stains. Taeko was crying, softly, while Omi and Etsuko lay sleeping before her like two small guard dogs. I stepped between them and tried to get her to sit upright. Her body was warm and heavy, and as I pulled her forward the kimono opened, revealing her bare breasts. I hurried to pour a glass of water to offer to her and, when she refused, sprinkled a few drops on her forehead. Her skin was death pale; the water upon it looked like beads of wax.

"Are you in pain?" I whispered, frightened somewhat. "Did you take an overdose?"

Her words were sluggish. After I listened for a while, however, they began to take shape.

"I want to go back. I want to go home."

I flung an afghan over her and sat down exhausted on the floor, and Taeko pointed to the TV, tuned to the Japanese station but with no sound. Pictures of the Imperial Palace were flashing on and off, the royal family. She pointed again. I turned the volume to a minimal level, then listened with eyes half lidded to a report that the emperor was dead, that he had died early that morning. "Oh." I nodded respectfully. "But you knew he was sick; he's been dying a long time. Taeko? He was a very sick old man." She resumed sobbing, while I did not move. I felt a slow uneasiness overtake me, as if I were back outside in the fog. Omi raised his head from the carpet for a moment and stared at me, without recognition, then went back to sleep, small fists clenched and body curled up tightly in reaction to the noises he heard.

It was dawn by the time I carried all three of them to bed, a pale sun beginning to burn through the mist and various birds starting up in a slow, disorganized chorus. I had been awake for almost twenty-four hours. I sat at the desk in my study and pulled off my tie, smiling at the mushroom stain from the night before. That all seemed to have happened years before, a silly memory from the past. I called Keiji, once again on impulse, and after about twenty rings finally heard him croak an answer into the phone.

"Uh."

"The emperor's dead, did you hear?" I said. "I just thought you should know."

Keiji made a strange half-asleep noise, like air leaking out of a tire.

"You woke me up for that?"

I toyed with the phone cord, wrapping it around first my fingers, then my wrists. A cup of coffee with milk scum on top sat in front of me, left from several days back, when I had been working at home. Also a banana peel, now black. Taeko was becoming a terrible housekeeper.

"He was so old," Keiji said. "He should have abdicated long ago."

"Emperors don't abdicate."

"Emperors are useless."

I yawned. "I knew you were going to say that." I swallowed nervously, ran a hand across my mouth. "Listen, I have to tell you something."

"What?"

Keiji sounded as if he was waking up, and I felt a need to hurry, to speak while he was still not fully conscious and therefore always leave the issue in doubt. I took a deep breath.

"Omi—Omi is not my son."

"Omi?"

"The baby, the boy."

"What?" There was silence. "You're sure about this?"

I nodded; my absurd habit of nodding while on the phone, as if face-to-face. Keiji made another hissing sound and asked whose child it was.

"Saito's—her orthopedist. I know it; that's why I can't stand him."

"Saito?"

"No, the kid."

"The kid? Don't take it out on the kid—it's not his fault. If you have to hate somebody, hate Saito, or Taeko. Not a baby. He's just a victim."

"Maybe." I stared at a piece of paper on the desk—a makeshift map of Connecticut, prepared for that day's meeting—until my eyes blurred. "I knew he wasn't mine from the start. And to think that's my only son."

"You shouldn't hate him."

"Yeah." Outside I could hear the dog yipping, probably at the birds, as Keiji asked again and again, "Shimada, are you all right? Speak up."

"Look, I have to go now," I replied. "I just had to tell you that. Goodbye."

I hung up. I put my head down on the desk and waited, half expecting the phone to ring, for Keiji to call back, but he did not. I stretched and stood and did a few deep-knee bends, then went into the kitchen to make coffee. The morning seemed so beautiful in its silence. I was not tired anymore. It would be a waste of quiet for me to go to sleep, I decided; out of reverence to the emperor, I would stay awake and work.

Beautiful pure silence. I nodded off at the kitchen table, then awoke to the timid clatter of Etsuko in her rabbit slippers, balancing a carton full of eggs and some milk and smiling, desperate to fix me breakfast.

◆

"I *know* you're married, but that's really your problem, not mine. You're the one who has to live with it. I'm not deceiving anyone."

Gina sat on the bath mat, with a towel wrapped around her head, speaking very clearly and distinctly, like a stage actress. The towel was a thick one and made a lofty turban. She seemed to be using it as a prop to keep a distance between us; she held her neck stiff and did not move as she spoke, staring straight ahead, eyes focused on the green-tiled wall with all its scabrous chips.

"That's a convenient attitude to have." I reached over and yanked the towel off. "No more Nefertiti head," I said firmly. Without the usual cloud of hair, without makeup, her face looked so pure I was almost ashamed of myself. Not a purity of body, obviously, but a purity of spirit—a truly sensual face. I thought of caressing the face with my fingertips, then decided against it. Gina did not react well to soft displays of affection.

"Please don't talk about my wife anymore," I said instead.

"You brought it up."

"I know, I know. . . . I'm tiresome like that."

"Well, it's obvious you still love her," she answered, matter-of-factly. "Don't worry; it doesn't bother me."

I was submerged in her huge claw-foot tub—a tub so deep it was the size of a small boat—which Gina had filled almost to the rim with warm water and several capfuls of oil that soothed my snaky skin. Chicago was such a dry city—I often felt I was shriveling. She began to soap behind my ears, using only the tips of her fingers, then continued upward to massage my scalp, one of her favorite tricks. I leaned back heavily and felt a rising expectation along with the slosh of water, an opening of all my pores; as she proceeded with her massage, I felt fluid and ageless, a sea creature, swimming toward the surface. The illusion was broken by the sound of a phone ringing, far off in another room. Much to my disgust, she went to answer it, calmly removing her other hand from my crotch.

"Why don't you get a machine?" I snapped, and threw the soap on the floor.

"Because I hate them." Ignoring the soap, she wrapped the towel around her body, then switched on the hall light. I noticed for the first time in silhouette the bowlike muscles of her thighs. "I'll be right back," she said. "I promise."

I lay quiet, trying hard not even to breathe, so that I could eavesdrop. Water dripped from the tap, loudly, and I plugged it with my toe.

She was speaking in Italian. I was surprised she spoke Italian so fluently; I had assumed that like most Americans, she did not know any other language besides English.

"Goddamn," I mumbled to myself. I did not know any Italian at all: only English, French, the tiniest bit of Spanish. I listened carefully and tried to piece together some semblance of a conversation. Certain words made sense: *viaggio, bene, Roma, aeroplano, ciao.* Somebody was planning a trip.

By the time she returned, I had noiselessly got out of the tub and gone into the bedroom. I lay on the rumpled sheets with the window open, smoking a Lucky Strike. The weather was oddly springlike for February. Just that day it had been over fifty degrees.

"There you are," she said, and came over to join me. "I thought you drowned. That was my uncle Gavino. He's going back to Naples."

"Vacation?"

"No." She examined her fingernails, hands in a half-cocked position. "He wants to die there. He has lung cancer. He's going on a tour to collect religious relics."

I put out my cigarette abruptly and sat up. "I'm sorry to hear that," I said. "Is he very old?"

"Seventy or seventy-one. I'm not sure. He's my great-uncle." She sighed. "What can you do?"

I wanted to mention how Taeko's father, diagnosed with lung cancer fifteen years before, had somehow overcome it, but then I stopped myself. That would be bringing up my family again, which I had been doing repeatedly all night—I had almost taken out a picture of Etsuko from my wallet at one point. Instead I asked if the uncle had taught her to speak Italian.

"Oh, no, he only knows a dialect. I learned it in college. Italian was my major, in fact." She laughed. "Don't sit there with your mouth open—did you think I majored in tea service or something? I'll bet you did."

"No. You're very smart. Why don't you get a job that uses Italian, like a translator?"

She answered vaguely. "I thought about it. But I like being at the Drake, seeing all the different people. It's so uncomplicated." She lay back against my legs, and I tensed them eagerly against the pleasant weight. "Anyway, I'll be off to Italy with him this spring," she continued. "I've never been there before; I can hardly wait."

"Oh?" I said lightly. "For how long?"

"Maybe six months, maybe a year." She laughed. "Maybe I won't come back!"

I closed one eye and then the other in disbelief, feeling like I had gone back to Asakusa, an amusement district I had frequented while growing up, only to find it deserted and closed, and myself with a pocketful of money, alone in the dark.

"But what about your life here?" I said. "Don't you have responsibilities? You can't just pick up and leave like that."

"Sure I can. What's holding me—not a job or family or anything serious."

"I'm here," I said, after a moment.

"Please." Her voice was reproachful. "Don't be like that. You're not here forever, and besides, you've already got two wives: your job and the one in New York. And you know you don't love me and I don't love you. Those are the rules."

"Fine," I said. I was beginning to feel dizzy from the suddenness of all this; the bed seemed to spin.

The phone rang again. I grabbed her hand.

"Don't get up, please."

"I won't."

She had a faraway look that annoyed me. The ringing stopped.

"Popular girl," I said. *You don't love me and I don't love you.* . . . "Ever had a Japanese before?" I asked, although judging from her apartment, the answer seemed too obvious. I wondered if she wanted to put my head, too, on the wall, perhaps use my hide as a rug. The floors were awfully bare.

"Yes, I had a Japanese before," she said. "I went with one for three years. American Japanese, but still a racist."

"A what?"

"A racist, like so many of you. It's inbred—there's a feeling of superiority on your part, I know it." She spoke in a controlled monotone, as if she had told this story many times before, and while her voice might be frank and casual now, at one point this had hurt her very much. "He wasn't really interested in me for anything lasting. I mean, we had loads of fun, but when the time came that he wanted to get married, he dropped me and found a Suzy Wong girlfriend instead. The usual type, you know. Submissive, sweet. Someone like your wife."

"Suzy Wong was Chinese," I corrected. "And my wife is not submissive, unfortunately." Although her words had annoyed me, it seemed pointless to protest further—my presence here was incriminating enough.

"Don't be so literal, Mr. Shimada," she said. "Here, I have a picture of him his photographer friend took." She switched on the bed lamp and rummaged through a night-table drawer full of odds and ends: playing cards, scraps of paper, spare keys, condoms. "It was on exhibit at a student show at Columbia College."

The photograph was of a young Japanese sitting in an old claw-foot tub much like Gina's, submerged in what looked like thousands of egg yolks. Very striking. Keiji would have paid good money for a photo like that.

"Are those *real?*" I asked.

"Yes. He shot it here. It was hell to clean up."

"What a terrible waste of food," I said. I stared at the photo, touched by a strange cramp of jealousy. The boy was built like an athlete and well-muscled, the samurai peasant type. His eyes were closed, and he had a smug, absorbed expression on his face, as if he might be masturbating. I envisioned him stepping from the tub with a huge erection, his body glistening in the portable studio lights. Gina would have wrapped a towel around him, the same thick one she had used on me. I dropped the photo to the floor and turned off the lamp.

"I suppose he fueled your interest in Japan," I observed quietly. "The books, the films. Sort of *slanted* you in that direction, so to speak. Ha-ha." I laughed alone.

"They were side effects, yes," she agreed. "But even before all that, I've always had a predilection for Asian things. A sensitivity. I like the culture, the way things seem so controlled on the surface but they're really not. Like you." She chuckled, leaning toward me. "And my old boyfriend used to say all the time that I looked Japanese from far away. He said that was what first attracted him to me." Gina examined the blunt ends of her hair, smiling along with the recollection. "Who knows—I can't figure it out. Some people pass for other races, you know; they'll have the features of one race with the complexion of another. Asian men have always been attracted to me, and vice versa. Maybe they can smell it. I certainly have fun with the situation."

"There's no arguing that," I said. "*I* was attracted."

We remained there, unmoving, like two people sharing a raft, and then I felt her hand press hard against my chest.

"And what about you?" she asked.

"What about me?"

Her thumb tickled my flesh. She put her other hand up to my face and turned it sideways.

"You don't see yourself as attractive to me?"

"Well, I don't know." I faltered, gesturing widely to indicate the expanse of her home. "In an odd way. You've obviously got a thing for Japanese. A predilection, as you called it." I eased "predilection" out, like taking a tight curve, just to show her I could pronounce it. I had a suspicion that she had used the word deliberately, because it was such a classic Asian pitfall—I was very sensitive about saying my "r's" and "l's" correctly.

She went on.

"And why is that odd? Are only Asian women supposed to be attracted to Asian men? Lots of white men like Asian women, and that's all right, it's understandable—they're supposedly so exotic, so submissive—but why can't anyone see the universal appeal of Asian men? I do. The shapes of their faces, their builds, the color of their skin. Their mouths. Asian men have some of the most beautiful mouths I've ever seen. It's not odd; it's obvious."

"Is that right?" I shifted a bit, growing uncomfortable and aroused at the same time. Gina continued.

"I picked you out right away. And not because you're a businessman and might have money to spend on me, but because of your appearance. I spotted you all the way across the room." She laughed again. "Really, just to look at you would be enough."

"You don't want my money, then," I joked. "Seeing as how I'm rolling in it. You don't work at the Drake just to pick up rich foreign businessmen, eh?"

Her reply was completely serious. "Not at all. I pay my own way, usually; that's very important to me. I like being independent. I like to do what I want, live how I see fit. And I don't get attached to people, not anymore. I just have adventures. So there's no need to worry about things getting messy, not with me. I'm a hedonist, I really am." It occurred to me that real hedonists didn't go around saying they were hedonists, but I kept quiet. She was entertaining.

I pinched each of her breasts fondly. "I can see that," I said. "Still, don't you worry just the slightest bit about your future— how you might end up, floating like this?" I realized I was inquiring not so much out of concern but rather from curiosity, the way I might question Keiji about his alternative life-style, had I ever had the nerve to do so.

"Worry?" she repeated. "I don't quite understand. Why would I worry?"

"Because . . ." I hesitated, not wanting to offend her. "Because, well, you're not getting any younger. This is all fine and good, having adventures for a while, but aren't you afraid you'll overplay your hand?"

She frowned. "Not at the moment, no. I'm only twenty-five, for God's sake."

"Yes," I persisted, "but even twenty-five is not so young. In Japan we call women over twenty-five 'Christmas Cake.' Haven't you ever heard that expression, in your travels?"

"No. Enlighten me," she said.

I nodded. "Women over twenty-five are just like seasonal cakes and cookies—once the holiday has passed, their value depreciates. You can pick them up at half price." I laughed. I was teasing again, although the concept really was fairly obvious.

"Well, this Christmas cake has a lot of preservatives in it." Gina bristled. "And I don't deal with timetables, remember?"

"Oh, that's right," I said. "Sorry . . ." I turned on my side. "Tell me what you do all day," I urged, suddenly. "When you're not at work. Tell me where you're from and where you went to college, who you spend your time with."

She shook her head. "No."

"No? Why not? You know about me. Why should you have all the secrets?"

She smiled. "You volunteered the information; it made it easier for you—you had to get it off your chest that you were married, let me know that this has no future. Which it doesn't. Why complicate things, why take this any deeper than it needs to go? Just enjoy yourself. It's not necessary to pretend you're interested in me."

"But I am!" I protested. I kicked my foot out of the tangle of sheets. "I don't like all the mystery and strangeness."

"Don't be angry," she said. "I should think you would prefer this—it's sort of like a teahouse relationship."

"Oh, you don't know what you're talking about," I snapped, then sighed so heavily I burst out laughing. Why was I bothering to tamper with an ideal situation? I didn't need any more information about her—I already could see what a unique person she was, willing simply to have sex. And to enjoy the sex totally, at that. Unless she was pretending, but then I figured my being Asian stimulated her. How rare.

"What's so funny?" she asked.

"Nothing." I poked at her. "No, I'm laughing at you, really. You do look Japanese in the dark."

"From afar," she corrected.

"Whatever," I said, then began to fondle her in particular spots, taking great pleasure in the responses my hands were producing. Small breezes like breaths puffed through the curtains, air that smelled like chocolate; someone must have been making brownies in the apartment below. She was so healthy. Even in the dark I could see the whiteness of her teeth, the strong armature of bones underneath smooth, serviceable skin. Perfect reflexes, machine-like, and like a machine, she never seemed to get tired. And since she appeared to want to be treated like a machine, I told myself, I didn't need to care about her; this was pure recreation, just as if I were sitting down to play pachinko. I placed my palm over her left breast and felt the nipple tighten reflexively between my fingers. The same response from the other breast, which felt to me slightly larger.

"How long have you been back in Chicago?" she asked, voice a little shakier than usual.

I dipped my head forward, embarrassed. "About five hours, maybe less. I made one stop before I came here, to drop off my luggage. I took the chance that you'd be home, since it's a Sunday night. People like to stay home on Sunday nights."

"Most people."

I had her struggling now, a fish on a dock. She opened her legs in a V and rolled over on her stomach.

"You must have really wanted to see me, to come here straight from the airport. You must be pent-up."

"Yes."

I slid my hand over her mouth and entered her from behind, full force. Like scissors on paper, her legs closed and tightened, again the perfect response, to hold me firmly in place. My sight blurred, and my back puckered with gooseflesh. I caught myself saying *I love you*, out loud, more of a moan that just happened to form words. I said it again, then again. After the third time I moved my hands over her ears. I didn't love this girl really, I couldn't— I had to stop saying that stuff. But she twisted her head and looked straight back at me. She was smart and brave: she knew. It was not the first time someone had said "I love you" to her in the dark—she had doubtless heard it on many occasions and received it with the same universal indifference and disbelief.

◆

Taeko had not called me all week. I lay on the bed in my room at the Nippon, balancing the receiver deftly between shoulder and ear and allowing the phone to ring on. I glanced at the travel alarm on the nightstand. Eleven o'clock—that meant midnight in New York. I could think of no reason why she would not be home; well, I could think of a reason, but for a tryst with Saito she would surely get a baby-sitter for the kids.

I put the phone down and poured myself a glass of Scotch, wondering whether she was not answering out of spite. There had been a bad day before I left, composed of several bad scenes. Omi, in the morning, had been playing with one of Etsuko's toys, and without thinking I had grabbed it away, told him to play with his own things. Suddenly, before I could stop myself, I had reached over and squeezed one of his fat little toes, like a baby grub between my fingers. I squeezed hard. Who was this stupid, soft-headed little creature—why was I responsible for him? Why was I responsible for any of the people in this house, why did they look at me with open beaks, why couldn't they take care of themselves?

Omi tilted back slightly on his pudgy legs, widened his eyes and began to cry. Taeko hurried in and called me a bully. I apologized and was going to take the dog for a walk, but Taeko persisted, running after me. She had been in the midst of doing her nails and came at me with beige foam wads separating her fingers.

"You treat that dog better than you do him, you know that? He's such a good little boy—why don't you love him?"

I looked at her in disbelief for a moment, then snapped the dog's leash from its hook by the door.

"Leave me alone," I said. Cho was racing around in circles now, frantic at the prospect of going out, and I felt his small teeth nipping through my socks. My shoes were on the porch mat, lined up with Taeko's suede boots and Etsuko's new high-top sneakers. Etsuko had begged for those sneakers for almost a month. After my last trip to Chicago, I had left a package under her bed—the sneakers along with a pair of pink flowered laces. I frowned. Of course I played favorites, but Etsuko was mine, not some mistake Taeko had made and was trying to palm off on me to save her own skin. Still, I remembered what Keiji had said. It wasn't the child's fault.

I hooked the dog's leash to his collar.

"Tell Omi I'm sorry." I slipped on my windbreaker and gloves and old knit hat, then glanced at myself briefly in the hall mirror but would not look at Taeko, reflected there. Cho was out of control, hurling himself against the storm door and whining. I stepped outside. The air felt brisk and inspiriting against my face.

"Why don't you tell him yourself?" Taeko called, but I merely let the dog pull me down the driveway into the street. She persisted. "He's only a little boy, Jun. He doesn't understand big things."

I turned back just as I was rounding the corner, where Cho had stopped at a lamppost to mark it. Taeko was hanging out the door, waiting, arms stiff at her sides. The sight of her in the flowered kimono housecoat, hair pulled up, so black, so heavy, round face so white: this Japanese woman who was my wife, against the backdrop of a Cape Cod house she was living in against her will—it seemed so wrong I almost felt sorry for her. The dog nosed around in a pile of dead leaves and kicked his hind legs. I waved to the Murphys as they drove by in their van: happy family, off on an outing. I often had a beer with the father when we were both out doing yardwork in the summer—he had been stationed in Osaka, briefly, during the Occupation.

I smiled. It was not such a bad life, being here, was it? The dog pulled me forward eagerly. I looked back for Taeko, but she was gone, inside consoling Omi, no doubt, as only a mother could.

The second scene came later, while I was in the den, presumably working but in reality doing a backlog of *Times* crossword puzzles, which I attacked with my American Heritage Dictionary and great excitement. Taeko saved them for me whenever I was out of town. "Aimless, wandering" was what I was stuck on, and as usual while looking through the dictionary for clues, I got lost in tangents, the definition of one word leading to my wanting to know the origin of another. But Taeko had come in then and loudly emptied the wastebasket—she was in the midst of cleaning, wearing pink rubber gloves and a pink headband—then she stopped and sank down in the chair on the other side of my desk. She looked furious, in a dazed sort of way; I asked her what was wrong.

"The hairs. I can't get rid of them," she said.

I put down my pen guiltily and closed the dictionary. "What?"

"The black hairs all over the place—on the floor, in the bathroom, on the rugs. No matter how much I vacuum, they're there. No matter how many times I clean the tub or the sink, they come right back. It's useless trying to keep a neat house; I just can't do it. And this house is so big, I'm always dragging things up and down stairs. I'll get all the way to the bathroom and realize I've forgotten the Windex to do the mirrors, then I have to go back down to the kitchen again. Or I left the bathroom cleanser in the kitchen. Then I clean, and you just go in and mess it up again." She eyed me defiantly, her soft mouth twisted. "They're mostly your hairs, I can tell."

I wasn't sure whether this was supposed to be funny or not, and

I waited, hoping she would laugh. She did not. Her face had a strange expression, almost vicious, as if we were talking about a life-or-death situation.

Without thinking, I ran my hand over my head and scowled back at her.

"What makes you say they're all my hairs?" I snapped. "You've got four people in this house, all with black hair. It's just as likely that they're yours, not mine. Or Etsuko's. Or even Omi's—he's got a lot of hair for a kid."

"They're yours, mostly. I can tell by their texture and their length." She snapped the gloves off her hands, which despite the newly done nails seemed puffy and waterlogged, then covered her face. "It drives me crazy! You go into that bathroom every morning and fling water all over the place, clog up the sink with hairs and beard stubble, and leave me here to clean up the mess."

"For God's sake, what are you wasting my time with this for? Maybe I'm going bald!" I turned on my calculator for no reason, tore off the previous edge of tape. "In Tokyo you were complaining you didn't have enough room, and now you—"

"I never said I didn't have enough room! I only said I wanted more outlets in the kitchen. I didn't say I wanted to live in a barn!"

"Yes, I know," I said flatly, tired of the subject, which although it had presented itself initially as unusual—the thing about the hairs—always came down to the same facts: a nagging tune I had to hear again and again. I continued:

"I also know you didn't pay the electric bill last month. We just got a second notice." She flapped the heel of her slipper against her foot; she was sitting in an uncharacteristically slutty position in the chair, one leg up over the arm.

"The Macy's bill is second notice too, and the checking account is almost overdrawn. Do you want to bounce checks? Is that your new hobby?" No answer. "I thought your job was to manage the house."

"I do manage," she said. Her chin was quivering.

"You do? What? Manage to watch it fall apart? You're a flake,

Taeko," I said. "I'll handle the bills from now on; obviously you can't."

I was at my wit's end with her, that was why I was being so gruff. The laissez-faire approach had not worked—perhaps what she wanted was stern authority and discipline, a touch of her father. I went back to doing the crossword puzzle, pretending to be absorbed while Taeko remained where she was, speechless. I could sense her anger, I could almost hear her heartbeat. I refused to look up.

Several minutes passed—she was still there. I glanced down at my sweater and saw a hair, one of my own, then very calmly picked it off and dropped it to the floor. She bolted. The chair she had been sitting in tipped over and fell, and I heard a clatter of things outside the study, in the kitchen—brooms falling, plastic bottles —and Taeko crying into her soap bucket, no doubt.

"Desultory," that was the word I was looking for: it matched the number of letters in the puzzle. "Oh, yes, desultory," I exclaimed to myself, acting as though it were the most important thing in the world. I filled the squares carefully, one by one, then, ignoring the sudden eerie silence around me, proceeded to the next space.

That night, at a funerary dinner for the emperor, Taeko looked beautiful, dressed somberly in a dark-purple silk, hair piled high, but she was mute and hardly touched any of her food. Explaining to the others that she was overcome with grief, I socialized double time to make up for her silence. I listened to Mrs. Azugawa's unending talk about her daughter's wedding—"The gown and the kimono are almost ready, and then we will have to choose the *hikidemono*, and then she wants dry ice for special atmosphere effects, and then they're going to Hawaii for their honeymoon."— and nodded with enthusiasm while Mr. Azugawa gave out tips on how to play better golf. At just past midnight, I felt Taeko tug lightly on the corner of my jacket, an indication that she wanted to go, but I brushed her off. We were the last couple to leave the restaurant; Taeko was fuming. Driving home, I blared the radio so she could not sleep, then when we were in the house insisted I was hungry and that she fix me something to eat. This bullying was a new sort of pleasure—it thrilled and frightened me. Omi and Etsuko were gone, sleeping at the baby-sitter's. The sitter was a good reliable woman, second-generation nisei. Taeko was fond of her and never trusted the children with anyone else. The woman was Saito's office nurse.

When Taeko was climbing the stairs, I snuck up behind her, circling my arms around her waist and nibbling her ear. I caught a strong whiff of perfume, a smell of musk and warm skin, but she was dead weight, leaning wearily against the banister. In bed, she put up no resistance yet offered no encouragement either. When I was finished I slumped back, ashamed of myself. Taeko had fallen asleep.

It had become quite stormy—a branch scraped repeatedly against the bedroom window. Taeko had already hidden her body with the blankets. I lay there, half expecting her to get up and take a bath, to purge herself. She was snoring lightly. I tapped her on the shoulder until her eyes opened, nervous, then I intertwined her fingers with my own.

"Taeko, you used to love me, didn't you? Maybe you never did. Are you that good an actress?"

She was whispering. "No."

"Then what happened?"

"I don't know."

"I'm not fat," I said. "I'm clean, I don't smell—at least I think I don't. I don't beat you, I make a good living and let you spend whatever you want. Right?" She nodded. A large tear oozed out of the corner of her eye and streamed sideways, into her hairline. I thought of licking it away, as I once might have done, but did not. "I'm not impotent," I continued. "I'm not bald or fifty years older than you. I'm a good conversationalist." I laughed uneasily. "So tell me what's wrong. Why are you in love with Saito?"

"I don't know!" A strange guttural noise came out of her throat, and she sat up abruptly, covering her bare breasts while I stared at them, surprised. Pear-shaped, with sensitive nipples. I had forgotten she was naked beneath the sheet.

"You're having an affair with him, right?" I took the silence to mean yes. I was almost excited: she would tell me now, it would all come out—it was necessary to drag myself through this, like lancing a boil. "Just nod your head, please. I need to know."

She nodded. More tears rolled automatically down her round cheeks.

"Well, what are you going to do about it?" I asked. When she said nothing, I gathered the mass of her hair into my hand and yanked on it as hard as I could. "Idiot!" Her head whipped back, the dull whites of her eyes showed, but she was still mute. After a moment or two she stood up and slipped on her kimono, then she got back into bed, waiting for me to continue.

"You could get a divorce," I said, my voice poisonously sweet. Taeko's father was old guard, with severe standards. He would most likely disapprove keenly of a divorced daughter, and Taeko, like her three sisters, idolized the man and went to great lengths to keep him happy.

I puckered up my mouth, martyr-like. "I don't want you to be miserable," I said. "If you're not happy, you should—"

"I should what? Since when have you ever cared whether *I* was happy or not?"

She had snapped her teeth at me, made the little sound a kitten makes when it's been played with too much. I hesitated a moment, flustered.

"What is that supposed to mean?"

"The truth!" She was sitting up now, a pillow bunched between her legs, breathing heavily. "You don't care about me, you liar. You moved me over here like a piece of furniture, away from my family and all my friends; you didn't even ask me if I wanted to go, you just announced it. And then you left me. I didn't know anyone here, I was always by myself—not like you and your stupid co-workers, never coming home, going off on seminars and business trips and fishing trips, company picnics and company dinners and company joint vacations. You don't even *look* at me anymore. You know you're wrong."

"You know what a man's job means to him, any worthwhile man," I said. "We've been over this a hundred times. Besides, I work to support you and those two children. Who pays all the bills? Where does all the food come from? I hand my paycheck right over to you. I let you do anything you like."

"Liar. You do it all for yourself."

I ignored her and examined my navel in the half-light. Taeko clutched my hand.

"I never see you, except in bed. Or maybe as your dinner partner, if I'm lucky enough to be included."

"But you never want to be included. I thought I was doing you a favor, keeping things to a minimum," I said. "And besides, other wives manage."

She shook her head back and forth repeatedly, nails now piercing into the flesh of my wrist. "Not this wife. I hate this country— filthy mess. To think my children have to grow up here!"

"You're the child, Taeko. This is a wonderful place."

"For you, maybe. You had no ties at home—no sisters; both your parents were dead. You speak English."

I pulled away. "Yes, fine, it's all my fault. I ruined your life. I forced you into an affair with Saito."

"More or less." She kept her eyes on me steadily. I looked away. Such calm, from Taeko, was unnerving. "He treats me like a person," she said. "He was my first friend here, the only one I could talk to. He looked at me when he spoke, he gave me compliments and told me stories and jokes. He asked my advice! He treats me like a woman, not a wife." She sighed. "You used to do the same thing, and then you lost interest."

As she spoke of Saito, a warm smile played around her lips, a softness, almost as if she were talking about him to one of her girlfriends. I had an urge to hit her—slap the smile off her face

—but instead let my hands dangle uselessly between my legs. I had never hit a woman in my life.

"Why don't you marry him, then?" I said. "Especially since he's given you such a fine son." I heard her gasp: such dramatics! This was as bad as any of those noodle dramas on TV. "Oh, don't deny it, Taeko—I wasn't even around when you got pregnant. I was in Chicago that month."

Small choking sounds were coming from her. She dropped to her knees alongside the mattress, which was raised slightly on a wooden frame set on pegs; Taeko insisted this was helpful for her back.

"How . . . ?"

I grinned, sadly. "He's so dark, just like his father. Saito's people are from Enoshima, right? Fishermen. Almost like a little Filipino, that kid."

My stomach was churning; still, it felt good to get the words out. I lay back, taking slight breaths; the odor of Taeko's perfume had become nauseating in the past few minutes—spermy, like her lover's cologne—and the room seemed to have shrunk down to nothing more than the square arena of our bed.

"But you won't marry him, I know it," I said. "He's a real playboy—I've seen him, always looking at women. If he's got you, he's got six more, for the other days of the week. The bachelor doctor. Did he make his move in the examining room, while he was feeling all over your back? Tell me. I'm interested in the small details."

She was crying, although by now I was so used to the sound of her crying that it no longer bothered me. Taeko could cry at the drop of a hat. Even normally her eyes had a moistness to them, an overfull look, as if at any second they might spill over, then well right back up again, with more liquid.

"I just—I just cannot be what I want anymore," she whispered. "It's so complicated. I can't bring things together."

Lying there, I reflected upon those words. Too complicated. Too many missed exits. "Yeah, well," I said. I did not touch her, yet I stroked the space at her side. For the first time in a long time, I felt myself speaking from the heart. "Isn't that true for everyone? That living gets in the way of life."

"Mmm, maybe," she agreed. "But I'm really lost."

I sighed. "What about your painting—can't you find yourself in that?"

She shook her head. "No, not now. I can't even think now. It's so empty inside."

Our argument appeared to have ended in a weary truce. Taeko remained exiled at the corner of the mattress, while I dozed on and off. I woke to the thud of the Sunday paper being thrown onto the porch, saw how Taeko had fallen asleep in her kneeling position.

"Ridiculous," I said. "I won't bite." I nudged her gently with my foot, and she jerked up, startled, a design from the bedspread creased into her cheek.

"Could you bring me some Maalox?" I asked. "I've got a sour stomach."

She hurried into the bathroom and returned with a glass of chalky liquid, which I drank down as fast as I could without breathing. Taeko watched, her movements suddenly small and wifelike. Complaisant. She was making me edgy.

"Jun . . ."

"Yes."

She began smoothing the hair just above my ear, with the queer affection one might give a dying pet. I dragged the pillow over my head.

"What do you want me to do?" she asked.

One of my cufflinks was on the floor—round, topaz: cat's eyes, they used to call them. I reached for it, but it was too far away. My arm seemed pale and scrawny in the daylight. Taeko repeated her question.

"What do you want me to do?"

"Oh, I don't know. Whatever you want. Go back to Tokyo," I said. "Go back and have a grand old time. Take a trip around the world. Move in with Saito. I don't care. I release you: run free. I won't make you live in the American dungeon anymore."

I laughed and then a moment later turned over to see her reaction. She was gone; only the new kimono remained, wadded up, still warm from her body. A kimono I had described in detailed letters to Mrs. Reiko Ogawa, who had made it to my design—lavender, with a border of red and yellow poppies, a black obi. A waste of time. I reached over and grabbed the robe, with it wiped the antacid from my mouth, then tossed it back into the middle of the bed, where it lay, a pile of filthy purple silk.

Taeko was humming along with the bathroom fluorescent lights. She obviously felt nothing for me anymore.

◆

In Chicago, snow was falling thickly but melting in a sloppy mush as soon as it reached the ground. Although I had left my rubbers at the Nippon, I tramped out at lunchtime one afternoon to buy Gina a present. I was beginning to feel a sort of pessimism toward the whole thing. It was very one-dimensional—I only seemed to see her in bed. That had been Taeko's complaint during our argument, but there were only so many hours to a day, and to go out, to take entire evenings off just to sit and chat and maybe dance with a woman, was next to impossible. Yamamoto, in Tokyo, phoned every day, sent orders, packages, relentless ten-page memos by fax. I found I could visit Gina only once or twice a week, especially because after each visit I was sucked dry, depleted, hardly in any shape to be running around an office. The more I saw her, the less I wanted to go to work, and for the first time in years I found myself thinking up excuses, ailments, reasons to call in sick. Not that she ever asked me to. She made no demands on me at all; I imagined that once I was out of her bed, she did not give me another thought until I was back in it. What she did with the rest of her time—whether she had someone else, any friends, hobbies—I still had no clue to, except that she was usually there when I called her. Usually.

She never called me.

Taeko had not answered the phone all week. I was planning to call Mrs. Nakashima, the baby-sitter, as soon as I got back to the hotel that night.

I decided on a set of Italian cordial glasses for Gina—crystal, with a gold rim—and had them wrapped. My original intent had been to give her a book, an illustrated *Tale of Genji*, but since the conversation with her uncle, she seemed to be losing interest in Japan; she appeared to be going back to her roots. I bought myself a Polish sausage with everything and ate it while walking back to the office, then threw the remains of the bun to some pigeons on the street. The pigeons were of various colors—tan, white, gray-blue. They looked at me suspiciously for a moment, then they all rushed forward to pick at the wad of bread. A group of older women in boots and fancy hats passed, turning off into an ice cream shop, their arms laden with packages from Carson's and Marshall Field's. Together they made soft cooing noises, similar to the pigeons'. A little after-shopping treat, I thought, although who could eat ice cream in this freezing weather? I stared at them briefly, in confusion, and wondered how people who didn't work managed to fill the hours of their day.

Back in the office, Yamamoto's Chicago assistant, Mori, was moving about with great agitation, preparing green tea. I paused to see if I had any messages. A frill of lace peeped out above her heavy calves, just beneath her skirt. I pointed.

"It's snowing down south," I said, smiling. I had picked up the idiom in my slang dictionary.

"Is it?" She thrust several pieces of paper at me without looking up. "I suppose they've got our weather too."

"No, no." I shook my head. "I meant your slip is showing. It's an American euphemism—get it? The white of your slip is like snow falling out of your skirt."

She tugged the skirt down and stared at me, arms folded. Mori was as much a bulldog as Yamamoto—nobody pushed her around. She was altogether different from delicate old Miss Ozaki in New York. Formally, I called Mori "Miss Mori," though in my mind and to my colleagues she was just Mori, like one of the guys. Big-boned, tough. She was also our best golfer in the all-company tournament.

Her lips thickened with a cruel expression, the henchwoman, and she rolled her eyes toward the corporate suite.

"He's back," she said. "He's back, and he wants to see you right away."

"But he's not supposed to be back until next week," I mumbled, really to myself. The sudden change from the cold outside to the overheated office had me sweating. I had been gone nearly two hours for lunch.

Mori stared at me from behind her nameplate, the dent underneath her lower lip growing deeper with aggravation. "Well, he's here today, and that's that. He's called for you twice in the past fifteen minutes."

The electronic kettle shot a plume of steam diagonally into the air. Dumping my package on my desk, I grabbed a legal pad and a pen. I bowed before Yamamoto's massive desk. He was on the phone, munching fruit slices cut up and arranged in a semicircle on a plate. Yamamoto ate fruit for at least two meals of the day. He had a deathly fear of colon cancer and refused to eat anything that would remain with him very long.

He set the phone down and yelled to Mori.

"Is it ready yet? Good, bring Shimada some too. Shimada, you have a seat."

Mori hurried in with a swish of nylon and two cups on a tray. In as abbreviated a version of the tea ceremony as she could manage—like a child hastily saying prayers—she poured water into the vessel with the tea powder and batted at it with a whisk. It occurred to me that Gina was at this very moment probably in the midst of the American version of this ritual at the Drake. Mori poured the tea and as an afterthought smiled mechanically before charging out the door. The slip had reasserted itself.

"How was your trip?" I asked. I sipped my tea only after Yamamoto had sipped his.

"All right. As I told you, the trouble was already settled by the time I got there. They took the first offer. I'd expected worse."

I nodded, trying to recall the exact situation. There had been a minor work stoppage at the plant in Kobe, nothing serious, but the press had given it a lot of attention. For some reason, although I had just read about the incident that morning, I had already forgotten significant details. "They're not much of a union," I offered.

"No, but they have a real firebrand stirring them up. He was representing a grievance about the quota hike. I met with him, just out of curiosity. He might be one for more than a section-chief position, with a little grooming. I don't think he'd be too hard to persuade." Yamamoto smiled broadly, showing his gold-capped back teeth.

"And how was the funeral?"

"Well, sobering, of course. I suppose you don't identify with Hirohito as much as I did; to me he was practically a contemporary. . . ." He broke off, eyes clouded over for a moment. "Well. A new era. I saw your wife there at the second day's services. She's looking well. Healthier than I've seen her in a while. More alert."

I had slipped forward a bit in my chair; her name flew from my mouth like saliva before I had a chance to stop myself.

"Taeko?"

"Quite sympathetic of you to let her go back." Yamamoto was watching me sharply now, stalking for information. What had Taeko told him? A million people at those funeral services, a mob, and he had to see her. To *recognize* her. She had gone home! She was gone; she had taken off, the bitch, snuck off behind my back. The thought of my sitting there for the past six nights at the Nippon letting the phone ring in a deserted house infuriated me further.

What had she told Yamamoto?

I tensed the muscles of my legs until they were rigid, while at the same time I eased the upper half of my body into the pose of a confident man, calm and smiling, generous enough to let his wife do whatever the hell she wanted. I jerked my hands up and clasped them together, took a breath and focused in on Yamamoto's bird-black eyes.

Peck, peck. "It's only for a short time, the visit," I heard myself say.

"Of course." Smoke was drifting collectively from the skyline behind Yamamoto's small, straight figure—heat smoke from the white slab of the Standard Oil Building, the Illinois Center, the trapezoidal Hancock Tower. "But isn't it a little capricious to take your daughter out of school like that? She is missing school, isn't she?"

"Etsuko's very advanced. She's already far ahead of her classmates in reading and arithmetic. We thought it would be more educational for her to see the emperor's funeral—of course it was all preapproved."

What was I saying? I had no idea if it matched Taeko's excuse. Yamamoto nodded, presumably satisfied, then lifted his knife to slice through a wedge of apple—first the flesh, then the taut green skin.

"She doesn't really remember anything of Tokyo, she was so young when we left. And the baby's never been there at all. He's never seen his grandparents."

"Hmm." Yamamoto peeled a banana with agonizing slowness while I sat waiting, my eyes closed against the view. Don't say anything else, I thought. Shut up. The fewer details the better.

"Now be straight with me, Shimada." Yamamoto's brows, tufted slightly at the corners, fused into a unit. Although his hair was white, his eyebrows were still black. His eyes were brown-black, and he wore no glasses—the warrior's gaze had not left him. Age had served him well. There was something to be said for being relentless.

He pressed his fingertips against the edge of his desk. "Shimada, are you having problems with your wife?"

"No, sir."

"I don't believe you."

"Please do."

I would not tell him, no, I didn't have to. This was not pertinent—not a family crisis or a disease or a gambling habit. Yamamoto already knew about my father, about Taeko's back and the fact that Taeko's father was having business troubles; he knew about Keiji; he knew how high the monthly rent payments were on the Cape Cod; and I suspected he knew about my little affair with Miho, the receptionist in New York. Yamamoto's network was extensive and ran efficiently under the guise of paternal concern. Right now he would start with one question, then slip in others— peel away the layers of skin, picking and probing expertly for truth with the precision of a coroner, the way he was going at that fruit. But this was too near the bone. I put my teacup down and thought before looking at him, trying to remind myself that this was just a person like myself, with a heart, a spleen, a brain, tissue, cells, fat, derma.

"Everything's fine, really," I said. "Although I appreciate your concern."

I had to fight with myself to keep the word "concern" from having an edge to it, a sudden Keiji-like tone. It did not work. Yamamoto stared back at me coldly.

"Don't lie, son. You might need time off to go to Tokyo, to patch things up."

"No, that won't be necessary, thank you."

"Oh, now stop it!" he yelled. "You're lying to me because you're lying to yourself!"

A silence followed, like the echo of pistol shots. I forced my fingers to release the arms of the chair beneath me, and the pressure of my sweating hands on the leather gave way to a small sucking sound, like a kiss.

Yamamoto's throat quivered. There was a hollow at the base of his windpipe, surrounded by wattled skin, the exact point where a blade might penetrate if he should ever commit seppuku. The skin, weak and loose, would offer little resistance. It tightened only momentarily as he made several short inhalations before resuming the interrogation.

"Shimada, do you love your wife?"

"Of course."

"Do you feel she's supportive of you and what you want to accomplish?"

Here I hesitated. I could never get away with a yes on that; Yamamoto was well aware of Taeko's lack of enthusiasm.

"She tries," I said.

"She tries," Yamamoto repeated. He was toying with a paperweight, a small crystal globe containing the gold Y that was the corporation logo. Everyone had this weight on his desk, from executives to mail clerks. I had two of them, as I was currently inhabiting two desks, at two separate branches.

It was at this point that Yamamoto seemed to have invaded my thoughts. He mentioned something about all the running back and forth from city to city having a bad effect on my marriage, and I found this an odd statement. Yamamoto had never cared one way or the other about my traveling or my marriage, even when I had had to miss things like anniversaries and birthday parties. I kept quiet. He then took off on a tangent about how he needed more American executives at the Chicago office, to ease personnel tension, then continued with a fable about the plum tree that was transplanted too many times and stopped bearing fruit. A slow suspicion began to form in my mind, and just as it crystallized, Yamamoto voiced the thought.

"I think it's best that you wrap things up in Chicago and resume full-time in New York. I need an American up front here, and besides, it would be cruel to move your family again. The Japanese community isn't as large in Chicago; it might be upsetting."

Yamamoto's words, so calm and instructive, were delivered with
a strange contempt. It made no sense. He had to be calling my
bluff. For months he had been telling me to prepare to move—I
would more or less be taking charge of the Special Projects unit
at the Chicago office. I was to start scouting neighborhoods and
new schools for the children. And now this. I could come up with
only two motives—Yamamoto suspected I had a mistress in Chicago or he knew about Saito. Either one would explain the polarity
of interests; this was not fair, being grilled like this, especially
when I had no idea how much he had grilled Taeko. He was
obviously applying the separation-of-prisoners tactic.

A ridge of perspiration had formed on my upper lip. I smoothed
it away as casually as I could, pretending to be deep in thought.

"It's unfortunate that you've decided to keep me in New York,"
I said, slowly. "My wife was really looking forward to moving to
the Midwest. She finds New York very hostile at times, too congested. She's worried about the children growing up there."

"Is she? How funny. She had nothing but praise for New York
when I talked to her, how she would hate to leave and move to
Chicago. But then perhaps she didn't want to offend me—she
wanted to wait until the transfer was official. Yes, I'm sure that
was it."

Weren't there any phone calls or meetings, any pressing inter-
ruptions for this bastard to attend to? It figured. Every time I needed
Yamamoto's undivided attention for business matters, Mori was
always barging in. Now nothing, just Yamamoto and myself in this
mahogany torture chamber.

"You and Taeko must have had a nice conversation," I finally
said.

"Oh, yes. Over lunch. It's the first time I've ever spoken to her
at length. She's very charming. And very attractive."

Goddamn: lunch. Lunch meant perhaps several glasses of white
wine, which Taeko had little tolerance for, particularly on top of
all her medications. Although she may have said nothing concrete,

she had probably given the old bloodhound plenty of clues, plenty of indication that something was wrong between us—a crack, a flaw, a sinkhole about to give way.

But why should Yamamoto care so much?

"Do you really love your wife?" he asked again, and again I supplied an affirmative answer.

"Even though she's carrying on with someone else?"

The snow that had been falling before was now needling the Thermopane window. I began to think fast, reshuffling my deck of thoughts, worry and caution pushed to the side and action and need about to come forward. I had to stay in Chicago with Gina. Even if she cared nothing about me, she gave me release: powerful release. There was no way in hell Yamamoto was going to confine me to New York.

"She told you this?"

"No. I'd heard rumors—well, in reality, my wife had—but after our lunch I was quite sure."

"I see." I let my shoulders droop and sighed, trying to affect the pose of the suffering husband. I made my face tragic, like Eiji Okada's, and said, "Ah. I've known of it for years but hoped she would stop, come to her senses." My voice swelled ever so slightly—subtlety was important; I was dealing with a consummate professional. "You see, there's much more than a marriage at stake. I love my children very much, and if we were to separate, Taeko would take them with her—I'm in no position to raise children alone."

I asked permission to light a cigarette, then puffed at it dejectedly, while deep inside my head a valve of steam hissed full force—to think I had to grovel this way and make an idiot of myself; it was as bad as if Yamamoto had been in bed with us during our last argument, sniffing all over Taeko's naked body and her kimono with its mixed male scents. I would kill her if I ever saw her again. I would break her aching spine for putting me through a scene like this. It wasn't her going back home, really, that infuriated me; it was her not telling me, the idea that I was some sort of monster she could not even talk to anymore.

I continued. "If I move here, I believe I could save things for us. She won't be able to see . . . ah . . ."

"Akira Saito?" Yamamoto volunteered.

"Yes, Saito; thank you," I said. Was there anything the man didn't know? Did he have a Yamamoto minicam in the toilet of every house? "She won't be able to see him so often, and to be perfectly frank, I think half his power over her is chemical—he has her on all these tranquilizers and painkillers. I think she's addicted. With all the going back and forth, I haven't had time to watch things, but if I'm permanently in Chicago, I'm sure our home life will be more stable."

"Hmm." Yamamoto took out his asthma inhaler and gave himself two blasts. "You seem quite determined," he said. "I say you're too good for your wife. She doesn't deserve you. Get a divorce instead."

I stared at him, shocked. Divorce was the last thing I had expected him to suggest.

"But I'll lose custody of my children," I said.

Yamamoto laughed. "Maybe temporarily, but if you remarry— an excellent woman, native born, of course—and you contest, you'll have them back right away. You're a model of propriety. Your wife's an adulteress, she abandoned you, she's a drug addict. What kind of mother is that? She's weak."

"But I—"

"Take my word for it. You'd have me on your side, which represents a good deal of the establishment. Don't worry." He broke off, jovially. "You think about it, and I'll reconsider Chicago. I want you to be happy, of course. I'm very fond of you, Shimada, despite all your tendencies."

What tendencies? I didn't dare ask. Yet I knew what he meant. My "softness," as he perceived it. My longing to be someplace else.

"Now we need to look at the annual report. Don't you have some drafts for me to review?"

"At my desk," I said. I felt drained. My tongue was dry. As I stood to go fetch the drafts, my knees wobbled, as if I had been seated for hours. Actually it had been only twenty minutes. I was surprised to see people still running around the office as I opened the outside door; I waited, expectantly, for Nurse Mori to bring me a powdered doughnut and some orange juice.

"And, Shimada," Yamamoto said, just as I was about to escape, if only for a minute. He beckoned for me to lean back in. "Don't do anything foolish; you know what I mean. Don't give in to bad habits—laziness, self-pity—or get mixed up with bad characters. Be smart." He began to recite: " 'Wild animals in the dark/taunt the dangerous instincts of man. . . .'

"The purity of our race is very important," he added.

I closed the door. I found myself limping, slightly stooped, to my desk, where the cordial glasses were, in their bag, waiting to be given to my wild animal.

Yamamoto had just quoted one of my father's poems. Racial purity.

There was nothing Yamamoto didn't know about.

The crackling on the wire matched the angry hum of thoughts inside my head. I allowed a piece of ice from my whiskey to melt beneath my tongue and waited for the connection to go through.

A woman's voice answered, dim, cautious. It was still fairly early in Tokyo.

"Jun-san! *Ohayō!*" Taeko's mother exclaimed. I cut her off. She gasped at my outright rudeness—the first trace of disrespect I had shown her in ten years.

"Put Taeko on the phone. I need to speak with her."

"Taeko's still asleep. Hold on. . . ." I waited while she yelled several times to rouse Taeko from her usual morning coma. A child's voice, piping and excited, carried through the background. Etsuko. I heard a sharp bark and remembered, for the first time in weeks, our terrier. Poor old Cho; she had made him suffer through another transoceanic flight. My eyes filled with tears. I had been drinking, steadily, for about an hour.

"Where is she?" I snapped. I wiped my eyes with the back of my wrist, then wiped my nose.

"She's sleeping; I can't get her up. Talk to Etsuko while I go wake her. Suki!" I heard small clattering footsteps. "Daddy wants to say hello."

"No! Don't give her the phone, goddammit!" I could not talk to Etsuko like this; I would break down. "You give Taeko a message instead. You tell her to make her visit permanent. You tell her I don't ever want to see her again. Go on, tell her! It's no joke."

My mother-in-law was making wild noises of protest that sounded like a wasp trapped inside the phone. I slammed it down full force and lay back, imagining that I still felt small electric tremors coming at me through the millions of feet of cable and cord. And within minutes, the phone did begin to ring. I paused in midsip and listened. Taeko. The ringing continued ten, fifteen, twenty times. I managed to crawl under the bed and unhook the black wire from a jack in the wall, then I sprawled on the carpet, exhausted. I had relayed my message; I had nothing more to say. I lay prone a little while longer, concentrating on the feel of my own wet lashes against my cheeks.

Numbness. I plugged the phone back in and dragged myself upright to call room service. I had run out of whiskey; the bottle was empty and tipped over on its side on the Chinese lacquer table. Whiskey, fast becoming my preferred drink. *Uisukī*. I liked it, its taste replacing saliva inside my mouth. I stared up at the long neck of the bottle, a little out of focus, then felt a drop hit me smack between the eyes, like a bullet.

I was severing connections. Taeko had sent a brief letter from her family home, requesting a divorce.

She had always had such beautiful writing.

I did not answer or phone with a response but on the next trip to New York settled matters about the house and began the process of dismantling and dividing. Taeko's things, or what remained of them, I had boxed and sent to her parents' house. The children's clothes as well. The children's toys and furniture I gave to Tsuda, one of the younger men at Yamamoto, with a bunch of kids; our own furniture was fortunately scant—Taeko had never got beyond the most basic decorating—and I sent it to Keiji. What better warehouse to dump it in than Keiji's empty loft, and the furious phone call that would result—how dare I inflict my useless material possessions on him, destroy his beautiful space—provided more of a motivation than anything else. My own belongings I managed to fit into the corporation car. Taeko's car I sold within three days—very low price, no questions asked—to the Murphy girl next door. I saw it, just before I left, moved only slightly from its usual position, now with a small Saint Francis on the dashboard and a *Syracuse University Orangemen* sticker on the back window.

How odd to be doing all this, taking steps I had never visualized in my plan for the future. Shuffling, weary steps. I had lost my wife. *I* had, this was happening to me, one of those drastic events you can never conceive of happening to you, like losing a limb or all your teeth. I wondered what could have broken down Taeko's father to consent to the divorce—normally the man was a ramrod of morality and structure, as bad as Yamamoto. Yamamoto. Perhaps that was the irresistible force to the unmovable object: Taeko's father's business was in financial straits. Perhaps Yamamoto had made a deal, pulled one of the many strings of his web. Yamamoto liked me, he wanted to keep me around, he saw how Taeko was expendable and how in his opinion she was holding me back, he had that niece he wanted to marry off. I felt my palms go clammy at the idea of such a deal and hoped that instead Taeko's father had yielded simply because he could see how despondent his daughter was. It was not likely, but I sustained the thought. Yamamoto, you see, never did anything without a motive.

On my last night in the house, now hollow, stripped of its furniture, I wandered around, getting aimlessly drunk. There were things I had missed: Taeko's attempts at pottery from two years before, hidden in the attic (I imagined her fine hands forming clay, her bud mouth pursed tighter as she desperately tried to replicate a Shinto piece); the dog's leash; one of Omi's socks, balled up behind the radiator; Etsuko's lunchbox, with a bitten-into Oreo inside (I ate the rest, although I had no idea how old it was). The carcass of a mouse in the laundry room, caught in a trap I had never set. I also found the fifth of Scotch Miss Ozaki had given me for Christmas and swigged it out of the bottle for lack of a glass. One of Saito's bills was on top of the refrigerator, and I ripped it up savagely—to think I had *paid* that bastard to rut my wife.

No ice for my Scotch, no food to sop it up; the phone had been disconnected, tomorrow the electricity would be. There was a patch on the wall where the scroll calendar had hung. I sighed. Three years in this house, all shrunken down to this one moment, this picture of myself, unshaven, in a filthy sweatsuit, straggling from room to room, sniveling at every clump of dog hair on the floor.

Was Taeko really going to divorce me? Was it as simple as that; all I had to do was nod yes, and it was over? I could not imagine myself divorced. The word itself connoted a degree of recklessness, of sophistication, that I had never imagined either myself or Taeko to possess. I kept seeing Taeko as she had been when I'd first known her, with that braid over her shoulder, wearing moccasins with flowers painted on them. And what about me—I still had trouble making eye contact with strangers in elevators. We were divorcés? I wondered what my mother would have had to say about all this. It would have hurt her keenly, I knew it would. She would have been so sad to see me go through this—after all, she too had been dumped.

Later in the evening I lay on the living room rug, my forearm over my eyes as if to shade them from bright sun. I was listening to Radio Yokohama on the small portable shortwave I usually kept in the bathroom while I was shaving. They were playing jazz, Thelonious Monk; the sound ebbed and flowed over the distance. Right now as I listened, no doubt several city lunch spots had this on too, preparing for the midday rush, especially Miyako's, where I used to go every day and order oden because it was so good and so cheap. My thoughts skated like waterbugs on a pond: I had no control of them.

It was very quiet. Here in the dark remains of the house I felt marooned; I felt I was the last living person on earth, a survivor of some nuclear holocaust, only I wished I'd been lucky enough to die with the rest. Why had we had that bomb shelter when I was a child? I wondered—would one really want to come through such a horror, have to deal with the carnage and mutations and radioactive waste, scratch out a new and pitiful existence? Obliteration sounded best to me, but then I could think such, couldn't I, lying safe on my living room rug. Morbidly philosophizing. I was of the soft generation, untouched by war and the atom bomb. We only cared about ourselves. I realized I could go out, get in the car and buy dinner, some cigarettes, perhaps a newspaper or a magazine or some other diversion, but my helplessness had swaddled me by now, like a thin filthy quilt I had wrapped tenaciously around myself.

The doorbell woke me. I jerked upright, sending my radio across the floor. My arm had fallen asleep and seemed a foreign body as I scrambled to go peek out the window.

It was Keiji, standing incongruously before a backdrop of suburban homes. I flung the door open and pulled him inside.

"I am not the municipal dumping ground," he said. "I do not need a toaster oven, an electric carving knife, a humidifier, or a love seat. Shimada, you've lost your mind. Look at you standing there: you look like a bum."

Keiji's hair was cropped short. The goatee and mustache had been shaved. He edged his way in, uncertain in the darkness, and plunked a heavy mass into my hand, something thick and textured like a rope.

"My queue," he explained. "You told me to save it for Etsuko. But Dios mío, man, where *is* Etsuko? What's happening here? Why did you send me all your stuff? I've been trying to call you for days, and just now I tried again from the station and I got a recording."

"The station," I repeated, blankly.

"Yes, I took the train out. I figured for ten bucks round trip I would come and see what was happening myself."

I turned and began shuffling through the house, turning on lights. My head was pounds heavier, as though somebody had poured concrete into it through my ear while I was asleep. I squinted at Keiji, trying to assemble some thoughts.

"I'd offer you a place to sit, but there is none. Nor is there anything to eat. Taeko's gone back home; she took Etsuko and Omi with her. She wants me to give her a divorce. Yamamoto wants me to get the divorce; in fact, I think he coaxed her father into allowing her to ask me. I'm by myself. I've been transferred to Chicago, which I think I had to sell my soul for. Yamamoto has that un-married niece—you met her—and I think he wants to bring us together. Everything's finished here, dead. I've been cleaning things up for two weeks. Do you have a cigarette? I'm dying for a cigarette. I ran out this afternoon, but I haven't had the energy to go get more."

"I don't smoke, remember?" Keiji smiled sadly. "I quit when I quit Yamamoto."

I slumped down and put my head on my knees, yawning. "Have some Scotch. It's the only thing I've got left, that Scotch Miss Ozaki gave me for Christmas. Maybe Miss Ozaki will take care of me." I laughed. "She's got a nice pension coming; I'm sure she could use a gigolo."

Keiji was unusually serious. "Let's get some food now, all right? You shouldn't drink on an empty stomach—you've killed half the bottle. It's a wonder you can walk. I think that's the key to your success, Shimada, how well you hold your liquor."

"Or how it holds me." I noticed something on the wall besides the scroll calendar patch—a pencil mark, in the spot where I used to measure Etsuko. Although I could remember measuring her several times, at least once a month, only two or three marks remained. The rest had worn off or become dull smudges. "She's going to be taller than her mother," I said, not particularly concerned whether Keiji understood me or not. "Suki—"

"Come on." I felt myself being lifted by the armpits and stood upright. "Is there anyplace in your pleasant little village that stays open late?"

We went to a delicatessen a mile or so away, walking because I was too drunk to drive and because Keiji, the perpetual city dweller, had never learned how. The delicatessen was part of a small mall, such as littered Long Island. I had noticed that no matter what the town, the malls were more or less composed of the same segments: a supermarket, a deli, a pizzeria, a Chinese restaurant, a pharmacy, and the variable—a video store, a beauty salon. Some teenagers were in the parking lot, flipping around on skateboards, monopolizing the sidewalks and cruising between parked cars.

"I think they're out of school this week," I said, almost apologetically. "Spring recess."

"Yeah." Keiji was stalking toward the delicatessen. "My former audience. You know at least one of them has a Yamamoto boom box at home." He paused. "Look, I count three, four Asians in the group. Look at those haircuts, those shirts. Asian kids are always into fads. They overcompensate, are extra cool. Believe me, I know. It's my life."

We purchased Swiss cheese, ham, roast beef, pickles, and a loaf of rye bread. The air inside was cool and spicy; the clerk behind the glass counter was on the phone—a conversation he did not bother to interrupt as he sliced and wrapped our order. I stood against a rack of snack cakes, waiting, watching the whole scene gone convex through the overhead security mirror. Keiji looked strange in such distortion, almost insectlike. I had meant to ask why he had cut off his hair, but I was not quite sure this was not a dreamscape; there was a certain hollow feeling to it all, as if anything could happen and I did not have to worry about being rude or impolite. Keiji was a hologram, I was a beam of light. My eyes rested on the tabloids and magazines for sale: *Good House-keeping*, *Esquire*, "Newborn Baby Sings Like Elvis." I wondered what kind of crossword puzzle the *Enquirer* could have. A technology magazine heralded a complete mobile office system ("Take Your Business Everywhere") produced by Yamamoto's chief competitor. In the row beneath this, a health magazine featured the benefits of Zen meditation and ginseng tea to combat stress while a travel magazine offered "Spiritual Vacations in Japan." In my more lucid moments, I had found it interesting how Westerners tore themselves in half with our products: mass producing, speeding things up with the electronics, and then attempting to wind down in the "Eastern way." It was rather like watching a snake consume itself.

I hurried to the register to keep Keiji from paying, but he had already done so and was examining his change and a lottery ticket. The counterman made a remark into the phone about Nips taking over the town. Keiji turned back. "And it's the best thing that ever happened to you, baby." He chuckled, then, once we were outside, waved his ticket in the air. ˉ

"What if I win this—can I keep the prize? I'm not a citizen yet, you know."

"How much did the food cost?" I demanded. "Come on now, let me pay."

Keiji waved a hand at me good-naturedly and slipped the lottery ticket into his pocket. "Oh, never mind, salaryman. Hard times are over, at least for me. I got a job, high-paying—that's why I cut off the queue." We walked on the main road and smelled from some point a cold, clammy breeze off the Sound. Keiji strolled along. "I took a position at an advertising agency, one of the big whorehouses on Madison Avenue, doing creative work. *Good* salary. The atmosphere is very liberal—I could have kept my hair long and the beard, but I suppose I wanted to shed them, to mark another change. They hired me straight off my portfolio, nothing else. That's what I love about this country: they never check references."

He looked at me with sudden fierceness, as if he had been insulted. "And what, I'm not allowed to have a job that utilizes my skills? I have viable talent, why should I deny the fact? I enjoyed the work at Yamamoto; it was the sanctimonious code of morality that drove me crazy. There are no morals in advertising. There'll be no *oyabun* to answer to, no enema of Japanese honor probing my subversive ass. I'll be very happy. Yes, I'm sure of it."

As he spoke, he held his head back, his broad hooked nose like the prow of a ship, his eyes dull and closed off to fear. Keiji never seemed to worry or vacillate about anything. Once he had chosen a course he pursued it, full speed and heedless, without any post-mortem of alternatives. Yet he was not totally reckless, no matter how he pretended. I remembered something Yamamoto had told me. "How's your friend Keiji Narata?" he had asked, as usual without waiting for a reply. "You know, I find it interesting that for all his contempt of us, he never bothered to sell his corporation stock. Must not be as foolish as I thought. That stock is worth quite a bit, as you're certainly well aware. A little piece of us he just couldn't bear to part with, huh?"

Now I smiled. "That's wonderful for you, Keiji. I'm very happy." I had meant to say more, but he seemed particularly argumentative tonight, feisty and ready to twist my words around. We were back at the house. I searched my pockets for the keys, then sank down involuntarily on top of a pile of lawn mower mulch, which was like a damp cushion. There was a pain in my stomach, a hot-bladed knife, and for a moment I thought I was going to lose control of my bowels. I sat, afraid to move further, watching the milky sky. The pain was bad, yet centralized, as though someone had jabbed in the knife, turned it sideways, then walked away. A marionette looseness jerked my limbs. I threw up.

"What! What's the matter?" I heard Keiji, far off.

My stomach would simply not hold down its slosh of Chivas anymore and tossed it back out—very fast and very neat—a stream of bitter liquid. Saliva spun from my mouth in one long thread. I felt tremendously relieved when it was over, as if I had been running and just caught a bus. I relaxed, touched the cool flagstone beneath me, while Keiji wiped at my mouth with one of the paper deli napkins, making small, maternal tsk-tsk sounds.

"Well, I'll say one thing for you, Shimada, you're a dainty puke. Look how nicely you did that. I hope it's not from practice."

I spit. "No," I said.

"You have an ulcer, don't you?"

"Ulcer?"

"The bad taste in your mouth you complain about. The heartburn. Throwing up. Your stomach has a hole in it. Can't you feel it all the time, opening and closing? Why don't you go to a doctor?"

Keiji followed me through the door and into the kitchen, where I slumped over the sink and let cold water run over my head. "And drinking like this! Ulcers are bad; they can kill you. They come from stress, gnawing at your innards, eating the lining of your stomach until you vomit blood—"

"Keiji." I raised my dripping head and shook it like a dog, splattering water all over the place. "Stop it. I don't have an ulcer."

"Yes, you do."

"All right, I do."

Keiji folded his arms and examined his long index fingernail. Like certain Chinese men, he had always insisted on having at least one long fingernail on his hand, for practical purposes, such as opening letters or scratching himself or picking things up.

"Well, are you going to let it kill you?" he demanded. "It's like a serpent, you know, coiled. You're never sure when it will strike."

"The serpent's hungry. Let's eat," I said, and sat down cross-legged on the bright linoleum floor without thinking, as always waiting to be served.

Later in the night, when we had both gone to sleep, I woke, startled by the flow of bright moonlight through the bare windows. The reek of my own body surprised me—I smelled sour, as if I had been on a binge—and for a minute I almost liked it, my smell. It was my own. Keiji and I had been talking for several hours, and snatches of our conversation floated like fish through my head.

"This girl, Jun, she seems a little risky to me." I had told him about Gina. "Not as far as Yamamoto is concerned, but for yourself. I wouldn't get in too deep, too addicted. But then I have a general mistrust of women, you know that."

There was something else he had said about himself, how one time he was riding the train out of Shinjuku station, crammed in as always, feeling almost the indentation of the buttons on the coats of the people around him. "Someone took my hand," he said. "Held it very tenderly, fondled it the whole trip home. There was a man and a woman behind me; I couldn't see either of their faces because it was so packed, but naturally I assumed it was the woman. I was young then. I held the hand back, and then I felt the size of the fingers and how the palm was rough, and I almost pulled away. It was the man—he looked thoroughly respectable, with a cap on, the herringbone kind some professors wear. But he was powerful. When he got off, I followed him, and afterward we went to a hotel and then to bed. That was the first time, for me. I never saw him again."

Keiji was out cold now, on the rug. He had taken off his sweater and wadded it up as a pillow beneath his head; his mouth was open slightly, eyelids twitching. I found myself crawling on hands and knees over to him and watching him while he slept. The train story had fascinated me. I tried to imagine two men together, giving each other pleasure: of course I was familiar with the mechanics of it, what they did; but what did Keiji look like alongside someone else? He was so tall and rangy. A long single hair grew from the middle of his chest, like a feeler. His abdomen was hard, with ridges; beneath his skin, veins crossed and intersected, close to the surface. He had to be sensitive, with veins like that. His eyes fluttered.

"What are you doing?" he asked, suddenly awake. I jumped back several paces and shook my head.

"Nothing. I was—I mean, you were just talking in your sleep. You must have been dreaming. I was trying to hear what you said."

"Really." He propped up on one elbow, then yawned. "Well. I often do that when I'm in a strange place. I can't be held accountable, though, for anything I say when I'm asleep."

There was a brief silence, wherein neither of us spoke, the only sound being the moan of a train whistle in the near distance. The house was just a half mile from the station. It had always been a convenient walk.

"Keiji?"

"Yes."

I wet my lips with my tongue and swallowed. The question had become unbearable to me, like an itch in a private place. "What do—what attracts you to men over women? I'm curious. I've known you for a long time; I feel I can ask you that. Do you mind?"

"No. If you really want to know." He frowned. "I don't like women; I don't like their bodies, I don't like their smell. I don't like the softness to them, I don't like their breasts. I think men are ridiculous about breasts, really, getting excited over two lumps of fat. I like bodies that are streamlined, and I like strength. It should be a fight, not some woman lying there like part of the mattress. And I don't enjoy flirtation or games. I went with a girl once, to a love hotel. It wasn't her fault, but I felt sick afterward, all greasy and sick, like I had gorged myself on potato chips. So I never honestly liked women, only a few rough girls I knew while growing up, but they changed as soon as they turned fifteen and went with the rest. They had to, I guess; they really had no choice." He pointed at me, smiling. "You've always liked women, I can tell. You have such a courtliness about you, more European than Japanese. That's why they love you back. I never gave them any respect."

"Who *do* you respect?" I laughed, but Keiji remained quite serious. I cleared my throat, speaking with an unusual bitterness that surprised me. "Women don't love me, really. Look at the state of things. Women don't want respect; they want abuse. They enjoy being treated nicely for a while, but then they get bored and sniff around for something else."

"But Taeko's sort of a masochist," Keiji said. "Remember that Sakamoto she hung around with? He used to humiliate her all the time, show those nudes he had done of her, those bizarre positions."

"No," I said firmly, forcing away the recollection. Although I had refused to view Sakamoto's exhibit, it was still a sore point with me, what I considered artistic exploitation of my wife. I was surprised that Keiji would bring it up. He could be so tactless. "Taeko's the same as all the rest."

Keiji got up and went into the kitchen, where I heard the running of the tap. When he returned, he sat down next to me, legs at angles.

"I'm so thirsty," he said. He belched. "There was enough salt in that roast beef to cure a whole cow. Hey, listen to this. A woman I work with, one of the art directors, she said she'd heard it's unspeakably rude to blow your nose in Japan. She wanted to know why we can belch and fart in public but not blow our noses. I tried to explain the difference, you know, blowing out snot versus a congenial belch, but she resisted me. I screwed her up then. I said using a handkerchief is what's unspeakably rude, carrying your waste with you. I said you should really just airmail it straight onto the ground—that's all right, that's no breach of etiquette."

"Good old Keiji," I said. I stared at him. "You know, you're going to get a rug burn, lying on it with a bare back. Look at that—you've got marks already." I stopped myself, horrified; my fingers had been tracing up and down his knobby spine. I pulled my hand away.

Keiji looked at me calmly. "I suppose now you want to know if I was ever attracted to you. The inevitable question." I said nothing. "You are appealing, yes, but I think of you first as a friend. I can see how uncomfortable you are about this, but you are liberal enough to be curious. I think there are great hidden things in you, Shimada, things you don't acknowledge. After all, your father was one of the greatest minds of the twentieth century, and you *know* he was your father, no matter how much you wish your father was a ricksha man or a fishmonger or the Great Yamamoto himself."

"I'm like my mother," I said stubbornly, "through and through. And besides, Yamamoto's given me more than my father ever did."

"Ah, yes, including an ulcer."

The heat hummed through the baseboards. How many times had I lain in this house in my bed, wondering if the heat was on high enough—Etsuko was susceptible to colds, always getting earaches, though Omi never got sick. Then of course, Omi had better genes.

I flopped down in a sleep position again, overcome by a new and sharper wave of depression. The night floated on, interminable. Keiji's feet were by my face; he was only wearing one sock. Keiji had the longest feet of any Japanese I'd ever known. His penis, the few times I had seen it during swimming or at the corporate baths in Tokyo, was also long and thin, more like a weapon than anything else.

"How do you pair off with other men?" I continued, still snared by the subject. "How do you know? How does someone know to approach you?"

Keiji turned over on his side, so that he faced the wall. "I don't like being questioned this way, for kicks," he hissed. "If you were sincere I'd show you—I could give you more than you've ever had in your life. But you're not interested in that; you're only full of voyeuristic questions. I told you I don't like games. Let's just go back to sleep."

I felt my face burning in the darkness. I tried to think of something appropriate to say back, but within minutes Keiji's breathing had become heavy and regular again, his body loose. He had to be pretending—nobody enraged drifted off that fast. More than I'd ever had in my life . . . What was that supposed to mean? Could it be possible? And of course, as always, Keiji had made it an issue of cowardice, *my* cowardice and bourgeois thought, which held me back from True Living.

I lay there shivering, half from excitement over our conversation and half from not having any blankets. Such a conversation, on a rug where my children had played, on the rug under which Taeko and I had swept all our troubles. And every conversation with Keiji ended in an argument, no matter what the issue. I wondered how the two of us had managed to stay friends all these years.

The silence deepened. I sighed and scratched at myself irritably, then rolled over and saw how Keiji's skin in the moonlight was the color of a golden pear.

In the morning we gathered the last of my things and left the house, stopping off for breakfast at a diner, where Keiji had pancakes and two large glasses of milk. He was a big milk drinker, said that was what had made him so tall. If Japanese people all started drinking more milk, he maintained, the height curve would shoot up. The milk left a froth on his upper lip like the old pencil mustache, a vestige of his former self. It reminded me to wish him the best of luck with his new self. We talked of baseball and where to buy good spring suits; after I had dropped him off at Union Square, I continued to the office, said my goodbyes to the New York staff and left. I was going to miss them—we had always gotten along very well, I realized retrospectively—but there was nothing left for me here.

As I made my way out, some members of the group followed, watching in consternation. They had never seen Shimada like this, so badly dressed, discomposed and with a bad case of dandruff, driving in an overloaded car toward Route 80, straight into the heart of the Midwest.

There are certain portions of this country a Japanese should not enter, even in this day and age, just as there are certain parts of Japan no Westerner should seek. I recall sitting in a truck stop deep in Indiana (the Vince Lombardi Comfort Station, to be specific), having driven nonstop for twelve hours, just grateful to be seated in a spot with scenery that was not moving, quietly eating a slab of peanut butter pie. The looks I received fell and gathered along with the dead flies on the counter; and then came the Where-were-you-in-1941 remark. I sat and looked at a pig-face clock. A bag lady had put that one to me and Keiji when we had first come here and were sightseeing on the Staten Island ferry. The woman's face was branded by a crisscross from a vent she must have fallen asleep on, but still she marched right up to us and yelled, "Where were you in 1941, Japs?" Keiji looked at her coldly. "I was dust," he said. "I was water in Tokyo Bay. I hadn't been born yet. Where were *you*, you old bitch?" A mob scene had nearly broken out; this was a bag lady, but she was an American, and she had her rights. I never said anything back to these comments—for one, it could prove deadly, and for another, I was a foreigner, off my own soil. You give up something of yourself whenever you visit another country—it's like exchanging currency. To me it was not important to prove a point or set an example; it was more important to keep out of trouble. So as I sat there in that diner in Indiana and heard that remark, I again said nothing. I merely got up and paid my bill and did not stop until I got to Chicago, where something of the tolerance of big cities hung in the fishy-sweet air.

I hoped.

A change had come over me on the road. Perhaps it was the driving itself, the semihallucinatory state, a compulsion to speed down the endless ribbon of highway alone and conquer it. I could just as easily have flown to Chicago—I had so few possessions left—but I insisted on driving. I had never really seen the country. Miles and miles of green, cows and cornfields, white farmhouses lit up at dawn, small industrial cities throughout western Pennsylvania and Ohio. I became something of a *rōnin* on that trip, a rootless person in limbo. *Rōnin* are generally what we call students who are waiting to get into university, but the definition goes much deeper. *Rōnin* used to be samurai without masters, those who had strayed or been ejected from the clan. Black sheep, loners, still valiant but no longer affiliated. The meaningless speeding I did down Route 80, between the old life of Point A—now gone—and the new life waiting at Point B, became more important than the points themselves. I was dressed in a filthy pair of chinos I had used for yardwork and a striped jersey from college; I let my beard go. My hair, which badly needed cutting, fell in a bang across my eyes, which I had covered with dark glasses because I was tired of seeing them and their broken blood vessels in the rearview mirror. In no time, I became very fond of the glasses, their potential, as they saved me the worry of my facial expression, whether I was looking attentive or enthused enough, whether I should make eye contact or respectfully look away. I wished I could wear them constantly from now on—to the office, to staff meetings, on the street so my race would be less obvious. I had taken them off to go into the truck stop. Big mistake.

For those fifteen or so hours I was no one; I had no obligations—I was just another car flanked by truckers on the road. The feeling was numbing and pleasurable enough so I did not need alcohol or even food. I observed the hard grip of my hands on the steering wheel, my pants double-patched at the knees, and I admired this new person. I felt I could drive forever, to the edge of the country and then beyond, deep into the Pacific, where I had come from. I did, of course, stop, but even when I had got back to Chicago and showered and shaved and put on the salaryman's uniform, the *rōnin* feeling persisted—it would not let go of me— ticking in my head like the sound of the engine metal once the car had been turned off, still burning hot after its eight-hundred-mile drive.

PART TWO

The Peking Opera was in town. I had been summoned by Yamamoto, with the request that I escort his wife and niece to the show, since he himself was going to be out of the city at an international trade conference. I accepted the three tickets and noted wryly that they were front-row seats. I knew for a fact that Yamamoto's meetings in Toronto would not start until the next week, but I said nothing and dutifully returned to my desk.

There was hardly a time these days when I was not drinking. Not staggering amounts, but enough to even my thoughts and soothe me—two whiskeys at lunch, then several after dinner, perhaps one during the lag of the afternoon in the building lobby bar if things were not going right. I carried gum and mints with me and began to wear a heavier cologne, and these seemed to me quite plausible defenses. If I did not drink I was inert, staring at the piles of work before me while detours of useless thought scattered my attention. If I did drink I could at least fulfill the social functions of my job—the meetings, the chitchat—for alcohol had always heightened my verbal powers, making me loquacious and benevolent. But it was the paperwork that was suffering, so many thousands of pieces of paper—memos, expense reports, letters, briefs—some bound, some loose, but all dry as dust between my fingers and embossed with the bright gold-and-black *Y* corporate logo. It seemed pointless to finish them, for once I did there would only be more. I was a rodent, trapped in a box, pushing through a mound of paper. I reminded myself of Etsuko's hamster, who had lived in a dry aquarium in a nest of shredded shavings that stunk of the animal's waste.

I was also tired of hotel living. Although the company had offered me several options in housing, I continued to stall on the subject, appalled at the thought of being in a corporate apartment, permanently, by myself. I grew quickly disenchanted with the Chicago office as well, almost all Americans, ruddy football players turned executives and blond-and-pink secretaries who regarded me with about as much interest as they would grant a plate of squid. I overheard something in the men's room once; I supposed they assumed I didn't speak English, these two young Americans, or perhaps they didn't care. "Doesn't it bother you," one said, "doing all this work to promote Japan? I mean, that's where the money comes from, and that's where it goes back. Japan's our economic enemy. Doesn't it make you think?" "Nah," the other one replied flatly, and rebuttoned his Bigsby and Kruthers fly. "I don't care, really, as long as I get my bonus." I tried to envision myself confronted with such a question, and I knew that I would only come up with a bunch of justifications. How both countries were really benefitting, how Japan and the U.S. were partners in a great joint-venture. This was just a matter of diplomacy, this attitude, of accepting a predetermined situation and working with it. I also tended to think in truth that Americans should perhaps be happy for the jobs we were creating. But that guy in the men's room, he had made no excuses—he had simply honed the issue down to himself. No extenuating circumstances—he could be at any company, producing anything, as long as he got his bonus. This was a cavalier attitude I both admired and feared. I imagined what a servile little dolt this guy thought I was.

My own group was composed of ten rather methodical, beelike Japanese, who joked very little and were nothing like the cosmopolites back at the New York branch. Some of them were not bad, the young ones, newly transplanted, who would engage in small-talk complaints with me about Chicago's dirty streets and unpredictable weather, how abrupt clerks were in fast-food restaurants and how erratically friendly they found their American colleagues. How nervous the all-company mixers made them, being forced to mingle and patiently give out mini Japanese lessons. "Oh, tell me how to say 'Good Morning,' " or "How do you say 'Mary Sue," or 'pencil,' or 'coffee cup' in Japanese?" Yet these fellow transplants edged around me warily, as if I was always on the verge of collapse. They knew, I supposed, that Taeko had gone home, that I was hitting the sauce a bit too much—somehow it had leaked out. It was virtually impossible to have a secret in that place; everybody knew your business, though you never told them face-to-face. Information passed through pneumatic tubes, I supposed, never through the anguish of discussion.

There was an anniversary party at Yamamoto Chicago my first week there—a marking of Yamamoto's thirty-fifth year in business. Held in the employee lounge, this was an all-staff event, not just for executives—a quick, after-five hors d'oeuvres-and-champagne affair that would run no more than two hours and thereby have all the suburban people on the seven P.M. trains home. Yamamoto was unable to join us—the Chicago office was such a small branch, and his presence was needed more in New York—but he was with us via videocassette: a taped message I had set up the big screen for. Yamamoto was seated at his Manhattan desk, beaming, telling everyone that no individual success was possible and only a team could win. He ended this boost with a guarded "Go Bulls!" as the Chicago basketball team was now in the playoffs. The tension cracked, smooth jazz music began to play in the background. That Yamamoto: he could really throw a party.

The Japanese hung together, out of defense against the full force of the American staff. I returned the Yamamoto tape to its case, then came over and stood by Hiroshi Udo. Hiroshi was an energetic character, comically ambitious. We were near the bar table, and I was drinking whiskey and sodas—one, two, then three, then I lost count—just to blur my senses enough to forget I was in Chicago alone, just to give me something to do. Every time I put my glass down, the hired bartender filled it, whether it was empty or not, whether I had indicated that I'd like another or simply was giving my hand a rest, and so to oblige him I just kept on drinking. Hiroshi was talking about his upcoming marriage, and then Aoki, one of the younger recruits, told us about his recent trip out West.

"Oh? Did you see the Grand Canyon?" I asked.

"No; New Orleans."

I laughed. "New Orleans is south, not west," I corrected. Aoki looked upset.

"But it's west of here," he said.

"No, not really. It's more parallel to Chicago, down the Mississippi. It's considered part of the *South*. Trust me."

"Yes. Shimada knows the U.S. well," Hiroshi concurred, though there was a slight sarcasm in his voice. He had a sort of worshipful envy of me, Hiroshi, the way one might feel toward an older brother. He was rather sly in appearance, short, with hooded eyes—the way many evil Japanese were portrayed in American World War II movies. He complained of people calling him General "Tojo" on various occasions. My eyes were wider, I was taller, more Western-looking. This needled him. "I think you like this country so much because it likes you back," he often said.

Aoki, in the meantime, was still not quite convinced about New Orleans.

"But I flew on South*west* Airlines," he persisted, then let it go, frowning, realizing that he had just supported my argument as well.

We were interrupted by two of the American marketing team—

a man, Frank, and a woman I knew only by sight. I'd been told that she had been pregnant this past winter, had the baby, and returned to work within three weeks. She was driven. She was also friendly and attractive, though her smile was more of a reflex, never anything truly for you; after encountering her several times I began to wonder whether it was activated by mere sonar presence, like an electronic door.

She gave us all the smile now; I picked up my again-brimming drink. That bartender was determined to have me on the floor by six o'clock. Frank and the woman associate, who was introduced to us as K. (we later learned this was a full name, Kay, and not just a letter), began to talk about a joint-venture meeting recently held. Frank cited a vice president from the New York staff, another American, and called him a moron. He then turned to me: "John, you've worked with him out there in New York—am I right or what? And he controls what happens to marketing here. We're strapped."

The vice president *was* rather ineffectual, and I could sense Frank's sincere frustration. But I merely shook my head and said I didn't know him well enough. Frank was obviously disappointed. Aoki, who had raised his eyebrows in reaction to so abrupt an approach, excused himself, almost out of panic. It was not correct to bad-mouth an upper-level executive so casually in general conversation, and at an office party. Criticism was to be done with discretion. I, however, knew from three years of working in the States that such talk was commonplace. Frank had not meant to offend; he had simply been airing a grievance. Aoki had perceived this as rude; I had circumvented it; while Hiroshi remained standing stiffly at my side. He did not like Kay, I could tell. He had a natural resentment toward women who were taller than he—added to the fact that in this country Kay was treated as an equal at work. She was talking to us now, and was to be listened to politely. That ate at him. I saw his mouth tighten as Kay asked us both what hotels we recommended in Tokyo, as a friend of hers was planning a trip.

"There's a Hilton and a Holiday Inn, don't worry," Hiroshi sniped. Kay stepped back a little, startled. I hurriedly cut in.

"Or probably best would be a Japanese-style inn," I said, speaking cautiously, not too sure, after all those Scotches, of my power over words. "They're reasonable, and you'll get a local flavor. Every guidebook has a list of them; otherwise, luxury hotels will cost you a fortune."

"Thank you, John," she said, her smile much more genuine, although to Hiroshi she was cold. She and Frank then drifted away. I saw them over by the exit, glancing back at us and shaking their heads.

"Kay thinks you're rude," I told Hiroshi, who made a little growl of indifference.

"Who cares. I'm sick of these people always asking me about Tokyo and where's a good sushi place here. Who am I—the consul? Leave me alone."

"She was just making conversation," I reminded.

"Yeah, well, who cares," he snapped back.

Aoki rejoined us, and we were each handed slices of anniversary cake and a plastic glass of champagne. I set my whiskey down, heard it being refilled again, but ignored it and instead swallowed all my champagne, then started on my cake. Champagne and whiskey and sugar combined on an empty stomach—with all my fiddling with the videotape, I had not eaten any hors d'oeuvres. All went straight to my cerebellum and nearly had me staggering backward. I shook my head, put the cake down next to my drink, then faced the bartender and his handlebar mustache with a grave smile.

"You win," I said. He winked. I turned back to Aoki and Hiroshi, who were scraping their forks against their plates, trying to get that last smear of icing. "I've had enough," I announced. "I think I'm going back to my desk."

"What about dinner?" Aoki asked. "Udo and I might go out. Join us."

"Oh, no, no—I'll just have a sandwich." I patted my stomach.

"Not very hungry." My perceptions were becoming strangely heightened: it was almost as if I could hear every word of every conversation around me, detect the clicking of saliva in all those mouths. It was deafening. How oily young Aoki's forehead was—I could see it, microscopically close—how annoying Hiroshi's tendency to blink every three seconds. I had to leave; I felt a sudden restlessness. I left Hiroshi and Aoki there, distracted by second slices of cake. And I of course had no intention of heading back to my desk: I was not capable of doing any work—I would only fall asleep on top of a pile of papers—yet I had the paranoid feeling that if I left by elevator, Hiroshi and Aoki would see me and follow me out. I found myself sneaking down the building stairwell instead. Forty flights down the stairwell—I think it took me a half hour. I kept on and on, sort of running and falling at the same time along a spiraling avalanche of steps—I reminded myself of something going down a toilet. Finally I hit bottom. My heart was pounding and I was about to puke, but I did not feel as out of control as I had upstairs.

"Agh!" I exclaimed, voice echoing up the shaft. I stared at a fire extinguisher for a moment, then spit in the corner; I couldn't help it. The serpent ulcer was twisting around inside, and I could hardly breathe, my stomach issuing up all kinds of froth.

"I don't want to do this anymore!" I gasped.

I emerged into the nearly empty building lobby, groped around for my employee ID card and showed it to the security guard, then got my legs to walk me out. I was on automatic pilot, though I kept jolting forward now and then, as if I were still going down stairs. I spit again, into a garbage can outside, then moved on, reflecting. I kept thinking: I'm here, nobody cares, nobody knows where I am now, I'm in Chicago, Illinois, drunk. Illinois—what does that word mean? When I reached Grand Avenue I stopped, spun around and nearly smacked myself with my open palm in the head. My hotel was six blocks south of here; I had gone the wrong way.

"Idiot . . . Have to go south, Aoki . . . I'm wrong too," I mumbled.

I found my sunglasses and put them over my face, then carefully retraced the exact route I had taken, step by wobbly step.

Several hours later, I was asleep on Gina's futon. She needed a new one—the cotton stuffing was displaced, the cover fabric worn. I had called her; she had taken me in; we had gone through our usual performance, only I was drunk and more sloppy than usual. I hit the bed like an overwhelmed bantamweight hitting the mat. She pulled a sheet over me and then dressed and went about doing what she'd been doing when I'd arrived—packing her belongings into boxes. She's leaving for Italy soon, I reminded myself, each time I woke and saw her sorting through summer clothes and old letters and shoes. She smiled at me brightly each time I opened my eyes. She seemed way too attuned to my consciousness.

"Why do you even bother with me anymore?" I mumbled, only moving one side of my mouth. Gina tossed an old Japan Air Lines poster into the trash—it looked old, maybe from the sixties.

"Because you're such a mess." She smiled again. "Ask a pitiful question, get a pitiful answer . . ."

"You threw that poster out on purpose, in front of me," I accused her. "It's symbolic."

"Oh, now you're being self-pitying again," Gina said. "I'm throwing it out because it's torn. Why don't you take it? You can have it if you'd like." She laid it out flat on the floor for me and I stared at it dumbly. Although she had on too much eyeliner, the stewardess featured in the poster reminded me of the way Taeko posed for photographs. Always with her head bent and the slightest smile on her lips. Or maybe I was just imagining that she looked like Taeko, that Gina was passing Taeko back to me and telling me to stop feeling sorry for myself. What would Taeko think if she could see me here, on this raggedy futon, with this foreign girl wearing a man's flannel robe and sweat socks. In a strange sense, Taeko might be impressed. She probably never thought me capable of such stuff. She probably thought I was too much of a company man. I wondered what Gina and Taeko would think of each other if they

ever met. Taeko would say Gina was too abrupt; Gina would call
Taeko a Suzie Wong. They seemed such separate entities, connected only by the ludicrous common denominator of me. I was uncomfortable being in the room with both of them at the same time.

Gina pulled a guitar out of her closet and began playing some
mournful tune. Every once in awhile her fingers would screech
against the strings, but she was quite competent. "I have an excellent ear for music and languages," she said when I complimented
her. Rather than protest the praise, like a Japanese girl might, she
merely augmented it. "I pick things up in a minute. Hum me a
melody once and I'll be able to play it for you."

I could think of no songs. I fell asleep once more, lulled, and
when I woke the guitar was back in the closet. The JAL poster was
gone as well, and although I snuck around the apartment searching
for it, it did not turn up. Everything was in boxes now and the bedroom had a clean-swept brightness to it. Gina was sleeping very
heavily on the left side of the mat; she did not hear me as I left. She
was tired, no doubt. She had packed all through the night.

I sat, finger to my chin, watching the adventures of Green Serpent
as she dodged the villain's spears. There was a great deal of color
on stage; a perfumed flesh and breath warmth to the audience, who
had been cooped up for some time now, watching the sinewy bodies
of the Chinese. Although they continued to laugh at appropriate
moments, they seemed to be growing restless, eager to be out of
their plush seats. Mrs. Yamamoto was enjoying the show greatly,
her snowy throat tight with excitement as she recalled her own
years of classical training in samisen and dance. She was to my
right. She looked very elegant this evening, in cherry-colored velvet, spangled diamond earrings that reminded me of chandelier
bobs. To my left was "Fran," Yamamoto's twenty-two-year-old
niece, whom both Yamamotos referred to as Yoko, although Yoko
herself did not follow suit.

Yoko was a modern girl, aspiring to none of the vivid frailty of her aunt; she was dressed well, in a linen suit of mannish cut, her body well exercised and streamlined. No makeup except for brownish lipstick that did not cover flakes of chapped skin on her mouth, and no jewelry except for a watch. Hair beefed up by a perm, triangular-shaped, not black but red-brown; I thought she might have dyed it. She was not unattractive. There was a straightforwardness to her, an intensity; as she sat nodding and following the performances, assiduously referring to her program notes, she reminded me of myself in my student days. There was even a breath of scandal to her: Yamamoto had hinted that she was going around with a white boy, a fellow student at Northwestern.

This fact, combined with Yoko's enforced presence tonight at the Peking Opera and my own marital troubles, clicked into place slowly, like a revolver chamber in my mind. I was not stupid; I could see what Yamamoto was up to. This evening was really a secret *omiai*, a premature meeting of bride and groom. Rather than being panicked, however, I couldn't help but chuckle to myself. Yamamoto had his hands full with this one, I thought. Yoko was not the type of girl who would ever be interested in me.

The music roared, as violent as wind. I turned away from the blast, while Mrs. Yamamoto smiled. I was fascinated by the texture of her skin, the dewy folds of it, so smooth and synthetic-looking, almost poreless. I was strangely drawn to her—she brought to mind Mrs. Ogawa. For a woman of fifty she was stunning: tiny ears, cupid's-bow mouth, beautiful swanlike neck. What kind of adventures had she seen as an actress? I looked her in the eye, hoping to fix her attention, but she continued to watch the stage, then leaned across me to Yoko to gently draw her hand from her mouth: absorbed, Yoko was gnawing her fingernails.

It was hardly ladylike.

At the Yamamoto apartment the web was drawn around me. Mrs. Yamamoto served sherry and biscuits; we chatted briefly about the performance, and then the phone rang and Mrs. Yamamoto disappeared to take a private call in the other room.

I faced Yoko alone, for the first time. Conversation faltered, like dimming light. Yoko had kicked off her low-heeled pumps and was pushing her feet through the silky pile rug. In the Yamamoto's U.S. homes, shoes were to be left on. Mrs. Yamamoto was very sophisticated about that. Yoko munched a biscuit and nursed her sherry with small, savoring sips. I had already downed mine. There was a certain awkward tension between us, but she refused to acknowledge it. She smiled warmly at me. I was beginning to find her moon face appealing.

"So you're getting an M.B.A.," I finally said, after several more revolutions of silence. "That must be exciting. I'll bet you can't wait to graduate."

"It is exciting." She nodded. "Especially at this point, you know, when you think of putting all you've learned to work. The real thing!" She laughed.

"To the top of the ladder, right?" I noticed that despite her Japanese accent, her voice had a friendly, Midwestern twang. Yoko had been in Chicago for five years now, I had been informed, and from the looks of her, she wasn't going back. "Do you like your coursework?" I said.

"Lots." She smiled, tugging impatiently on her skirt. "We just did a study on the tier system in the Japanese corporation. It was so funny—everyone in the class was staring at me. But you know the model, right? The *ringi* and *nemawashi*—"

I cut in. "I'm afraid I'm only a foot soldier, not a strategist," I said. "You should ask your uncle. He'd talk your ear off."

She looked at me shrewdly. "Uncle? Hardly. He refuses to even acknowledge that I'm in B-school. He says it's 'inappropriate.' "

I could see myself in the oval mirror, myself and the bushy back of Yoko's hair, blocked partially by a Heian vase. A clock of pure and perfect tone chimed ten times. I frowned. This was a subject not to touch. I myself had never known a woman to pursue such a degree—we had women at Yamamoto, of course, but no Japanese women executives. Yamamoto had not mentioned any serious career pursuits for Yoko. It seemed unlikely that where she was concerned he would approve of anything but marriage.

She went on. "We're on the outs these days anyway, Uncle and I. He's upset because I'm dating an American."

"Oh, are you?" I feigned surprise.

"Yes. Business student, just like me. We plan to move out to California together after graduation. There's tons more Asians on the West Coast, and more mixed marriages." The smile was gone from her face, and she was watching me for any hint of reaction. I gave none. "I don't like Japanese men; they're jerks. They take everything for granted, especially women. No offense, of course."

"None taken." A last swallow of sherry remained in my glass, but I ignored it and instead got up boldly and went to the bar to pour myself a Scotch. If they were going to keep me prisoner here, I should at least have something decent to drink. I didn't really mind. The conversation was picking up.

"I suppose I'm sort of a maverick," Yoko said, tossing her head back. "That's how they refer to it in class, the Japanese who want to break free of tradition and take risks. I think the country is stagnant; how creative can you be when you're running out of space and you have a homogeneous population? If I went back there now, I'd be bored to death, walking around, looking at so many similar people. Know what I mean?"

It seemed hardly possible that she was blaspheming so in the temple of Yamamoto, and I waited for a violent trembling of the building beneath us. I felt very stiff, not sure how to respond, just as I had whenever Keiji bad-mouthed home. I looked up. Keiji. That was an interesting subject to veer off onto.

"I believe you may have met a friend of mine, Keiji Narata," I said. "He used to work at the New York branch. His opinions were closer to yours than my own are. I've always been somewhat conservative, coming from an unstable home."

That wasn't altogether true—after all, I had wanted to come to the States—but I *was* a foot soldier, and I had to be discreet.

Yoko smiled slyly. "Oh, sure, Keiji. He was one of Uncle's first attempts. We did have a lot in common, sure, but he's so bitter. He doesn't want to progress; he only wants to complain."

"One of Uncle's first attempts?" I asked, again feigning surprise. Yoko was examining the sole of her foot.

"At matchmaking," she elaborated. "He's always trying. Last Christmas it was that Hiroshi, who is about four inches shorter than me; and Kenzo and Nobu and Ichi, that hick from Osaka. But it was most ridiculous with Keiji. Keiji's not interested in women."

"Excuse me?" A stiff, unsteady smile crossed my lips.

"Well, sure. I hope I'm not shocking you. I figured it out soon enough. But we always got along well, once he forgot I was a woman, I think, and realized *I* wasn't the one with designs on him, it was all Uncle's doing. Perhaps Uncle thought I could straighten Keiji out. Even though he was rebellious, Uncle always said he was one of the brightest men on staff. You see, Uncle's very upset. He can't accept the fact that I'm going to marry David and I don't care about being disinherited or cut off. For the first time in my life, he's powerless. I'll have my degree, I'll be able to earn my own living. And if he never speaks to me again, well, I won't wither away. My parents will still love me. Besides, families are a wonderful thing, but sooner or later you have to break free and start on your own."

If only Taeko had followed that philosophy, I thought. "Your uncle wants what's best for you," was what I said, evenly, for lack of anything else. Was this Yamamoto's idea of a good wife for me? Ironically, I liked her for all the wrong reasons. "He has very high standards."

Yoko bounded up and retrieved her cream-colored jacket. "Maybe. But I think he confuses what's best for himself with what's best for everyone else. He means well. He's very fond of you. In fact, he's been talking about you so much lately that I thought this was another setup, but then of course I remembered that you're married, with kids. I met your wife at the summer barbecue—we talked about abstract expressionism." She yawned and then extended her hand to me: at this point I was semirecumbent on the couch. "I've got to fly; I've got Risk Management at eight-thirty tomorrow morning. I enjoyed meeting you." She smiled, nodding. "Tell Aunt Michi I said goodbye and that I'll call her this weekend, will you? And thank you for taking us to the show. Aunt Michi's been looking forward to it for months. Oh, don't get up; I've got my car in the garage." She jangled a set of keys, as if to convince me. "It's only a twenty-minute drive back to campus, no trouble at all."

"But it's so late, Yoko-san," I said, surprised by the note of urgency in my voice, at the realization that I rather liked her and didn't want her to go. She was a diversion. I liked her even better, seeing how we were so totally mismatched.

"I've been out later by myself!" she caroled, keys still in hand as she walked vigorously through the foyer. "And don't call me Yoko —it reminds me of Yoko Ono. It's Fran to you and me." Her nose was an appealing snub blur in the distance. "Bye now! Be good."

The door slammed from what seemed miles away. A maid appeared to refill my Scotch glass and wipe biscuit crumbs off the chair where Yoko had been sitting, then she disappeared again, as noiselessly as she had come. Of course, I thought, Yoko wants to get home to her boyfriend, the white man who gives her free rein, not sit here with a pallid bag carrier who wouldn't even discuss the tier system. I sighed. As she was leaving, I had nearly yelled, "I think you should marry whoever you want," but in true bag carrier fashion, I had demurred, deciding she didn't need my encouragement.

I stood by the window, waiting for Mrs. Yamamoto, staring down like a child at the lights strung like fine gold chains over blocks of buildings. The view of the city was spectacular. I thought of how Etsuko would be just as awed by this view. I could almost imagine holding her up against me, how her small shoes would kick against the back of my leg and her fingers grip around my lapels. She would search my pockets—she always did. I always let her keep whatever loose change she found.

"Where's Yoko?"

Mrs. Yamamoto was standing by the empty sofa, hand on her

hip. From this distance she, too, looked spectacular, so red and black and white. Purely cinematic. I blinked several times and moved toward her, like eyes to a flickering image.

"She left. She asked me to say her goodbyes—she has an early class tomorrow, and it is late."

"Why, yes, I suppose it is." Her voice trailed off sweetly, into weariness. "I'm sorry to have been gone for so long—that was Yoshi on the phone. He'd been trying to get me from Toronto all night."

It was hard for me not to smirk—Yamamoto holding a long conversation with his wife! Normally even his most crucial business calls lasted no more than five minutes. And why would he have been trying to phone all night when he knew this was the date of the Peking Opera, when he had arranged the whole evening himself. It had been a setup, just as Yoko and I had suspected, an excuse to leave us alone. Mrs. Yamamoto was now so elegantly drowsy—she had probably been napping in the bedroom for the past half hour.

"I suppose I should leave too," I said, but made no motion to go. The room was beautiful and still; I hadn't any desire to get back to the hotel room, which in its perpetual stark emptiness had become cell-like, as bad as my cube at work.

"Why don't you have another drink?" she said, and although I wanted to prolong my departure, I told myself, You've had plenty. Already I was drunk enough to feel a peculiar warm affection for her surface and resurface, something I usually had no trouble repressing.

"Only if you'll join me." I smiled. "Yes, come on now, you've been a terrible hostess, abandoning me with your poor niece. She was bored to death."

"Just as I bore you, no doubt," Mrs. Yamamoto said. She was carrying a glass of white wine, and I marked this as a small triumph—I had never seen her drink. I replenished my Scotch and we sat on the couch. She drank her wine leisurely, eyes closed and musing. "Besides, I'm sure she was hardly bored. You're very close in age, close enough, whereas there's nearly a generation between you and me. Remember we discussed that, at the Drake, where you kept staring shamelessly at that tea waitress."

Women! I hated the way they noticed everything, with an almost reptilian sixth sense. I kept a smile fixed on my lips and drew in a deep breath.

"The waitress? Oh. She reminded me of our neighbor's daughter, where I grew up. The parents were a mixed marriage—an American who had stayed over after the war and his Japanese wife. I went to school with the girl. She looked a great deal like that waitress; there was really nothing more to it than that."

"I see," Mrs. Yamamoto said, somewhat disconcerted. I was watching her intently, half in hopes of getting her off the subject, but also because I had never allowed myself to look her up and down before—I had always been too nervous, flustered by the presence of Yamamoto. Her legs, emerging from the cherry-colored gash in her dress, were slim and white, tapering into delicate, if not scrawny, ankles, small narrow feet. Her waist was still quite defined, her breasts firm beneath a sculpted ledge of collarbone. Yamamoto should consider himself lucky to have a wife as well-preserved as this, but then he had undoubtedly picked her out with that in mind. She was his second wife, whom he had married after the death of the first, following an appropriate period of mourning. She herself had been twice married, once widowed: to a diplomat, who had died; and when she was eighteen, to the film director who had discovered her and whom she immediately divorced. When she was younger, she had been popular for an admirable span of time—I could remember a cousin of mine doing her hair up in what was then known as the "Michiko twist."

And now I was sitting with her, staring at her legs, far on the other side of the earth. It struck me distastefully as something my father might have written a short story about—the fleeting beauty of women, their too short season.

"Tell me what you thought of Yoko," Mrs. Yamamoto said. Her glass was empty; she set it down lightly on the Italian marble coffee table, then folded her hands in her lap.

"Huh? Well, she's very independent—aspirations of a career and all that. She seems quite happy with the way she is. I think you're wasting your time with marriage efforts."

Mrs. Yamamoto frowned slightly, faint eyebrows drawn together. "Did she say that?"

"No, not outright, but from the way she was talking I just assumed . . ." I hesitated. "I think this country has an unusual effect on people. Some get a taste of different freedoms and want to stay, others hate it and can't wait to go back. I myself don't care much about the freedom, but I can't help being fascinated by how much opportunity exists—it really is a fascinating mess. Look at all these people here: Koreans and Chinese and Italians and Germans, Mexicans—why, you go up into the neighborhoods and you won't believe the sights, how they've all adapted, how they can scratch something out of the earth, get these Americans to eat their food and buy their products. It's almost limitless!"

She was staring at me curiously. I realized I had gone off on an excited tangent.

"Do you visit the neighborhoods often?" she asked.

I backed off, wary. Of course she was going to tell Yamamoto everything. The ice in my drink fizzed, as if it were in pain.

"I explore. There's much more to the city than just downtown. But what do you think of this country? I've never heard you say one thing or another about it."

"Yes, that's true. I enjoy living in foreign places, though. I was born in Manchukuo actually, my father was an officer there; and with my second husband I lived in Paris; and of course now with Yoshi, Chicago and New York." She spoke clearly but very softly, in the slow, halting tones of Kyoto, her head now lolling against the back of the couch. "I'm very sorry your wife disliked it here so much."

So she knew, I thought. "Yes, well, I—" I muttered.

She startled me by interrupting. "And you're such a handsome man. She's very foolish."

"I'm honored that you think so," I said. My mouth was dry. She was staring at me now, eyes all pupils and liquid black. "But how do you deal with all the free time on your hands?" I ventured. "President Yamamoto keeps a grueling schedule."

She smiled. "Me? Oh, well, I keep busy. Perhaps it's because I'm older. You learn to expect less from a husband as you get older. Have you seen the rest of the apartment?" she continued. "I know you've been here several times, but I don't remember your seeing anything but the living room. I'm very fond of it myself. The apartment in New York has such low ceilings—you've been there too, of course."

"And to the one in Tokyo. And to your villa."

Her gaze drifted off into the distance. "Yes. We really are accumulating many homes." She laughed. "So many places to live, and no children to fill them. That's why Yoshi is so fond of all his nieces and nephews, like Yoko. He has no one else."

"Hmm," I said. I drained my Scotch and flung my head back, almost as if to clear away the sad and poignant image of Yamamoto she had raised. Without much thought, I got up and began to wander about, knowing she would follow. An invisible thread seemed to join us, made of spun silk. There was a cool draft flowing through the rooms, and it was silent; no noise of cab horns or street sounds penetrated the windows, their panes curved slightly to accommodate the tremendous winds at this height. I ventured to the kitchen, the dining room and Yamamoto's den, which was nearly empty except for tatami matting and a wall of unpatterned shoji screens: his place to think, and meditate—just like the bathroom's cedar tub. The apartment had its *tokonoma*, an alcove reserved for the dead; I was most impressed by the way Mrs. Yamamoto or her decorator had mixed things up here—a little traditionalism, some nouveau design, a Tokaido view in a gold-leaf frame, a bonsai garden on an eighteenth-century credenza.

I touched one of the piano keys, wondering who played. The note hung low and solemn in the air, like a man clearing his throat.

"This is my room," she said. We had just gone down a hallway slanted on a diagonal, which angled off to two closed doors. She stepped past me boldly, mouth taut with a small smile—it was obvious that she was quite proud of this upcoming room, her own sanctuary.

It was rose-colored. Thick carpet, chiffon drapes, velvet chairs and dresser cloths—all nearly the same shade, the color of a blush. Even the phone was pink. The bed, high and Western-style, was surrounded by a canopy parted to reveal a satin coverlet with matching satin tube-shaped bolsters. A bamboo birdcage hung from the ceiling, draped by the canopy material.

"These are my finches," she said. She lifted away the cover to show me two small birds huddled together, sleeping; they stirred slightly and shoved tiny budlike faces farther down into their breasts.

"Male and female?"

Mrs. Yamamoto nodded. "Kesa and Morito. I love that story, don't you? I've had several different pairs of birds, but I always name them the same thing."

Kesa and Morito, a famous tale of infidelity. Lady Kesa and her soldier lover, Morito, and their plot to kill her husband, gone awry . . . The cage was immaculate and free of any litter—no seed shells or droppings. I remembered, uncomfortably, the presence of the maid somewhere in the apartment and shoved my hands into my pants pockets.

"Where do the other doors lead?" I asked.

"One to the master bath and one to Yoshi's room. Yoshi prefers morning light."

She had sat down at her dressing table, before an arrangement of perfume bottles—so many different shapes and sizes they looked to me like a miniature skyline. I was directly behind her, still standing. She smiled into the mirror.

"We make an interesting couple, don't we?"

I nodded at the reflection, transfixed: the effect in the mirror was as a portrait, almost mother and son but not quite. I had not looked at length into a mirror for a while. It was a shock to see the new gauntness in my face, the way my suit no longer fit but

merely hung across my shoulders; how my skin had become so dry
and tight, the color and texture of parchment. No, she did not look
that much older than I at all.

My fingers stretched out involuntarily and undid the Michiko
twist. I could not help myself. The rope of hair uncoiled of its own
accord, slowly, like a living thing, a long anaconda snake, longer
than any hair I had ever seen on a woman. I heard her sighing.
The sigh became a low laugh. The skin at the back of my neck
tightened, a sure sign that I was in trouble.

"What have you done?" she asked, amused. I apologized repeatedly and said that it had just happened, I had not meant to
touch it.

"Please forgive me," I begged.

"That's quite all right." The brassiere beneath her dress pushed
her breasts into soft mounds; a bustier—that was what they called
it. "I know you wish I were younger," she continued. "That's the
hardest thing a woman has to contend with, her age, losing the
attention of handsome young men like you."

"I'm very sorry!" I stammered again.

She was looking at me sadly, her throat a slope that glistened
with iridescent powder, and she was not so much seeing me as
seeing an amalgam of all the ghosts of young men she had known.
And there had been many, I was sure, many in her life; yet here
she was stuck with Yamamoto. A possession of Yamamoto's, really.
Surely he did not satisfy the full realm of her emotions or measure
up to what she was used to—he was so gruff and abrupt, so old,
and she so quiet at his side. She was withering away, mooning
before her vanity table. It was sad. I heard the ticking of my watch,
the intense slam of my heart within my chest. I still could not
believe I had touched Mrs. Yamamoto.

"Will you stay awhile?" she asked.

"Stay?" My face was stiff. "I really should be leaving. It's so
late. I—"

She had turned back to the mirror and was brushing her hair as if nothing had happened—twisting it up into place, her arms raised slightly, smooth and white.

"Yes." She nodded. "Perhaps you should."

"I—" I broke off again, not really quite sure of what I wanted to say. She had to understand my plight, how it would be impossible for me ever to do more than touch her hair—she was Yamamoto's *wife;* it would be an unpardonable offense.

"Just go," Mrs. Yamamoto said. "I'm afraid you've overstayed your welcome tonight."

There was a small spot of wetness on her smoothly powdered face. It hurt me to see it there, as ugly as a scar.

I took several steps backward, bowing despite myself, then turned and banged into the settee in my hurry to get out. My shin screamed in pain; one pant leg had hiked itself up over my sock. I stumbled like a bad comedian, leaving a rose-colored trail.

As I rushed through the apartment, head bent, I caught a glimpse of the maid through the open shutters of the kitchen, calm and stolid, surrounded by white shells and eggs. She did not look up as I passed. It was only when I was in the hallway that I realized how unusual that was, for a maid to be awake after midnight, peeling hard-boiled eggs. Such devotion—it was exhausting. I slumped against the back wall of the elevator and pushed the button, then allowed gravity to further drag me down.

◆

The corporation's annual meeting, held in the Mimosa Room at the Nippon, began badly. It had been my task to refine Yamamoto's speech for the event, the text of which was to be projected from slides in a presentation, along with charts and photos and narration by the top American executive. Yamamoto did not want to handicap the essence of his message with his accent, and he felt it would be more enjoyable for the primarily American staff to have one of their own at the podium. But I had procrastinated so much on the project, and Yamamoto had made so many finicky changes, that I was late in getting the text shots camera-ready for the slides. At seven A.M. the morning of the meeting, I had gone myself to the twenty-four-hour photo lab, not daring to trust anyone else with the task or admit to such stupidity.

To my horror, I was told that the slides were not ready, nor had any such order been placed.

I nearly threw up. In approximately ninety minutes, employees from all branches would be filing down the cedar steps of the hotel and past its miniature waterfalls, into the Mimosa Room, and there would be no presentation. I had already lied and told Yamamoto the slides were done—what could I possibly tell him now? Nothing; I would have to quit, disappear, disembowel myself, change my face and fingerprints and drop off the face of the earth.

"But that's impossible!" I yelled. I pounded on the speckled Formica counter, trying to force the clerk, a small Hispanic girl with high-piled hair, into action. I stared dully at the filigree cross dangling at her throat, the YO ♥ JAIME button on her lab jacket. "I brought the film in here myself, to the man with the mustache. I was told they'd be ready at seven—I need them right this instant! Otherwise we would have done them in-house. We're paying you a fortune!"

She looked at me stolidly. The air smelled of chemicals and perfume, and from within the panel of doors behind her I could hear a hum of photoprocessing machinery. I was shaking. Already fluid was rising from my empty stomach up into my mouth.

"Sorry. No slides for Yamamoto."

I clawed the side of my face, wondering what I would do now; what would life be like without a job, without work? For a fleeting instant the thought was almost pleasurable—it would take me only minutes to pack my things, an hour to get to the airport, buy a ticket to some obscure city I could get lost in easily enough, maybe Seattle or Portland. As Yoko had said, "There's tons more Asians on the West Coast." One more in the crowd.

But then I rallied, snapping upright, clenching both hands into fists.

"Check Shimada," I said.

"What?"

"Shimada: S-h-i-m-a-d-a. Please, take a look. Maybe that's what name the slides are under."

Her long red fingernails moved with agonizing slowness through the order bin, and then stopped, retrieving a small pouch.

"Thirty high-gloss color?"

"Yes!" I lunged forward and snatched them from her. An envelope that fit into my breast pocket: so this was what life had boiled down to.

Even she was smiling in relief as she told me what was owed. She waited while I fished out the money and waved away the change. "Oh, *thank* you. You know, you had me real scared for a second. I thought you was going to faint."

I grabbed my receipt and the envelope and bolted out the door, jaywalking across brilliant sunlit Wacker Drive and back to the hotel, where I meticulously checked each slide in the men's lounge, then put my head between my knees. They were all there. And what if they weren't—what was I planning to do then? How close can you shave it? I scolded myself. Still, I felt relief. I was going to be Yamamoto's bag carrier for at least a little while longer, I thought.

God, did I need a drink.

Polyps of black-and-gold balloons, each embossed with a *Y*, hung tethered in a net overhead. At the end of the meeting they would be released in a joyous outburst, for the staff to keep as souvenirs, just as three hundred fifty small lucite digital clocks with YAMA-MOTO: THE TIME IS NOW printed in the corner were to be distributed as this year's employee-appreciation gift.

I was seated up front, along with the other members of the staff, at a long banquet table that appeared to extend for miles. Far off, at the helm, was the VIP contingent, the only members of the audience allowed to smoke: Yamamoto; old Tanaka from Tokyo, chairman of the board; Kurahashi from Los Angeles, whose corporation, Globe Electronics, Yamamoto had just swallowed whole; and finally R. R. Magill, the American vice president, who sat large and awkward amid the three old Japanese, a stag among okapi.

Yamamoto caught my eye momentarily and nodded. I had not seen him since the night with Mrs. Yamamoto—our only contact had been via telephone. I gave a bow-nod to both him and Tanaka, then as nonchalantly as I could eased my gaze to the other side, to Hiroshi on my right. Hiroshi was nibbling at a piece of crumb cake, already scribbling copious notes. He was not one for wasting time. A new gold ring encircled his stubby finger—he had been off for the past three weeks on home leave, a traditional spring wedding. Hiroshi was small and frail but tough-hearted, his voice inconsistent with his body—gravelly, deep: a whiskey and cigarette voice. Ruthless. He sounded like a syndicate hood. Already I could feel him nipping at my heels, taking on what work I could not, voraciously gobbling it up, demanding more, and Yamamoto of course noticed these things. I stared at Hiroshi's ring, morosely. It was so new.

"*Yakuza*," I said to myself, aloud.

Hiroshi looked up. "What?"

"Nothing." I took a sip of my coffee, which had gone cold. Directly behind me, the slides were being loaded into the projector, reminding me of my earlier panic.

Hiroshi patted the newspaper by his plate. "You see the *Yomiuri Shimbun?*" he asked. "Prime Minister Takeshita's going to resign—they think maybe next week." Hiroshi wet his forefinger and picked the last clumps of streusel off his plate. "It's all over for him."

"You think so?"

"I know so, yes. It's a terrible disgrace. But I could tell he was crooked from the start."

The lights dimmed, and a gradual silence ensued as R. R. Magill took his place at the podium, which was draped, like the banquet tables, in black and gold cloth. His salutatory remarks were low and majestic, following a bit of trouble with the microphone, which he had to adjust to his full height.

"My friends, I would like to welcome you to the annual Yamamoto America Electronics Corporation meeting. . . ."

A heavy Boston accent: Magill had played football at Harvard, class of '48, after a brief stint in the Pacific. His enemy embraced. He was rather phlegmatic, almost haughty, but he nonetheless inspired more confidence from the employees than Yamamoto ever would. Following the preamble, the slides began to flash overhead. Briefly the focus of attention turned to Yamamoto, then back up to the white-lettered slogans of inspiration, read out in the Boston accent.

"We must avoid cowardly hesitance and pursue the New Frontier. Aggression equals Progression. We must not fear adventure, the unknown, the *unwalked* path. . . ."

I sat with my thighs tight, waiting for a slide to be missing or out of place. But they all followed with rhythmic beauty, just as I had planned them: the pie chart, with its two-tone yen/dollar layout; the text; the employee expansion graph, with its bold red upward bar; more text; the photo of last year's company picnic.

"We must make our mistakes faster. Life is an adventure for all."

Hiroshi was jotting away with furious vertical strokes. I disliked him intensely at that moment, so much energy and enthusiasm, a new wife. Life is an adventure for all—what a laugh. Corporate adventure, but don't step outside your cubicle. There was a brief spatter of applause—they were giving out Employee Appreciation certificates, hand-lettered on rice paper. Hiroshi, who had been assigned the job of photodocumenting the event for the staff newsletter, jumped up with his camera and hunched before the group, doing his best silly-Nip-tourist imitation. Everyone laughed. He repeated the stance for the second group, and then for the third. By the time the fourth pack of certificate winners had passed and Hiroshi had leapt up again, I was ready to fling my coffee in his face. I folded my arms and sat back. No Japanese staff members ever received certificates—Yamamoto would not allow it. He preferred to have a "shadow staff" of Japanese, with the Americans working up front, receiving all the parties and prizes. Nearly everyone got a scroll of sorts, either for extra motivation and effort or for perfect attendance and punctuality. To me it seemed almost pointless, just like the annual promotions back in Tokyo—what was so special about a promotion when you knew you would get one no matter what?

The lights redimmed. A steely slim man in a gray suit sprang on stage and began to give his presentation. The author of the corporate best-seller *Achieve/Excel*, he was received with great interest, more so than anyone else. His remarks seemed rambling and unfocused, full of more idioms than even I could handle, but the Americans laughed and relaxed and yelled out comments. It appeared more like a nightclub act than anything else—he had broken away from the podium and was dragging the microphone around with him, entertainer style. Yamamoto sat smiling indulgently, not quite listening but watching with approval the looks of avid attention among his flock. I imagined what sort of life this *Achieve/Excel* man must have, going around speaking to groups, hotel suites and first-class flights, a California beach house, a Porsche, blondes and redheads and exotic restaurants, a smile as exquisitely tailored as his suit.

"Hey, that company's motto is 'Be on Time and Don't Steal the Furniture.' What more can you ask for? Life's what you make it. Don't beat around the bush, do it right. Achieve/Excel: *You* are the one that counts."

Odd speech, I thought, for a corporation that professed team effort. But then I supposed Yamamoto knew he was only going to motivate so much with the Japanese ethic—these were Americans, they were individualists. Whatever worked—that was probably Yamamoto's game. Whatever revved these people up. Hiroshi frowned in confusion and nibbled on the tip of his pen, then took a picture for lack of anything better to do.

The presentation ended with a slide of a sheep, captioned: "It All Boils Down to Ewe."

"Don't *be* one of these. Lay down your own law. An outfit's only as good as its people. So take that ball and run with it, all right?"

"All right!"

"Thank *you!*" he gasped.

"*Ewe!*" the audience yelled back, some baaing like lambs.

The balloons were released in a cascade, bouncing all over the room to shouts and thunderous applause. Magill and Yamamoto and Tanaka exchanged a series of clumsy handshakes, and then Magill went off with Mr. Achieve/Excel, who lit up a great cigar, triumphant after his performance, and allowed people to approach him and pump his outstretched arm. The staff began to filter out through the main entrance, some carrying balloons, all carrying their clocks, a few going back to the buffet table to pick up extra slices of cake or steal cream containers and sugar packets for later use. I yawned. Hiroshi took my picture. I waved him away, disgusted, as if I were fending off paparazzi.

Yamamoto had come up to us. The small approving smile from before was still on his face, and it deepened as Hiroshi and I bolted out of our chairs in respectful greeting.

"A foursome of golf on Saturday, at Blue Lakes. Kurahashi-san, myself, and you two young men. We tee off at ten A.M. sharp."

We both nodded. I smirked, quickly—here was one area where I outdid Hiroshi, who had no finesse whatsoever at golf and swung at each shot as if he wielded a baseball bat. I grinned with enthusiasm, put in the obligatory remark about how successful the meeting had been, then waited for Yamamoto and Tanaka to go first into the slow stream of semicharged employees trickling slowly back to the office.

"Come on, Mr. Pressman," I said. "The party's over."

Hiroshi snapped a quick shot of the ruined ballroom, and then another, and then, satisfied, smiled and pushed his thumb down hard to rewind the completed roll of film.

"*Say Cheese!*" he cried. I ignored that, masterfully, and wondered how much it would hurt him when I pulled his tongue like a rip cord, all the way out of his head.

❖

I had seen Gina nearly every night for the past two weeks. She was most accommodating. The trip to Europe loomed somewhere in the near future but she was never definite about dates; she merely laughed whenever I asked: "Oh, I'll be gone soon enough."

Our relations were very cut-and-dried—there was really no more than a dog's pleasure to it. She was friendly yet impersonal; she allowed me to do anything I wanted and played me skillfully, like a harp, long fingers touching every string. I told myself I did not care anymore—I did not care who she was outside of bed or what she did—and when I went at her I tried to imagine the Amerasian girl riding her bicycle at night in the dark, its small headlight beaming, and not Gina, this headstrong, heedless girl who now represented my social life.

I wondered whether I should be giving her money. Perhaps it would help me to be objective.

I remember the Friday following the corporation meeting quite clearly; it was the only time I ever saw her that we did not have sex. Normally, we only met at her apartment and not at my hotel —I was paranoid about Yamamoto spying on me, perhaps having Hiroshi stationed behind a potted plant—but that night she surprised me by coming to my room unannounced. I hustled her in quickly. I had not planned on seeing her that evening—I had the golf game at Blue Lakes in the morning and would need my rest.

I expected we would go right to bed.

But *nothing* happened, and I was oddly excited by the change of pace. I was lying on my stomach on the bed. She came in with a container of yogurt and a bag full of small rice cakes, apologizing for bringing food with her but she was starving, she hadn't eaten since noon. I apologized back.

"Oh, no, I'm sorry I can't call room service," I said. "But they'd send the company the tab, and I don't want that."

"Of course not." She sat down at the food of the bed and ate quickly, offering some to me, but I refused. "Wouldn't that be fun, though," she continued, "like in *Tampopo*, that scene where the gangster who loves food so much uses it to make love to his girl-friend. Puts a raw egg in her mouth and kisses her. Puts salt on her breast, a live prawn down there"—she pointed to her lower abdomen—"and tickles her with it. Did you see that movie?"

I shook my head. "No, I saw the other one."

"Which? *A Taxing Woman? The Funeral? A Taxing Woman Returns?*"

"The first one you mentioned."

"You should see *Tampopo* too."

"Okay, I'll make a note of it."

We watched television for a bit, guests I did not recognize on *The Tonight Show.* I stroked Gina's hair, intrigued by the slight currents of static I was creating.

"Long day?" I asked. She did not look back at me.

"I've been busy, yes."

I gathered the hair into a short knot. "With your other activities?"

"Actually, no." She disengaged herself and tucked her feet neatly beneath her. "I've been running around with last-minute details. You see, I'm leaving tomorrow."

I felt a gradual pressurized sensation pass over me, as if I were trying to go all the way down to the bottom of a pool. So this was it, this was the last night. I said nothing, then lit a cigarette and watched the smoke from it stretch upward in long, funereal spires.

"You might have given me more warning," I sighed. She came and lay beside me.

"You knew it was coming. Originally I wasn't even going to say goodbye in person—I was going to do it over the phone."

I removed my shirt and socks, loosened my pants, yet when she made a move to switch off the light, I stopped her. I was feeling sadly conversational. "No, no, wait. Got your ticket?"

"Yes. I've had it for several months."

"Excited about your trip?"

"Yes."

"What about your apartment, your things. Your job. What'll become of them?"

She shrugged. "The apartment's been sublet, my things I either sold or gave away, the cat's gone to a new home, and today was my last day at the Drake. I was training my replacement this afternoon."

"Ah. Does she look like you?" I joked. "Maybe I'll pay her a visit."

"No, she's a big blonde." She was about to give me a soft karate chop, only I intercepted and made her do it again—hand held at a proper angle.

I covered my mouth, yawning. "Oh, a big blonde. Might have to switch gears for that." I studied her frankly in the lamplight, my head cocked. "You don't look so Japanese anymore, anyway. You've changed."

"No, I haven't."

"Yes, you have."

"Maybe you've changed," she countered. I said maybe I had, at that.

"What did you do with all your Japanese stuff? Your books, your Eiji Okada poster."

"They're in storage."

I frowned. "Won't you miss them? Or they'll miss you?"

She stretched and nestled her head back upon a pillow, then turned to me almost demurely.

"Don't worry," she said. "We'll all get back together someday."

"How about the cordial glasses?" I persisted. "The ones I gave you."

"I've entrusted those to a friend." Her face brightened. "Then when I come back I can fill them up with some real Italian liqueur. Won't that be nice?"

"Have a shot for me," I urged.

She nodded. "Of course."

We remained so, neither of us initiating any action. Sober as I was, I felt no sparks. She was leaving tomorrow; I kept dwelling on that. It should have propelled me on, spurred me toward one last thrill, but instead it had only filled me with a sense of numbness. She was waiting, ready and willing as always, but I couldn't do it. It was as if my lower regions had been anesthetized. Finally I patted her knee.

"I appreciate your telling me in person. From you that's a great gesture."

"Are you tired?" she whispered.

"Yes, sort of. *Heto-heto:* dog-tired. Sorry. Not much of a farewell night, huh?"

"Oh, we'll see. . . ." She leaned over and began kissing my throat, even biting it, which usually got me started. Slid her hand beneath my armpit, tickled, prodded, teased. Still I lay there, unmoving, only very lightly handling her neck. I just couldn't do it this evening, come away from her exhausted, stumble to the bathroom with urine burning through my penis like lye, have her leave me there, charred. Since this thing had had no dignity throughout, I felt it ought to assume some now. She pulled away.

"This is becoming difficult, isn't it," she said.

I smiled. "Afraid so."

"Would you like me to go?" she asked. I said yes. She hesitated a moment, then retrieved her jacket and gloves from the chair she had flung them on and went toward the door. Just like that.

"Gina, come back here," I called. "Please?"

"Yes?"

Her eyes were focused on me—although they were lazy, they never seemed to blink. Yellow-brown eyes, not plain brown like my own. Or coffee brown, like my wife's. I couldn't get Taeko's face out of my field of vision, in fact—it had superimposed itself over Gina's in a strange montage. I blinked; the image quivered; and I had to force myself to see Gina as she was: her jewelry, her knowing looks, the fine rims of liner on her lower lids, her high forehead, her larger, stronger arms and legs. She would have a fun time in Italy, this girl. She would have a fun time anywhere, because she had the right attitude. A wide-open mind. I took a good last look, then slowly pulled out twenty dollars from my wallet, all the money I had on me.

"For cab fare, nothing else." I pressed it upon her. "Because it's so late. And don't pocket it and take the elevated anyway." She laughed. "I don't want you to die before your trip. You have a lot to look forward to. Adventuress. Lean down, closer." She did. I tugged on one of her hoop earrings. Her eyes were now somewhat cloudy. She gripped my arm hard.

"Listen," she demanded. "I want you to take care of yourself, get yourself back together. Do you understand?" I nodded. She stepped back and put her hands on her hips, her flat shoes splayed firmly against the floor, her large mouth pursed tight; her entire body seemed to be fighting something off, perhaps a sentimental impulse. "I won't worry about you—I refuse to. You're a grown man, you can fix things up. You're able. I mean," she went on, "I know this is a whole other issue, but think of my uncle, who I'm taking the trip with. He's got cancer, he's got a death sentence. There's no second or third chance for him. He is *dying*. You are not. That should put things in perspective. It does for me. Do you understand?"

"Mmm," I said. Her words hit me like rain on a rock—I could perceive them, recognize them as good, no-nonsense advice, but they slid off me and away from my person; they did not penetrate.

"You just take care of your uncle," I urged. Was it really her uncle, I wondered, or was that a euphemism? And did it matter? I smiled again. "Make his last days worthwhile. Don't worry about me, please. Life goes on, in all forms."

"Don't you worry about me either," she insisted back.

"You?" I lit another cigarette, laughing with difficulty. "I'd worry more about the men you bump into—I hope they know 'the rules,' as you call them. You'd better be sure to tell them, straight out. Like you did with me."

"Of course. Now goodbye, Mr. Shimada. *Sayonara.*"

I nodded approval at her accent. Her *ear*. She paused one final time, before opening the door. "Don't I even look Japanese from here?" She laughed.

I squinted. "Eh, maybe. Maybe if you turned off the light." She made an obscene gesture, before slipping noiselessly out into the

hall. I could hear her footsteps and then the whoosh of the elevator
. . . and then I heard nothing. Absolute silence. All quiet on the
western front, except for my own slow breathing.

When I had energy enough to stand up, I munched a few of the
rice cakes she had left behind. There were no other remembrances
of her around, so I chewed at them reverently, thinking of her and
washing them down with a glass of tap water. What godawful
things—tough and tasteless and full of stale air. They were unlike
any rice cakes I'd ever known; no sweetness, no snap—more like
Styrofoam wheels. Poor Gina, fancying those to be authentic rice
cakes. Surely she deserved better.

She was gone; she was on the Lake Shore Drive at this moment,
no doubt, being ferried home, untouched. My last chance; perhaps
I had wasted it.

"Now you're really alone, Shimada," I observed, gazing out at
my city view. I licked some fibrous crumbs from my lips and turned
off the television, then fell forward and crashed straight into bed.

That night I had a dream that repeated itself over and over, like
a demonstration tape in a department store. I was young and rather
small, wearing my serge school uniform and sitting on a bench in
the school hallway, waiting for something. There was a woman
calling me—I knew it was my mother and could almost see her
smiling in the distance, with her round pleasant face, her pointy
front tooth like a tiny fang. But when I tried to go to her, I found
I could not walk—the speckled floor was slippery with wax. I fell
once, twice; my hands slipped, and I fell onto my chin. The wax
accumulated like butter between my fingers. "Stand up, Jun. Stand
up or someone will know you're sick," my mother urged. Still, I
couldn't do it. I demanded that she carry me, knowing that all I
had to do was ask. But she laughed and told me I was too old for
that, then she left, and although I yelled to her several times, until
my throat ached, she would not turn back.

In reality I had been in that very situation once, when I was
being sent home from school sick. My fever was so high it left

bruises all over my body, and my excitement at being sick and having a legitimate vacation from school was so great I could hardly walk. I could hardly contain myself—my mother had had to half drag me along the ground, laughing; I was sick for two weeks. I remembered it as one of the happiest times of my life—nothing to do but be waited on and lie in bed. "Sickness is our only escape, the body's vacation forced upon itself." My father had written that line. He knew.

I had never missed another day of school or work since those two weeks, never had more than a cold or a headache: I had always taken great pride in my health, and now I was falling apart. I realized then, in a corner of my subconscious, like someone whispering a secret, that I was doing it on purpose—drinking, not eating right, encouraging an ulcer: I was trying to give myself the excuse of physical collapse to get out of my job. I realized that during the dream—my thoughts were unusually clear. It was so obvious. I awoke, with a slow, calm opening of the eyes, to small harmonious things around me: the whir of the air vents; the beep of my alarm, which I mistook for a bird; sun slanting across the ruined bed. I stroked my cheek, beard very heavy this morning. Saw how the clock read 8:43—not 6:43, as I first thought. Of course it wasn't 6:43; the sun was too strong. I bolted up, wild-armed; I had mis-set the alarm. If I did not hurry I was going to be late for Blue Lakes.

I ran around in a circle for a moment, like a dog after its own tail, not quite sure what to do first. Shave—no, that was out, however much I needed it. Shower—no, forget it. "Shit, shit, shit," I muttered, rushing into the bathroom and washing my face and hair at the same time. I found a new polo shirt, ripped the cards and pins out of it, transferred everything in handfuls from my trench coat of yesterday to my windbreaker of today. Threw a hanger across the room to vent my frustration at having overslept, scrambled down the hall past breakfast trays being wheeled to various rooms and wished I could be enjoying one of them. I held my temper with a lackadaisical cashier giving me an advance on my

Japan Credit Bureau card, then raced through the revolving door and straight into a cab.

Once in motion, I looked up, tried to relax somewhat, hastily composing an excuse. My heart was pounding so fast, straining; calm down, I urged myself, don't die, not over this. I took my own pulse. Sickness; I would use sickness, of course, as my excuse to Yamamoto—sickness was my only escape. I stared out the window, sighing. It was a beautiful day, blue skies, vague stratocumulus clouds like bird tracks. Perfect weather for golf, I thought, and then glanced at my watch. Perfect for golf or a hanging.

Lunch was being prepared, to be eaten out on the terrace. The smell of salmon grilling drifted from the small electric hibachi in the kitchen to the five of us drinking highballs outside. Mrs. Yamamoto, wearing some sort of translucent peach chiffon dress, had captivated Kurahashi just as she captivated all of Yamamoto's associates, and was continuing to engage him with a story of how she had once danced with Emperor Akihito. She was ignoring me. I took refuge in her silence and merely sat listening, quietly getting smashed, watching small private planes head for landing at Meigs Field. Hiroshi was not drinking but was instead nursing a bee sting he had got on the links; and Yamamoto kept wandering on and off the terrace, concerned with the maid in the kitchen and the performance of the electric grill, which was a test model. He felt it had a tremendous yuppie market. At one point, however, he laid a hand on my shoulder. It was the Grip.

"Shimada, come with me," he said.

I swallowed a fragment of ice. There was something ominous in his tone. I rose from my chair, noting Hiroshi's sharp look. Hiroshi knew what was up. At Blue Lakes, after I had finally found the group of them, Hiroshi had stood at the eighteenth hole, watching Kurahashi make his shot and pointing to my open-collar golf shirt. "You've got a mark on your neck," he commented dryly, eyes still fixed on Kurahashi.

"Hives?"

The mark, although I could not see it just then, turned out to be a bite from Gina, complete with two toothprints. I had not noticed it in my scramble to get dressed, although as soon as Hiroshi mentioned it, I had a sinking feeling as to what it was.

"It's from my dress shirts," I said, as evenly as I could. "They seem to be too tight in the neck these days—I must be gaining weight."

"Oh, really? Funny, you look like you're losing weight more than anything else." He smiled and handed Yamamoto the putter, caddy-like. Yamamoto glanced over at me, and I bent my head. Although Hiroshi had spoken softly, with that raspy voice of his, it was possible that Yamamoto had heard. The course was impossibly quiet—not even a bird song. As soon as I had a moment to myself, I fastened all but one of the buttons stiffly shut.

Now I hurried to follow Yamamoto, squinting a bit as my eyes adjusted from the bright outdoor sun to the filtered light within. I was a little light-headed, from drinking on an empty stomach. I had had nothing to eat since a corned beef sandwich at my desk the night before, that and what I could stand of Gina's rice cakes.

Yamamoto was leading me into his den. I caught a glimpse of Mrs. Yamamoto's room, the door of which was slightly ajar—I saw the folds of rouge silk, heard the finches, now singing loudly and flapping around their cage. Maybe she had told him, only warped the whole story and said it was I who had been the aggressor. Maybe that was the reason for this little aside; and if that was the case, I would walk right out there and throw her fifty-nine floors off the terrace. I clenched my fists in anticipation. Yamamoto stopped, so abruptly I walked into him. He entered his den, removing his shoes first (I did likewise), then sat down on the tatami.

There were several moments of the piercing stare, although in casual clothes Yamamoto was much less intimidating than in a business suit. He was, in essence, a frail man, with smooth, unlined fingers. My own hands looked more aged, and the skin itself seemed older, tougher. Yamamoto had the hands of a girl who put on glycerin and gloves at bedtime. He cleared his throat.

"Your illness today, Shimada—what exactly was wrong? I'm concerned about you. You haven't looked healthy in months."

"I, ah, my stomach. I was queasy all night, that's why I overslept." My fingers rubbed against each other as I spoke, as if I were priming dice. "I think it may have been food poisoning from a sandwich."

Yamamoto nodded slowly. "But you haven't been well in a long time, I've noticed. Your skin is very sallow, and so are the whites of your eyes. You're drinking too much, without eating. Is it depression over your wife?"

"Of sorts."

"Do you miss her?"

I focused on the woodwork behind him, smooth and brown, walnut. It reminded me of the color of Gina's hair. Suddenly I didn't want to be reminded of that. I thought of Taeko.

"I miss my wife, yes, and I miss my children. I also miss my home. I don't enjoy living out of a hotel."

"Of course. But we've offered you corporate housing several times, and you've refused it."

"Yes, I know," I said. I smiled, despite myself. "Unfortunately, as much as I dislike the hotel, I dislike the thought of an apartment even more. It wouldn't be a home, not like what I've been used to. I haven't lived by myself ever—I went from my family home to a dormitory to living with Taeko. It's a matter of adjustment."

"Yes. But people have adjusted to greater hardships, don't you think?" Yamamoto was cross-legged in almost a lotus position now, spine straight. This was after all his private room, where he practiced meditation and tai chi. His eyes were questioning. "I must say you're of a softer generation than myself; you don't remember the war. People had greater sacrifices to make, which brought forth greater effort."

Ah, yes, the famous *moretsu-gata* speech. Yamamoto was frequently upholding the virtues of the previous generation—the *moretsu*, like himself—versus the laziness of the "beautiful people" around today. I couldn't help but stiffen up a little at this, in defense. I had always thought of myself as more *moretsu* than beautiful.

"Your situation is difficult," Yamamoto continued. "But it isn't hopeless. One might think you would take refuge in your work, but I see your work has been slipping more than ever. Have you got a mistress?"

I bit my lip. "No," I said.

"Good. I advise you not to get mixed up in that, not if you ever expect to have custody of your children." He pressed his girl's hands firmly together. "Son, I've overlooked quite a bit where you're concerned these past few months, such as your lackluster productivity and poor attitude, but I'm afraid I can't overlook them any longer. You've got to shape up. Look at Udo: he had a broken engagement and was unhappy for some time, but he devoted himself to his work and now he's married to a nice girl, a schoolteacher from Nara. His mother arranged the whole thing."

And my mother's dead, I thought. Of course Yamamoto would throw Hiroshi in my face—he had established the competition between us; he knew all the soft spots.

"Udo never went to university, you know. High school men are much more cooperative, harder workers. University graduates are difficult—like you and your friend Keiji Narata. You get a taste of that academic life-style, skipping classes, radical clubs. You expect too much." He was pushing his tongue against the side of his mouth, as if he had something stuck in one of his molars. "Perhaps business is not your true calling, after all," he said. "Perhaps you're more like your father, made for the easier, intellectual life of the academic."

I nearly groaned aloud—this was the ultimate insult. Yamamoto and I supposedly shared a contempt for academics.

"In any case, Shimada, you've got to start using your head. The quality of your work has to improve, and you must pay more attention to your colleagues. You've been a virtual loner since you came to Chicago. Office relationships are important, as are punctuality and effort: I shouldn't have to *tell* you this, Shimada; you've always been a good employee in the past. I want you to move out of the Nippon and get an apartment, establish a place for yourself. Try to enjoy solitary living; many people do. Take home leave if you'd like, to go visit your children. Stop drinking so much, have a physical and perhaps some B_{12} injections, get regular sleep and exercise. We have a program for alcoholics at the company; you're aware of that. As far as female companionship is concerned, well . . ." He paused. "My niece Yoko is an attractive young woman, intelligent, unmarried. Why don't you contact her? I understand you got along well the night of the Peking Opera. Listen to me, Shimada, will you? This isn't a poison antidote I'm trying to give you, it's a formula for success. The values of the *bushido:* filial piety, a sober life, justice and integrity. Take it. It's a code you can follow all your life."

No, I wanted to say. The *bushido* doesn't work for me; I've left the clan. I am weak, I am tired, I don't want to play anymore. Leave me alone, please. You don't need me on your team.

But the words, like bile, were swallowed back into my stomach. My face was flushed; I said nothing in my own defense except, after several respectful seconds, "I'll try to improve my performance, sir."

Yamamoto nodded. "Very good, young man. You're important to us, remember that."

We both stood up—I had a bit more difficulty than Yamamoto, having just had my blood let—and we returned to the terrace. Yamamoto patted my back and allowed me to lead the way. Mrs. Yamamoto, eyeing me coldly as I sat down, spread her linen napkin across her lap. Yamamoto beamed.

"Let's eat!"

Kurahashi, after two or three bites, pronounced the salmon excellent. "Tastes like it was cooked over a fire," he said. "That's a fine product you've got—I'd like to have one for indoor grilling myself."

Yamamoto smiled, pouring a full glass of wine for everyone except me, for whom he poured out half. "We must get you one, then," he said. "The hibachi goes to test market in your western region first—people are more experimental out there, more attuned to an outdoor life-style."

"Our cook is quite skilled, don't you think?" Mrs. Yamamoto asked. "She used to be with the prime minister's house."

"Oh, yes," Kurahashi and Hiroshi both agreed.

Yamamoto laughed. "Then we brought her here and she married a Korean! Imagine that—somebody so used to refinement and elegance marrying a Hun of the Orient!"

They all laughed. I smiled, staring first at the outline of Mrs. Yamamoto's breasts through the diaphanous fabric of her dress, then down at my beautifully arranged plate: salmon, fluted crepes, vegetables in a flower-fan shape. I was having difficulty bringing the food up to my mouth; although I had been hungry before, suddenly I had lost all appetite.

That evening I called Gina from a pay phone. Just to make sure she had gone. The number had been disconnected; no further information was available. "Please make a note of it," the recording said. I did not.

Just for kicks, I rode the elevated to her apartment. I sat on the train with my eyes dulled, just like all the other commuters, staring only at the pictures of missing children and the beauty school advertisements on the panels overhead. The el seemed to rush through houses; it stopped and stalled frequently, lights dimming. I imagined myself following such a routine every day. I got off, as I had been instructed by the conductor, at a stop guarded by police dogs—lean, alert, wire muzzles over their snouts—then read the signs in English and Spanish prohibiting graffiti. The signs were covered with strange codes and conquistador emblems of the Latin Kings. I wished I had my camera to take a picture to send to Keiji. Keiji had always been a great fan of graffiti in New York.

I had never walked the streets surrounding Gina's apartment— I had always been in cabs. The area was a hodgepodge of things: Korean auto repair, Chinese cleaners, German apothecaries, *ta-*

querías, and a bar every block. As I turned her corner, a smell of wet feathers and excrement surprised me, as did the crowing of what sounded like roosters. I stopped. There was a live poultry shop on the corner; I tried to look in, but the windows were opaque with steam, and the smell was enough to make me sick. On the street, loose down floated everywhere. Dirty, a mulch of slush. This country was so determinedly dirty, ramshackle businesses all over the place, so much space. I kicked a Coke can full of feathers and continued on my way.

The windows I had stared out of on that first snowy night were dark and stripped of their rice paper shades. Her name was off the mailbox. I remained in the vestibule for a moment, thinking of how charged and nervous I had been then, how excited. How foolish. Looking for an adventure, I had found one. Trying to do something impulsive, I had stepped off the predetermined path.

I glanced up. A moth was circling the light, and I squinted at it, amazed. Its shadow was as big as a bird's. I went back into the street.

It had begun to rain, the first real thunderstorm of spring. I noted a strange odor and realized it was the smell of thawing earth. As I cut through the alley next to the building, I recognized pieces of Gina's furniture heaped by the Dumpster; amid Hefty bags and pizza boxes, I saw her weary futon mattress, folded over in a heap. It was as if I were seeing her naked corpse lying there before me, so much did I associate her with that bed.

And then the first pang hit me, the feeling of withdrawal. You see, it's quite easy to say, Oh, I'll stop drinking or smoking or taking those sedatives, when one is still full of their effect— perhaps even oversatiated by them. That is generally when the resolutions are made. The night before, in the hotel, with her there at my side, it was not so much of an effort to abstain, to think, All right, now this pleasure is going to be taken away from me, and I'll just have to learn to live without it. But here, now, by the compost heap of her belongings and alone, I truly realized what had happened. My insides knotted and my knees wobbled at the thought of never being able to touch that body again, those smooth, bony flanks, hips like a rocking horse. It was gone, she had really left, she had taken off. She had brought the senses up to the skin, quivering; she had stimulated all of those senses and then left them there, to flop around pathetically like creatures from an overturned aquarium. And I had so willingly become an addict; that was what depressed me most. I thought of her laugh. I could still hear the sound of my own moaning.

I had not loved her; she would not let you love her. In essence, I still loved my wife, and I believe Gina had known that. But I had taken to her with the same morose enthusiasm I now had toward alcohol, and now, as with the alcohol (which fortunately was still available to me), the dependence was showing its effects.

I began to drift, past laundromats and liquor stores, past gangs hanging out on the corner on a warm spring night. Once I had reached a main intersection, I flagged a cab and stepped into it gratefully. I had no desire to take the el train back—it had begun in a cab and should end in a cab, a brief adventure, as much as I was capable of.

I would not be coming back here anymore. As I bounced and jolted on the cab's sprung upholstery, racing through alleys, a million miles from home in this exhausting mishmash of a city— a war zone, a minefield—I seemed to feel my last tie with the hub of life give way. A chain spun around wildly, broken, disconnected; I lit the wrong end of a cigarette. At the odor of burning filter, the driver glanced back at me in consternation. He had a beautiful long gazelle's neck, a name of many vowels, which I could not pronounce. I heard tiny scratching sounds in my head like mouse claws—my thoughts, trying to get back in line—so many scrabbling little feet, desperate to march in unison again.

New cigarette, the filter soaked with saliva. It refused to light. I sucked on it anyway, sat sweating, my head between my knees. The air was so moist and warm, smothering, like a woman's breasts. It was hard to breathe. Where was I going? I had been on these roads before; I had done everything. Here in Chicago, a universe away from home, I felt pitiable—in pieces, smokeless in a cab, jittery and red-eyed: no better than a junkie who had just lost his best source.

◆

Promotions were given in May. I did not receive one. Although the excuse was offered that it was because I had so recently transferred I was not yet eligible for a promotion, I knew better. It was a slap in the face. Hiroshi was promoted to Special Projects Assistant. Since my own title was Special Projects Assistant, it was clear now that we were equals; I had no comfortable big-brother edge over little Udo anymore.

I sat in my cube a bit dazed that morning, too embarrassed to do much of anything else, then at lunchtime went for a stroll. The warm weather had finally settled over the city, and today was even more beautiful than it had been at Blue Lakes. I wandered midway across the bridge at Wells Street and stood by the rail, having a cigarette, feeling the rush of people and traffic behind me while I stared out at the murky river and the statues in the Merchandise Mart. Those statues had always bothered me—I could see them from the hotel. They were busts of eight prominent Chicago businessmen—Field, Armour, I didn't know the rest—set up on poles. The sight reminded me of guillotined heads on pikes, like illustrations of the French Revolution in history books. The sun was warm on the back of my neck; I felt I could stand there for hours, not moving, just feeling the surge of activity behind me, below me, while I myself remained stagnant. This morning I had found it difficult to invent three good reasons to get out of bed. It was rather pointless, except perhaps to eat or urinate. I sighed, wondering why standing on a bridge always produces such predictable thoughts of suicide, then I flung my cigarette out into the water and turned around to go back to the office.

There was a letter from Taeko waiting for me that evening. I opened it with a sort of eager nervousness—the last communication I had received from her, weeks ago, was very brief and curt, about the divorce. Since then a period of awkwardness had settled in between us. This letter was long, and I could tell by its small, timid characters that it had been difficult to write. I brought it over to the armchair by the window—the days were longer now, lots of bright light, even though it was still just fool's spring and we had had snow just the other week.

Jun:

I hope this letter finds you in good health. Mother saw on the news how it is still cold in Chicago and I thought of how you always walk around with your coat unbuttoned, no matter what the weather. Here it is quite pleasant and there are cherry blossoms. Sometimes it is almost dizzying to look at them and smell their heavy perfume.

Etsuko is back at school and doing well. She had some difficulty at first being teased because she had been in the U.S., but as time passes she seems to be adjusting. They were pretty cruel to her, calling her *gaijin* and ignoring her, but she is persistent and very proud that she speaks English better than anyone else. I told her that you would be proud too. She thanks you for the Ichimatsu doll that you sent her in advance for Children's Day. She misses you and asks for you often.

Omi caught bronchitis but is feeling better, particularly with the drier weather. He has lost a bit of weight, but you always said he was too chubby.

I have started painting again, out in the tea cottage. Since Father has stopped insisting on having formal tea ceremony out there, he has let me turn it into a studio. I am using oils more than watercolors, and dark tones. I think it is a reaction against the cherry blossoms, don't you?

I am sure you will be insulted by this letter, but I am sending it anyway. No doubt you hate me and have good reason to, but I want you to know I left because I was not a good wife and I felt we were both unhappy. You may tear this letter up, but please read it to the end. I do miss you. It is unfortunate that our society makes it all or nothing between two people. I am not sure what it is I want to do, but I do know I am happier here at home.

I told Etsuko that you might pay a visit this summer or that she might spend a week or two with you in Chicago. I promised nothing. I do not know how you feel about entertaining a child on your vacation, but she does ask about you quite a bit. You should see her. I think she is going to be *tall*, maybe closer to six feet than five, and these days she is all arms and legs. Extremely precocious. I was thinking of ballet lessons to give her good posture. Otherwise she may be a bit gangly, especially as she hits the teenage years.

I thought it funny the other day that Etsuko is closer to being a teenager in years than I am. I am fifteen years past all that, while she is only six years from it. It doesn't seem so long ago—I remember it vividly. How strange to feel yourself growing older. You know.

If you choose to write back I will be very happy. If not, I understand. I hope work goes as well as ever. There was an article about Mrs. Yamamoto in *Women's World*, with pictures from all her films. She is still beautiful, isn't she? I find it hard to believe she is older than Mother!!

Best wishes,

T.

She had run out of room on the page and not signed her name —only "T," the roman letter, which hardly like her. The tissuey paper had an oily feel between my fingers, and then I realized it was scented—not any true scent I wanted to have from Taeko, like the smell of her hair or the vague almondy odor of her skin, but still I sniffed it several times appreciatively and reread the pages until I felt a numbness pierce the cavity of my chest. What was it? Longing; no, it wasn't as simple as that. Humiliation, discomfort, embarrassment—that was more like it. The longing caused humiliation and embarrassment, which in turn produced discomfort. I thought of Taeko, how for so many years she had tried to be there, washing plates I had eaten off, folding my clothes, carrying a child I had launched into her body, bringing newspapers to the table, feeding me and the children and the dog, and now she was not there: it was as though a clock had stopped, an erratic one that had trouble keeping the correct hour, yet one to which I had turned impatiently for the time.

I folded the letter back into the envelope, wondering if I should call her or simply write back. She would appreciate a letter more, and it would save me the ordeal of direct contact, particularly with Etsuko. Later. Ironically enough, that very afternoon I had been glancing over a mention of the upcoming Children's Day in the corporation newsletter. It was just a brief account of the ceremonies, really just to inform the American employees of our customs, but it touched off my own recollections of the holiday and how my mother had hung out a carp flag every year in my honor. The flags were brightly colored windsocks—carp was the symbol for boys. I couldn't recall ever hanging out such a banner for Omi; perhaps Taeko had done it. He was only old enough to have celebrated two Boys' Days, and the circumstances surrounding his birth were indeed strained, but still he was a boy just like I had been. He deserved his holiday, he deserved acknowledgment. He was just a casualty of unfortunate human interaction, like I myself had been. Just a fat, shiny-faced baby who had already learned not to come near me because I was mean to him. I was *mean* to a baby. He had perceived that. I felt very sorry for us both.

It was almost dusk, muted blue and orange across the river, unnatural colors of a neon twilight. The first of the evening cruise boats was gathering people at the river's edge, trains clattered over the bridge, although I could hear nothing because the windows did not open—it was a hermetic environment, just like the office.

I stood up and poured a cup of sake, which I sipped cold. Sake was easier on my stomach than the hard liquor I had been giving it before, and in drinking it I did not seem to be disobeying Yamamoto as much, seeing as it was a "home" product. Amniotic fluid—a warmer effect. Within an hour I had killed three quarters of the bottle; within two hours I was nestled in the armchair, mouth half open, dead to the world, asleep.

My analysis for Yamamoto on health-care expenses, exquisitely prepared, received no comment. Likewise a summation of first-quarter activity for the board meeting, on his smooth black desk two days earlier than expected. Normally several comments or a curt "Good job" was given, but now there was only silence and another assignment. My work was dry and clinical of late, no "special projects." Just what I had always wanted. I wondered why it disturbed me so.

Hiroshi, on the other hand, was moving into the inner circle. Every time I returned from the copier or the washroom I would glance down the hall through the glass doors of the executive area and see Hiroshi's small body in Yamamoto's office, perched on the edge of the very chair where I had so often sat, about to fall on his face in rapt attention. The other Japanese staff members were noticeably indifferent toward me and had stopped asking me to lunch. At noon every day I would hide in the library area, pretending to be researching Standard & Poor's, waiting for their boisterous laughter to fade as they gathered and hurried to a nearby restaurant.

"Where is he?" I heard young Aoki ask once, standing over by my empty desk.

"Shimada? Oh, he's sobering up," Hiroshi answered snidely, and they all tramped out.

I had never been excluded from anything in my life. Belonging, at least superficially, had been as easy to me as the smiles and conversation that accompanied such efforts. But now I was on neither side—not the Japanese or the American—and I felt an unfamiliar sense of resentment. I took to having lunch back in my hotel room, so as not to eat conspicuously alone and in order to drink in peace and thus fortify myself to finish the day.

I began to understand how Keiji had felt and—as always on impulse—called him in New York. A receptionist answered the phone with a string of names and replied that Mr. Narata was in a brainstorming session and would be tied up all afternoon. I smiled. The girl's heavy Long Island accent made me homesick for a place that was not home.

One day I returned from a solitary lunch and found Hiroshi in my cube. I popped a Velamint into my mouth and stood angrily in the entrance. Hiroshi grinned and explained that he had been writing me a note, although it seemed to me that several things had been moved out of place on my desk.

"Did you want something?" I asked.

Hiroshi bowed slightly, more of a swaying gesture. His bows were meaningless. Behind the fine wire of his glasses, his eyes were hard and bright.

"I wanted to invite you to dinner, to meet my wife. She arrived last week and would like to get to know my co-workers. She's a wonderful cook, real old-fashioned. Please come."

I sat down at my desk, reclaiming what little turf I had. I could see very well now that all my project folders had been disturbed, rifled through, and very slowly and deliberately I began to put them in order.

The rasp voice continued. "It would be just the three of us; there's not much room. We only signed the rental agreement on our new house yesterday, so we'll be in the apartment till July."

Hiroshi's intercom was sounding—a summons from Yamamoto. He nodded apologetically and hurried off. I followed, watching as the little ferret gathered together whatever pertinent material he needed for the inquisition. A familiar enough pattern, although I myself never seemed to go through it anymore. I had been under the impression that Yamamoto was out of town all this week.

"Excuse me," Hiroshi said.

I raised my hand. "No, no, excuse *me*. I am unable to accept your invitation—I'm very busy, trying to keep up. You understand. Perhaps another time."

Hiroshi's mouth snapped shut. "Fine," he said. I walked away, face burning, and laid my head down on my desk. It was not very professional to refuse an invitation to a colleague's home. My thoughts spun in crooked circles. It was so damn hot in this place—didn't the air-conditioning ever work? Either it was freezing or I was sweating to death. The hermetic world of skyscrapers . . .

Exactly five minutes later, my own intercom buzzed, and I jumped up guiltily, startled. Had Hiroshi really told on me—said I wouldn't come to his house for dinner? Idiot. I straightened my tie and slipped on my suit jacket, ate another Velamint, then strolled as slowly as I possibly could into the executive area, making sure not to use the handle and instead leaving a lone sweaty hand-print on the smooth glass door.

Mori, upon seeing me, frowned, which was her customary greeting for all in-house staff. I felt some relief over this: had she smiled at me or been courteous, it would have been a sure sign I was getting the ax. She was furtively eating peanut butter and crackers at her desk. Poor Mori never seemed to get to take lunch.

"Udo's still in there," she said. "He'll be right out." She took a quick sip of tea and resumed typing, while I sat down on the reception couch, eavesdropping—Yamamoto's door was ajar.

"Find out what the rent is on the thirty-eighth floor and the amount of space available. I think we should move Personnel and Purchasing down there and expand the corporate area. Also find out how much it would cost to have new phone and computer lines put in. Then add a receptionist—we'd need another receptionist. Find out what we started the one here at, and . . ."

I closed my eyes. It was almost a relief not to have to be in there myself, although this was a fairly easy project. Hiroshi bustled out. I wandered in. Yamamoto was eating gumdrops, discarding the green ones in a separate pile.

I cleared my throat. "Excuse me for interrupting, sir . . ."

"That's all right." Yamamoto was smiling. "Just a quickie—to invite you to my niece's graduation dinner this Saturday. It'll be just the four of us."

"Very good," I said. I was very popular today—so many invitations. Yamamoto was still up to his tricks with his niece, obviously.

"And your birthday is Sunday," he added. I flinched. "We'll have to celebrate both occasions."

He resumed with his gumdrops. "I think we'll go to Spiaggia's; both ladies will like that. How about you make a reservation for six P.M. And say, Shimada, have you decided on an apartment?"

"Yes," I lied.

"Where? Chicago Towers?"

"Yes," I lied again. Chicago Towers, like the Hotel Nippon, was owned by a Japanese development company, which in exchange for free electronic equipment provided Yamamoto with free space. There was no place I despised more than Chicago Towers, a hideous elliptic building with boxlike apartments, only three blocks from the office. From my cube of a home I could run to my cube at work. I squirmed a bit at the thought of it.

"Well, it's about time," Yamamoto said. "We'll get busy on arranging things. Oh, and Shimada, one more question . . ."

"Yes?"

"You are going to the promotion celebration tomorrow after work, are you not. It's always good form to show support for your colleagues." He smiled acidly.

"Yes," I said.

A red gumdrop fell to the floor; Yamamoto made no move to retrieve it. It lay there on the magnificent Persian carpet—a panic button I did not have the guts to push.

"Leave it be," he said. "The cleaning people will get it." He smiled again. "You're looking better, Shimada, I must admit. See what a difference healthy living can make?"

"Yes," I lied, one final time, then turned and clicked my heels together, imitating Hiroshi.

As much as I wanted to, I could not hate Hiroshi. Yes, he was ambitious; yes, he was ingratiating; but nothing he had earned in the past months had been the result of dishonesty or deceit. We were oxen, yoked together: I was slacking off, falling apart—he was merely shouldering the load. I realized as I watched him hard at work, stepping into Yamamoto's good graces, that perhaps other men had once resented me in the same way. I sensed that the week of promotions would be my last. I decided to step aside, gracefully, before I rolled into the ditch.

Hiroshi acted hurt at my refusing his invitation to dinner—he did not even look at me as he walked back and forth past my cube, skimming from one task to the next. I had always liked his walk —quick, quasi military: not the real march of a general like Yamamoto but rather the way dancers portray soldiers in ballet. Perhaps he was once a gymnast. Oftentimes, when he thought no one was looking, he did silly, endearing things: karate jumps into an empty elevator; munching on plum buns or candy bars hidden in his desk; and while his English was not great, nobody imitated the Chicago accent better than he did, like a parrot: "Oh, I gatta getta brat-woorst; I hadda taste fer one ayl day. . . ."

I approached his desk cautiously at day's end, the dark seal head bent over a copy of *World Press Review*, its cover story "The Japan Problem: It Will Not Go Away."

"Udo," I said. "Want to get a drink?"

He blinked in confusion, and I remembered being more familiar with his face, before it had become the comic mask of My Enemy—we had actually been friendly once.

"Well, I was just finishing up here, but . . ."

"Good," I said. "Then let's go."

He slipped into his small coat, draped neatly on a hanger in his cube, followed me out to the elevators and continued to walk behind me even after we had reached the lobby. I knew he was suspicious.

It had been a month since I'd agreed to socialize with anyone from the office.

"Where to?" he asked. I suggested a karaoke bar farther uptown, and together we made our way against the swarms of people let loose from their jobs, all charging along frantically toward Northwestern station.

Once seated at a window table in the bar, I immediately ordered a drink. I decided to take it easy that evening and start with beer. Two men sat in the corner, each with a big bottle of Suntory, and I knew that was what I wanted—my nerves were singing out for it, like crickets in the grass. Hiroshi asked for the same, along with a plate of tempura and tuna maki. The air was blue and smoke-filled. We recognized several people we knew—from Yamamoto, from Kansai Bank and Financial—and we nodded. There seemed to be more American executives than Japanese. It made sense. Karaoke bars, with their video toys, had become quite popular of late.

I took a long draw off my beer and grinned at Hiroshi, who looked back at me with his head turned, one eye squinting, like a boxer.

"Congratulations on your marriage and your promotion," I said. "You're a new man."

Hiroshi acknowledged the toast, then snapped his chopsticks apart and began to attack his sushi rolls, first dipping each in horseradish paste. I envied his appetite. Even when I was hungry I did not like the fish in this country—it had a metallic taste.

"Not eating?" he asked, mouth full. I picked a breaded carrot petal off his plate and held it under my tongue without chewing, in the way I imagined people took communion wafers. I enjoyed watching him savor his food so much—the quick up-and-down motion of his pointed chin; how he closed his eyes gratefully with each swallow of beer, then lit a cigarette and sat back, taking long, siphoning puffs.

"You know, I tried to get in to see Kroft three times today about the software project, but his secretary kept telling me he was in meetings." Hiroshi shook his head. "These guys here, these Americans, they sure have a lot of meetings. You can never just go at an idea, straight away—they keep on forever, all this power play. That's why it takes so long to get anything done."

"Yeah," I said, without much interest, although I knew what he was talking about. We often joked that an audience with the Pope would probably be easier to get than ten minutes with any high-powered American executive. And the elusiveness sometimes seemed deliberate—an establishing of self-importance. Giving you that "you're here on my turf" feeling—"you're here and you play by my rules." Here was where individualism reared its ugly head: corner offices, car allowances, protocol. Such things were discouraged at Yamamoto America, but still they persisted; essentially, no matter how well we pretended to work together, we remained two very distinct groups, each showing great interest in the other's culture yet deep down convinced of the superiority of his own. After all, we had been enemies not so long ago. The whole thing seemed rather extraordinary, almost like two large animals who have been trying to kill each other all their lives suddenly forced together into a zoo cage to mate.

I refilled Hiroshi's glass, transfixed by the way the orange and green floodlights from the karaoke area shot through the amber liquid.

"How's your wife liking it here?" I asked.

"All right, I guess."

"No complaints?"

Hiroshi shrugged. "She's not one for complaints, or excitement either, really. She's very even-tempered."

"That's a good quality."

"Yes, I know," he said. "Hey, isn't that Hashimoto?"

We began watching those singing along with the karaoke speakers, some swaying back and forth with microphones in groups, some doing solos. "My Way," "The Great Pretender," "Mack the Knife"—the choice of titles was extensive, hits from the fifties, sixties, seventies and eighties, country western, standards. You were provided with a sheet of words and the microphone, and then your voice and the background music were broadcast together. Hashimoto, a surly, dark-skinned guy with a cowlick, was struggling with "Surfin' U.S.A." It helped to be drunk. The bleat of pachinko machines from the downstairs lounge cut through the laughter and the intermittent pauses in the songs. Hiroshi and I were drinking plum wine now, out of red lacquered cups. I raised my cup to him, and he raised his, but it was an empty gesture—neither of us seemed willing to offer another toast.

"Again, to your new marriage and your new responsibilities," I finally said, then added, "You've become the opposite of me, riding the up escalator while I'm on the one going down."

Embarrassed, he knocked his drink back quickly and measured out another, spilling a little onto the oval tabletop. Hiroshi was not much of a drinker—maybe because of his size; I don't know —and up against me in my current alcoholic marathon he really had no chance. He was beginning to slip, ever so slightly. His gestures were wider and more abrupt; his face had a troubled look, flushed.

"You're just going through a bad period," he said. "It happens to the best of us—you have to fight back."

"Could be." We each took another cup of wine. I felt very warm and generous from the heat of it within me, a potbellied stove. Hiroshi pressed his palms down against his knees and moved up onto his haunches, into what I had dubbed his forward-diving position, the avid pose he so often took while listening to Yamamoto.

"Yes, you have to snap out of it, Shimada. You can't become sloppy and fall apart—look at all you've done."

"What's that?"

"Are you fishing?"

"For compliments? Hardly." I took one of his cigarettes, as I had neglected to bring my own, and Hiroshi jumped with matches to light it, so abruptly I was startled. "Thank you," I said. "Such a gentleman."

"No, you're the gentleman. Gentleman Jun."

"Oh, yeah?" I didn't like the way he had used my first name, insidiously; I did not want a familiarity between us.

"Yes, you are. You have something I can't ever seem to grasp, a grace, even now. I don't know how to explain it." He sighed, removing his glasses and slowly massaging his eyelids. "I resent you, you must know that. Everything I've had to work for comes to you naturally, but you don't care—you don't realize all you've got. Like you were born rich."

The host came and refilled our cask of plum wine, smiled and bowed deeply, then walked off with a strange, penguin's gait. Hiroshi gulped down two cups before I had a chance to touch my own, so fast he upset the arrangement of lilies between us with his motions.

"Easy there," I said. Grains of yellow pollen were scattered all over the table.

"Huh. What do you know?" he said.

I smiled. "Not much."

He swung his head around, blindly. "I'm short, and small," he exploded, motioning to himself. "At home it wasn't such a problem, but here I'm ridiculous. Do you know how much I weigh? One hundred twenty-five pounds, and that's the most I've ever been in my life. People laugh at me; I hear it. Women treat me like a monkey."

"The women treat us all like monkeys here," I said, although I was thinking with a bit of forlorn nostalgia of Gina and her tolerance. Still, I wanted to make Hiroshi feel better. "They think we have no dicks."

"No, not all of us. Some of them look at you; I've seen it."

"Oh, come on, Hiroshi. You have a wife—what are you complaining about? I'm so good-looking my wife left me, remember?"

"And you speak better English; nobody makes fun of the way you talk."

"You can improve your accent."

He continued, trancelike. "Just yesterday I asked one of the secretaries if I could borrow a pencil, and then I smiled and thanked her for it. Well, then her stupid blondie friend who had overheard came by and said, like I wasn't even there, like I didn't even exist, 'At least you could find one who's better-looking and can speak English.' Imagine that—like I didn't even exist!" He broke off, bitterly, and pressed his cheek against the slightly fogged window of the bar. We were facing the street, a view of a man panhandling by a bus stop. "Yamamoto likes you better too," Hiroshi said. "He always uses you as an example."

"He's pitting us against each other. Competition produces results, especially in unfamiliar surroundings."

"No, he likes you. I'm his mule."

"Udo! Do you know what Keiji Narata used to call me? Yamamoto's bag carrier! Think of that. We're all mules. Besides, Yamamoto's a fair man. He rewards hard work. Who got the promotion?"

"But that doesn't mean he likes me as much. Or respects me, the way he does you. He's even giving you his niece."

Although I had been deflecting his remarks easily, one by one, that particular arrow passed so close that I frowned.

"He's not *giving* me his niece; we've only met once. And from what I understand, you had the chance before I did."

"Except she didn't like me, I was a joke." He chewed at a bit of green onion left on his wood-block plate, as if to fuel himself. "Your self-pity kills me, you know that? How dare you start to slip? You just don't realize; you take everything for granted. You never had to bust your ass like I do, to get a job, to get a wife, to get people to take you seriously. I never went to university, I never had connections."

"Are you implying that I did?" I asked. He ignored me.

"Did you get beat up at school?"

"Well, for awhile, yes, but then I—" I had been about to say, "but then I got taller."

"Well, I had the shit beat out of me till graduation. Till the very last day—they got me in the cloakroom after the ceremonies. What do you think of that? Oh, fuck." Our wine cask was again empty.

Hiroshi pushed it away, muttering, and flagged down a passing waitress, who wore a light spring kimono.

"Get me a Scotch," he said. "I'm sick of this piss water; I want a real drink."

"Hiroshi," I warned, "don't mix the grain and the grape."

"I *want* a Scotch." The waitress nodded and turned to go. "Hey, she's not bad," Hiroshi said, squinting. "Nice hips."

The girl was pretty but also big-boned and tall. I suspected she might be Korean.

"Bring us some rice too, and some pickles," I told her. Hiroshi was going to need some sort of blotter in his stomach; he was falling apart, joint by joint, before my eyes.

"I don't want rice," he snapped.

"Well, I do—two bowls' worth. Aren't I allowed to eat?"

"Actually I would like some nachos," Hiroshi said, suddenly quite sad. "But I don't think they have them."

"Eat the rice instead."

Hiroshi got up and followed the girl, on the pretense of going to the bathroom, and while he was away I watched the sushi chef behind his glass display of fish prepare the evening's dishes. So methodical and absorbed, chopping, rolling, garnishing; he took a puff on a nearby cigarette between orders or stood waiting with a calm grace. I wanted very badly to be him at that moment, with such an important yet uncomplicated job, a dignity. To literally put food on the table for people. No, maybe not as a sushi chef; maybe something more adventurous. I did not like to cook Japanese food much myself; I liked to experiment. But still I could see myself standing there in the white garb. Why not me. He probably slept like a stone every night.

Hiroshi sat back down, and then our waitress returned with two bowls and Hiroshi's drink. He gobbled up his own bowl of rice as voraciously as he had attacked the sushi before, and then he ate up mine as soon as I pushed it toward him. Next he went for the Scotch. His eyelids tightened at the first taste, and he struggled with it, glass tilted but not swallowing, until he flung his head back and drank it in one bolt. It was a full drink, neat. Even with the rice inside him he was going to be sick.

He gasped.

"You know what I think," he said, when he had his wind back. "I think you're letting everything go because you never earned it in the first place. That's what I think. You just don't know how lucky you are," he sneered.

"Them's fightin' words," I replied, and made my finger into a pistol.

He was goading me now, trying to get a reaction—his small face eager, like a child looking for someone to play with.

"You're just afraid of losing your rival," I said. My calm was maddening to him, I could see that. I was using the sushi chef for inspiration. Hiroshi's jawline stiffened into a hard underbite.

"Shimada, have you—have you been listening to me at all? To a single word?"

"Of course I have. Shall we go?"

Horns blared between us—they were playing that song "The Lady Is a Tramp." I couldn't remember the words but knew they were something about Harlem and pearls and Chicago being damp. The crowd started shouting out the Chicago lines in boozy chorus. I turned back to Hiroshi.

"I appreciate the pep talk," I said.

"Pep?" He looked at me, incredulous, rising. "Oh, I've had it with you, Shimada," he sputtered. "You're worse than a woman."

"That's right," I said flatly, then smiled and poured him into his coat.

His wife was waiting for him in their apartment on floor twenty-five of Chicago Towers, or the Honeycomb, as I had taken to calling it. I had thought the night air would do him good, only I had to more or less drag him all the way. Hiroshi had a certain reluctance to return to his wife and was pulling the dead-leg trick children so often use when they don't want to go to bed.

He clutched at my sleeve as we entered the ficus-filled lobby.

"Remember—remember the time we went tie shopping, you and me and Ikeda? And then we went to Rush Street and then we watched those porno movies on the VCR?"

"Yes," I said.

"I'm wearing that tie now, see? And I remember your tie was paisley too, only when you held it up against your suit, the salesman said that you looked so distinguished. Remember?"

"Uh-huh," I said. This was from a long time ago, my buddy-buddy days with the group.

"Don't you see what I mean?" he said, desperate, no longer clutching at my sleeve but clinging to it with all his might, so that we both leaned sideways. "My tie was almost the same, but he said nothing to me. Don't you *see?*"

"My tie had blue in it, and blue's my color. That's the only reason," I said. Hiroshi groaned, exhausted. I straightened the ties in question, first mine, then his, then allowed Hiroshi's wife to take him away, so apologetic for coming down in just her bathrobe and slippers, her hair in pigtails, murmuring sweetly, bowing, her fine eyes tired behind thick, black-rimmed glasses: The Salary-man's Wife.

The following day I did nothing, on purpose. For me to do absolutely nothing at my desk was even more difficult than finishing all the piles of work, but I stuck with it. I completed the crossword puzzle in the *Tribune*, and when I was through with that I did the one in the *Sun-Times*, along with the Jumble. I read the dictionary, word-hopping, then took a very long lunch break and walked to Burnham Harbor to watch the sailboats. When I returned, Hiroshi was there, a little pallid but still operational—I heard the whir of his calculator through the partition between us, listened to him talking on the phone with Yamamoto, who was in New York. I listened to the typewriters, the copying machines, the water cooler. I contemplated the view of the west side of the city from my desk: trains and burned-out buildings, the golden domes of Ukrainian churches. I sketched my own hand, in idleness. No guilt managed to penetrate.

Hiroshi came over once, to see what I was doing, then quickly
darted away. He returned again later with some bean jelly candies
he had got as a wedding present—they were shaped like tiny
cakes—and gave me a number of them, presumably as a peace
offering. I ate them slowly, one by one, as if my only purpose in
life were to sit and savor their mealy taste. "Resign," I said to
myself, and drew the character for "resignation" deftly on a scratch
pad. To resign; to resign oneself to . . . to what? I departed at five
with the nonexecutive staff—the secretaries, the customer service
people—leaving poor Hiroshi to watch the sunset from our common
view and to finish his fifteen-hour day; poor Hiroshi, now running
a solitary race.

◆

Saturdays. Now that Gina was gone, I had no idea what to do with
them—the weekends sprawled before me like a vast desert, sparse
and unpopulated.

I had struggled with a letter to Taeko all week, but each attempt
sounded stiff, like a business communication. I felt a new affection
for her, touched not by any hope of reconciliation but rather with
forgiveness. I retrieved her photo from my suitcase, a shot I had
taken last summer—Taeko holding Omi, smiling beautifully, one
long curl arranged like a vine tendril down her shirtfront; Omi
smiling to the point of squealing, wearing a little pair of overalls
and nothing else. I set it on the nightstand, next to the photo of
Etsuko and the portrait of my mother. Stacks of newspapers and
magazines littered the floor; my slippers waited under the bed.
Cigarettes and sake, a box of saltines and a jar of jam: strangely
enough, this hotel room I had always despised was becoming a
home.

I dialed the number of my in-laws and waited. Saturday evening
in Tokyo: I imagined the glare of televisions everywhere, cars
streaming along the metropolitan expressways, millions of lights.
Here it was so dim—I always seemed to be squinting. I wondered

whether the lights were brighter in Tokyo because everyone there had darker, denser eyes.

Taeko answered—her low-pitched voice so distinct from her mother's, high and oversweet.

"Moshi-moshi?"

"Hello, old woman," I said.

"Jun!" She sounded almost as she had when I'd first known her, a note of enthusiasm combined with shyness. "Did you get my letter?"

"Yes. Thank you very much."

"And how are you?"

"All right." I glanced at myself in the bureau mirror, naked except for a pair of boxer shorts, unshaven, drinking sake out of a coffee cup. My ribs were showing, but my stomach was distended. Just that morning I had been vomiting. In the squalid room, I had closed the blinds to keep out sunlight, and the air smelled stale, of dirty laundry and cigarette smoke. Saturdays. "I'm quite fine," I said. "I was glad to hear from you. I don't hate you, Taeko, not anymore. How's Cho?"

She laughed. "He's okay. He had a tick on his ear, but Father burned it off."

I snapped the waistband of my shorts. "And your boyfriend?"

"Excuse me?"

"Oh, come on, Taeko—do you talk to him anymore?"

There was a soft pause, then a sigh. "No."

"I'm sorry."

"No, you're not. But I'm fine. My back is much better—I've been taking acupuncture treatments. That and the painting have been great therapy. Also I've joined an art society—we meet weekly. Happiness is found in the contemplation of beauty."

"No joke. Don't give them any money," I said.

"Oh, shush."

I asked her about the sketch she had done of me when we first met, hoping she might send it as a gift, but she explained that it had been lost for years, before we were even married.

"I might have thrown it out," she added.

"That figures," I mumbled back.

"Excuse me?"

"Nothing. Look, you tell Etsuko she can get on the plane all by herself and visit Daddy this August. That's her birthday present —I'd love to have her. Omi can come when he's old enough, if you think that's right."

As I had expected, Taeko was dissolving into tears. "Don't cry," I said. "This is expensive."

"I'm sorry. Are you—are you living in a house?"

"No, still at the hotel. I'll be in an apartment soon. I can't wait to get back to being a cook."

"Really!" She laughed. "You were always better than me. Send me some recipes."

"Sure." I sat on the bed, staring at her picture. "How are the proceedings?" I asked. She had said nothing about the divorce in her letter.

"In review. It takes a long time, even uncontested. You haven't changed your mind?"

I hesitated, wondering if she had, thinking of how easy it would be to pull myself out of the dumps, back into the old life. One word would do it: yes. I looked at my *rōnin* reflection again, watched it mouth the word "no." There had been problems with that life too. Besides, I wasn't ready, not just yet. Somehow I had to flounder out of this on my own.

"No," I said, aloud. "No, I haven't."

Silence. "Neither have I, Jun."

"Well, that's that, then. But you tell Etsuko what I said, and tell her to study hard. I don't want to talk to her just now, you understand."

"Yes."

"And give my best to your father."

"I will."

"And keep on painting."

She laughed again. "But what about your birthday? Who's taking care of you?" she asked coyly. "You must have someone else."

"No, old woman, I'm a mess. I'm going to spend my birthday in a bar."

"Liar."

"Goodbye now."

"Goodbye! Call again soon!"

I hung up, drained by the performance. But it was somewhat refreshing to me—I had not bantered with Taeko like that in years, and the prospect of having Etsuko for a visit would drag me through to at least August. I lay back against the bedsheets and balanced my sake coffee cup upon my bare chest. Outside the door, the hum of a vacuum sounded in the hallway—the maid making rounds—but I had put the DO NOT DISTURB sign on the knob. All right, the call to Taeko was accomplished—one less thing to do. Taeko wanted to be my friend, not my wife. Hiroshi had my job, and a wife, whereas I couldn't even hold on to a mistress. The next day I would be thirty-one, born in the Year of the Dog. Dogs are modest and honest, loyal and dutiful, yet wary of everyone, including themselves. Dog tired, doggone. Oh, well. You must accept the star you are formed under.

Now the only question was, What will drag me through today?

By five P.M. I was feeling quite ill. Chills racked my body. I was sick again in the bathroom, betrayed by both ends, and as I held my head between my knees, I was surprised by the cold sweat— like condensation on porcelain—covering my skin. I had nothing left in my stomach but bitter sake to throw up, and soon spots of blood appeared. My bones felt as if they were coming through the flesh. I lay on the floor in an S shape, bewildered into thoughts of dying.

What if I did die: what would it mean? Would they call it suicide? Would they say, He had no other choice, he comes from a suicide chain? Up front it would be just the death of a salaryman, and many people would attend my funeral; salaryman colleagues of mine would be upset and realigned with their own mortality, but what would it really mean? I had accomplished the right things, yes, stored them in my bomb shelter in tall stacks, but now I was hiding behind them like a petrified mouse. Yamamoto would be impersonally sad, as if he had lost a man in battle; Mrs. Yamamoto would sigh as she contemplated her own face; Taeko would feel guilty; Keiji would be angry; my children would cry and be frightened for a month or two, then forget as other months and life impressions pushed the earlier memories away. Doctors would do an autopsy on me, because I was so young. Perhaps they could use my corneas and ventricles and whatnot; with a little bit of flushing, my kidneys and liver could be redeemed. When they cut my heart open, they would find an underdeveloped muscle, flaccid. There would be a box inside full of expensive but useless objects—watches without stems, Mont Blancs with chipped nibs, silver lighters without fuel—beautiful things without function, which had ceased to work. Melted down or stripped apart, these would be worth money for their various elements, or they could be repaired by someone who found joy in junk.

I remained there, shipwrecked. At some point there was a knocking on the door, and although my first impulse was to ignore it, I realized that probably no one would knock again for a long time, and if I really was dying, I needed help.

"I'm coming!" I croaked, flushing the toilet first and pulling up my underwear before walking, doubled over, to the door. It was the longest walk of my life. My teeth were chattering so hard I bit my tongue twice.

A woman in blue stood before me, radiating perfume. I recognized the smell even before I could focus my eyes on the woman herself—sweet, funereal. Mrs. Yamamoto. I fell toward her involuntarily, like someone being taken out of the electric chair, and saw her hold her gloved hand to her mouth, either in horror or because of my own, sour smell.

"Shimada-san! My! What's the matter with you? I thought you'd be ready to go. We're all downstairs in the limo, waiting."

But the strain of answering the door had been too much for me, and I blacked out. Vague sensations of pleasure ensued at the touch of a woman's hands all over my body, wiping me clean; I lay there obediently, allowing myself to be washed and stroked like a prize racehorse.

"Poor darling, look how thin you've become. Let me take care of you; let me call a doctor; you'll be all right. Just relax. . . ."

I flinched, weakly, beneath her fingertips. It had been so long. I had even stopped bathing much these days, so as not to focus on my own nakedness or feel the touch of soap against skin. Several harsh voices, male, invaded my peace. I came to again to the sickness, to being buoyant on a stretcher amid the murmur of an astonished cocktail-hour crowd, to the wail of a siren, which made my throat hurt. The smell of Lysol and vomit. A nasal woman, Southern. *What's his name?* Yamamoto's cold reply. *How's that spelled?* A needle in the ruined muscle of my ass. The dream of being in the school hallway, with my mother calling me, which seemed to be the only dream I had left.

I awoke to the squeak of rubber soles on a floor. There was a tube in my arm, pale-green curtains all around, and I was wearing a paper gown. A nurse, young, very pretty, black, was placing a strip of plastic on my forehead.

"Hello, Mr. Shimada," she said. She had a space between her front teeth. "How you doin'?" The plastic strip was a digital thermometer, which she threw away. "One oh one point six. Fever's gone down, at least."

I stared at her, vaguely embarrassed. "Why am I here?" I asked.

"Oh, you're just run down. Malnourished; you got a virus, alcohol poisoning, and an aggravated ulcer. You're a mess, but you'll be all right." She smiled. "You'll just have to stop working yourself to death. Now take your meds and go back to sleep."

I sat up, accepting two pills and a paper cup full of water.

"Meds?"

"Medications. Muscle relaxants and Tylenol. The IV drip's 'cause you're dehydrated. You need to get fluid back into your system—and I mean the *right* kind of fluid."

"Have I been here long?"

"Six or seven hours. Your friends left—the Japanese couple. The young lady who came with them had to leave too." She smoothed my sheets taut, then placed her hands on my hips. "No parties for you; you need rest."

I swallowed the pills with difficulty; my throat was scraped impossibly raw. My voice sounded like Hiroshi's now, a rasp.

"How long will I be here?" I asked. I was so tired. Already the heavy sleep was reclaiming me.

"Only a few days. We'll need to run some metabolic tests, do a cobalt for that ulcer. I don't know if you'll have to detox or not. You'll be all right. Nice vacation in the hospital, nothing but lying in bed." She glanced at her luminous watch, yawning. "Get some rest now. I'll see you in a bit. My name's Didi, okay? You got a call button at your side if you need me."

I wanted to thank her, but she drifted away and became nothing but soft light. Still I heard the sound of her voice floating in the distance; it had replaced, very easily, the sound of my own thoughts.

No visitors were allowed as I slept for twenty hours, interrupted only by Didi and by another nurse, whom I did not like as much, Jane. With each drop downward in sleep, I felt more and more of my soul come back. Once I opened my eyes and saw my father on the bed, lounging and smoking a cigarette.

"You can't smoke in here," I said. "People are sick."

My father merely smiled. He was wearing the kimono he kept for writing, its sleeves tattered. My father was so good-looking: hair shoulder-length; round, double-lidded, almost Caucasian, eyes; brooding lips. He appeared to be drugged.

"Don't stay here, Junichiro. Find your own retreat. I don't want you to live that life anymore."

"Oh, shut up." I tried to kick him off the mattress, but the IV held me back, tethered. "Go away," I said. "You don't know anything about life; you can't tell me what to do."

My father's eyes were half-slits, suddenly framed by colored glasses. His voice was sad and wailing, muffled, as if coming through a tin can. I remember thinking how much he sounded like the ghost in *Rashomon*. Even in delirium I keep track of my details.

"I was born on the day of the Tokyo earthquake. . . . I was never meant to live in the first place." He smiled again, a thin stream of spittle spinning from his lips. "I'll take Veronal, you know that. A fool's life has an early death. I'm not strong like you."

"Coward," I said, though I was shaking. "I hate you."

"No, you don't."

"Yes!"

"But you're following in my footsteps."

"Stop that shit! Go away! I'm not like you at all."

"Oh, but yes." He smiled, slowly. "Yes, you are. You'd better get used to it." He lay back on the bed as if to sleep, still smiling, and no matter how violently I kicked at him, he would not budge. The weight of him became so great the room seemed to tip forward. He began to moan softly, until I squeezed my own eyes shut, afraid to open them again, to hear anything further he might have to say.

When I did open my eyes, there was a man in the chair by my side, another man, dozing slightly, one thin leg crossed over the other. Yamamoto. I had never seen his features in repose before, and I struggled to get a better glimpse. His mouth was childishly sweet. I wondered how he had slipped past the nurses—it was still early: even through the heavy hospital drapes I could sense the grayness of dawn. His eyes opened and mine closed. He made a quick coughing sound and caught his breath, then I felt his hand on my forehead, index finger and thumb on either temple, pressing lightly. Humpty-Dumpty, plucked from Buddhist hell, that was me, here with the king himself trying to salvage my shattered egg's skull. "You're my real father," I wanted to say, for both his benefit and my own, but the words stuck in my mouth like bean paste, and I had to go back to sleep.

"He's the cutest man, my Japanese boy. Last night he was whinin' for a kimono. Isn't he adorable? He looks just like a little doll, with those long eyelashes."

I laughed at Didi, despite myself. I had just had juice after two hours of tests, then a bowl of wallpaper-paste oatmeal while I watched *The People's Court* on TV. Colors were so bright, smells so strong, noises clear and sharp—it was as if I had been retuned. At nine the phone rang, and although I was not sure if I was supposed to answer it, I did so anyway, just to stop its loud trill.

It was Yamamoto. "Shimada. How are you feeling?"

"Better, sir, thank you."

"You gave us quite a scare, you know."

I thought of him at my side in the chair. "Yes." I gestured emptily with the phone. "I'm sorry I ruined Yoko's celebration. Please apologize for me."

He cleared his throat. "You're a good man, Shimada. I want you to take a month off, nothing but rest. Don't worry about the office; we'll be fine. You just concentrate on getting back your health. There's a wonderful spa outside Montreal—hot springs, tranquil atmosphere, everything. Perfect replica of Kinosaki. Would you be interested? I'll have Mori make reservations."

Kinosaki. That was where my father had killed himself. It had to be a joke, of the thickest, blackest humor. But Yamamoto was serious—he went on with descriptions and flight details. I gave up. This was not a vast world, a planet in the universe, it was merely a Hollywood set. In reality there were only about five cities, with fifty or so true inhabitants; the rest were all extras, there to fool you, paid by the hour.

"Thank you, sir. I'd welcome the cure," I said. I noticed for the first time two large floral arrangements on either side of the room: mums, roses, phallic purple tulips with black stamens. A Happy Birthday card. So I had spent my birthday unconscious.

"Take care of yourself, son. My wife will be in to see you tomorrow. And all of us from the office send our best."

I hung up, depressed by the sound of tenderness in his voice, at the recurring image of him seated next to me the night before. Now he was sending his wife to see me; Mrs. Yamamoto, no doubt already preparing for the visit next day: the perfect outfit, the perfect disconcerting gestures to embarrass me with. I sighed, glancing down at myself. Small bruises the size of peas dotted my arms and legs.

Sickness is our only escape, I thought. I wished I did have a kimono, dark with vertical stripes, like my father's, because it was so drafty in here and because the stiff hospital gown had begun to chafe me intolerably, suddenly, like a hair shirt.

◆

My stay at Kinosaki North America—KNA—set somewhere in the Laurentian Mountains of Quebec, was paid for by Yamamoto, as were my plane fare and my hospital bill. When I returned from this retreat and felt strong enough to go back to work, I was to participate in an alcohol abuse program, this, too, sponsored by the corporation. It was a comforting and stifling feeling, like a mother's love. On the flight north, I closed my eyes from time to time, peaceful at the knowledge that someone cared for me, but then I would force them open immediately and try to dredge up anger that I could keep on with this womb-to-tomb existence.

The resort was a perfect replica of its prototype, the traditional hot springs, not the yuppie *onsen* playgrounds with massage beds and neon waterfalls. From what I had heard, here the springs were artificially stimulated, effervescent, but the main lodge, the gardens, the pine forest surrounding, were all just as beautiful as the original, and just as conducive to meditation. I had a small room, white-walled, wooden-floored, with just a tatami mat, a lamp, and a closet. In contrast with its spareness, we were provided with big feather pillows, so densely packed your head did not make an imprint. I hugged mine at night. All personal gadgets such as

watches and radios and pocket calculators were taken away: con-
fiscated, to be returned upon release. All Western clothes were
taken also, and each person given a *yukata* and cotton undergarments. The *yukata* you had the whole time you were there, while
fresh undergarments were provided daily. My robe was pale blue.
The ends of its sash were discolored, bleached, as if the previous
wearer had been tugging on them nervously with sweaty palms,
again and again and again.

We lived in separate quarters. I did not see any women, besides
the maids, who were all older and nothing more than efficient.
Contrary to the camaraderie encouraged at work, here we were all
solitary except for meals, where the almost monastic aura of the
place inhibited conversation. There were six of us who ate together,
regularly, but I could swear I saw others—different faces—on my
walks by the carp pool or in the garden, and when I went to and
from my own room I counted more than six pairs of slippers outside
the other doors. I wondered why we didn't all eat together; I wanted
to know those other people too—perhaps one of them had the
answers I needed. I asked the friendliest maid if there wasn't some
sort of conspiracy going on, but she just looked at me with an
incredulous smile and said it was easier to serve food in shifts.

The food was very simple traditional fare: fish, rice, tea, *yōkan*
and pickled radishes, *dashi* broth made with kelp. No coffee or
sweets. I had not had food like this consistently since I was a small
kid. My diet had deteriorated since then, in the past year especially, my palate dulled by sugar and salt and alcohol, so much
so that at first the food tasted bland and I merely picked at it. But
on the third or fourth day, after ambling through the chill of a
mountain twilight, I sat down to dinner with relish. I tasted an
oyster, so fresh it seemed to quiver for a moment in resistance
before sliding down my throat. I sucked on a bit of ginger root that
had escaped pulverization in the sauce; felt the old familiar tight-
ening at the back of my tongue at the true bite of cucumber rolls
in sesame oil, vinegar and soy sauce.

"This isn't fish from New York," I said to Murakami, the only one of my six companions with whom I had formed some sort of conversational relationship. He was a vice president at Soroban Leasing, late fifties, heavyset, with thinning hair and calm, untroubled eyes. I seemed to be younger than every other man there. Whenever Murakami passed me outside or joined us at the table, he greeted me as "kid." Rather than finding it patronizing, I warmed to him right away.

"No, it's flown in," he explained, examining one of his own oysters by holding it up between his chopsticks, dripping with brown juice. "You tasted the difference, didn't you. You tasted the Japan Sea."

We ate fish for breakfast as well, along with the usual dried plums and a raw egg and rice. This was difficult for me, because no matter how fresh or sweet the fare was, I still preferred Western food in the morning. Murakami seemed to notice this and nudged me with his elbow as I stared down into my plate.

"I bet you'd kill for a doughnut right now, wouldn't you?" he said.

"Oh, yes," I groaned, jokingly. "And some coffee with powdered cream!"

"*Powdered* cream—well, I can't say I'd ever miss that."

"I do. It's one of those tastes you hate at first but then you grow to crave."

He laughed, nodding, but ate his food enthusiastically nonetheless, along with the others.

I tried very hard to find my health. I searched for it under rocks, in trees, in the center of my sushi rolls and in drops of glacier water. Still, I remained tense despite the peaceful surroundings. Panic wires had overcome sinews in my body, leaving me with a sluggish nervousness, a feeling of obligation: I should be getting better, I should be getting better. My head seemed to be full of the insects that swarmed outside my windows, my thoughts black bats that flitted from corner to corner. I remember no dreams during this period. Before, there had at least been that one about my mother, but now there was nothing, only deep dark sleep pricked with starlight, as dense as the sky itself.

Lonely and bored, around ten P.M. of my sixth evening there I wandered down to see Murakami, who was reading in his room, feet tucked into the *kotatsu*. The nights were chilly here. I peered in at the doorway, requesting permission to enter, then joined him by the small brazier. He was more settled in his room than anyone else, with books, the brazier, even an armoire full of clothes. He had been smoking a pipe, and spirals of heavy fragrant smoke floated around him, flattening into nothing as they reached the crossbeams of the white ceiling. That was the unusual thing about this place—while its practices and foods and patrons were thoroughly Japanese, its lodgings were not. I decided to ask Murakami about it. He seemed to know everything about this retreat: every shrub and bush, every pebble; who was who; that it was owned by the Japanese Business Association and that corporations paid dues for clublike privileges.

"Oh, didn't you know?" Murakami explained, calmly as always. "This used to be a monastery, until about forty years ago. There was a terrible homosexual scandal affiliated with it—they found all sorts of interconnecting tunnels to the rooms, love letters, you know. The poor men . . ." He nudged back his glasses, then successfully swatted at a mosquito on his arm. "Ah, full of blood—my blood, no doubt. I thought I felt him get me on the back of the neck before."

"No wonder I feel a little repressed," I said. "Seeing what the history of the building is."

"Oh?" Murakami asked. "Are you feeling repressed?"

I hedged somewhat. "I don't know. No and yes. I'm not feeling any different, except stronger, and sober. There's still that strangeness, though, that—"

" 'Indefinable anxiety'?"

"Yes, you could call it that."

"That's a quote from Akutagawa," he said, smiling.

"The writer?"

"Yes. He used it to describe Japan's state of mind after the 1923 earthquake."

I hid my face in my sleeve, yawning. It seemed that no matter where I went, the same tedious facts continued to dribble out of the mouth of some person quoting a writer.

"Well, that's how we used to feel, perhaps," I said. "We feel no 'indefinable anxiety' anymore—we aren't in fear of the West as much. We have our own position and our identity."

"Yet you complain of anxiety," Murakami said, teasing, but I wriggled out of it.

"Only because I'm not *good* enough to be Japanese." I laughed. "I've had my spine broken by the West. Besides, indefinable anxiety is universal, like ennui or angst. Let's not give Akutagawa all the credit."

"Who was?"

"I don't know. You."

"Oh, Shimada . . . ," he said, softly. In fact, "soft" was the key word here—Murakami seemed to be too soft and refined to be vice president of a leasing corporation, where the hard sell was everything. I began to get nosy.

"What are you here for, anyway?" I asked.

"Me? I come here every year, on retreat," he said vaguely. He closed the book he had been reading, a translation of Boccaccio's *Decameron*, with Japanese demons and victims on the cover, and stared back at me. "I take two vacations—this one, and one with my grandchildren."

"Your wife?"

"My wife's dead."

"Oh, excuse me," I said.

"That's all right. She was sick for many years, so when she did die it was a relief. For everyone, I mean, particularly her. She was too strong to die in pieces. How about you? You've got a wedding ring."

I explained my situation, then, after outlining the trouble at work: "You're right; it is indefinable, I guess. Nothing happened

—I never made a grave mistake or insulted anyone. I wasn't fired. I just stopped performing, that's all. Slowly but surely I . . ."

"Ran out of gas?"

"Yeah, that's it. Engine trouble; sugar in the tank." We both laughed lengthily, until I decided to continue. "I feel guilty, though, being here. The company's paying; I'm supposed to re-cuperate and recharge and come back better than ever. But I don't see it coming; I won't even try. When I think about my job and what I used to do, I simply want to go to sleep. Do you suppose it's temporary?"

"Perhaps." Murakami stoked the brazier gently, a poker in his pawlike hand.

"What do you mean, 'perhaps'?"

"Do you see yourself doing any other work?" he asked. "Have you ever wanted to be something else besides a businessman—a composer or an artist; something unusual, like a parachute jumper?"

"No."

"You have no wild dreams? No fantasies to get out of your system?"

"No." I then thought a moment, remembering my night out with Hiroshi at the karaoke bar. "Well, maybe to be a chef." I frowned. "But it seems ridiculous to waste my education, to become a chef." I felt disappointed, that I was so lifeless and uninspiring a com-panion. I forced myself further. "You see, I've done nothing true with my life; I see that now. I'm afraid to take risks; I had no wild dreams because I felt it was frivolous to encourage them. So I bypassed them, took the safe route. I tended to view it all in black and white: to go off *that* way, toward art or music or parachute jumping, was to be unsteady all your life. I wanted security—you see, my father was a writer, and he was always miserable; he made a career of it, eventually killing himself. There's that proverb— it's in our office manual, and I'm sure you've heard of it—something about how a busy man has no time for depression. My father thought too much, he was too introspective. I didn't want to be like that;

I didn't want to worry about the effort of individual striving; I wanted to be given a nice, safe path, and I would follow it. Besides, I don't think I have much of a creative spirit, and that's fine, that's all right. But now I see I don't want to be in the corporate army anymore; I want to lag behind. I'm not a good soldier—I don't care about the campaigns and the camaraderie and the decorated uniforms. I've lost everything I've built up, so why not try a different approach?"

"You mean desert?" Murakami said, cheeks flushed and shiny from the fire. I, on the other hand, was squatting on my haunches, shivering.

"I suppose so, yes. I still want to work at something, of course—work is important. I don't want to go on welfare or anything like that."

"This happened so suddenly," he said. "Don't you think it possible you are being a little hasty?"

"Did it happen suddenly?" I mused, half to myself. "Or was I just too busy goal-jumping to notice. To *keep* myself from noticing. We become jolt junkies, I see that—we get jolts of sugar, jolts of salt, sexual rushes, alcohol shots, meet this deadline so you can get on to the next, promotions, bonuses, superficial conversations, thirty-second attention spans . . ."

I launched, abruptly—like a garbage disposal backing up—into my theory about crammed geese, which, having read an article about French cuisine on the plane, I had used my leisure time at KNA to formulate. Just as certain geese are "crammed" or stuffed with food in order to engorge their livers for the richest pâté possible, so I had been crammed—not with food, of course, but with facts and goals and objectives: all through school and university, to pass one exam after another; then further, at work, with more facts, personal data about fellow employees, information on contracts and other companies, phrases of English, knowledge about cities, states, airports, international business practices, information for Yamamoto to prepare his speeches and reports; then in my own life—American brands, how to be a good consumer, base-

ball statistics, what tie to wear with what suit, lovemaking tech-
niques, parenting tricks, makes of cars and golf equipment,
periodicals, journals, what movies and books to discuss, finance
charges, routes, maps, addresses, chunks, scraps, all gobbled up
by me as voraciously and stupidly as any goose. And here I was
with this tremendous liver to absorb all the aquae vitae I could
pour through it, the very stuff that was killing off the brain cells
and memory chambers that had bloated my liver in the first place.
The irony amused me, for a moment. It also seemed to amuse
Murakami.

"Ho," he said finally, winded with laughter and wiping his eyes
with his sleeve. "What an analogy, crammed geese. Maybe you
should be a chef, at that. You poor kid!"

"That's right." I smiled wryly back. "Poor kid indeed."

"At least you have a sense of humor about it. You don't see it
as the pursuit of knowledge, then. Rather it's the *consumption* of
knowledge. They stuffed you to death."

"Yes," I said. "And I'm no leader, I know that, so I never
applied it toward my own good, to advance myself. I only spit up
facts. I'm a bag carrier, a fetch man. I do what I'm told."

He looked at me thoughtfully, now serious. "You don't suppose
this is a midlife crisis?"

I shook my head. "Uh-uh. That was happening when I was
eighteen years old: *that* was the middle of my life."

"Yes, yes." He chuckled. "But remember, thirty is the old age
of youth and forty the youth of old age. *Sixty* is when the second
half of your life is supposed to start. You'll see how less fatalistic
you become as you get older."

As always after confession, I felt embarrassed. I apologized for
having taken up so much of his time, then rose to leave.

"Please don't repeat what I've said," I added hastily. "Just take
it as the ramblings of a self-pitying salaryman. I'm sure I'll be back
at work in a month."

"No, I doubt that." He motioned for me to sit down again, and
although I pretended to be tired and ready for bed, he was insistent.

I went back to my side of the brazier, this time closer to the heat. From a many-tiered box he removed a second pipe, identical to his own, and a calfskin tobacco pouch. "Ever smoked a pipe?" he asked. I said no. "Here . . ." He filled both bowls carefully and lit mine first, then his own. I had not even been smoking many cigarettes since arriving at KNA, and the rush went straight to my head.

"Let me tell you a quick story before you go. A while ago, before I came to the States, I knew an automotive section chief whose wife had died like mine, in a long, disfiguring fashion. This man had been quite successful up to this point, a Waseda graduate, hardworking, respected, but the death of his wife made him turn to alcohol. The alcohol killed his concentration—like you—and eventually he became so insubordinate he lost his job. Both his daughters were married and had lives of their own, and he felt no longer needed. A great weakness had overcome him, along with the alcohol, and he could not keep up. So he dropped out, he became a bum, out on Sanya skid row. You've seen men like him, right—of course, not so many at home as in the States, but they exist. This man wanted no more than his *shōchū*, that cheap shit, and an occasional charity meal. Wouldn't go live with his daughters, didn't want them to see him in such straits. He lay there in an old suit that had been tailor-made and drank, staring at the million people passing every day, on their way to work or family or whatever. Then one morning he saw a woman who looked frighteningly like his wife—so pretty and fresh—and she held a handkerchief to her nose and forced him to take a thousand yen. Something further snapped within. With the yen he purchased some gasoline, which he then doused himself with, setting himself on fire. It was a horrible, hideous death—he died before any police could reach him. The skin crackled right off his bones, like roast chicken. Imagine that."

I stopped puffing inexpertly on my pipe, now fully nauseated. Murakami added more tobacco to his own and tilted his head back; against the half-light of the brazier, his face had such a kind expression—it reminded me of netsuke carvings of Hotei, the god of benevolence and greatness of soul. He continued.

"I knew this man because I lay alongside him for nearly a year, brought down by almost identical circumstances. Fortunately that woman did not give any money to me, or I might have taken the same action. You never know. You get drunk and desperate enough."

"You were," I stammered, "you were . . ."

"A bum, yes. Kishi was my friend, or as good a friend as two drunks can be. After I saw him burn, though, I couldn't lie there anymore like that. Even in the army I don't think I saw anything so grotesque."

"You went back to your job?"

"I went back to a job, yes. I'm not with Soroban, no, although I was for twenty-three years. Now I work here. I manage this resort, so that perhaps people like myself or yourself or Kyoshi can have a place of refuge and contemplation without feeling a need to take more drastic measures."

The flame of Murakami's oil lamp sputtered on a bad piece of wick. I shook my head in confusion, then moved it from side to side.

"Why did you lie to me, Murakami?" I said. "Why didn't you just tell me outright?"

"Because you needed to think I was worthy of giving advice; you needed to see me as a senior colleague, not an innkeeper. And you had to speak first; you didn't need to be spoken to. You've had enough of that all your life. Goose." He chuckled. I did not. Instead I sprang forward and grabbed him by his shoulders, shaking him furiously.

"How could you let me run on like that, like an idiot!" I was screaming. "So stupid, so insignificant—nothing's happened to me that I didn't deserve. My wife's not dead, I wasn't fired; I didn't even fight in the goddamn war! You must have wanted to spit in my face. Such bullshit! How could you have listened to a word I said, with all you'd been through. Murakami!"

Although I was thrashing him so violently that my own neck was stiff, when I was through and slumped exhausted on the bare floor, Murakami simply fell back into his previous sitting position, like an otter. He propped me up and slapped me lightly on the cheek. I slapped him back. He slapped me again, with greater force. I pointed to his robe front, the way they do in slapstick routines—to get him to look down—and when he did I punched him under the chin. He brought the *Decameron* down hard upon my head; I pulled his ear. Finally we both began laughing, and I collapsed face-first into his lap. My laughter was desperate, more lung contractions than anything else. It shook me uncontrollably. I laughed for a long time, and so did he.

"Oh, shit," I gasped.

Both our pipes were lying over by the doorway, bowls down and burned out. My hair was sticking up here and there, in tufts. I imagined there should be blood all over the place.

Several minutes passed, maybe hours. Murakami remained motionless, his breathing so relaxed I wondered if he was sleeping.

I jumped to my feet.

"Why don't you have any geisha at this place?" I snapped, in mock exasperation. "So we can get laid—like in *Snow Country*."

He glanced up. "You read that?"

"I saw the movie."

"Do you want a woman?" he asked, quite serious.

"No. I was only kidding."

"It can be arranged. It often is, albeit carefully."

I realized the difference in our ages then, our separate generations of salarymen. Murakami was from the generation that frequented Turkish baths and hostess bars and went off on "sex tours" to foreign Asian fleshpots like Bangkok and Seoul. Not that my generation was completely innocent, but that sort of thing was less common. Infidelities were still frequent, but hurly-burly sex, the recreational stuff, was not so widespread.

"Are you sure you—"

I cut him off. "Yes. Let me just say that I owe you my life,

that's all." I bowed. "But I must go now, I really must. It is im-
perative."

He smiled slowly, suspicious. "Oh? Why's that? You're still
upset?"

"No. It's because I've wet my pants."

"Shimada!" Murakami sucked air through his teeth and motioned
to hurl his book at me again. "You slob."

It was true. I had laughed so hard, I had been so furious, I had
actually wet my drawers, which were now turning cold and soggy.
The maid would be repulsed. I did a little jig.

"Go tidy yourself up, Pisspot," Murakami said, then snorted.
He kept on laughing as relieved and almost weightless, I bowed
and minced with small shuffling steps sideways, out of the heat-
filled room.

That night I dreamed I had become the Yamamoto chef. I poached
an egg for Mrs. Yamamoto and fed it to her tenderly; I prepared
Yamamoto's fruit plates with exquisite skill. "Shimada's a wonderful cook," Yamamoto boasted to all his friends as I carried out
a towering baked Alaska. "We've recycled him; it was the best
we could do—I'm quite happy with the results. So go on, please,
dig in. . . ."

After the initial dip into the hot-spring bath, my skin puckered;
what few hairs I had on my chest stood upright slightly, alarmed.
But as I allowed the bubbling warmth to take over my body, I felt
myself almost dissolving. All around, the whoosh of wind through
the pines and new mimosa flowers, the moan of doves, the gurgling
of water against rock, continued and made me, temporarily, devoid
of any thought. I was a drop of water, a vein on a leaf; I was
integral, yet thoroughly insignificant. This was not a manic dis-
location, like the *ronin* feeling. This was a faceless peace.

I slipped down a bit lower, submerged to the neck. There were
lotus blossoms—probably flown in from Japan with the fish—
scattered along the spring's surface.

A heavy splash, followed by a thud, jolted my tranquillity. Murakami, with his Buddha breasts and stomach, had climbed in with me.

"Still thinking about a woman?" he whispered, sotto voce.

"Me? No, why?"

"You looked so dreamy."

"Actually my thoughts were so pure they vaporized. I had no thoughts."

He nodded, then we closed our eyes and soaked in silence for a half hour or so, until a maid brought Murakami's eyeglasses and some sake on a tray (only for him: he had proprietor's drinking rights) and reminded us, gently, that dinner would soon be served.

The meal was oysters cooked in miso and served on chrysanthemum leaves. I ate them with reverence. I knew this would be my last meal here and wanted to enjoy it as much as I could. I had already told Murakami I would be leaving the next day, and he nodded in understanding. The others knew as well, and after dinner all offered me their *meishi*, which I accepted with a hollow gratitude, as always holding the business card with both hands and studying it earnestly before inserting it into my case. I did not give them a card back, but this they also seemed to understand, which made the offerings they had made me particularly poignant. Normally you are nothing without your business card.

As I was getting ready for bed, swallowing the various gastric medications I was now on, Murakami stopped in to say good night.

"It'll be goodbye as well," he said. "Tomorrow the maids will give you your things—I'll be in town on business."

"On business . . . ," I echoed.

"Yes. It has been a pleasure meeting you, Shimada. I wish you the best of luck. *Gambatte kudasai.*"

Hang in there: that, in essence, was what he meant. I bowed. Tears were forming, slowly, in my eyes.

"Best of luck to you too," I said. "You're a very noble man. I hope you enjoy your second life."

"Likewise, likewise." He continued to nod his head, then his eyes met mine. "Good night."

"Thank you; I owe you much for your kindness," I called. There was no further reply.

I heard him going down the hall, Murakami-Hoiti, keeper of the hearth, padding, with calm determination, back to his permanent roost. Outside, wind shook the eternal pines gently, beyond the walls of a Quebec monastery now filled with Japanese.

◆

I had wondered often in my life what I would do if I ever committed a murder, where I would go next. Since the *rōnin* half of me had more or less smothered the salaryman with a feather pillow, I found myself faced with the same decision.

I felt a need to hide out.

Because Montreal is so close to New York and because they were not expecting me at the office for another week, I decided to visit Keiji. In the disjointed world of an airport I could be anyone, going anywhere. At Dorval I had a delay before my flight, and I went into the restaurant for a cup of coffee. We of course had not been allowed coffee at KNA, and I assumed I would gulp mine down at once, but as soon as it was actually before me, I had no urge to touch it. I sat and smoked instead, heavy Canadian cigarettes, listening to the curious mix of Franglish around me, nasal and melodic. The airport was done in aqua and white, and despite the fact that this was Canada, it reminded me of how certain cafés in Tokyo were decorated to achieve the American 1950s look.

It was early yet—I was pretty much alone in the place. I yawned but still did not touch my coffee. A very old man came over to the next table, assisted by a very young waitress. He was a little crazy, I think, with dingy white hair like a feather duster; he wore a suit but no socks on his scrawny ankles. He sat with a roll of the eyes and great pathos, and tugged on the arm of the waitress, to whom he still clung. He complained that his coffee was not hot. The waitress pulled away.

"*Il est très bien chaud, monsieur,*" she snapped, with that appealing bitchiness Frenchwomen have, and flounced back to her counter. She reminded me of Gina. The old man glanced down tragically, as if this were just too much to bear. I put out my cigarette, smiling. He glanced up again, seemed to pierce through me with a pair of blue eyes like fish milk, and muttered.

"*Japonais,*" he said.

I was surprised by his perspicuity—knowing I was Japanese. We faced off for a moment, in silence, and then I noticed how my own coffee was still steaming—I hadn't yet put in cream or sugar. The old man's mouth trembled. His whole universe was floating in his unacceptable cup. It was too sad. I got up and set my coffee in front of him, nodding.

"*Il est très bien chaud, monsieur,*" I repeated. "*Je ne touche pas.*"

I hoped he understood me. He hesitated, then wrung his hands together. I motioned for him to drink.

"Go on," I said.

He gave me a crazy salute, arm extended, which I hoped was a compliment; and as I left, he bent down and went at my cup with little pig-trough noises, slurping, as if he hadn't had coffee in years.

Such a simple gesture, yet it had made me feel so good. I had wanted to give him the coffee, and I had done it without a second thought. I was going to do that from now on, I decided, walking along. I was going to do what I wanted, from instinct, as long as it didn't hurt anyone. Want, do, be: one fed into the other. There seemed no reason to live otherwise. I paused at the boarding gate, taking out my ticket and trying to summon up a sense of purpose. I had to become more imaginative. I recalled a saying from somewhere: "the embarrassment of choice." I had never seemed to have this problem before, of choosing—the paths had been rigid and predetermined, and I had followed them quite willingly. Now there were no paths, except the one leading up to this plane. And there was no real reason for me not to do exactly what

I wanted to, except of course the embarrassment of not knowing what to want.

The offices of Peltzman Anderson Peck were surreal. Peach walls, red sofas and blue carpeting, paintings hung off center, blood orchids in green vases. A Dalí nightmare. I swam to the front desk.

"I'm looking for Mr. Narata, please," I said. The curly-headed receptionist glanced up from a copy of *New Woman*, smiled and informed me that Keiji had just gone to the men's room.

"A minute ago," she said. "Have a seat; he'll be right back." She took a quick breath. "Would you like some coffee, tea, Calm Time Decaf, Coola Cola, Diet Coola Cola, Sunny Meadows Fruit Juice, Big Apple Seltzer or High Cloud Mineral Water?"

"No, thank you."

Confused, I wondered why such emphasis on brand names, until I remembered this was an advertising agency. Samples of ads for all the brands she had mentioned hung in frames above her head. I studied them, while she went back to her magazine, pausing only to answer the phone, which rang every half minute or so.

"Very impressive," I said, between calls, pointing to the posters.

"Oh, yes," she answered proudly. "We're in the top five."

That meant they were probably number five. Still, I was surprised to see all the accounts they had, and to think that Keiji, born and bred in Japan, had so much to do with the American media.

I felt something like a gun in my back. I tried to turn around, but an iron hand gripped me and prevented my moving. "Give me all your traveler's checks," a voice commanded. I panicked—after all, this was New York—and looked at the receptionist, but she was laughing. Finally I wrenched free. Keiji was standing behind me, jamming a stapler into my kidney; Keiji, wearing a screaming Hawaiian shirt and a tiger-striped watch.

"Asshole!" I blurted, then glanced back to the receptionist in apology. "Oh, excuse me."

"She can't understand Japanese; don't worry," Keiji said.

He had gone through another transformation, it seemed. His hair was very short now, almost shorn, and his eyes were luminous in his thin face, no longer mud brown but gold. He fit in well with the cacophony of colors in the office. He blinked.

"Contacts," he said.

"Do they make everything golden?" I asked.

"Oh, sure. You look like a Brancusi standing there. You're wearing the same clothes as when I last saw you."

I nodded. I was indeed—the ratty pullover and my *rōnin* pants, mere fibers hanging to my lower half.

"So what brings you to this place, Shimada?" he said. "Job hunting?"

I shoved my hands into my pockets, full of Canadian change, and pawed my left foot back and forth.

"Not really. I just thought I'd visit for a spell and take some lessons on being liberated."

"You quit?"

"Not yet. But I'm planning to as soon as I write a letter of resignation."

"Always a rule man, till the bitter end," he jeered, though his voice was kinder than it had been before.

"Yes," I said.

"You want to stay with me?"

"If it's not an imposition. Be honest."

"No imposition. Come on, I'll show you where I work."

"Your receptionist is quite nice," I said, as we filed down a long hall.

"Patty? Yes, she is. I feel sorry for her, chained to that desk. She wants to be a copywriter. I don't know how she does it, answering that bloody phone all day long, saying 'Peltzman Anderson Peck' with any kind of enthusiasm over and over again. I can only assume she drinks heavily at night. Here we are. . . ."

He hung a sharp right, into a maze of cubicles with nameplates, an open area bordered by drafting tables and foot-high stacks of magazines.

"Looks like Yamamoto," I said, regarding the cubes.

"Look again."

The resemblance did end quickly. Each cube was very individualistic—people had clippings up, toy airplanes dangling, radios. Their attire was equally nonconformist. Some even wore shorts.

"We don't meet much with the clients," Keiji explained. "Therefore we can more or less dress the way we want. Creatives can, that is. This is called the Creative Area, where the ideas are hatched. I'm a Creative—that's my job title. Did you ever hear of such a scam?"

Keiji's desk was covered with neon highlighters and large pads of paper, a picture of Malcolm X and another of a geisha with the head chopped off, a goldfish in a small bowl, an aloe plant.

"The fish helps me concentrate when I'm blocked," he said. "And the aloe is for my paper cuts. I'm always slicing myself."

"Does the fish have a name?" I asked.

"Yes. Fabian," Keiji said.

Another Creative, hearing all the Japanese, peered over the edge of his cubicle and made a face at Keiji, pulling his eyes up into slants with his fingers.

"Hey, fuck off." Keiji laughed, not missing a beat. "This man is a visiting dignitary. Show some respect."

"Yeah, sure," the other said, and dropped back out of sight.

Keiji picked two flesh-colored things up off his desk and began playing with them.

"Earplugs," he said. "Goldman Earplugs. The client wanted a new slogan, away from what they had before—Sounds of Silence, which could imply any earplug—to a better identification with the name." He laughed again, savagely. "It was so easy, it took me twenty minutes. Silence is Goldman. I didn't even have to open my *Ten Thousand Clichés* book. Silence is goddamn Goldman."

"Your eyes are Goldman too," I said. I was still unsettled by their stare.

Keiji yawned. "Here, let me give you the keys. Same apartment, but better furnished." He wrote the address in bright pink. "Don't go anywhere till I get home, or if you do, try to be back by seven, eight o'clock. Otherwise I'll be locked out."

I accepted the keys and looked around one last time. Fabian was burbling at the water's edge, gasping for air. I felt useless; this goldfish seemed more important than I was. I had never been in an office I wasn't part of before, unless I was meeting someone else on business. It was a strange feeling. Keiji, perhaps sensing it, was steering me back toward the door. He had work to do, work he liked.

"You should probably take the subway; it's fastest," he said. "Just don't stand too near the edge of the platform, and don't make eye contact. You'll be all right."

"Will I?" I asked, vaguely.

Keiji hit me on the back with the heel of his hand. "Without a doubt, Shimada. You always land upright."

I left. I walked to his apartment anyway, some forty blocks. It was such a nice day, I didn't mind; and besides, I had plenty of time.

Keiji was unhappy, I could see that. He had his new job and appearance, yes, his uncensored channels, but a certain raw edge remained. He could not calm down. He spoke in short, clipped sentences, continually thrust his hand over his cropped head; he reminded me of the younger American men at Yamamoto—the jargon, the rapid-fire delivery, the minimal level of interest in the person he was speaking to. He talked about his job constantly— ads he had done, ads he planned to do: no matter what subject you raised, it all went in a circular motion, back to himself. There were grooves from his nose to his mouth, and beyond the flashy clothes he looked haggard. When he stopped jabbering, the lines on his face became more evident, the drawn look he had became almost frightening, and I think he knew this—he wanted to distract you with activity and speed so that no one would pick up on the shocking void that constituted the rest of his life.

I found it on the verge of unbearable for about two days. I tried to tell him about the hot springs—the food, the peaceful surroundings and my discussion with Murakami, how it had put things into perspective, but he kept bouncing the conversation back to work. His work was different, he insisted; he throve on it, it wasn't a trap. "Are you sure about that?" I questioned. "It sounds like you've become a little too engrossed."

He glared back at me sternly and replied how people who lived on mountaintops had no business telling others what to do. "That's unrealistic. The peace will last only so long, then reality invades again, so you'd better learn to confront it, head-on."

I couldn't reach him. I remember listening to him talk about his portfolio, watching his bony, intolerant face and thinking to myself that at some point even the best of friendships should be put to sleep. The thought saddened me, like a glance at a grave. Then the following day we got drunk together, and everything was fine again.

Alcohol and spirits. You might wonder, with concern, why alcohol is such a major and accepted part of our life, why every meeting involves drinking—heavy drinking—why being able to hold one's liquor and drink for hours is the sign of a good man. We are reserved by nature, that is why. Various internal valves, as in small aqueducts, control the flow of emotions. This is necessary, it is inbred from birth—you do not get to know a person in a day; a person is assumed to be complex and multileveled. Long-term relationships, business and otherwise, are encouraged. It is not stiffness or inhibition that holds us back; it is respect for the other person. Also, a real man does not become sloppy or belligerent when drunk—he merely lets himself open up some of the valves and makes others comfortable to do likewise. My limited success as a salaryman was based a great deal on my ability to listen—not to pry, but to sit and listen, and never to repeat anything that was said. Even with Keiji, my best friend, I knew not to push. I waited, propelling things only by drink, and drank along with him until he was ready to talk. I wasn't supposed to drink, but I felt I had to. It was like taking a trip with someone despite the fact that you're in no mood to travel; you go along because the journey will be a significant one and you know the other person does not have the nerve to go on his own.

The slow, dislocated drunk of the afternoon. We were watching baseball on TV, a Mets vs. Phillies game; there were quite a few people from Philadelphia within the New York crowd, wearing maroon hats and heckling loudly. Keiji had been in a funk all morning—sullen, glum. It was Saturday and he wasn't going to the office, a sacrifice for my benefit, as I assumed he normally went in Saturdays; Sundays and holidays too. He sat, eyes hooded, in a low-slung chair. His eyes were his normal eyes, behind glasses, though they did not seem to focus. His mouth was down at the corners, and he had not used it to say anything for an hour. It twitched slightly as he sat there, like the lid on a simmering pot.

I wondered what I had done. I made a few attempts at wisecracks, but he remained unresponsive, staring at the game and perking up only when the commercials came on. At the third inning I went out to Happy China Groceries for cigarettes and also bought a bag of pretzels and some beer. When I returned, I set down one bottle for each of us and put the rest in the old Frigidaire. Keiji took the beer without emotion.

"Thanks," he said. "I didn't want to drink in front of you unless you started. I thought it would be rude."

"No problem," I said, equally laconic. "I can drink beer; beer is harmless. It's whiskey and sake I can't handle."

"Okay," he said. We drank on.

I was sprawled on a chaise longue thing he had—my bed for the week—just wide enough to accommodate a slim person, although it was upholstered and padded and very comfortable. I was getting tired—having been off alcohol for three weeks, my system was hypersensitive. It seemed that this beer was incredibly fizzy in my mouth, little geysers around my back molars. I kept forgetting what brand it was and had to look at the label to remember.

"Oh, yeah—here we go!"

I jerked up and squinted at what I thought was the game, but we were watching a commercial. Keiji was slung forward in the low seat. He punched his fist hard into his open palm.

"I did this one, for World Electronics," he said. "Man, it was great to do work for the competition, just to kick Yamamoto in the grill."

The commercial was blue and black and white, oddly lit, with a Japanese woman in a body stocking descending a staircase of televisions, each with a different picture. Newscasts, soap operas, video games, a Bogart movie, a samurai flick. A cappella choir music in the background. Dreamlike. I couldn't help but be impressed.

"You're wasting your time with ads," I marveled. "Get into cinema—this is too good for a commercial."

I wasn't sure how he would take this, but he looked pleased enough. The smallest lift of the lips. The smallest twitch of those warrior eyebrows.

"I'll reach more people through advertising," he replied, started on his third Kirin, and then there was silence till the stretch.

I was falling asleep: I wasn't going to be much of a drinking partner today. I had walked all over the place in my three days in New York, through the safe zones, down Wall Street, up all the avenues—especially Park. I had always loved Park first thing in the morning—past the Yamamoto Tower in the shadow of the Empire State Building. I went to Times Square and looked up at all the Japanese billboards; had a coffee and a whole-wheat doughnut; went to Lord & Taylor to use the bathroom. I walked past the Pelican Bar and farther uptown to the Nippon Club and on to where I had spent my first night in Manhattan, the Essex House. I wasn't depressed—they were just places, areas I had inhabited for a brief while, and now I was walking away. Still, I felt somewhat ghostlike passing by them, surrounded by people rushing and running and waving for taxis. Cabs, another thing of the past. Cabs did not seem to fit in my new and low-paced future.

So I had walked until my feet were bloody stumps. Even now,

as I lay there inert, my calf kept throbbing rapidly, of its own accord.

"Can't hit for shit," Keiji was saying. "And these guys are so fat they can't run either. Look at the ass on that guy, and the gut. It's amazing they got him off the bench."

"Hmph." I felt myself drop a few levels, floating on my chaise longue. I dragged my eyes around the rest of the apartment in an effort to keep them open. He had new furniture in here, yes, some of it from my old house—the coffee table, the lamp. I supposed he had sold the rest of it, and good riddance. The best in electronics, precision quality; he had painted away the blotches and stains on the walls, put blinds on the front window, burglar bars on the back. It was more like a home, less like an airplane hangar. But ironically he appeared less at home than he had in its former barrenness.

My whole body snapped like a fold-up knife—that spasm you sometimes experience while you're drifting off—and I almost fell. The television was remarkably loud.

"Are you frightened?" I heard Keiji ask.

"No. Just falling asleep."

He laughed. "I mean of going forward, finding a new job."

I used the beer to prime my mouth and with effort said yes, maybe a bit. The words were hard to pronounce. As I said them, I felt the indefinable anxiety return again, just a tiny prick, like a draft hole in one of the valves of my heart.

"You'll be all right," he reassured. He was hunched forward now, smoothing his hand over his shaved head. His voice was muffled.

"You keep saying that with such confidence," I complained. "That I'll be all right. What makes you so sure?"

"I know you. You have a way with people, you accommodate. You're a fish out of the main stream now, that's all. You'll jump back in. But I'm very proud of you for what you did—I am, goddammit. I never would have thought you'd have the courage to quit."

"But it's all talk now," I insisted, modestly. "I haven't *quit* quit yet."

Keiji was slumped over, spineless. It was a most uncharacteristic pose.

"You've quit in spirit. That's really all it takes."

"You think so."

"Yes, I do."

The afternoon was like an old tourist boat chugging around a harbor. The game dragged into extra innings. A little time passed. I turned sideways. Keiji was staring at his wrists.

" 'A fish out of the main stream,' " I asked. "What did you mean by that?"

"Precisely what I said."

"That I'm so conventional?"

"No." He got up loosely and swiveled the TV away from the setting sun, which was throwing a glare on the screen. Every time he moved, his bones cracked. The front of his shirt was tucked in, but the tail hung out. I wondered if that was deliberate. He frowned.

"What I meant is that you *can* swim in the main stream without fighting it. Parts of you incline in that direction."

"Such as?"

"You have a wife."

"Had."

"You had a wife; you'll have another. Maybe you won't, I don't know, but at least you'll be with women. Women and wives are acceptable. You'll have children to populate your life, you'll have a network."

"*Had* is the proper word," I stressed again.

"You still have them; they're not dead," he snarled. "You can put a picture of them or of a woman on your desk at the office, and everyone will think you're normal. That you function right. That you must have fucked a woman at least twice in your life."

I had woken up fully now. I began to react slowly and cautiously, as if a wild bird had landed on my shoulder.

"Aren't you happier now?" I asked.

"I'm doing my work, yeah, that's something. I can justify myself with that."

"But?"

"But what? Socially I have no life. I have no close attachments—my profession doesn't allow them. It's too cutthroat. I have a lot of acquaintances. There's no one I can trust as a friend. You have to understand the nature of New York life, paranoid. That's bad enough, but single city life, homosexual city life, is worse. And to be Asian on top of it. I'm prey to so many weirdos, and others you might feel safer with you just never know—there's too much disease. Understand? I'm very fearful, though I act otherwise."

He was not looking at me as he spoke. When I replied, I did not look at him. It seemed easier, that way, to say things. It seemed easier not to have any sort of expression.

"Isn't being in an ad agency helpful, though? A better atmosphere?"

"Better? It's jokeland, satire all day long. Joke, joke, jab, jab. It's the nature of the beast—I mean, look at most advertising, how it stereotypes people, how superficial it is. That's okay: I exploit that. I've got my finger on the pulse. I join right in in the fag humor, because I don't want any Achilles' heels for them to hit." He paused, then slowly mouthed the beer bottle, contemplating it. "I just want them to say, Damn, that bastard's brilliant. And you know me, how closed off I am. I'm like an alien—hydroponic. I don't even have a network from the past. It's tiring at times, tiring and pointless. You become subterranean within your own body. Even if I turned straight, I'd still be alone—it's the nature of my beast."

"Turned straight?" I repeated.

"Most unlikely," he said. "If anything, as a very last resort, for convenience. If I were starving to death."

For some reason I felt relieved over this, although it only per-
petuated his problem. But for Keiji to imply compromise would be
more disturbing than anything else. I would have really begun to
worry.

"Maybe it would be better in another city," I offered. "Where
you could at least get the paranoid burden off your back. A friend-
lier place, like Chicago. Surely there are ad agencies in Chicago."

He took off his glasses and pinched at the red welts on either
side of his nose, as if he had a headache. Exposed, his eyes had
a blurred, angry look.

"No, I don't think so," he said. "Not like New York. New York
is the ad center—you know, Madison Avenue."

"Then you could be a big fish in a smaller pond."

He chuckled. "A smaller main stream? Nah. I've never been
one for that. I think you should go to the top. I think you should
stand in the screaming vortex of it and let it rip you limb from
limb."

I sat up, and as my feet touched the floor they stiffened at the
prospect of more walking.

"Shimada?" Keiji said.

"What?"

"Let's drop the subject."

I let it go, as lightly as I had received it: the bird on my shoulder
flew off with heavy wings.

Keiji stretched and yawned. "I'm buzzed," he said. "I've drunk
three times as much as you. Want some coffee?" I nodded. Keiji
went into the kitchen, where I heard him put the kettle on and
measure out two cups' worth of instant grounds.

"So what are your plans?" he asked. "You're not going to stay
here and be my houseboy, even though I'd love to have you hang
around and cook. What's on the horizon?"

I gestured slackly. "Dunno. To go back first and tie up loose
ends. To deal with Yamamoto."

Keiji howled along with the teakettle. "Uh-oh. Fate worse than
death. But after that, then what? That's what really counts."

"I suppose I'll get a job and start over?"

"What sort of job?"

"Maybe translating. I would enjoy that, and there's plenty of work. Or I could always flip hamburgers."

"Oh, yeah? Where?"

It was good that he was voicing these questions, the same questions and in the same pattern that I asked them of myself. I never answered them, though; I only came up with more questions and more alternatives until my head ached.

"Chicago," I said.

"The scene of the crime? Why there?"

"I like it, and I know how to get around. I like the lake, all the different ethnic groups. It's so different from home. It's a cheaper city than New York, but there are just as many jobs. It's big enough to get lost in, and there's always plenty to do."

"But you could go anywhere you wanted now; you say you have no ties. L.A., Paris, Budapest. Anywhere. Don't pick someplace like Chicago."

"No," I said decidedly. "Chicago has an edge to it. It's a start. I don't have to stay there all my life."

I felt a new wave of energy, just having said something so concrete. A glimmer of want. I could not see myself in Budapest or Los Angeles or anyplace else. When I closed my eyes I saw myself in Chicago, riding anonymously on the el.

"Sure, I know you're disappointed," I added. "But that's what I've been looking for. The luxury of disappointment."

"It's your call," Keiji said, sticking his head into the freezer for a moment. "London's a great city," he mused, amid swirls of frost.

"London!" I laughed out loud at this, surprised. "With all the tea and Brits? The changing of the guard, such decorum—that's someplace you'd like?"

"There's a whole underside to it, beyond the pomp, really. Pakistanis, Chinese, Turks. And it has style, much more than France. And what's wrong with tea? I'm a tea drinker myself."

"Then why not live there?" I asked. "*You* live there, if you like it."

He slammed the refrigerator door shut, glasses fogged, and waved me away. "I'll live there when I'm old," he said. "When I'm just there for the scenery. Hup! Game's over."

He brought the coffee over and sat down. The Phillies had won. We watched a few of the batting highlights.

"Chicago has two baseball teams, right?" he asked. "Ever been to the parks?"

"Wrigley Field only. I went last year, with the Osaka people."

"No more corporate box seats for you," Keiji said, smiling. "Now you'll be in the bleachers with everyone else."

I smiled as well. Keiji began reminiscing about a Met game that he and I and the Yamamoto group had gone to, how someone had hit him in the head with a plastic cup.

"Remember? What a free-for-all they are here," he said. "*That's* nothing like home either. It's a laugh."

At home, baseball was an extremely organized recreation; oftentimes during a Tokyo Giants game you sat back within the vast homogeneous crowd and imagined even the jeers to be in unison.

"The Mets just aren't the same on TV," Keiji lamented. "You miss all the atmosphere."

I threw a handful of pretzels at him, then a bottle cap.

"There. Any better?"

He pointed at me menacingly, then brushed the salt and crumbs off his lap.

"Pan-face," he muttered, pretending to be pissed, but as I tramped around him to clean up the mess, it seemed a few of the harsher lines around his mouth had eased away, if only for a moment.

I was walking the last mile. I had my shoulder bag, and in just a little while I would be off to Grand Central, where I would catch the bus to La Guardia. No more cabs, I again told myself, no more limos and no more airline business class either. No more company car. That was all right; I didn't much like to drive. Living in such congested cities, you were better off walking, something I was becoming quite good at.

It was June 21—summer solstice—the longest day of the year. Going to Chicago, I would gain yet another hour of light. I needed as much as I could get. The sun was high and strong even at this hour, before noon. I went into Macy's for some air-conditioning, to look at the suits and ties I would no longer be wearing. Translators didn't need suits; they never had power meetings. I would have to redo my whole wardrobe.

Macy's was full of Japanese, Japanese signage here and there, Japanese buying and buying, indulging their yen. Whenever I approached a clerk I saw smiles widen to near hysteria: Here comes another one, they thought, here comes the next commission. But I bought nothing. I noticed a woman by the cosmetics counters— a slim, pretty woman in a slim, pretty flowered dress. The way Taeko would dress. Hair like Taeko's, shimmering at the roots, neatly pulled back; I stood watching her, knowing just how that hair would feel between my fingers. I pretended to look at chiffon scarves. She was testing lipsticks and powders, putting little smudges on the back of her hand. She started by Shiseido, continued to Charles of the Ritz, Lancôme, back to Shiseido. The salesgirl there spoke Japanese, and the woman completed her purchase, but prior to that, at the other counters, she had struggled along in English, laughing, communicating via the universal language of mattes and frosts. I thought of Taeko with her nail polish. But you could see how much of an adventure this woman was having, how she was having a fun time. I followed her out the revolving door, maintaining as discreet a distance as I could. I didn't want to lose sight of her.

She glanced around as she walked, lightly guarding her handbag. She had a sweet, merry face—it wrenched at me—so placid and indifferent. She had no idea I was behind her, and if she did, she didn't care. At Rockefeller Center she bought some ice cream, pink with red spots, perhaps black cherry, and then she went to the promenade and sat down. She ate her ice cream like a little cat, licking the spoon each time it emerged from her pursed mouth, her toes wriggling upward in their sandals from the sheer taste of it, from the heat of the sun. When she was finished, she took a small New York guidebook out and studied it earnestly, one shoe now off. Her hand was still splotched with the little palette of cosmetics. There was also a ring on the hand—she was married —but I didn't care, I only wanted to watch such a spirited person, again like a cat out preening on a rock. The flowered collar of her dress lifted and fell. I watched, intent, but hidden behind sunglasses. She was modestly ignoring me. A man in a jacket bearing a Daiwa Securities emblem came over and joined her. She showed him her purchases and indicated something on the guidebook map. He smiled, poking her in the thigh. Their knees were close together, both her narrow feet now out of the sandals and resting on his. I suddenly felt I was intruding, and I left.

On a furious postcard to my soon-to-be-ex-wife, I asked her why she had never eaten ice cream; why she could never wait calmly and sit in the sun. I wrote fast and hard with a lousy postal pen, illegible bird strokes, and then I reread it. To her it would make no sense, I realized, but I mailed it anyway. It was a postcard of skaters at Rockefeller Center. I dropped it in the slot and checked not once but twice to make sure it had fallen in. I had signed it "Your Friend in the U.S." She would know who it was from, though perhaps I would prefer it if she didn't; I didn't know if I could explain these strange new palpitations of my heart.

Chicago was rainy when I arrived; wild thunderstorms kept the plane circling for twenty minutes, while Armageddon bolts of lightning flashed pink through pewter clouds. It was the rainy season in Tokyo, too, now. Children such as Omi and Etsuko would be

wearing bright little raincoats and carrying Mickey Mouse um-
brellas as they tramped to school in their colorful boots, instead
of the geta clogs of yesteryear. My mother used to tell me how she
would kick her clogs up high in the air to see how they landed:
right side up, sun tomorrow; right side down, more rain. Funny.
That is how we Japanese are—we make a sport or tradition out of
everything, even lousy weather.

Back at the Nippon, I packed my suitcase quickly, then left fifty
dollars on the glass table where all my newspapers and magazines
had been stacked. The maid had had to clean up a terrible mess
in here after they'd carried me out. It was hard to believe that this
would be my final ride down in the elevator with the digital panel
and the mechanized British computer voice naming all the floors,
so very proper. *"Going down. Watch your step."* I turned in my
key to the desk clerk—there was no bill to pay—then once I was
finished, went over by the pay phones to call the office. I had
wanted to be ready to bolt before I made the call. I didn't want
them rushing over with handcuffs, trying to drag me back.

Mori answered at half-ring. On the ball, as ever.

"Is Mr. Yamamoto there?" I asked, impeccably formal.

"Mr. Yamamoto is out of town. Who's calling?"

"Mr. Shimada."

"Mr. Shimada? Jun Shimada?" she exploded, and then her
voice changed to awkward gentleness as she remembered I was on
the mend. "He's at the home office through mid-August. Where
are you?"

"In the city. I'd like to schedule an appointment with him, as
soon as possible after he gets back."

"Schedule an appointment? I don't understand; just go in to
see him—"

"That won't work," I said, cutting her off. "You see—"

She cut right back. "Udo's here. Do you want to talk to him?"

"No. Now, Miss Mori, I know what I'm trying to say, so let me finish. I'm scheduling an appointment because I'm no longer with the company. I need to present my letter of resignation."

"But we've just gotten your apartment ready!"

"I won't be needing it, thank you. Pencil me in for the first thing three days after he gets back. That should give him time to recover from jet lag. Is he free then?"

"Yes, August sixteenth, but—"

"August sixteenth it is." I wrote the date down on a piece of Nippon notepaper at my side, in the most unlikely event that I might forget it. I would be more likely to forget my own name at this point. Mori persisted:

"Why don't you let me get him on a conference call right now, and you can speak to him directly. It'll take one minute. Hold on—"

"I wouldn't do that if I were you," I caroled. "It's two in the morning there." I grinned happily. I had flustered Yamamoto's Foo dog.

"Oh, yes, of course. But he's been so concerned about you!"

"And I am indebted to him. I've checked out of the hotel, and my car is in the garage, with the key at the desk. Please keep this in confidence, Miss Mori. I would like to tell him in person, face-to-face."

"Shimada-san! No, no, this isn't at all right. Let me put Udo on the phone, please."

"See you on August sixteenth. Bright and early."

"Shi—"

I hung up and rubbed my neck, feeling as if I had just been wrestling with an octopus: the phone cord still swung back and forth, a tentacle that might grab me at any second. Time to go. I hobbled out, lugging all my worldly goods, past a demonstration of the hotel's restaurant workers before the front entrance, big weary-looking men in white aprons. They carried signs: JAPS ARE SLAVE DRIVERS / SUPPORT UNION WORKERS. I kept my head bent and scrambled on, then stopped at the edge of Dearborn, turning left, turning right, trying to find another place to live.

◆

I went into a bookstore and bought all my father's works available, even the one I dreaded most: *The Death Notes*. Translations—I wanted to practice my English. It was a small extravagance, as there were only three works available. I bought them and then left them on the bureau of my furnished room.

I had found a room in Hyde Park, by the University of Chicago; I knew that any university would have a lot of Asians nearby. Bookish ones, meek, preoccupied, just like myself. I hadn't the courage to live in Chinatown, like Keiji, seeing as I looked more evil dwarf than he did and knew so little of the language; and in New Chinatown, full of Thais and Vietnamese, I might have reason to fear for my life. It might seem simple, fitting in anywhere as an Asian, but really it is not. North and South Koreans kill each other to this day in Chicago, as do Serbs and Croatians; long-standing feuds from Mexico go on—I knew all this, I read the papers. So Hyde Park it was. It was a strange apartment-hotel by the lake, filled with a combination of foreign students and what looked like blues men down on their luck. The street was lined with old Lincolns and Eldorados; the building lobby was decrepit but colorful, with a radio always tuned to WBEE and a switchboard operator with an antiquated headset. I believe I may have caught my breath when I first walked in.

You didn't sign a lease, you didn't need references. All you needed was cash each month and a face the lady manager happened to trust. She trusted mine, purred about how Asians were so neat and courteous. She called me Mr. Watashi, and I tried not to laugh. Watashi was the alias I had given her, not wanting to be found by anyone: watashi meaning "I," as in me, myself. Only Keiji knew where I was. Antagonist or not, Keiji was my preferred link with life.

So I bought my father's books and ignored them, until on the seventh day I unfolded my Murphy bed and flopped down with *The Death Notes*. Most un-neat and un-Asian, I munched on handfuls of roasted beans and dried sardine bits and swigged at a beer. I was not allowing myself much alcohol anymore but needed it sometimes, particularly when approaching a precipice such as *The Death Notes*. The bed smelled musty. No bugs, but I had seen millipedes wriggling around the bathtub. That was all right; you got used to it. You shook out the sheets every morning and checked them at night. You could get used to anything in time.

I propped the book against my chest, trying to concentrate, but it seemed to be in a language other than English—the characters snarled together and locked up against me, like a foreign alphabet. Cyrillic, maybe. I held it upside down. No better. I sat up and brought the page closer to my face.

◆

Through the mangle I saw the characteristic moaning words I associated with him: *sadness, loss, suicide, hell*. I sighed. This was not what I needed; this was like a full bottle of whiskey. Hell. I lit a cigarette. Hell to me was good, hell in the Buddhist sense. Hell is change. Hell is run by Emma-hoo, a frightening but strong man who determines your stay, your duration in limbo. Hell is only a temporary thing, a passage to reincarnation, a purging of the negativity and indecision that result from a false life. My hell was of paper pushing, of always acting agreeable and accommodating, of simulating enjoyment and following the crowd just so I could take refuge within a large structure. It was the hell of conformity, of trying to assume a false shape. I had my jiffy Buddhism, but it seemed to me that my father never got out of hell, or, getting out, dragged himself back in. Writers are like that, amorphous—always observing and recreating. Their souls are in constant flux, always having to act as mediums for other people, for characters and bits of dialogue—they are something like actors, protean men. Their own life is secondary. I felt a little for my father the man, thinking this. I also imagined a skull-and-crossbones on the cover of the book, and decided to put it aside again.

I managed one line before I dumped my beer and went to fix a cup of tea. *I live in twilight*. I pressed my finger to the page, gently.

Not I: the night outside was black, the lamplight bright (especially since I had taken off the pink shade, something out of a bordello). Hell is twilight, dim sounds, vague outlines. I brewed a cup of scalding hot tea in my kitchenette, turned the radio loud; I picked up the book, saw how I had broken its spine in my efforts at deciphering it, then carried it like a dead thing back to its spot on the bureau. I didn't need to read *The Death Notes* now; I had got its message. I sat down at the table and drank my tea instead, burned my tongue, cursed, stared at my reflection in the window and smirked at it briefly, glad to see I could stand to be alone with myself at this moment, glad to see I recognized my own face.

Wandering up and down the beach, resting on a flat rock. To my left hung the skyline of the city—it seemed to hover over my half-mast eyelids, so close, a distortion owing to the curve in the shore and the crowded arrangement of buildings directly north. I was alone, observing speedboats and bathers here and there, hearing laughter, smelling barbecues from the park. On the rim of other people's lives. I felt the heaviness of my own body, as if it was its own world. Being so long alone can get to you, particularly in summer. Summer is a social season. And I had been alone for a long time: first my alcoholic withdrawal; then the time at Kinosaki; then ghostwalking all over New York, which, though I had been staying with Keiji, was for the most part a solitary session. Now here. Nearly two weeks without human contact, I had begun talking to myself in private, simply to exercise my voice.

That afternoon I had gone to the Drake at teatime, just for the diversion of memory. It had not changed. The same harpist was there, yes, the same sort of crowd, but of course Gina was not— I hadn't expected her to be there. There was another young woman, nothing at all like her, moving around graciously, wearing the demure black dress. I wondered what Gina was up to now, at this precise and specific moment, and further entertained myself by calculating the hour in Rome—dinnertime. A hot night on the piazza, with motorcycles roaring by and Gina before her *aperitivo*.

Laughing. And here I was, like a piece of medical waste beached upon the shore, in her city. But then again it was everyone's city, wasn't it? I had taken her place. I wondered whether she would be surprised to learn I had settled here by choice. I wondered whether she thought of me at all.

I went on to the movies, alone, to a university showing of *Stray Dog* by Kurosawa. I have always liked that movie—it can stand up to any melodramatic crime story of its era; Toshiro Mifune even looked like Clark Gable. On screen before me, he was like an old friend, playing a man who had had hard luck, who could have tilted toward either good or bad and chose good, with a lot of screaming. I sat through it twice. After the movie I had iced coffee in a deserted Thai restaurant, walked home and sat reading the paper in my apartment. My heart thudded uncertainly, skipping beats. It seemed to need a metronome of outside activity.

I went to bed early, at nine, and woke up four times in a disconnected sleep, on the rim of other people's lives. . . . I kicked at the sheets, trying to relax, counted backward from a thousand, dreamed Toshiro Mifune came to deport me, but I had forgotten my native language.

At first light I got up, stared out the window, went back to bed. I remembered something, exactly, the quote from the Yamamoto manual I had referred to in my conversation with Murakami: "A man who is busy thinks of no one but himself. A man engrossed in work becomes one with his accomplishment."

I got dressed. Idleness would kill me, no doubt, I thought, pinching myself. I needed work to do soon—right now, in fact. It was as plain as the very plain nose on my face.

My attack was two-pronged—well, at first it was one-pronged: the procuring of employment I could stand and that would support me, which when I closed my eyes and practiced visualization I could see as nothing but translation work. I tugged on a flimsy connection and managed to arrange an interview and a barrage of tests. The tests were on Friday. The interview would be the following week.

I had really had to "sell" myself over the phone, something I was not fond of, and if this didn't work I didn't know what I would do. All weekend my stomach did flip-flops; I imagined myself blacklisted by Yamamoto, unable to get a job, going through all my savings, living on rice, drifting, drinking again, sponging off my friends, embittered and foolish. "He used to be a president's man," they would say. "But now look at him—makes you think, huh?"

I consoled myself and said I could always work as a clerk or drive a cab. America was full of overqualified people, surviving. I wouldn't starve. But was that all I wanted now, mere subsistence? No—but yes. What I really wanted still eluded me, no matter how hard I strained to push it. I was frightened of a world without structure, yet bit by bit I had let every last iota of structure around me erode—*everything*—except for the essential, my skeleton and the skin around it. A structure thirty-one years in the making. In my mind I had no landscapes other than cut-and-dried translation, no schemes or thought-out plans. Screen blank: nothing would come up. Except perhaps cooking, but otherwise I had no urge to be my own boss, own a franchise, become a diplomat. I decided that subsistence would have to do for a while, just to keep me from forcing myself into further mistakes.

The second prong of the attack came out of nowhere, unexpected, like a mutant bud. I was wandering again, walking through alleys and streets—walking, I had noticed, was the way I exorcised my panics. You walked and walked until your lower half was numb, till your pelvis creaked in protest and settled to about five times its normal weight onto the sagging cradle of your legs. My feet now had a layer of callus I could stick pins into without feeling pain. As I walked I thought, and when I got tired of thinking I looked around, peeked into apartment windows and shops, porches, the never-ending sprawl of Chicago. Walking was free, it was a diversion, it could be done alone, without comment. When I got tired of thinking while I walked, I went on automatic pilot toward home, where I would peel off my shoes and collapse each joint toward bed, blisters throbbing, muscles contracting even in sleep.

You slept deep after a marathon walk, deeper than alcohol would drop you, with no shakes or pallor in the morning, just stiffness, which went away as you started to move again. I hadn't drunk much since the day at Keiji's, though I had often wanted to, in which case I would stick my finger down my throat to promote a gag reflex. A Clockwork Orange effect of sorts. It often worked; sometimes it did not. I would then try to remember myself at my worst point at Yamamoto, sitting in my cube, full of sugar and alcohol, never quite sure of what I was doing. Of always drinking and smelling heavy odors in my piss, of waking up with bloated fingers and puffy eyes, of feeling my stomach like a gutted fish writhing around inside me. *Of being out of control.* This generally stopped me.

I lay on the bed, miserable, or I went out and walked fifteen miles, but I stayed sober. I wasn't sure if I enjoyed not drinking, but I kept to it. I enjoyed the lucidity of my thoughts and the ever-increasing speed of connection between mind and body. I even kept up the doses of antacid powder I had been prescribed; although lack of alcohol had eased the ulcer, I took the medicine in the same way people make offerings to a dormant volcano. I didn't like the fact that because of my own weakness people had mocked me: Hiroshi's words, "Shimada? Oh, he's sobering up . . . ," rang in my ears. If it was only subsistence I wanted now, at least I had to be in charge. To get by and wake with a clear head, painfully aware of every worry and problem. That didn't seem to be so much to ask for, I felt. All I wanted was my own newly washed hide.

I wandered past the back of a restaurant. Wine crates were stacked up in the alley, big cylinders full of garbage; from inside came odors of melted butter and meat, fish, garlic. Very subtle odors, so I assumed it must be a French place. I was right: the name *Côte d'Azur* was painted on the garbage pails. The kitchen door was open, revealing lots of white tile and light, men in white attire smeared with sauce and blood. It was near eleven, closing time for most restaurants in Chicago, where people eat and go to bed earlier and tend to lead less neurotic lives than in New York. I was going to have to hop public transportation home. I was on the trendy North Side, way off base.

An intense man of about forty, with hairy wrists and a look of mystification about him, was out on an overturned crate, sipping cognac. He wore whites like the others, yet did not join in their camaraderie as they partied around the ruins of the kitchen. Something about him suggested that he did not ever mix with the others. Sitting out there among garbage, so aloof as he savored his cognac, he reminded me of exiled royalty. It was an aura. I felt in my bones that this was the Côte d'Azur's main chef.

I couldn't help but gawk at this man. French food has always represented the epitome of the craft, and this man—I assumed him to be a premier French chef—assumed celebrity status in my eyes. He glanced back at me, annoyed, wiped a smudge of something off his glass with elegant fingers: deft fingers that danced over sauces, trimmed gossamer slices of veal and cracked three eggs at a time.

I approached him haltingly, and I could tell by the way he regarded me, in my careless clothes, that he thought I was a tramp, about to hit him up for a meal.

"If you're looking for work, we have none. I'm sorry. It's a small staff."

Not a trace of an accent, but a curious elasticity to the words, which were Berlitz perfect and well-enunciated like my own, which led me to believe that English was not his first language. His face was tired and nervous at the same time, flushed across the cheekbones from constant exposure to ovens and steam pots.

I laughed. "I'm not looking for work, or food. I only wanted to ask if you're the chef."

"Yes, I am," he drawled. "Why?"

I revved the charm up to high gear, explained that I was an amateur cook and someday wanted to learn the best—*la methode française*. He shrugged.

"You can learn from books, even videotapes," he said. "There are many classes. I myself taught one, La Bonne Cuisine, full of Winnetka housewives."

There was a crash of plates, which caused him to wince and hurl cautionary epithets back into the direction of the kitchen.

"Oafs," he muttered. "I can only wonder how they handle their women."

Uninvited, I sat down on the curbstone and attempted to keep our feeble egg-white conversation going.

"Is it hard work?"

The chef raised his eyebrows and peered down his long, thin nose. He was rail thin, from facial features to feet; ironically, it appeared he did not eat much of any food.

"Hard? Of course it's hard; it's excruciating. I put myself into all my dishes, and I own this restaurant, or I will as soon as I've paid my investors off. We do very well, but I'm still in a hole. That's why I came up with a prix-fixe menu, twenty dollars for four courses. Volume, crowds and crowds. I must make a reputation. Chicago's a cheap town; you cannot charge outlandish prices here—people will just go to an ethnic restaurant instead. But"—he swallowed the last of the syrupy yellow cognac—"it's also unbroken turf. No French restaurant in the city has three stars—*none*—only La Française out in Wheeling. It's my challenge. So of course I kill myself every day."

"You're American?"

"By nationality, yes. I was born here. Then I trained in France, under Vervé. You've heard of him?"

I admitted that I had not. The chef sniffed.

"Well, he marked me as one of the masters of our generation. I have that prophecy to live up to, because he is a man I deeply respect. I repeat it to myself every day and night, you know, like a mantra. I repeat it now, sitting in an alley with you."

He went back into the kitchen, where I heard him complain about grease buildup on the range, then give supplementary instructions on how to correct it, first in English, then in French, then Spanish. I heard scouring noises. "*Throw* yourself into it, don't just pour on ammonia. A filthy range is a disgrace. We have health regulations, you know."

He returned with two glasses of cognac and a sour expression. "Here, have a drink. I like you," he pronounced. "You're sincere."

When I did not touch the cognac, he leaned sideways, hand on his hip. "What's wrong? You don't drink cognac."

"I'm an alcoholic."

"Oh." He snatched the snifter away and poured the contents into his own. "More for me, then," he said, yet leaned back elaborately to let me know everything was all right.

"You really want to cook? I mean professionally—any slob can serve up sandwiches and sweet and sour pork in disgusting pink sauce."

"I enjoy cooking, yes."

"You want to be a chef?"

"Oh, I don't know about that. It's kind of a strange fantasy I have, nothing more."

"Then why are you talking to me?"

"Admiration."

He shook his head, gleaming brown hair combed with oil or pomade—something; I could smell it—with an odd white streak up front.

"You can admire the performance without becoming an actor," he said.

"True."

"What do you do now?"

"Nothing."

"At all?"

"I'm between careers."

"Lots of culinary school graduates out there," he warned. "It's quite competitive."

"I'm sure of that," I said. "And I enjoy cooking, but maybe if I took it on seriously, as a career, I might grow to hate it."

"Oh, well, there are several questions to ask yourself." I felt guilty for a moment, hardly worth his interest, then I realized that he was probably a lonely man, put off by his crew inside for being a martinet, able to communicate with few others the essence of his work. I let him go on. The preparation of food had always done something for me, pressed a hidden central button that made me feel good. It was physical—tactile, really—yet required judgment and the use of a brain. In its highest form it was like art. Meals meant so much to people, brought them happiness, brought them together, nourished them and raised their energy levels, fueled them for other activities.

"Do you want to be rich and famous?" he asked.

"No. I never have."

"Good—you won't be, being a chef. Restaurateurs become rich. They don't care about quality—they'll ask you to do something 'chic' with chicken wings, just to make a fast buck."

He relayed this information with great disgust. One could see that inhuman requests such as that had been made of him and had left a hundred scars.

He eyed me shrewdly. "What did you use to do? You're not a kid."

"Corporate executive. Midlevel."

"Oh, my! And I thought you were sincere!" He laughed.

"But I am."

"Of course you are; I was only kidding. Name?" I told him. "Ah, the Japanese appreciate food. You're second generation?"

"No, native," I said.

He stared down at the myriad smears on his apron, as if trying to recall the exact ingredients each of them was composed of.

"Well, Jun, what do you do on Sundays?"

"Loaf mostly. Why?"

"You have a means of support?"

"I hope to start translating, yes."

He lowered his voice. "If you're interested, you could come down Sundays and clean up—wash pots, sweep, haul trash, that sort of thing. Dirty work, but in exchange you could hang around and watch me and the sous-chefs, the preps, and see if this is the life for you." He dropped his voice again, so low now it was hardly more than a hum. "You'll be getting an edge. Some of these kids go to school and get *certified* and end up with no better than clean-up. Especially in a restaurant of this caliber."

"Why only Sundays?"

He stifled a yawn, then straightened up on his crate as if to remind himself that the night was not yet over.

"Our regular clean-up plays flamenco guitar at an Argentinian nightclub on Sundays. He's a musician; he couldn't turn down the chance. Only Sundays, though. I don't want to put Miguel out of a job. Are you interested?"

I looked into the kitchen, and I looked back at the chef. My Sundays were exceptionally empty of late. I said yes.

He smiled warmly. The smile disappeared. "You do have a green card, right?"

"I have a work visa."

The smile returned. "Good. I wouldn't want to get fined. Well, Jun, show up next week, and then I'll introduce you." He indicated the crew with a twitch of his head. "And don't tell them about our conversation. Don't be too obvious watching. Egos are frail here. There's a very high rate of turnover in this business. We'll pay you minimum wage, so it looks up-front. No special treatment."

I, too, was smiling. Minimum wage was half of what the mail clerks made at Yamamoto.

He got up and took a deep breath, flexed his wrists and prepared to go back inside.

"Oh, my name is De Mornay."

"Very pleased to meet you," I said, and I bowed.

He returned to his restaurant. I wandered away in much improved spirits, pausing at a junction of streets and making note of them, so as to be able to find the Côte d'Azur again with a minimum of difficulty on Sunday, my first day of work.

And so, incredibly, I began to clean up after everyone. As promised, the atmosphere was very high-charged and hot—in both temperament and temperature—and my work was filthy. Fish guts, beaters jammed with hardened pastry, knives, whisks, counters, the hoods on the ranges. My hands were parboiled all the time, covered with cuts and scrapes. Helping my mother had been nothing compared to this: in addition to kitchen duty, I was responsible for loading the tableware and china into the dishwasher (which was an autoclave, set to Sanitize, as per health regulations) and vacuuming the dining area. De Mornay was getting his money's worth. Still, I enjoyed almost every chore I did. The sous-chefs and preps tended to ignore me, and I was able to watch them and De Mornay undetected. It was pure theater—sautéing, garnishing, mincing, fussing. Between dishes they gulped mineral water out of the bottle; De Mornay went for grapefruit juice. "Cleans the palate and gives you a vitamin C rush," he explained when I asked him, in private. He never acknowledged me outright, but sometimes, while working on a stock or coulis—complicated things—he would call me over and have me stand there by his side, presumably to catch all the utensils he was flinging into my plastic bin, but in reality he was allowing me to watch. I think he enjoyed that, the performance aspect, the instructing. The others, though they idolized him and jumped at everything he said, were still resentful and waited for a slip-up, a chance to step in. They depressed me, the chorus boys. With the exception of the fish cook, there was not one I would have trusted to give me the correct time of day.

The interior of the Côte d'Azur's dining area was done in yellows and blues, colors of the Riviera. I knew every inch of it soon enough, running the vacuum here and there, although I always saw it when it was empty of customers. I did not get to watch them enjoying the food they ate or see the presentation of it on the cream-damask tablecloths. I was glad of this, in a sense. Education or not, although I enjoyed the menial labor and the grunt work, I certainly did not want anyone to see me doing it. I had come far, but I had not come that far yet. I didn't think that it was necessary that I should.

One thing I noted wryly as I came home and removed my filthy clothes was that they smelled. They reeked of the oil and fish and meat and food I had been so desperate to get away from while growing up. At this restaurant, no matter how prestigious, how haute the cuisine, I was doing the things I had done for my mother as soon as I was old enough to be put to work. The smell was essentially the same; food was food, whether you put it on china or in a chipped blue-and-white noodle bowl. I had come full circle. Only now I liked the smell. I liked it, and I liked the work. No one was telling me what to do—that was the issue. I cleaned up pots and I stank of food, yes, but it was *my* smell; I did it of my own accord.

It was funny. I hoped my mother was having a good laugh.

I knew I was.

◆

"So you want a job?"

I nodded. I was having breakfast with Mr. Hideki Ito, head of East-West Translation Services. The breakfast was my interview: Mr. Ito was a busy executive, a maverick, as Yoko might call him. It seemed as he slurped up his egg with his chopsticks that I didn't have much time to present myself.

He was a small, sloppy man, about my age but with not as much hair left. He reminded me a comedian in Japan who sneaks up on people and yells at them at top volume. I kept waiting, hand by my ear, for the joke to follow. Nondescript gray suit, brown shoes: a terrible fashion faux pas. Still, he conveyed great enthusiasm and had the waiters hopping as they served our Japan-style breakfast: miso, fish, pickled vegetables, a poached egg. You could only get this sort of fare at two hotels in the city: the Nippon, of course, my old stamping grounds; and the Four Seasons. We were at the Four Seasons, where in a suite upstairs East-West Translation had its offices. I should say office, really—Mr. Ito's office—for the majority of translators working for him were free lances. A secretary received clients and answered calls; a proofreader typed text and checked for errors. We had used East-West at Yamamoto, for lengthy documents. I had always envied the come-and-go life of a translator.

Ito sucked in a piece of salmon.

"You did very well on the tests, that's for certain," he said. "And you work fast; I like that." He cocked his head. "What makes you want to give up a corporation job, though? Such dignified duties and perks. With me you'll have to deal with everything, all the garbage—boring stuff, crazy stuff, instruction booklets, letters, articles, even recipes!"

We laughed, I a bit more nervously than Ito. "You won't have a desk," he cautioned. "You get your assignments and then work in a library, or at home."

"That's all right," I said. "I don't want a desk job anymore."

"We are busy," he mused, eyes shut. I looked around at the salon we were in: lace curtains, brocade chairs, just me and Mr. Ito—it was only 6:40 A.M. "And even your handwriting is good. Some guys, they write so awful in English it drives the proofer nuts. Well . . ." He glanced at his watch. "You only get paid by the hour; a good wage, but strictly hourly and by assignment. No more salaryman."

"That's fine." I pronounced it like a prayer, head bent. I didn't want to push, though a certain desperation frothed inside me. I really wanted this job.

"Well, I'll try you out. Can you start today?"

"Yes, *yes*," I said, and bounced forward despite myself, bowing. I was going to be a *translator*, for God's sake. I had a tremendous urge to pour my glass of cold water on my head.

"Let's go, then." He tossed his napkin into his bowl, ready to leave, then glanced at my own arrangement of dishes. "But you've hardly finished," he said. "Aren't you hungry?"

"Too nervous," I offered, smiling. Actually the food had been a disappointment—the salmon metallic-tasting, the miso weak and the green tea yellow and underbrewed.

Ito sniffed. "Nerves, huh! You got spoiled at Kinosaki, I bet." He watched my face stiffen and blanch. I hadn't known he could so thoroughly check my record. "How did you know?" I gasped, and yet suddenly it became obvious. KNA was run by the Business Association. Ito apparently had some friends in convenient places. He sniffed proudly. "I have my sources," was all he said. "The food was incredible there, wasn't it?"

"Yes, yes, it was."

He nudged my arm. "Now, Shimada, don't look like a leaky balloon. I know you were there, but I don't hold it against you."

"You also know why I was there? For alcoholism and depression?" I spit it out; I had to. If I didn't, the weight of it would hang upon me like a millstone and ruin even the most renegade translator's life.

"Yes. But I said I would try you out—you do deserve a chance. Besides, you look okay to me now—am I right? No worse for wear, not too skittish?"

"No, sir." I held my hands up, smiling lamely. "Steady as they go," I said.

They were just turning on soft dining music—not Muzak but Mozart, this being the Four Seasons.

"Have you been to Disneyland?" Ito asked.

"Disneyland?"

"Yeah, I want to take my kids there for vacation. You said you've got two kids—so do I."

"No, we never made it to Disneyland," I said, a little sadly. Not the American one at least: we had taken Etsuko to the Tokyo Disneyland when she was a toddler.

"No matter." He pushed himself away from the table and grabbed his copy of the *Yomiuri Shimbun*. He then showed me the check: thirty-six dollars for the two of us. For breakfast.

"Now that's where the Tokyo authenticity comes in, the price," he said, laughing. "But I just can't stand American food. Let's go. You need to brush up on your Spanish."

"Excuse me?"

His small eyes widened. "Spanish—tremendous need for Japanese to Spanish. Come on, I don't have all day."

He charged out, with me fast behind him. The waiters jumped out of our way. In the elevator, Ito stomped about, penned like a rodeo bull. He again checked his watch. I checked my own: 6:51—an interview of seventeen minutes. A brief hell, but a productive one, all before seven A.M.

You never forget your first piece. I worked very hard on a translation for an art dealer, a letter of twenty-five pages postmarked Ueno, all about ukiyo-e pornographic prints.

Summer was here. In the summer Hyde Park had a peculiar, heavy odor, almost palpable, maybe a hangover from the stockyards, from when Chicago was a big-shouldered, cow-killing town. The population of the neighborhood was slightly diminished, the students dispersed, and the lake sent occasional cooling breezes. I had not spent a summer in Chicago before. Just one year earlier I had been commuting back and forth. I tried to remember the last summer in particular, but it became a blur with all the rest.

The ukiyo-e stuff made me think of Taeko, with some discomfort. She was so very classical-looking. It seemed hard to believe that there was no one around now for sex, that I would have to start all over again. It made me nervous. This was why they encouraged salarymen to marry young and get all that horny distraction out of the way. I was missing just living with a woman, with Taeko. Merely seeing her scattered toiletries in the bathroom had filled me with a sense of purpose. It wasn't the housewife issue—I didn't mind cooking and cleaning for myself. (She had been right—there were hairs everywhere.) It was a matter of presence, the idea of having a better half, a feminine presence that intertwined with yours. It was beginning to seem natural, as I set up house again.

Alma, almendra, almohada . . .

I was at the cherrywood secretary in my room, trying to study Spanish. It was broiling hot. The back of my shirt clung to me, then pulled away as I moved forward to start another sentence.

The desk was old and lustrous, with a cache of tiny compartment drawers. Barely scratched, it was the nicest thing in the room, perhaps in the building. Seated at it, I felt like Thomas Jefferson.

The phone rang, and I froze up immediately, the hairs on my head prickling. The phone had never rung before—it had no reason to. The sound was low and staccato, like a phone ringing out of the past. The switchboard operator from downstairs was on the other end.

"Mr. Watashi?" she said dreamily. She had a marvelous phone manner. "Mr. Watashi, Mr. Anata calling long distance. Want me to put him through?"

Mr. Watashi, Mr. Anata. I, you. I smiled and said yes; yes, please. Keiji was calling.

"Where are you living!" he exploded, as soon as we were connected.

"In hell." I laughed. I elaborated a bit. Keiji got a kick out of such things.

"Send photos," he said. "Anyway, your wife wants to get in touch with you—she called me for your number. Should I divulge it?"

I turned the ukiyo-e material over quickly. Taeko: how eerie. I hesitated for a moment, not knowing what to do. Maybe Yamamoto was behind this.

"She says your kid is supposed to be coming here, and she wants to make arrangements. She wasn't sure if it was still on your schedule."

Etsuko's summer visit. "No, we'll have to postpone it," I said mournfully. I had looked forward to Etsuko's shy excitement on arriving at O'Hare with her pint-size travel bag. But it was impossible. "I can't watch her or take her anyplace—I need to get established. I'm working now."

"Where?"

"East-West Translation and the Côte d'Azur restaurant. I clean up and get to watch the chef. He's a *cordon bleu.*"

"Sort of a food groupie thing," Keiji observed, with perception. "That was fast."

"Everybody needs something to do. I'm not too good at soul searching."

"It's an art." I heard some crackling booms on his end of the line. It was the Fourth of July.

"Well, should I give her the number?" Keiji prodded.

I hesitated again. "No, you'd better not. I'll use my AT&T card and call her from a pay phone."

"A little paranoid, aren't we?" He laughed. I explained without humor that I didn't want anyone from Yamamoto to find me until I had the letter of resignation done. Such a letter was generally lengthy and apologetic, a written confession of sorts, often presented in a folder of the finest quality. I had not managed to progress past the first line: My name is Jun Shimada. It seemed I had nothing further to say.

"Sorry you had to get involved in all this," I told Keiji. "Taeko calling you and all. I should have remembered Etsuko."

"Oh, that's all right. I always liked Taeko, you know that, and she's loosened up a lot. She sold a painting."

"What!"

"Yeah, some woman from Boston was on a trip and saw one of Taeko's paintings in a show. She's a fashion person. She said it was just the thing for her boutique."

I was amazed and for some reason embarrassed. It had never occurred to me that Taeko might have any genuine talent; her attempts had been so halfhearted. I felt very stupid and small. Taeko was actually painting, and making money from her work. And I had always been so condescending, referring to it as a hobby. In the years I had known her, she had always been so unfocused, starting things, abandoning them—the only project she had seen through was childbirth: she didn't have much choice.

Keiji cackled at me. "Yeah, I know you wish she'd become fat or a lesbian painter like in *Beauty and Sadness*, but she hasn't. She's fine."

I was confused. "*Beauty and Sadness?*" I echoed.

He groaned. "Am I the only person who reads in this world? How am I supposed to communicate with you, Shimada? You don't read novels, you don't read *Rolling Stone*. It's like we're on different planets."

Before I said goodbye, I inquired how he was. He said all right, that the agency had got the King Kat Kitty Litter account they had been dickering for.

"I may be moving into my own office. The chief Creative is on his way out; he's got AIDS."

"How convenient."

"Yes. The slings and arrows of contagious fortune."

I didn't know the original phrase, which he clarified for me, and then I winced, even though I detected a shaky undertone to his voice. "Narata, you can be vile sometimes," I said.

"Who, me? *Au contraire*—I'm just full of quills. There's a soft little animal underneath, crying."

"Indeed," I said. I asked if he was planning his vacation.

"I suppose so," he grumbled. "I get three weeks. It's not a good time just now."

"Go to London," I suggested. Keiji said he'd see.

"You went to work today?"

"Yeah, for a bit."

I smiled. "But it's the Fourth of July," I said.

"So? I don't celebrate the holiday, I'm not American. Do you?"

"Sure." I looked around at the paper-strewn room, the crusts of a festive cheese sandwich I had eaten. I had been inside since noon, alone with my dictionary. "Independence Day—that's very meaningful to me. How did the fireworks look in New York?" I asked. "Do they compare to the ones on the Sumida River?"

"No—here you can't tell them from the gunshots. It was good to talk to you, Shimada. Now call your wife," he said, and hung up. He had calcified again, a fringe dweller. Keiji had never even celebrated holidays in Japan, and Lord knows we have enough of them: Respect for the Aged Day, Golden Week, Sports Day . . .

I felt hollow after talking to Keiji, as if I had lost my heart and spleen.

A conversation with my artist wife. I went through it haltingly, like a student reporter conducting his first interview.

"What's all this about not eating ice cream?" she chided, tired of so many polite questions.

She had just done another painting, yellow and green peppers on a chopping block, which was to be included in the Yamamoto yearly calendar. I asked whether Yamamoto had tried to pump her for information.

"He phoned, yes," she said. "I told him I honestly didn't know your whereabouts. Then he came by to look at my work. I never expected he'd be interested."

She sounded bubbly. I was calling from a public phone by the Walgreen's, in the pit of night. Buses roared by. A kid of about ten began spraying the plexiglass walls surrounding me with unintelligible symbols.

"He only asked about you once," Taeko continued, as if to put my mind at ease. "Then he started talking to Father about the wood beetles in his summer cottage. Father was very honored to be asked such questions by Yoshi Yamamoto. They talked for a good while." She giggled.

"Will Etsuko be upset?" I asked, almost hoping that she would, that somebody out there might be longing just a little bit to see me. "Has she been looking forward to the trip?"

"Oh, she'll be all right," Taeko said. "She can learn to swim this summer instead."

I gave her the East-West office address and told her to communicate through it. Taeko then began to interview me.

"You go there every day?"

"East-West? Yes. I pick up my assignments."

"And you work at home?"

"Pretty much."

"And why won't you tell me where home is? Are you living with a woman?"

"Hardly. Are you with a man?"

"I don't want a man. Are you eating well? Where do you have your lunch?"

"Strange question. At the coffee shop in the Palmer House."

"Is that near where you work?"

"No, but it's near where I used to work. I've always liked it."

"You go there every day? I thought you didn't like hotels."

"No, but I like their coffee shops. They give you melon with your sandwich, even in winter. And it's an interesting mix of people. I don't have to eat surrounded by businessmen."

"Well!" she said. I heard her earring scrape the receiver. "Do you miss me, or have you forgotten me altogether?"

Why did she always ask me that, if I missed her? I tugged on the collar of my T-shirt, feeling prickly hot, as if I were sunburned all over. I was not good at this gay-divorcée-type banter.

"I miss you a great deal," I said thickly, in an elephantine way.

Her voice softened. "No, you don't. You just miss the comforts of a wife."

"Meaning what? I cook better than you, I keep a cleaner house."

"Then you miss the sexual comforts. You're not used to bachelorhood."

She was whispering now—someone must have been in earshot. I, on the other hand, began talking louder, excited. Normally she clammed up at this point.

"Sex is easy enough to find, you know that," I lied. "Besides, I can't recall having much sex or anything with you over the past few years. In fact, I can probably count all the times on my fingers. I even—"

"Jun." She interrupted, sweetly. "Are you angry now? Are your eyebrows up and is your hair flying in every direction?"

"Exactly!" I gasped. "Can you see me?"

"Yes. I'm in the building across the street."

"I wish you were."

"No, you don't," she replied, as she had done before, and the rare charged moment between us ended, as abruptly as it had begun. "We'll write to you." She prepared to say goodbye.

"We?"

"Etsuko and me. Who else?"

I watched the spray paint dripping down the booth outside me and crossed my eyes. A breeze went up my pants.

"You haunt me, Taeko, you know that?"

Pause. She made a deep noise—a purr—from the throat.

" 'Haunt'—what an interesting word," she said, and then cut me off before I could tell her anything else.

I went back to my ukiyo-e and my sweating. Around midnight, a mouse skittered across the floor and dived into a heating unit. A very healthy mouse, kissing cousins with a rat. My companion. I laid my head on the desk and felt the waves of something radiate over me.

I ran a bath, the water ice cold. I let the water go over my head. The tub was just like Gina's, an antiquated claw-foot. The drain was rusted. Under water, I heard every noise as an explosion. I thought of the iron fish from World War II: men had lived for months in submarine vessels barely bigger than themselves. History put one's problems into perspective. I tried to stay under for a full ninety seconds. My father was in the room, I could sense it, anxiously watching at tubside. For once that did not bother me. I welcomed him, wherever he was. Sixty-one, sixty-two, sixty-three . . .

From the depths of the pine salts I emerged, gasping, and asked my father to please keep an eye out for the mouse.

◆

July began with a limp, but by midmonth its pace began to quicken. I had a good deal of work to do: Ito, having taken an interest in me, gave me the meatiest assignments. He even went so far as to have me out to his newly constructed home in Buffalo Grove, a lengthy drive, during most of which he yammered into a car phone and cursed traffic.

"This area is booming," he said proudly, giving me the tour. 'Lake County is a smart place to make investments, if you're interested."

Ito was a partner in several real estate deals here on the diminishing prairie. He spoke of starting his business, and some of his commuter fatigue eased away.

"I was in California, working import-export, and we needed something translated in Chicago. It took us hours to find a capable person—I had to call the consulate. In a major city! So I saw the void and I filled it. I used to work out of a phone booth." He grinned and swung into a U-shaped driveway bordered by new trees. "Things have changed."

His wife had dinner waiting. She was pleasant and genial and Caucasian, smiling down at her high-energy husband, click-clacking around the house in thongs. I'd had no idea Ito had a white wife—it had never occurred to me that a Japanese businessman could have a wife of another race and still be very successful. There were some mixed matches I had heard of, yes, but they were rare. You needed a great deal of courage. And here was Ito married to a woman with green eyes and at least four inches and twenty pounds on him, and he dashed around, master of his universe. Of course I had had my own involvement, with Gina, but then Gina didn't really count—practically a B-girl, she had had that half-caste look, and I had taken solace in it. And it had been subversive: an affair, not a marriage. Ito was the true maverick. Although he breakfasted on fish and miso, I watched him gobble up corn on the cob that evening and realized that here was truly a man who had come to the United States.

I flicked a look at his wife, her freckled throat. I had the same options now too, I supposed, and it made me a little nervous to entertain them all, to have the embarrassment of choice.

The twelve-year-old daughter and I played a few games of badminton at dusk, while the seven-year-old son caught fireflies. They were unusual-looking children, tawny, with Asian features and hazel eyes. Exotic. I imagined the daughter as a model when she grew up. They did not remind me of my own children at all, which made it easier to be around them. Still, I wondered what strangers would come and play badminton with Etsuko, and I couldn't see how she would remember me much longer. I would visit her maybe once a year from now on; she would become a teenager, become preoccupied with boys and music and makeup, be famous among her school friends as the girl with the father in the U.S. Her colt-legged ghost galloped across the lawn. I let Ito's daughter win, and she graciously ran inside and got me a soda. Then I went over and joined Ito, who was set up in a lawn chair, working on a lap-top computer. His wife was doing needlepoint. I was grateful for this particular American custom, of ignoring one's guest completely and letting him roam free.

"Bonnie's got a crush on Shimada," Ito said, not looking up from his midget screen. Bonnie was the daughter. "She missed *21 Jump Street* to play badminton with him." He shuddered, and twisted his face into mock trauma. "What's this world coming to?"

"She's taping it," his wife advised, and we all laughed.

"Shimada looks like a teen idol—he's got that soulful sort of face," Ito said.

"Hal," the wife admonished, but she was smiling as she knotted a yarn end.

Ito said little more to me the rest of the evening but in general seemed happy to have me around. We really talked very little, inside or outside the office, but he inclined toward me, wanted to know I was around, watched over me and set me in position so that some of his own good fortune might spill over into my mouth. He was like that—all action, few words. He disregarded all the fussy niceties that the birdcage of Japanese business is made up of. One time when I had made the obligatory conversational remark about the weather, Ito cocked his head and put his hand to his ear, said he hadn't heard me, that the words were too small. I never made small talk again. With Ito, silence seemed to be preferable.

"I expect you're kind of lonely," he said that night, straight out, as he was dropping me off at the station to take the ten-fifteen train home. I scratched at my arms and ankles. Suburban living: I was covered with mosquito bites.

"Sometimes," I replied. "I'm getting used to it. I'm glad to have my work."

"Yes, work is good," he agreed. We were in the family van, not his car, more a miniature school bus than a personal vehicle—paint sets and soccer balls in the back, fuzzy stick-on animals on the steering wheel. It had a certain coziness to it. I would much rather have slept on its narrow seat than endured the long milk run back to Northwestern station, then another train ride to Hyde Park.

"It's too bad your work's not particularly social, though," he continued, and hit the button to clean the windshield for lack of any other available task. "You come in, you go out, you work at home. You need people around, I think."

"I'm all right," I said. I explained with surprising candor my other vocation, that I was washing pots. Ito, open-minded success story that he was, ate it right up.

"Very interesting. Still, you're behind the scenes, and all those expensive restaurants usually just have waiters and male chefs. You need to mix with people socially. I myself met my wife at work."

"Where?"

"The import-export firm. She was a secretary there."

I peered at him through the green glow of the dashboard. "May I ask you something?"

"Sure."

"Your wife—weren't you nervous about approaching her, of being smaller, of being from another race? Of being so different?"

Ito dipped his thatched head, straightened his slouched shoulders reflectively. He turned on the radio—the bongs of a newscast sounding the hour.

"Maybe; I don't recall. We got along well. She has a good sense of humor; I liked that. And I liked her, so I followed my instincts. I always follow my instincts, otherwise I can't sleep at night. They've never failed me."

The bull only sees the flag, he doesn't care what country it represents. I spared him this analogy.

"You would make a good general," I said instead, and Ito laughed.

"Oh, I don't know about that. I have no finesse. Sergeant, maybe. Just someone who motivates. But back to my original statement. Anything brewing in your life?"

"Brewing?"

"Women-wise."

"Oh. No, not at present."

"Well . . ." He hung over the steering wheel, brooding. I noticed for the first time that he had heavy, almost sensual lips.

"You can always marry my daughter in ten years," he offered. "She likes you."

"That's a comfort," I said, and we laughed again. The approaching train cut a thin arc across the flats surrounding the area. I unhooked my seat belt. "I'd better go." He nodded.

"See you tomorrow."

I scrambled up onto the platform and waved my arms just to make sure the conductor saw me—I was the only person waiting, and the train, like all trains in the dark, was moving fast, speeding as if it did not want to stop. Ito honked and drove away. I slept well with borrowed domesticity that night.

My friend the mouse, who nibbled my shoelaces and scratched around in the garbage, met his fate in an open-mouth jar of sesame oil. I had a big can of the oil, but it was too cumbersome to keep lifting all the time, so I had poured a ration out into an empty peanut butter jar. I left the lid off one night when I was too spent from the heat to clean up the mess from dinner. The mouse was drowned in the oil by morning. I felt terrible for him as I fished him out by his slippery little tail, poor gray body oozing, claws outstretched, whiskers drenched. Awful expression on his face. Such a terrible death—I wished I hadn't been so careless. Dead mice were becoming milestones of my life. I found them in bomb shelters, in laundry rooms and in bottles of oil. I decided to look for another apartment. I could not conceive of starting over again, with a new mouse.

I found a place that had been lived in by generations of students, its walls and cabinets slathered with another layer of thick white paint each time a person moved out—I nearly dislocated my shoulder forcing open the windows. Still, it had two small rooms, an adequate kitchen, and an octagonal sun porch. I signed the lease with my neat Western signature, put SHIMADA on the buzzer and the mailbox. I didn't care anymore if they found me—it was nearly the final week of July. At this point I would be happy to see them, have them sit on the floor of my home and drink coffee out of Styrofoam cups—although I hadn't a stick of furniture or a dish to my name, I would be a gracious if not desperate host.

Hiroshi passed me on State Street one day around lunchtime. I saw him coming, antlike, dragging a huge sack of what looked like bedding. Forever the ant, Hiroshi bought things like down comforters and quilts in the dead of summer, which of course was when they were cheapest. I froze up, then relaxed, knowing he would turn onto Madison, back toward the office—but he did not; he kept on straight. There was really nowhere for me to duck into, except for a wig shop, which would have been ludicrous, and pointless, for by now he was only a step away. He looked at me sharply: this was it, I thought, he was going to perform a citizen's arrest right there on the sidewalk. We would wrestle, he would win by binding me in a cocoon of blue goose down. But Hiroshi didn't see me as me, he was merely eyeing me with apprehension. I had become dark from all my walking; my hair was longer than it had ever been before—shaggy, by now all different lengths; I was wearing sunglasses, casual clothes, worn loafers (Ito's usual frumpy attire did not encourage me to gussy up: one did not want to dress better than the boss). I had the day's work in a nondescript manila envelope against my hip, strolled along with no briefcase, no watch, no tie, no wedding ring—no signs of respectability. Hiroshi was a little worried about me, that was it—all those years of being beat up on had made him edge around every thug.

A thug, that was what I looked like. To me he had always sounded like a *yakuza*, but to him I now looked like one. I crossed the street indolently and tried to keep up my shifty presence, then ducked into the Palmer House, where I had planned to eat lunch anyway, and watched him from the corridor. The revolving door sounded like a person being flogged. Hiroshi had not recognized me: I had almost wanted to seize him by his pubescent shoulders and shout, "It's me! It's Shimada! Don't you know?"

Incredible. I went into the coffee shop and drained a glass of water at a gulp, there at my usual booth. I took a great breath and laughed quietly to myself. Hadn't even known me at close range. I supposed I would need to see a barber before August 16.

As I was paying my check, a hollow-cheeked woman in black approached and grazed her hand against my arm. I stood back, startled, and gave her a closer look—she was Asian, yes—and then I felt the same frozen stance come over me as when I had seen Hiroshi. It was Taeko. Taeko, hidden in a baggy dress with no belt; Taeko, about ten pounds lighter, so that she seemed transparent; Taeko, a coy smile across her lips. Her hair was shorter now than my own, severe and cadet-like. I could hardly recognize her but knew within seconds it was my wife. Her eyes were moist, the clearest of browns. Before I could stop myself, I had shoved her away.

"Good *God!*" I said, dropping my manila pouch. She picked it up. I clutched it, then held it like a shield between us. "You can't just appear like that! I almost had a heart attack!"

Bea, my usual waitress, was regarding me sourly, having seen me shove a woman. I was normally so good-natured and polite, she made a point of giving me extra wedges of melon. I hurried back to my table and left her a heavy tip to compensate, then ushered Taeko out. People were staring. Taeko, *here*. I could hardly believe the feel of her small elbow between my fingertips.

"You told me you ate at the Palmer House every day," she said as we rode the escalator up to the lobby. "I thought I'd surprise you." She glanced at the ornate lobby ceiling and gasped softly. "Oh, that's just beautiful. Almost like a fresco. When was this hotel built?"

"Eighteen ninety? I don't know. Do we really want to discuss this?" I plunked her down on a plush sofa amid a convention of Shriners milling around the reception desk. "Now, why are you here?"

Black canvas shoes on her bare feet, as shapeless as the black dress. No makeup, no jewelry, no ornamentation whatsoever. I was not used to seeing Taeko stripped down like this, except in the morning, but even then she had always had the distraction of her hair. I assumed all this was what made her seem so different to me, but then I realized when she spoke that it wasn't that; it was the fact that she was looking me in the eye, that she had no hidden expression—not contempt, not guilt, not boredom. Her expression now was calm, maybe a little peaked. I wondered when she had flown in. She had only a large rattan bag, no luggage.

"Why?" I repeated.

She moistened her lips. "I had already bought Etsuko's ticket when I called you. It was a special price. Rather than return it and lose half the money, I decided to come myself. I've never seen Chicago, and you don't have to watch me during the day. I'm an adult."

"Oh, are you? When did that happen?" I couldn't help it—like the shove, it had just slipped out. Although I couldn't stop looking at her, I was still annoyed by the whole thing. Skipping off to see me, as if I was there waiting, with no life of my own. This was true, in a sense, yet something hard lodged in my stomach and prevented me from showing any pleasure. My ulcer cramped for the first time in two weeks.

"What's wrong?" she asked. "You said you missed me."

I stared in disbelief. "You took off on me," I began coldly. "You left me—you were too childish to even tell me where you were going—you took away my daughter and made me look like an idiot. Forgive me if I don't bound up to greet you. Even the stupidest dog hangs back after you kick him in the head."

Her lips were now pale. She moistened them again, seeming to draw back into herself, then surged forward.

"I am sorry, and I cannot apologize enough, I realize that."

I sputtered. "No—no, you can't."

"But I'm not going to let it ruin the rest of my life."

I lit a cigarette. She took one for herself, unasked, inhaled meditatively, her eyes narrowed. The gesture amused me, despite myself. She never smoked—I think she just wanted to show me she was composed, that or allow us equal conversational weapons.

"It shouldn't be forgotten," I said.

"No," she agreed. "But neither should the circumstances around it."

"Which were my fault." I leaned toward her. "Well, while we're divvying up the guilt, let's not forget Dr. Saito. I'm afraid I can't forget that."

"I was unhappy. Did you want me to kill myself? Are you that old-fashioned?"

"Who, me?" I laughed briefly. "If I were old-fashioned, I would have been the one to kill you."

A Shriner sat down in his purple fez, gave us a look, one-dimensional, as if we were a pair of Nips talking about all the things we could buy here in Chicago. He murmured to his buddy, producing great guffaws. I boiled at this—I wanted to go over and kick him in the gut, knock that stupid cylindrical thing off his head. Then I realized he'd probably fought in the Pacific or Korea; he was of that age. Gook wars, bad wars; a horrible time in his life. I turned away with the same wary resignation I'd had in Indiana. Some people you could never reach: it was the same on both sides.

Taeko was examining her cigarette between her slim fingers—as if she didn't know how to smoke it—yet when she did puff, her cheeks went in and her nose crinkled with enjoyment. She nudged me with her foot, so wan and appealing.

"Haven't we discussed this all already, Jun? If you want to remember it forever, then remember it. I was stupid, I wasn't very strong. I'm not thinking we can live happily ever after—I only had a chance to come visit, and I did. I wanted to see you now, see all these changes. We've both changed, haven't we? I think it's kind of exciting."

I asked her how her flight had been.

"Interesting. Economy was full by the time Dad dropped me at Narita, so they put me in first class." She flushed. "I felt so guilty: all those hot towels and caviar—I only paid for a regular seat in coach. Even the headsets have more padding around the ears. I saved you parts of the grooming kit they gave us, the razor and the shoehorn. I kept the kelp soap and the sponge—you don't mind, do you?"

"Why should I care?" I replied.

I saw her studying me in more detail now. I had last seen her six months earlier, after Hirohito's death. Our two selves back then were so young and plump; it was as though a whole outer layer had been peeled away. I remembered how soft a face I had had, how tender—I was only just starting to really drink.

We went on for a moment, examining each other.

"What luck, your getting in first class. Those seats cost a fortune—that's how Yamamoto flies."

Taeko had aged a bit, though it was only around the eyes—not lines or bags, but a gravity of expression.

She nodded. "All you do is eat. I told you I felt guilty—at first."

"Then you gave in."

"Yes."

"Enjoyed yourself."

"I did. It was a good omen for the trip."

Like my rose petals. I patted my work folder, which was quite full. Prior to Taeko's showing up, I had been happy for so much. Now I wondered how I was going to go on.

"How long do you plan on staying?" I asked.

"Eight days. I have things to do; I won't tie you up," she added, intuitively. "You won't need to worry about entertaining me at all."

"Things to do?"

She had a leather cord around her wrist, a bracelet of sorts, under which was a thin white line of skin. Pale as she was, she must have had some sun of late. The line circled and intersected with fine blue veins. It seemed inexpressibly beautiful, like decoration on a vase or a piece of china.

"What's your itinerary?" I said.

"Museums and galleries. Sightseeing. I should be quite busy."

She brushed my knee, presumably just a light touch, the hand of a wife on familiar terms with her husband's body. My knee, however, stiffened.

"Eating ice cream?" I offered, although I was still pretty dour.

She laughed. "You never did explain that to me, the ice cream postcard."

She mistook silence for anger. "If you want, Jun, I'll go to a hotel. I have money budgeted."

"You'd be better off at a hotel," I said. "I just found a new place, and there's no furniture. You'd have to sleep on the floor." I looked at her bitterly. "Might be bad for your back."

"No," she said. "It would be better, at that. Hard surfaces are preferable, really."

"Is that right?"

"Yes. I told you I was taking acupuncture, didn't I? Also I do exercises and take calcium supplements. Etsuko's taking them too. It's best to catch these things early on."

"Right."

She sat up straight, as if to show me her progress, then brushed her hair away from her temples. The hair lifted slightly, then fell into a geometric arrangement. Her fingers were unusually sallow and puckered, which she explained was due to turpentine and solvents.

"Don't you wear gloves?"

"No. Too fussy."

"You're really serious about painting now, aren't you?"

She spread her ruined fingers with a delicate sense of pride. "It fills my time. I know it's hard for you to imagine me serious about anything," she said, then smiled. "But then it's hard for me to imagine you *not* serious. I still have my moments of laziness, though. But I do like to paint, and I have been productive. It's my outlet."

I moved over next to her and grabbed her arm, holding it, almost pumping it in desperation. "Why couldn't you have painted in New York—why not then? I asked you that before, remember? Why didn't you make that your outlet then?"

She stared ahead. "I wasn't capable of painting. I was so miserable I couldn't even get out of bed. You don't understand; you can't. Everything was awful then—it took me hours to decide whether to do laundry or dust; it took me hours to get myself together just to go grocery shopping. I couldn't think. When the baby was asleep I used to sit in the cellar, you know, down by the hot-water heater, in the dark, and listen to it go on and off, warm and quiet, away from everything. I was happy there. That made my mind go dark and quiet too, and I liked that. I knew I needed an outlet—that's always the answer, to keep busy—but I couldn't stick to anything. I had no ideas; I didn't even want to do copies or sketches. I didn't want to waste the canvas. I didn't want to depress myself even more with the results."

Taeko down by the boiler, on the filthy cement floor. The bowels of the house; while upstairs, dishes sat heaped in the sink and the dog clawed in concern on the cellar door, Long Island sun came through the windows and spread across the walls, solid plaster walls, which were always cool and damp. A young woman in the prime of her life, curled up next to a hot-water heater. I sighed and loosened her arm, rubbed my thumb against the small biceps area, with its constellation of tiny moles. I just couldn't be angry with her anymore—it was like a muscular pose I had assumed to make my physique more impressive and that I couldn't continue to maintain. What was the point of it anyway? She had suffered, she had hit bottom; she had had to admit failure and humble herself before her father so he would take her in; and she was now humbling herself before me, simply by coming back to a place she was so afraid of. Perhaps it was just a goal she had set, to test her new strengths—it had nothing to do with me; I was only a convenience, her friend in the States. Perhaps, yes, yet perhaps it was best not to overanalyze. Perhaps I had been wrong too. She had cut off her hair, and this alone indicated something to me. Taeko had always been tremendously vain about her hair.

I let a portion of my anger go with another sigh, felt myself relax and expand. Excitement ensued among the Shriners, as in the upper lounge the Winetasters of America were setting up their reception to celebrate the new Zinfandel and were giving out samples. I went over and got a plastic goblet of it for Taeko. She had always liked wine.

She sipped appreciatively. "None for you?" she asked. I made a face.

"It looks like cherry soda," I said, pointing.

"Mmm. This will only make me more tired."

Everything seemed to happen to me in Chicago hotels, I thought, great lavish hotels like stage sets I had wandered onto. I had met Gina at the Drake. I had fallen apart at the Nippon. I had been hired by Ito at the Four Seasons. And I had been surprised by Taeko at the Palmer House.

"Are we divorced yet?" I asked, something I had been meaning to find out for some time; I had always got deflected onto other subjects.

"Not yet. I told you it takes a while."

"How long?"

"By year end. You can start the new decade with it all behind you."

She was holding a good bluff: no change of eye contact or expression; no change of voice. I was bluffing as well, blasé. I suggested
that we leave, and she accepted with equal politeness; we hopped
a bus, talked about the sights, hopped off the bus and walked to
my home. Taeko asked for a glass of water, being dehydrated from
the flight.

"I've been awake forever," she said, almost swooning.

I unrolled the futon, drew the shades and sealed her off in the
bedroom, where she fell asleep, still in her black shoes and dress.
I tiptoed around happily—I caught myself being happy, but I didn't
like it, tried to stop, yet the feeling persisted like soda bubbles.
I sat in the kitchen at a card table I had bought from the Salvation
Army and managed to do some work. Each time I finished a page
of the Sumitomo Foreign Auto Parts Catalogue, I couldn't help but
walk over to the bedroom to listen to Taeko breathing. And I *could*
hear her, the place was so cavernous and empty. It was a reassuring
sound.

I went and found her purse. I extracted from it a smaller bag,
full of travel-size bottles, lotions, the kelp soap and sponge from
the airline, a toothbrush. These I carefully arranged to look dis-
arrayed around the bathroom sink, then stood back, pleased with
the effect. Before, it had been just a razor and a bar of Ivory, my
own toothbrush and a new tube of striped toothpaste, almost pathetic with its merry colors. Now it looked like someplace, a man
and a woman living together, enforcing each other's presence. At
least one quarter of the apartment had a personality. I went out
into the remaining three quarters and skidded in my socks across
the old wood floors. It wasn't big enough for a family, but I didn't
care to think of anything like that. I told myself that I just wanted
to be selfish and enjoy my guest, yet somewhere in the eaves of
my mind I was thinking that if we put Omi on the sun porch and
Etsuko on a fold-out couch in the living room, we all might manage
to fit. They were hidden thoughts, sappy thoughts I didn't care to

admit. "To forgive is *easy*," I jeered out loud. "It has absolutely nothing to do with being divine."

The letter of resignation was going nowhere, and there were only nine days remaining till my meeting with Yamamoto. Although I set aside time to write it, I was generally too hand-cramped from translation to do anything but scrawl the word *compassion* over and over again on a yellow scratch pad. Yamamoto must have been furious with me by now, all those weeks back from Kinosaki, which as far as he was concerned had been a wasted treatment. He wasn't getting a reformed employee; he was getting a deserter. Still, I remembered how he had sat by my bedside and pressed his hand against my head. He was not a demonstrative man. If he cared about me that much, he wouldn't want me to be unhappy. All that "son" business over the years—what did it really signify? The true son was someone with filial piety, not a prodigal. With the buffer of elapsed time, however, I realized that I was no longer afraid of him—I actually missed him in an odd way; it had been so long. *Compassion, compassion*, I scribbled again. I imagined an enraged pair of eagle eyes turning toward me.

I fell asleep. Sometime around daybreak, I heard water running for a bath. I lay there in discomfort, my shoulder blades and knees planing into the boards of the living room floor. It reminded me of sleeping on the floor with Keiji on my last night in Glen Cove, only then I had been drunk and more relaxed. Taeko was bathing. I heard her give a little chuckle: was it at her things arranged on the sink's ledge? did she understand? I continued to listen. The splashing of water, water in the hollow of her delicate armpits, down between the valley of her breasts. Buttocks rubbing against the tub bottom. I closed my eyes.

When she was through, she emerged in a pajama top and stood in the hallway, watching me as she combed her hair. For twenty years she had had long hair, and she geared up still for deep strokes, then ended each of them with a surprised jerk of the wrist, dragging the comb through mere air. She was trying to tell if I was still asleep. I pretended to be. How times had changed! She went back into the bedroom and turned off the light, and I smiled.

I wasn't ready to go near her just yet. It wasn't so simple, as if we were snap-together pieces of a toy. We were different now— the body shapes had changed. She had said before that all I missed were the sexual comforts of a wife, and I wanted to disprove this, more to myself than to her. And if I enjoyed it, I would be miserable when she left—I had learned my lesson with Gina, I thought. It was so strange to have a woman around again, even stranger than getting used to being alone. I told myself all this, there in the dark. I shouldn't make it easy for her; she shouldn't be able to win me over like that. Then I ground myself back into the floor and realized that every part of me was fully awake.

"Well, your performance has certainly improved," she remarked the following morning over breakfast. "Did you have an affair?"

I slid a rice omelet onto her plate, then cracked two eggs with one hand and beat them to prepare my own. I had bought all sorts of cooking things as soon as I had settled into this good-size kitchen. I had also bought the *Larousse Gastronomique*, a ten-pound volume, which I pored over avidly every day, caught up in the incomparable world of soufflés and reduction sauces. It had been De Mornay's suggestion. Although he was nouvelle, he insisted that you couldn't be inventive if you didn't know the classics.

"Yes, I did," I replied, just as casually, knocking the pan against my hip so that the eggs spread evenly.

She looked a little sick. "Oh. When?"

"Started last December, ended in April." I spooned a mixture of rice and minced onion into the omelet, folded it over and joined her at the table. "Surprised?"

"A bit."

"Can you blame me?"

She rolled her eyes. "No . . . but all the moralizing you did. Really, you had no right!"

I buttered a wedge of toast. It was a very nice spread—toast, omelets, marmalade, juice, and a bowl of fruit in the center. I was quite proud of myself. This was really *my* kitchen.

"You started, Taeko."

She wasn't touching any of her food. This distressed me more than anything else.

"But the moralizing, the guilt you heaped on me. That was hardly fair!"

I sprinkled some salt. "My affair was casual," I said. "Nobody got pregnant."

"You *can't* get pregnant!"

"*You* should have been more careful."

"Oh, I don't believe this," she said.

"Eat your breakfast," I urged. "It's getting cold."

She managed a few bites, then threw down her fork.

"Who was it? I want to know."

I swallowed, carefully. "Well, there were two. The first was the receptionist at Yamamoto in New York—"

She interrupted. "Miho?"

"Yes. You knew her?"

"Of course. I spoke to her every time I called you at the office." She covered her face with her hands, but she was not crying. "Oh, I can't believe this."

"It was only a few times, after the Christmas party. You had had Omi, and if I recall, we weren't even sleeping in the same bed."

She waved me away. "And the other—the long-term one?"

"That was an American, a tea waitress at the Drake. She was an unusual girl, sort of a free spirit. I didn't love her. But it was what I wanted at the time."

"An American!" she exclaimed. "Did you use condoms?"

I nearly choked juice out of my nose, laughing. "Taeko. What kind of a thing is that to say?"

"An honest one. You said she'd been around."

"I did not. I said she was a free spirit."

"Who'd been around. And I don't want to talk about it anymore."

"You brought it up."

"As a joke." Her cheeks were bright. She picked up a piece of the newspaper and pretended to read it with an intensity I knew she wasn't capable of—her English had not surpassed the third-grade level, and it was the business section she had grabbed. I wondered if she was truly upset. Yet she wasn't crying, miracle of miracles—Taeko, who cried so easily, who fell apart at the slightest touch. She only seemed to be breathing hard, with a bit lip. I pushed the paper aside.

"You can't be mad," I said. "You have to realize how this affair helped me—no, really, it did. It was a catalyst, I think; it brought me down so low, made me focus so much on physical feelings that I had to redeem myself by bouncing back. Prove I was something more than just a bunch of urges. It was a shock to the system. I needed one. Don't you think it was to my benefit?"

"I can't talk about it now, as freely as you," she said. "I'm not that *sophisticated*." Still, she let me hold her hand. There were hard little pads on the palm. I pressed each one.

Taeko then spoke: "All I'm mad about is the wounded-husband act you put on. Acting like I was the only one in the wrong. You should have told me then. It might have made a difference. I felt so guilty, I thought I had to leave you. You should have been honest."

"It never occurred to me," I replied. "Or to you, admit it. We swept it under the rug, didn't we? Both of us."

She shook her head, then illogically said yes. Whispered it.

"But there aren't any rugs here." I laughed, rubbing my foot against the bare floor. "Everything's up-front, huh?" My raised voice echoed through the rooms.

This time, however, she gave no answer. She had big shadows under her eyes this morning, yet she appeared less drawn than she had the previous day, following her trip. She delicately buttered her toast, set it down and complained that she liked rye bread better than wheat. "And this omelet's runny," she continued.

"That omelet's perfect," I said. "Don't try to get to me through my cooking."

"Your cooking stinks." She chewed on, then let out a great moan, clutching the bottom of her jaw. "Shell fragments too! Mr. Big Shot, cracking five eggs at a time. You might pay more attention to what you're doing."

"Taeko!" I said. She was laughing, but with effort.

"You know something, Jun, you're just as dumb as I am. Here I thought you were superior. You're not."

"We're dumb in different ways," I conceded. I had taken her omelet away from her and was examining it closely.

"Is this tea waitress out of the picture?" she asked.

"Very much so. She's not even in the country anymore. She went to Italy—abandoned me, just like you did."

"I'm sorry."

"Don't be sarcastic."

"But I'm not. I *am* sorry; I've told you so many times."

I gave her back her plate. "Just forget it. I don't want to hear about it anymore. The score's tied. All right?"

"So who's in the picture now?" she persisted.

"No one. I'm abstinent. Couldn't you tell last night?"

She liked the thought of last night, I could see that. She began rolling an orange between her palms, studying it. Her hands among objects were trained and supple. I imagined they would be the same way when mixing colors or choosing a brush, although I had never really seen her at work. It was strange, how I suddenly perceived her as having talent. I wondered if it was a ploy she had deliberately thought up: making herself seem serious by stripping down her own good looks. I asked her about this.

"Yes, I did it on purpose," she admitted. "My looks were of no help to me. They were the wrong type, too obvious—they attracted all the wrong sort of attention."

"Like me?"

"Mmm, maybe. I just got tired of it, all those peaches and pinks, silk, hair ribbons, men gawking through my clothes. None of that was what I wanted. Now you have to look hard to see something. I know I'm beautiful, somewhat. But it gets tiresome centering your whole life around that. When I started painting, the hair got in the way, so I cut it off. The looser clothes were more comfortable. I like seeing my naked face, and I like to force it on other people. You have to be really at ease to do that—it took me years to be able to go out in public without makeup. You don't like it?"

I smiled. "Actually, I do. I've always been fond of the anemic look."

She set the orange down on the table and stabbed it hard with a knife. Her teeth were bared.

"That's *your* face, Jun," she said.

"Oh, is that so?" I was now squeezing her hand. I had never liked Taeko so much in my life.

She laid her head down on the table like a tired child and kept quiet for a while, shoulders hunched, a large hollow the size of an egg cup on either side of her collarbone.

"Let's take a walk someplace," I suggested. With all the hot air of confession around, it had become rather stuffy inside.

"Where?"

"Anywhere. Around the block. Around the world. Okay?"

She raised her head and looked at me sadly.

"Two flings. One wasn't enough."

"You should feel, uh—*vindicated*," I said.

"Maybe."

She came over, took my hand and placed it on her slight breast.

"This is only a visit here," she cautioned.

I gave her a half-smile.

"That's all right," I said. "What more can I expect?"

❖

Slides. The last time I had been involved with them was the day of the corporation meeting. It had been warm that day, not so long ago, yet when I thought back on it all, I saw it happening not to me but to Toshiro Mifune as he'd been in *Stray Dog*. As though it had happened to another person. It had.

Taeko was at the table, arranging slides in a plastic sleeve. She was preparing to bring them to a gallery that had expressed interest. The slides were all numbered, catalogued and detailed in tiny type. She had done a total of thirty-six paintings over the past five months. I had peered at a few and been astonished: a young punk shaving, a train at night full of dozing commuters, a policeman soaking his feet. I had no idea where she had come up with such things. I had always assumed Taeko would be a woman's sort of painter, limited to flowers and landscapes.

"You're ambitious," I said, and the observation unnerved me.

She pursed her lips and went on arranging. "Just making up for lost time, I guess."

"We started with slides, you know," I reminded her, bringing up our first meeting in the library.

"Yes, I know," she said, and although she was smiling slightly, she did not look up.

She was trimming my hair. I was seated backward on the closed lid of the toilet, my head bent, while Taeko took precise and gentle snips.

"Old man's got some gray in here." She laughed. "Should we save the clippings?"

She rubbed at my shoulders and neck with a towel. I stood up and took a look at myself, and I didn't like seeing my old round face. The hair had made it seem tougher, with more character. Now it was a boring magazine face, with the obligatory side-part haircut. I walked away. Taeko followed.

She had tacked something up on one of the walls, an art postcard. I pointed to it.

"What's this?" I asked.

"The beginning of your collection. It's Foujita. I bought it at the

Art Institute. He was an expatriate, lived in Paris with Picasso and the rest. This is a self-portrait."

She spoke with that quiet and shining devotion you see in young nuns.

"Is he your favorite?"

"Mmm, not exclusively. I like Van Gogh too, and a bunch of others."

"Going to work here?" I asked.

She brushed some of my hair off the oversized shirt she was wearing. She was certainly dressed for painting.

"I don't think so; I'm on vacation," she said. "Though the light's very good on that porch. If I lived here, that would be my studio."

"I thought we'd put Omi out there," I joked.

Taeko thought for a moment, thumbs to her temples. "No. Omi could fit in the pantry."

"But that's so small!"

"So's Omi," Taeko said.

"How about the back porch? The cold night air's good for a kid."

I kept hitting balls to her, just to see how she'd react. She rallied well.

"You'd give the dog the master bedroom, of course," she said.

"Of course!"

"You know the dog misses you most of all?"

"Sure. I figured the dog would fly here to see me before you would."

Later, when I was about to leave for the restaurant, she called me over. She had transit maps spread over the floor, visitor guides, scribbled handwritten directions. It looked like command central of a tourist office. I squatted down and listened to her explain where it was she wanted to go: another gallery. I nodded and dropped two city tokens into her palm.

"Piece of cake. You'll have to take the bus and then another bus. Or you can switch to a train if you want variety. Ask for a transfer."

"Is it a bad neighborhood?" she asked, one arched eyebrow arched higher in trepidation.

"Not really."

"Are you just telling me that, or is it bad?"

"It's not bad. I don't want you to get murdered—if anything happens to you, I'll have to deal with your father. He'd hold me responsible; he'd cut off my fingers."

She poked me with a pencil. "Come with me," she said, then a split second later shook her head. "No, don't. I'll manage."

"I'll go with you if you want," I offered. "Are you afraid?"

"No." She turned back to the map. "I'll manage."

"Good," I said. "And even if you don't, you'll have tried. I'll respect you greatly."

"How nice," she replied, then regarded me for a moment. "You're really going to this job—to wash dishes?"

"Pots. Yes, I am."

"But I'm only here another two days. Can't you take the night off?"

"No."

She traced the pencil over my lips. "This *is* serious, then."

"I think so." I ran the back of my hand over her cheekbone, simply to reconfirm its presence.

"Then go," she said. "I don't want you to be late."

I tucked in my T-shirt, found my keys and wallet. As I bounded out the door, I was overcome by a silly urge to steal Taeko's shoes, so she couldn't run away in my absence.

De Mornay fired the vegetable prep that night. A blond, blue-eyed kid in his twenties, the vegetable prep had, despite his angelic appearance, a swift and nasty temper. He mouthed off, something about the ratatouille looking lousy because De Mornay gave him watery "seedbag" tomatoes to work with. He then flung a tomato against the wall. There had long been tension between them. The vegetable prep was a graduate of the Culinary Institute of America and was frustrated by his small duties. "I could have done this in kindergarten," he had muttered to me once. He walked out in mid–rush hour. De Mornay stared at the remains of the vegetable prep's station and at the exploded tomato, his face thickening as if he might spit blood, and then he smiled coolly, turning to us all.

"No elaborate garnishes tonight; it's as simple as that. All garnishing will be done by me. Jun, you will come over here and wash and peel the vegetables. Forget the pots for now; anyone who finishes a pot will wash it himself. The vegetables are of supreme importance. We have orders coming in."

He motioned me over from where I stood, paralyzed, behind the sink.

"Jun, I said to come here. I'm not joking."

He explained much too quickly what it was I had to do. My legs quivered, so that I had to grip the counter.

"This is not as easy as it looks," he threatened. "I want uniform cuts. And don't let them sit out for a minute—keep them moist. *No brown edges!*"

"Poor Chinese bastard," I heard the fish cook mutter under his breath. I didn't bother to correct him. The sympathy was enough.

For three hours I washed and sliced vegetables—bright, ripe produce from Mexico—sweat forming on my forehead, running and beading down my nose. I felt I was performing open-heart surgery. I kept waiting for an outburst, a horrible shriek at some misshapen chunk of eggplant I had tried to pass off, but De Mornay said nothing. Time blurred. I began to hallucinate. I saw Taeko's peppers on a cutting-board painting, only instead of peppers, there before me were my own fingers, hacked off by a raging chef.

After the ordeal I slunk back happily to my ceiling-high stack of pots (not one person had washed his own, as instructed, only toward the bitter end, when we had run out), and I sudsed around. My hands were still trembling. I cut one of them open on a chafing dish that had broken in half. I got blood all over myself; I bandaged myself up. I kept washing. Only when the evening was over did

De Mornay come over and tell me, tartly, I had done a good job, then as the real reward showed me several shimmering pans of fruit terrine he had prepared earlier in the day. He watched me sweep and packaged a bunch of glacéed grapes and cherries for me to take home.

"Go ahead," he insisted. "We can't use them after today."

I left with my hand bound and stains on my pants, bloody yet triumphant, emerging from battle. It was a beautiful hot night, the sort that sucked the wind out of you. Storm-tossed. I was exultant. What doubled the pleasure was that I had someone to tell the story to at home, and I could hardly wait. Taeko, however, was curled up on the futon, her knees drawn up to her chest. The lights were all off. For a moment I thought she had gone back to the depression, that she was no better at all, and I felt a thud of deep disappointment hit me, like a kick in the ass. The scene was far too familiar. She rolled over at my touch, though, and told me irritably that she had menstrual cramps.

"I'm all right, or I will be when the pills take effect. You know how I get. Acupuncture doesn't help this."

I offered her some of the candied fruit, but she pushed it away. With my good hand I rubbed at her midriff, which did seem rather tense and distended.

"Does this help, or is it bothering you?" I asked.

She kept her eyes closed, face immobile. "It's sort of a help. What happened to you?"

As calmly as I could, I described the vegetable prep incident, my manner much more subdued than when I had been rehearsing it on the train. She was silent when I finished. There was a pleasant odor to her, of kelp soap and perspiration.

"That's something," she said, after a long moment. "Think of how the sukiyaki chefs are about vegetables. I'm surprised he didn't do it himself."

"He had a pigeon consommé going; he couldn't break away."

She laughed. "Ugh. Pigeons like you see on the street?"

"Yes; exactly. And people *pay* to eat them. I catch them with flour sacks in the park." I crammed a cluster of cherries into my mouth. The sugar was coursing through my exhausted body; I felt a sharp buzz, as if I were drunk.

"Do you understand why I'm doing this, or does it amuse you?" I suddenly said.

She lifted her leg and let it fall, groaning. "Mmm, I can't understand it really, but it doesn't amuse me. I mean, it amuses me when you tell me kitchen stories, about the prima donnas, but I don't think *you* are silly. Does my painting amuse you?"

"You've gotten money for your painting." I laughed. "You must be on the right track. I'm hardly being paid for this at all, for doing *clean-up* work. The lowest of the low. All my training down the drain."

"Yes, but you're learning. Isn't that what you want?"

"Maybe it's a phase."

"And what if it is? Who cares? I don't. It's an experience." She removed my hand from her stomach, which I was now kneading to death.

"Sorry," I said.

"Could I have a grape?"

"Of course." I slid one into her mouth, touching the edge of her tongue with my pinkie. She was so nice and fever hot, like something out of the oven. I wanted to open her up and crawl inside.

"You don't want to be bothered now, do you?" I asked.

"Not really."

"They say intercourse relieves these symptoms." This was true—I had translated an article on the subject for a women's magazine.

"Do they?" She twisted up again, sucking on a grape. "I wouldn't advise it," she said. "It's like a vise in there; you'd probably never come out intact."

"No, thanks. I understand." I hesitated, then straightened the sheet over her lower half. "You understand too, it seems. Don't you, Taeko?"

"I try," she said.

I left her there in peace and took my fruit into the kitchen, sitting by the window to watch the tremendous storm brewing, feel the alternate gusts of warm and cool air on my face. Tin cans went rolling along the alley. Car alarms sounded. It was a wild night, like the screaming of demons. I enjoyed it thoroughly from my refuge inside.

Morning came, with everything green and cleansed and pelted into pulp. Hail had accompanied the storm the night before; the battered geraniums in the yard had a wrecked but hopeful look. It was Taeko's last day. We went around with a solemn awkwardness—I ignored her while she packed. She was leaving next day in actuality, but so early that it didn't count. After I had picked up and completed my assignments—fortunately small ones, Ito having gone off on that trip to Disneyland—I joined her for sightseeing. Along with alarming numbers of other Japanese (and Chinese, Canadian, German and unidentified) tourists, we made the pilgrimage to the Field Museum, the Shedd Aquarium, the Water Tower and the Sears Tower. Taeko had been to the Art Institute, so we skipped that. It was a familiar route for me, as I had set it up so often for Yamamoto's visiting cronies. In the evening we would take the boat ride, up the backward river.

I let her do as she pleased; it was her holiday. It was important to me that all her memories be good ones. She was wearing a dotted jersey and harem pants, billowing along like a priestess, and like a priestess, she made a grand ceremony out of everything, even choosing postcards at Woolworth's. Up in the observatory of the Sears Tower, we stood very close to each other by the window, facing south. I murmured in her ear.

"There's Indiana . . . see the smokestacks of Gary; and that's Soldier Field, where they play football."

She leaned back. "Interesting," she said. "Sort of like Tokyo Tower."

I grazed my lips against her bare shoulder. "We need to talk," I said.

She replied, "Yes, I know," and then we both immediately moved away from each other and the subject.

At an outdoor café on Michigan Avenue, she wanted to have a cappuccino.

"Outside?" I asked. "Don't you want air-conditioning?" The cool of the morning had worn off. Already it was back to ninety degrees.

"No, there's a nice breeze here. Plus outside we can watch people."

Taeko was that way, able to sit and dawdle over coffee for hours. I had never been able to match this stamina, the ability to keep motionless and sun for hours, like a lizard on a rock. I had always blamed my restlessness on my job. Now I recognized it as sheer restlessness. I sat there, however, for Taeko's sake. Taeko massaged her feet.

"You're killing me," she grumbled. "I think we walked about twenty miles."

"You said you wanted to sightsee."

She licked the cappuccino foam off her spoon. "Seeing and walking are two different things."

"What did you like best?" I asked.

"The Yamamoto Netsuke Room at the Field Museum."

"Be serious."

"Mmm, this. . . ." She extended her arm. "Michigan Avenue is beautiful. The sidewalks are all diamondy—did you ever notice that? What was *your* favorite?"

I pulled open two plastic half-and-half containers and dumped them into my coffee, stirred, then poured the coffee over the glass of ice I had requested. After a moment, I drank. By doing this, I saved the extra ninety cents it cost for iced coffee.

"What's going on with us? We need to get down to business." I spoke calmly and with confidence. The edge of the Cinzano umbrella over our table flapped like a sail. It had been such an unexpected and successful span of days that I no longer cared about protocol or pride. I only wanted to know, so that I could continue on without doubts. "That's my favorite subject at present."

Taeko slipped on her sunglasses: a bad sign. She wanted to hide.

"Okay, businessman," she said. "What is it?"

"Don't be coy."

"I'm not."

"You're going home tomorrow."

"Yes."

"And then what?"

"What do you want?"

I lit a cigarette, then put it out. In such weather, smoking seemed redundant.

"Taeko, we've been sleeping and living together again. You visited here of your own accord. That was all very nice. Now what do you want to do? That's what I'm asking. Was it just a holiday? Do you want to go on with the divorce?"

She nodded. "Yes, if all it is to you is convenience."

"How so?"

"I told you before—you're used to being married, having me around. It's hard to start over again. It's hard to be lonely."

"I know. But I was lonelier when we were married."

"Mmm."

"Take the damn sunglasses off," I said.

She took them off and folded them, looked me straight on for as long as she could stand, then looked away. I smiled.

"Why did you come here? Tell me again."

"I was very curious. I wanted to see you, all of a sudden."

"And? Have you seen enough? Did you lose interest?"

"Not yet." She knotted her hands together, then tugged them apart. "But it's such a mess from before! And it's too soon to tell, it really is. I don't want to get in your way, myself and the children—you have a small apartment. And what if you want to go to cooking school? You won't go if you have to support us. And then things will get bad again."

"You could get a job," I offered.

"But I want to paint! I'm just starting to do something with that."

"Well, your father supports you at home. Why not have him

support you overseas? Tell him it's an education. Or do you want to stay in Japan? Is it still the issue of the U.S.?"

Some Osaka tourists whom we had seen on our rounds were now eating ice cream and listening to our conversation as if they were watching a soap opera. Taeko saw this first and smirked, nudging me with her shoe. We tried not to laugh.

"And you had to have a sex-change operation!" I said loudly, to their open-mouthed astonishment. "There went all our savings!"

She hid her head under the table, laughing, and emerged with a balled-up tissue in her fist, like a wailing rag. Taeko tended to weep when she laughed. The Osaka group realized what was happening and turned away sheepishly, back to their whipped cream and fudge sauce.

"Omi," she finally said.

"I've come to terms with Omi. And I miss Etsuko very much. She's going to forget me soon. Look," I said, and seized her hand. "I'm not ready to have the whole lot of you come back either— I don't know what I'm saying, I'm talking before I think. I just don't think we should dispose of the whole thing so quickly."

"You won't live in Tokyo?"

"No. I like it here. We've gone over that too."

"Yes. Well. I was hoping you would have changed your mind." She glanced around. "I suppose I could consider living here. This is not such a bad city."

I nodded encouragement. "Do you see? Do you see how things are different from New York?"

"Mmm, maybe. It's still dangerous, though."

"Taeko, you've got freckles on your nose," I whispered. "You'd better keep out of the sun. You're such a delicate flower. So delicate, I'm sure you'll outlive us all."

"You shut up," she said. She swallowed the last of her cappuccino and peered down into her empty cup. She had such resignation in her eyes. I told her not to be so serious.

"Think about it, that's all. Go home and think, and I'll do the same."

"But you said you wanted an answer," she exclaimed. "Right here, right now, snap to it!" She imitated businesslike behavior. I laughed.

"A visceral answer, from inside. I didn't say I wanted the whole tribe of you tomorrow at the door. Just a gut reaction. I need things in black and white—I can't stand living in gray."

Nearly all the ice in my glass had melted, leaving me with lukewarm coffee. *Il est très bien chaud, monsieur*, I thought. I finished it nonetheless. Too many important words had come out of my mouth, and I had an intense thirst.

"I don't think you want a divorce," I hinted, grinning.

"Neither do you."

"No."

"Then we're back where we started," Taeko said.

"Oh, no," I insisted. "We've covered tremendous ground."

"We'll be separated?"

"For the time being."

"Then we'll decide."

"Yes."

She frowned. "Aren't we in a shade of gray now?"

I crossed my eyes. "Oh, no. We're in charcoal tones. There's a difference. You're an artist, you should know that."

"Jun?"

"Yes?"

"Is there a deadline for when you want to know for sure?"

"No." I laughed at some residual amusement from long ago. "Our only deadline is death."

"Very witty," Taeko said.

"I stole it from Keiji," I confessed. "He's the real wit."

"I'm going to put my glasses back on now, all right?" she asked. She already had them on. The sun beamed orange against the green lenses, reflecting myself and the scenery around us.

"That's fine with me, Taeko," I said. "We've finished our conversation."

"Mmm, for now," she agreed, yet she relit my discarded cigarette, handed it to me, then asked for another cappuccino, and from the way she stretched herself and leaned back in her chair, it did not seem as though she was planning on going anyplace, at any time soon.

◆

I was fixing a duck as a joke for Taeko, duck being the symbol of marital fidelity. It was a fresh bird, so fresh I had had to pluck it myself. I did not believe in singeing, so I pulled each pinfeather out meticulously, with a pair of tweezers. Cautiously I snipped the skin just above the knee, pressed the foot and ankle down and cracked the joint. The tendons came smoothly out and lay—still trembling, I imagined—on the white counter. Excited, I continued to slit the breastbone and slip my hand through the incision, where the warm gizzards and entrails lay. I removed them, as well as the kidneys and lungs—fibrous and bouncy, like sea sponges between my fingers—then I extracted the oil sac. The liver made a sighing sound, full of juice. I took a step back, hands on my hips, the various parts assembled before me, glistening. I was extremely proud of myself and couldn't help smiling—usually I messed up at some point or made sloppy cuts. But there it was before me, a perfect duck, waiting to be stuffed and roasted. Taeko had gone souvenir shopping—I was by myself in the apartment; I had no one to share my accomplishment with, just myself and the bird, with its fatty yellow-purple flesh.

I took the duck, tenderly, into my arms and washed it in the kitchen sink. I hummed to it and fondled its massive drumsticks.

"Little friend," I said. "Wait there."

I dried my hands and went into the other room to have a smoke. I wanted to savor this moment, my time with my first perfect duck. You couldn't just shove something like that into an oven.

I went out on the sun porch, amid the plants and the bamboo furniture Taeko had helped me choose, and I smoked my cigarette, still humming—a tuneless song I realized was music to a commercial, only I substituted "Yamamoto, Yamamoto is coming back" for its actual words, which I couldn't remember. I yawned. Yes, it was time to face the tuneless music. My hair was cut, my shoes were polished, my suit was pressed and hanging in the closet. I had hidden in my hermit's chamber long enough—now the emperor waited, sternly, in a mahogany corporate suite.

I couldn't go empty-handed.

I thought, perhaps, that I should give Yamamoto my duck. Stuff it with bits of myself: a tie, a shirt scrap, a mechanical pencil, an airline ticket, a crossword puzzle, a wedding ring. Carve the character for "compassion" on its breast; baste it in a whiskey sauce and roast slowly in a convection oven until the flesh "crackled from the bone." That was what I could do. I might.

Still, he deserved better than that.

I sat up. I would write that goddamn letter of resignation tonight if it killed me. I would lock myself out here on the sun porch and sit with the expensive parchment, pen and ink I had bought specifically for the job and do it. Perhaps my father could help me. Perhaps he could show up and sit on the windowsill and guide me through this, coax the crammed-up words out of my mouth with his little finger, arrange them into the simple but exquisite sentences he was so famous for—give me a document that he and Yamamoto and I could be proud of.

If he really wanted to make peace with me, he would.

Afternoon light streamed in and burnished the air; a shadow pattern of dappled foliage shook with the breeze against the floor. The essence of everything seemed for the moment to be around me within this small room. I finished my cigarette and got up to return to the kitchen, stopping to look in the mirror along the way. My face had a certain smoothness to it that surprised me. There was a spot of gizzard under my left eye: it matched, perfectly, the mole under my right. I left it there and continued on, in balance.

"Madman," I said to myself, even though it wasn't true, then I went back into the kitchen, ready to get on with my meal.